DRY ROAD
TO
NOWHERE

DRY ROAD TO NOWHERE

The Frontier Overland Company

WILLIAM W. JOHNSTONE

AND J.A. JOHNSTONE

Pinnacle Books
Kensington Publishing Corporation
www.kensingtonbooks.com

PINNACLE BOOKS are published by

Kensington Publishing Corp.
900 Third Avenue
New York, NY 10022

Copyright © 2024 by J.A. Johnstone

PUBLISHER'S NOTE: Following the death of William J. Johnstone, the Johnstone family is working with a carefully selected writer to organize and complete Mr. Johnstone's outlines and many unfinished manuscripts to create additional novels in all of his series like The Last Gunfighter Mountain Man, and Eagles, among others. This novel was inspired by Mr. Johnstone's superb story-telling.

All Kensington titles, imprints, and distributed lines are available at special quantity discounts for bulk purchases for sales promotion, premiums, fund-raising, educational, or institutional use.

Special book excerpts or customized printings can also be created to fit specific needs. For details, write or phone the office of the Kensington Sales Manager: Attn.: Sales Department. Kensington Publishing Corp., 900 Third Avenue, New York, NY 10022. Phone: 1-800-221-2647.

First Pinnacle Books mass market printing: June 2024

ISBN-13: 978-0-7860-5095-6
ISBN-13: 978-0-7860-5096-3 (eBook)

10 9 8 7 6 5 4 3 2 1

Printed in the United States of America

CHAPTER 1

Tucker Cobb could feel the whiskey was starting to get to him and did not mind one bit. "I told you before and I'll say it again, Butch. I'll leave when I'm good and ready to leave, Butch, and not a moment sooner."

His partner, Butch Keeling, stood beside him at the bar. He had pushed his empty glass away from him half an hour before and had not allowed Cobb to refill it since. "Our coachline hasn't been exactly thriving since Hagen put the word against us. I hate seeing you throw away what little we have on a woman who doesn't want to see you anymore. Jane's moved on and so should you before you drive yourself crazier than you already are."

Cobb closed his eyes. *Jane Duprey.* Just thinking about her gave him some small measure of comfort. He had not known how much she had come to mean to him until she shut him out of her heart. He had been a bachelor his entire life—content to roaming the open country without any real aim or purpose—until he had met her.

He had once prided himself in the fact that he had made it past forty without allowing a woman to get her hooks into him, but Jane had him hooked good and deep.

He had been a fool to allow her association with "King"

Charles Hagen to come between them. He knew that now, but feared it was too late to remedy the situation. He had seen whatever affection die in her eyes that night when they quarreled in front of the hotel all those weeks ago. She had gone on to open the Longacre House since then and, by all accounts, it had been a success.

But no matter how much time Cobb spent waiting for her to come down to see him, she never did.

"We've got bigger concerns at the moment," Butch went on. "We need to keep our wits about us if we have any hope of fighting off Hagen."

Cobb's mood darkened as he thought of Charles Hagen. The king of the Wyoming Territory. The industry titan's hatred of them had spread far beyond Cobb's love life. It had been several weeks since Cobb and Butch had refused Hagen's offer to buy their Frontier Overland Company.

Business had been rough ever since. Hagen had already purchased or controlled most of the stagecoach lines in the territory. Cobb and Butch were among the last of the hold-outs and were paying a heavy price for their independence. None of the respectable hotels in their part of the territory would recommend their stagecoach line to their guests. They pushed them to ride on Hagen-owned lines instead. Some even went as far as refusing to allow them to rent rooms while they were in towns along their route. The two men had been forced to stay in the haylofts of the same liveries where they kept their team of horses. Lately, some liveries had even begun to refuse their business out of fear of reprisals from Hagen. Cobb expected that number would only increase as Hagen's vendetta against them spread.

Cobb tried not to think much about it, for when he did, he felt like he was on the edge of a high, steep cliff.

"Sometimes I think we just should've sold out to him like everyone else."

"Now I know you're drunk." Butch took the glass from Cobb's hand and placed it on the bar. "We didn't start this business because we liked working for other people. We started it because we wanted to be our own men, and we can't live like that under Hagen's thumb."

"I'd say we're already under his thumb," Cobb said. "Look at the kind of trade we've got now. We're lucky if we roll only half full and that's on a good run. All we get are widows and drunks who can barely pay their fare. I've lost count of how many times we've had to wash down the inside of that coach in the past few months."

Butch was not so easily persuaded. "That'll get better in time. Besides, we've managed to keep ourselves going by running freight, haven't we? That's helped some."

"Barely." Despite his present drunkenness, Cobb had not lost his head for business. "But there's only so much our rig can hold. It's only a matter of time before Hagen finds out what we've been doing and puts the stop to that, too."

"Hagen might be a powerful man, but he ain't God, Cobb. He'll lose interest in us soon enough and things will get better." Butch tried to ease his friend away from the bar. "Hell, they already are. We've got that big meeting with Colonel McBride in the morning, don't we? He's never been one who looked kindly on drunkenness. You'll need your rest if you hope to be at your best for it. He's trying to help us, and I think he will if we let him. He's always done good by us and vice versa."

But Cobb would not be moved. At six feet tall, he was bigger than Butch and weighed a solid thirty pounds heavier. He could easily see over the heads of the men drinking around them while scantily dressed women acted like they were hanging on their every word.

Cobb eyed the ornate wooden staircase in the middle of the place and the plush red carpet secured to the stairs by gleaming brass fittings. It was a staircase worthy of a queen. Worthy of a woman like Jane Duprey.

"She's got to come down here sometime," Cobb said, "and I aim to be standing right here when she does."

Butch did not take his hand away from his partner's arm. "Leave it alone, Cobb. You're killing yourself over a train that's already left the station. And no amount of whiskey or heartache will be enough to make it come back."

It had not been too long ago that Cobb had been obsessed with concerns like time and reputation. About drumming up new business for their stagecoach line and keeping schedules. But all of that seemed silly to him now that he felt like he had a hole right through the middle of him. A hole that could only be filled one way and not by whiskey.

"Why won't she see me, Butch? Why won't she give me only a few minutes of her time? She has to know how much it would mean to me."

Butch sighed as he pushed his hat further back on his head. "Which is probably why she won't give it to you. Jane's still mighty sore about you not trusting her like you should have and she's making you pay for it. Some women get mad. Some yell and throw things. I've known one or two that liked to throw a punch when they were angry. You should count your blessings that Jane's not that sort of gal."

"She won't even let me apologize. She won't let me tell her how sorry I am."

"Just give it time, Cobb. That's the only thing that'll work right now. Time and sleep." He pulled on his partner's arm. "Let's go."

Cobb remembered something his partner had told him

when they had first returned to Laramie. "You said you saw her. What did she say?"

Butch pulled him away from the bar. "I already told it to you. Repeating it won't do you any good, but I'll do it if you start moving."

Cobb let his partner pull him along, but was desperate for any attachment to her. Even a second-hand story he had heard a hundred times was better than being ignored like this. "Tell it to me again."

Butch began to lead him through the men and sporting ladies toward the door. "She had me come upstairs to talk to her in her rooms. The place still smelled of drying paint and wallpaper paste. It's done up in red velvet and fancy furnishings. I practically begged her to let you see her for a few minutes, even if it was down here with her customers, but she refused. She said your lack of faith in her wounded her deeply, and it's best if you both forgot about each other. She said she's got a new enterprise here and won't change it on account of you or any other man living or dead."

Cobb had heard all that before but hoped, with each retelling of it, that he might find some nugget of hope he could cling to in these darkest of times. "Did she sound angry when she said it?"

Butch politely pushed through a group of men in evening clothes as he said, "She sounded hurt more than anything. She doesn't hate you, Cobb. She just doesn't want to see you anymore, and you've got no choice but to take her at her word. You've been down here pining for her every night in the week since we got back, but she won't come down to see you. That ought to tell you everything you need to know even though it's not what you want to hear. It's best if you do what you do best. Move on and leave the past behind you."

But Cobb could not move on, not from her, which had been the devil of it. He had spent his life being careful to not allow himself to feel much in this world. Besides Butch, he had never bothered having many friends, much less business partners. The world was tough enough without the burden of being tied down to one person or place.

Butch had been different. They had formed a friendship somewhere along the many miles of cow trails between Texas and Nebraska. Jane had just been another pretty lady who had bought a ticket on their stagecoach to take her from North Branch to Laramie. He had not been looking for a woman to love then but had grown to love her anyway. He had not realized how much until he had been foolish enough to question her loyalty to him over "King" Charles Hagen.

Cobb glanced at the staircase again as Butch led him toward the exit, hoping he might catch a glimpse of her. But all he saw was one of her hostesses bringing a drunken customer up to one of the rooms above. His eyes filled with tears, and he looked away.

"We'll be back in a week," Butch assured him, as they cleared the crowd. "A week can be a long time when it comes to a woman's temperament. Hanging around here won't do you any good, but a few hours of sleep will. The colonel wants to see us bright and early in the morning, remember? And from the sounds of it, we might be looking at a decent payday for our troubles."

But Cobb did not care about Colonel Louis McBride or paydays or reputation. He only cared about getting back in Jane's good graces.

"Maybe you're right," Cobb said, though he didn't believe it.

"Now you're talking sense." Butch pulled Cobb past him and gave him a hearty slap on the back. "Once we're back on the road, you'll be as good as new. I'm bound to think of another way I can talk Jane into seeing you again. You know I can be mighty persuasive when I put my mind to it."

As they passed through the red drapes on their way to the front parlor, Cobb saw the doorman step out in front of them. He was a skinny man with bad skin and longish hair already going gray, though Cobb doubted he was much older than thirty yet. He had narrow, quick eyes that never settled on any one thing for long but did not miss much.

"Hold on, you two," the doorman said, when they got closer. "I want to have a word with you."

Butch urged Cobb to keep going. "We've had more than enough words for our liking for one night, mister. We've paid for our drinks and now we'll be going on our way."

But the doorman held his ground. "I told you to wait, so you'll wait."

Cobb tried the door, but it was locked. The emotion he had barely been able to tamp down began to rise within him. "Open this door."

But the skinny man with bad skin did not. "Not until we get something straight. You two have been coming in here every night for the past week."

"And paid for our drinks every time," Butch said. "We didn't even complain about how expensive they were, either."

The man opened his hands as if revealing the parlor for the first time. "A place like this costs money and it doesn't run on selling whiskey alone."

"Whiskey's all we were in the market for," Cobb said. "Now open this door and leave us be."

But the man made no effort to look for the key. "You leaving things be is why we're having this conversation right now. You haven't been too friendly to our hostesses.

Haven't shown them the least bit of interest. That hurts their feelings."

"Not to mention your pocket," Butch said. "We know what this place is and what you are. We don't come here for that, so you'll just have to take what we buy in whiskey."

"Lots of places in town serve whiskey," the man said. "So, if that's all you're here for, you can find that anywhere else in town. I can even recommend one or two saloons for you. But if that's all you want, don't come back in here. This here is what you might call a quality establishment, and I don't like a couple of trail rats like you taking up valuable space that a couple of sporting men could put to better use."

Butch tried to intervene, but Cobb squared up to the man. "This is your last chance to open that door before I start looking for the key."

The doorman's lips drew into a sneer. "You really don't know who you're talking to, do you, mister? I'm Lucien Clay and I run this place for Miss Jane." He offered a slight shrug. "Well, Miss Jane's true employer, anyway."

Cobb's left hand shot out and snatched Clay by the throat. He pushed the smaller man against the wall as he grabbed hold of the breast pocket of his jacket and tore it away. As a handkerchief fell to the floor, Cobb pulled off the pockets of the jacket. He had ruined the second pocket when a key dropped out.

Cobb kept squeezing Clay's throat as he tried in vain to break the coachman's grip. "Pick up that key, Butch, and let's get out of here. Looks like we've worn out our welcome with Mr. Clay."

Butch picked up the key, opened the lock, and threw the door open. "You'd best let him go now, Cobb."

Cobb pulled Clay off the wall and hurled him out into the street. The doorman stumbled off the boardwalk and fell into the thoroughfare on his backside. Passersby gasped and moved back at the sight of the man splayed in the mud and mess on the ground.

Cobb moved outside and pointed down at Clay. "Let that be a lesson to you, boy. I come and go in here as I please. The next time you raise a hand to me, you'd better have some friends around who can back your play."

Clay's small eyes grew even smaller. "Next time? There won't be a next time."

In one swift motion, Clay rocked up onto a knee and pulled a knife from his boot before launching himself at his attacker.

But Cobb saw him coming and threw a roundhouse right that connected flush with Clay's jaw while the smaller man was still in the air. He was unconscious before he landed on the floorboards of the boardwalk. His knife clattered away and into the street.

Cobb stood over the fallen man. "I have half a mind to stay here until he wakes up so I can be sure he got the message."

Butch looked down at Clay. "Judging by how hard you hit him, I'd wager we might be waiting a long time for him to wake up. We'd better get out of here while we still can."

"No one's going anywhere," a man called out from behind them.

Cobb turned, fists up and ready to swing, but lowered them when he saw it was Rob Moran, sheriff of Laramie. He was fast approaching with one of his deputies close behind.

Cobb had learned through bitter experience that it was best to stay away from lawmen when he could, but Sheriff Moran was a different sort. He liked and respected the man.

As was his custom, Butch stepped forward and did the talking for both of them. "It was a fair fight, Sheriff. That fella pulled a knife on old Cobb here, and he had no choice but to defend himself."

"Was that before or after you threw him into the street?" Moran asked. "Clay's the doorman of this place. He had a right to ask you to leave if that's what this was about."

"We were leaving, anyway," Butch said, "but he locked the door on us and refused to let us go. Wouldn't let us leave until he spoke his mind. That's got to be against some kind of law, don't it, Sheriff?"

Moran motioned for his deputy to tend to Clay as he said, "Only Butch Keeling would try quoting the law as he's leaving a whorehouse." He surprised them by taking Cobb's arm. "Let's go, Tucker. I'm locking you up for the night until you dry out."

Cobb was too surprised to be taken in hand to resist. "But I'm not hardly drunk."

"Drunk enough to start a fight," Moran said. "And dumb enough to have spent every night this week in there mooning over a woman who doesn't want anything to do with you." He pulled Cobb closer. "You don't think people talk about this? You think you're the first man to be thrown over by a woman? Especially *that* woman? Her kind break hearts in there every night of the week."

Cobb balled his hand into a fist, but the cold look in Moran's eye made him stop.

"I've seen this play out hundreds of times, Cobb," Moran said. "Tonight, it was Lucien. The next time it could be the bartender or one of the customers or worse. You'll never get Jane back by turning into a drunk, and I'm not going to waste my time worrying about you every time you pull into town. A night in a cell will do you some good. Probably more than you know. Now get moving. I'd hate to have to force you."

It was only then that Cobb noticed all of the people

on the street who had stopped to look at him. He had not realized he had raised that much of a ruckus. He looked back inside the Longacre House in the hope that all the trouble he had caused might have been enough to bring Jane down from her room to see what had happened. Just a glimpse of her would have made all of this worth it.

But all he saw were potential male customers peeking outside with drinks in their hands and cigars in their mouths. A couple of sporting ladies were fussing over Lucien Clay as Moran's deputy tried to get him back on his feet.

Cobb felt all of the fight go out of him. He felt ashamed. For what he had done and for what Moran said he might do because, deep down, he knew he was right. "I won't fight you, Sheriff."

Moran kept hold of Cobb's arm as he led him out into the street.

Butch trailed after them. "How long are you fixing to keep him locked up, Sheriff? We've got a meeting with Colonel McBride tomorrow morning, and I'd hate to have to explain Cobb's absence."

"If he behaves himself," Moran said, "I'll let him go around sunup. But if he so much as looks at me or one of my men sideways, I'll keep him in jail for a week until he cools off."

Cobb's shame only grew worse as he heard Butch stop following them. He took a final glance back at the house of ill repute and could have sworn he saw a curtain on the second-floor drop back into place. He liked to think it had been Jane looking out at him. It was not much of a hope, but it was all the hope Tucker Cobb had at the moment.

CHAPTER 2

The next morning, as he sat across from Cobb at Colonel McBride's dining room table, Butch could see his partner was in a bad way. The dark circles under his reddened eyes were almost the size of saddlebags and his skin bore a yellowish tinge to it. He looked like he had not slept a wink in jail, and Butch imagined alcohol was only partly to blame for his sleepless night. His sorrow over losing Jane's favor and his violent run-in with Lucien Clay had likely played a part in keeping him awake. He knew Cobb was a man of great pride who was capable of feeling great shame on those rare occasions when he allowed his emotions to get the better of him.

But although Cobb looked the worse for wear, he managed to remain attentive to what Colonel McBride had begun to tell them.

"I've asked you gentlemen here this morning to discuss a matter of grave importance and urgency," the colonel explained. "I'm asking you to help not only me, but your country."

Butch had been expecting McBride to hire them for a private charter, not this, but said, "We'll help if we can.

You know Cobb and me owe you for getting us out of that scrape with Hagen a few weeks back."

"Doing a decent deed is its own reward," the retired colonel said, "and doesn't require gratitude. If you agree to do this, I'll be the one in your debt and so will the army."

Butch did not know Colonel Louis McBride well, and he had not known him long, but he knew McBride was not given to exaggerating. The former army man was about sixty with iron-gray mutton chops that did little to hide how jowly his face was becoming. His suit was expensive and had been tailored to fit his roundish frame. But although age was beginning to gain the advantage on him, his deep-set eyes were as clear as they were intense.

"Sounds serious, Colonel," Cobb pointed out. "Might as well lay it out for us so we can give our answer."

McBride cleared his throat. "The matter concerns Fort Washington, which is only an hour's ride from here. I take it you're familiar with its location."

"We've ridden past it a few times," Butch said, "but we've never had call to go inside yet."

"Colonel John Carlyle is the commanding officer of the fort. He was an artillery officer who served under me during the War between the States. He was only a major then, but received a battlefield promotion that was made permanent after the war. I'm sure I don't have to tell you that almost every such promotion was rescinded after the hostilities ended. John kept his rank. That should give you some idea of his merit as an officer."

Cobb said, "I can't imagine an army colonel like that would have much use for a couple of mule skinners like me and Butch."

"Unique problems call for unique solutions," McBride explained. "Jack is a sick man. His doctors believe he is suffering from a cancer that has spread to most of his innards.

They don't believe he has much longer to live. The colonel sent for his daughter as he would like to see her one final time before he passes on. In fact, she's upstairs sleeping right now. Her name is Eustice, but she goes by Tess for short."

Butch saw Cobb bring his hand to his mouth as his empty stomach growled and cramped. His body was beginning to make him pay for his excesses from the night before.

Butch spoke quickly to cover his friend's obvious discomfort. "We're sorry to hear about your friend, but Cobb was right earlier. I don't see why he can't send some of his men to fetch her and bring her to him."

"Under normal circumstances," McBride said, "that's exactly what he would do. Unfortunately, these aren't normal circumstances because Fort Washington is currently under attack."

The colonel spoke over their expressions of surprise. "I only learned of the attack last night when a rider from the fort managed to escape under cover of darkness and bring word to me here. A band of Lakota and Cheyenne warriors have laid siege to the place. They attacked a supply wagon train more than a week ago, and when Colonel Carlyle sent a patrol to find them, the warriors attacked them, too. The fort has been cut off from the outside world ever since and is in desperate need of supplies."

"A siege?" Cobb said. "I've never known a tribe to attack a working fort. They like to hit and run in the open ground."

"I fought a different sort of enemy in the war," McBride said, "but this time they seem intent on using the army's foolishness about fixed fortifications against them. Those soldiers have been trapped behind their own walls for the past week and are running mighty low on provisions.

That's why I'll need your help. Not only to bring Tess to her father, but to get those soldiers the supplies they so desperately need."

Cobb's mouth dropped open. "You mean you want us to run a stagecoach laden down with supplies and a woman through a band of hostile Indians on the warpath?"

McBride nodded. "That's exactly what I want you to do, Mr. Cobb. And, what's more, it needs to be done this morning. Without delay. Both Colonel Carlyle's condition and the condition of his men demand it."

Butch knew there had to be a better way. "Did you send word to one of the other forts? The army's better able to take on Lakota and Cheyenne warriors than we could."

"The young private who brought word to me here also sent a telegram to all the forts in the territory," McBride explained. "The tribes planned their attack well. The closest forts are short on men as they've already sent out their regular patrol. Fort Laramie should be able to send men within a couple of days, but those men in Fort Washington don't have that much time, hence the urgency. I hate to say it, but Colonel Carlyle's desire to see his daughter before he dies has become an afterthought."

Cobb sank back in his chair. "What you're asking is suicide, Colonel."

McBride arched an eyebrow. "Having seen the extent of your valor back at Delaware Station, I'm disappointed in your hesitation."

When Butch saw Cobb's face redden, he spoke up before his partner's mouth got them in trouble. "Valor's one thing, but keeping our hair is another. Cobb's right. We can't outrun those warriors, and there's not enough of us to fight them off. Do you even know how many are out there?"

McBride shifted in his chair. "At least twenty, but likely more."

"Words like 'likely' don't do much against Lakota or Cheyenne," Cobb said. "Butch and me have ridden by that fort plenty of times, and what you're asking us to do won't be easy. There's a thick band of trees that circle the fort at a distance. There's a narrow clearing in one place, but we're as good as dead if we try to use it."

McBride frowned as he was clearly growing frustrated. "I'm quite familiar with the land, Mr. Cobb. Colonel Carlyle is an old artillery man. That tree line is exactly one thousand yards away from the fort. The rest is open ground. John insisted on that distance because he keeps a couple of twelve-pound howitzers hidden behind the walls. The Cheyenne and Lakota may think it provides cover for their warriors. They don't know they're sitting in a tinderbox. One exploding shell in the heart of those trees will be enough to set the whole place alight."

Butch wondered when the army would realize that fighting Indians was not like fighting soldiers. "But he ain't used them yet, has he? Probably because he knows they'd just scatter as soon as they caught sight of that cannon. And I'd bet my last cent that they already know he's got them. Besides, cannons won't do us much good."

Cobb picked up where Butch left off. "Since we can't use that gap in the trees, we'll have to ride through the trees before we even catch sight of the fort. The roots and overgrowth will threaten to flip us over every step of the way. Even if we make the clear ground, which will take a miracle, a heavy coach has no chance of outrunning braves on horseback."

"I didn't say it would be easy, and I'm not asking either of you to do anything I'm not willing to do myself,"

McBride said. "I'll be putting myself in harm's way right beside you. I plan on accompanying both of you to Fort Washington." He held up a hand to stop any attempt to talk him out of it. "My leg may forbid me from moving around as well as I used to, but I don't need my legs to work a rifle from inside the coach. I intend on helping you boys repel any of the attackers who are certain to descend on us once we reach open ground. And the trees will provide as much of an obstacle to the warriors as they will to us. I've fought in heavily wooded areas before and it's a great equalizer. I know it can be done because I've done it. The messenger assured me that the men at the fort are awaiting us. They'll ride out to help us as soon as they see us."

Cobb ran a hand over his mouth as he thought it over. Butch imagined his partner had the same empty feeling in his stomach. Only in Butch's case, it was not due to too much whiskey the night before.

Colonel McBride cleared his throat again. "To put a finer point on it, I wouldn't have asked you to do this if I wasn't confident that you're the right men for the job. And I assure you, I'll personally see to it that you're well compensated for the trouble."

Cobb slowly lowered his hand. "We can't spend money if we're dead."

Butch added, "And we've heard what the Lakota like to do to their captives. They won't make it quick if they catch us, and it'll be even worse for the woman."

"It's certainly a possibility," McBride admitted, "but I ask you to take Private House's accomplishment into account. He found a way to escape the fort and ride here to Laramie right under the noses of the warriors. I've spoken to him, and he's quite sure he can get us to the fort safely. I have every confidence that he can do it, too."

Cobb glanced at Butch before saying, "This Private House tell you how many other messengers tried to escape the fort and failed?"

McBride frowned. "Three."

Cobb frowned, too. "That's what I thought. I know what you did in the war, Colonel, but you've never gone up against the likes of these men before. I've faced them a time or two, and Butch here has had plenty of scrapes with the Apache and Comanches down in Texas. They don't fight like you're used to fighting, and the only reason why your Private House escaped is because they let him escape. I wouldn't be surprised if that was their aim all along. To draw the cavalry into some kind of trap. They're not the mindless savages that folks back east think they are. They're smart and ruthless and they're not afraid to die."

Butch had not known Colonel McBride for long but could tell he was disappointed to the point of being insulted. "I've forgotten more about war than either of you could ever hope to know. I didn't expect you to relish the idea of this request, but I certainly thought you'd show more backbone than this."

Butch knew Cobb was still raw from the night before and feared he might lose his temper but was glad when his partner showed restraint. "You might be right if it was just our scalps I was worried about. But you want us to take a girl right smack dab in the middle of a siege."

"I'm not a girl, Mr. Cobb," a woman said from the hallway.

Cobb and Butch got to their feet as Mrs. McBride escorted a tall woman into the dining room. She had straight black hair pulled back into a tight bun and wore a plain floral dress devoid of lace. She had a longish face with high cheekbones, dark eyes, and a thin line for a mouth. Butch supposed some men might have called her ugly or plain, but there was a certain quality to her countenance that he found appealing.

"Gentlemen," Colonel McBride said, "this is Eustice Carlyle, the colonel's daughter. She also happens to be my godchild. You already know Mrs. McBride."

Cobb and Butch bid the ladies a good morning as Mrs. McBride gestured for them to sit down. "No need to stand on our account, boys. We've just finished packing Tess's things and decided it was time for some coffee."

But Tess was not as pleasant as her hostess. "We managed to hear some of your concerns as we were coming down the stairs just now, Mr. Cobb."

Cobb blushed, which was the first hint of color Butch had seen in his partner in a week. "I didn't know you'd be listening, ma'am, or I'd have chosen better words."

"Plain speaking is important in times like these," Tess said, "especially when you happen to be right. One of the sacrifices of being a soldier's daughter is that we aren't often spared from the dangers our fathers face in this part of the country. I have no misconceptions about what those warriors might do to me if our plan fails, but I'm willing to take the risk. But the burden of seeing my father before he passes is mine, not yours. Don't let my Uncle Louis here bully you into risking your lives on my account. I'll just have to return to the fort with Private House on horseback later this morning. We'll just have to make other arrangements regarding the supplies. The private and I will carry as much as our horses can bear."

Butch spoke over Cobb's objection. "You can't do that, miss. That private was lucky he got out of there in the dark. Riding to the fort in daylight is just plain crazy."

"Then I suppose I'm quite mad." Tess smiled. "Others have said as much about me before. But my father's condition does not allow for delay. He needs me, and I intend on being there for him to help ease his passing. Each one of my siblings would do the same if they were here, but as they're not, the task falls to me. You needn't trouble yourselves about the matter any further. It's settled. Private House and I will go alone. I bid you both a good day."

Cobb and Butch began to rise as the women left the dining room, but Tess gestured for them to remain seated.

There was something solemn and resigned in that simple gesture that struck Butch at his core. He found her bravery touching and felt ashamed of his lack of it until now.

The colonel rested his hands on the armrests of his chair. "Well, gentlemen, it seems that the matter is, indeed, settled. As you can see, my niece is a headstrong woman who speaks her mind. She's much like her father in that regard. I'm sorry for having wasted your morning. We'll have to find another course of action."

But although the colonel began to stand, Cobb and Butch remained seated.

Butch watched Cobb begin to turn over the prospect of the matter in his mind. It was clear that Tess had succeeded in shaming him into considering it, too.

"A stagecoach won't move as fast as free horses on open land," Cobb said. "It'll be louder, too. They'll hear us coming and they'll see our approach from a long ways off."

McBride cocked an eyebrow. "True, but the hostiles would be facing five guns instead of just one. Tess is more than a fair hand with a rifle and pistol. Her father made sure all of his children knew how to fight."

Butch felt the burden of his own doubts begin to lift. "It *is* mighty flat land, though. After those trees, I mean. And our coach runs better than most its size. With me and my rifle up on the roof, I might be able to bring down a few of them up front." He looked at McBride. "With you and Tess shooting out from inside, it might be enough to slow them up some until those horse soldiers ride out to meet us."

"And ride out they will." McBride's eyes were bright with pride. "You can rest assured of that much."

"Rest and assurances don't play much of a part in this," Butch said. "Do you have a rifle of your own or do you need us to get one for you?"

"I have my pistol from the army," McBride said, "but I won't be able to take it with me. I haven't told my wife of my plans to join you, and I want to keep it from her until the last possible moment. And yes, gentlemen, I'm more afraid of crossing Mrs. McBride than I am a band of warriors."

Butch admired the older man's grit. "We'll get one you can use and plenty of bullets to go with it."

Cobb asked, "You still want to head out this morning?"

"Before noon, if possible," McBride said. "I took the liberty of purchasing provisions for the fort. There is a pile of goods waiting for you to pick up at the general store. We can put them inside the coach to help center it while weighing it down. It won't make for comfortable accommodations inside the coach, but this isn't a pleasure ride. My niece and I will gladly suffer it."

Cobb stood, followed by Butch. "Looks like we've got a lot of work ahead of us, Colonel. We'd better get to it. And if you change your mind about coming with us, we'll understand."

McBride leaned on his walking stick as he stood, too. "I'll be ready to travel, gentlemen. And so will Private

House and my niece. We'll give a good accounting of ourselves."

Butch did not doubt it as he followed his partner out of the McBride home.

Once they were out on the boardwalk, Cobb asked his partner, "What did we get ourselves into just now?"

Butch was beginning to wonder that himself. "Hopefully a good story we'll live long enough to tell one day."

As they loaded up the goods from the general store in the stagecoach, Butch decided it might be a good time to tease his partner a little. "Judging by how you're moving all this stuff, I guess what they say is true."

Cobb slid a sack of flour into the coach. "And what do they say?"

"That there's nothing quite like the prospect of losing your hair to cure a hangover."

Cobb grinned as he grabbed another sack of flour. "I think I'd prefer the hangover, but since I've already got one, it doesn't matter."

Butch took the last box of McBride's provisions and slid it inside the coach. The volume of supplies reached from the floor of the coach to the roof, with just enough space for Tess Carlyle on one side of the bench and for Colonel McBride on the other. "That niece of the colonel's shamed us into doing this, you know."

"Yeah, I know," Cobb admitted, "but she was right. I wouldn't have been able to live with myself if we let her and that private ride out there alone. Would've been like Delaware Station all over again, only this time, we wouldn't be able to double back and help them. Besides, it sounds like those soldier boys need all this stuff."

Butch knew they did, but he was bothered by one question he could not quite shake. "I didn't know the Lakota and the Cheyenne were on the warpath again. I'd have thought we would've heard about it before now if they were. This sort of thing doesn't just happen overnight. There are usually rumblings about it before it starts."

"Everything's got to start somewhere at some time, I guess." Cobb shut the door of the coach. "We've found ourselves on the beginning end of it is all."

Butch had seen enough brawls and skirmishes in his life to know it did not take much to set men against each other. White, black, red, or yellow did not make much of a difference when it came to violence.

But of all the tribes he had encountered in Texas and in the years since, he never saw a warrior do something without a good reason. Getting members of two different tribes like the Lakota and Cheyenne to ride together—even against the army—did not just happen. These were not a couple of braves who got themselves worked up over something a loudmouth said over a cookfire. There was more to this than that. And he had a feeling McBride knew what that was but doubted he would tell them. He did not think it would make a difference if he did. Cobb had already made up his mind and that was the end of it.

"Let's just hope that Private House the colonel mentioned has enough sand to ride against them Indians a second time around."

Cobb shut the coach door, climbed up on the running board, and used his weight to try to test the balance of the coach. "If he was brave enough to reach safety and go back, I'm sure we can count on him to do his share of the fighting." Cobb stepped onto the loading bay of the general store and put all his weight against the coach.

"She'll ride a lot heavier than normal. We'll have to move slow over those trees if we don't want to risk cracking an axel."

Butch knew the coach faced another, even greater difficulty. "Hauling so much weight will mean the team will be near played out by the time we get there. But they've had a good long rest here in town this past week, so we ought to be able to squeeze enough speed out of them when we need it most."

Cobb jumped down from the loading dock. "Getting there's only half of it. Getting out again will be harder."

Butch did not think so. "I figure we'll be safe enough if we just stay behind them high walls they've got around the place. Keep our heads down until those horse soldiers arrive from Fort Laramie. The colonel said they ought to be there in a couple of days at most."

"You know how the army is," Cobb said, as he climbed up into the wagon box. "Two days is just as likely to turn into a week. They'll want to save their men, sure, but the Lakota and Cheyenne will have something to say about how fast they get here."

Butch climbed up next to his partner and took his Henry rifle from the bench before sitting down. He always kept the rifle in fine working condition, and it had never let him down yet. He hoped this time would not be an exception.

"Did you think to get some cartridges for that shotgun of yours?" Butch asked his partner.

"Two boxes worth." He released the hand brake and snapped the reins, sending the team into motion. "We'd best go pick up the colonel and his niece. I just hope that soldier boy who brought that message is ready to ride. The more I think about this, the less I like our chances."

For one of the few times in their friendship, Butch found himself with nothing to say, for Tucker Cobb had just said it all.

CHAPTER 3

Colonel Louis McBride stood in front of his home, looking up the thoroughfare in anticipation of the arrival of the stagecoach. He did not want to risk his wife detecting something in her husband's demeanor until the last possible minute. She would do her best to talk him out of such foolishness, and he feared she might be right.

But in his heart, he knew this was not a foolish venture. It was far from just an aging soldier's desire for one last taste of battle. Helping his friend's passing by bringing his daughter to him was beside the point. The fort was under siege and good men were running low on supplies. He knew what it was like to fight on an empty belly with the sharp blade of death looming only inches from his throat.

Louis McBride knew he may not be in uniform anymore, but he would never stop being a soldier. The army was as much a part of him as breathing. He was in a position to help it in its hour of need, and by God, he would do just that.

There were other concerns, of course. Concerns he had not shared with Cobb and Butch. They did not need to know, and if all went according to plan, they never would. Some secrets were worth keeping at all cost and this certainly qualified as such.

Secrets were why McBride had resisted the urge to let Sheriff Moran know that Fort Washington was under attack. Moran was a good man and would undoubtedly offer to raise a posse to help free the fort from the threat of hostile warriors. But a posse, no matter how well-intentioned, was no match for a band of mighty Plains Indians. A lot of good men would get killed, leaving the city of Laramie undefended and much the weaker for it. This was not Moran's fight. It was up to Louis McBride to do something about it.

A tactician by trade and experience, Colonel McBride might not have thought much of their chances against such an enemy, but something deep within him convinced him that his plan would work. Tucker Cobb and Butch Keeling were not just a couple of mule skinners with more pride than brains. Each had proven himself to be tough and resourceful in the direst of circumstances. They had acquitted themselves more than adequately at Delaware Station all those weeks ago, and he had no doubt they would rise to the occasion now.

He felt the old exhilaration of battle begin to stir deep within him now that the hour of their departure grew near. That unique elixir of fearful anticipation and possibility of victory against overwhelming odds that only a man who had survived battle could know or understand. He did not try to deny it, but he could not explain it, either. It was against common sense to equally welcome and dread an occasion at the same time.

It was a feeling the young soldier standing beside him had not yet known, and it would be a waste of time trying to explain it to him. He glanced at Private House, who was standing rigidly beside his horse, waiting to mount.

"I'm no longer an officer, Private," McBride told him. "You don't have to stand at attention on my account."

Private Stephen House relaxed, but only a little. "Yes, sir. My apologies, sir. It's just a habit, I guess."

"No need to call me 'sir,' either. Colonel McBride or Louis will do. There's no place for formality in the face of the gaping maw we're all about to ride into."

"Yes, sir." House cringed. "I mean yes, Colonel."

McBride could not blame the boy for being tense. "This your first encounter with a hostile element, House?"

The young private said, "I've only been in uniform for about a month. Fort Washington is my first posting. I haven't even had the chance to go out on patrol yet. They had me mucking out the stables at the fort until all of this happened."

McBride was not surprised. Officers often saddled the least experienced men with the most mundane tasks. Mundane, but still necessary. "Well, if we live through this, I'll see what I can do about getting your duties changed. It took a lot of bravery for you to ride through their lines like you did. You should take heart in that."

"I was just following orders," House admitted. "If I'd had a choice, I probably would've let one of the others do it. A few fellas got themselves killed doing what I did. I was scared the whole time. Couldn't hardly hear anything else over the sound of my own heartbeat in my ears."

"Of course, you were scared," McBride said. "Only a fool or an idiot wouldn't be scared under such circumstances. You were scared, but you did it anyway. Not everyone would."

He shifted his weight to relieve some of the pressure on his leg. "And if it makes you feel any better, you won't be the only tenderfoot out there today. This will be my first entanglement with the red man, too."

McBride watched some of the parade ground starch fade from the private's demeanor. "I never saw the likes of them, colonel. They rode right up to the fort no matter how many of us started shooting. It was like they weren't afraid to die. Like they weren't human men at all."

McBride knew what House meant. He remembered his first battle in the war, how General McClellan had wanted older men to lead his soldiers in the battle. He believed his troops would be more willing to trust orders from a man with a little gray in his beard than a younger officer.

But in all his years, nothing had prepared McBride for that first time he came under fire. How the rebels cut loose with a shrill, rebel yell that was cold and clear enough to cut through the soul of even the most Union man. And how they kept coming in waves, only growing angrier and more determined than those who had fallen before them. McBride remembered the exhilaration of surviving the onslaught only to know there was still more to do in the face of an enemy that would rather die than relent.

He imagined that was, at least in part, some of what Private House was feeling now. "The Lakota and Cheyenne are human enough. An animal would have the good sense to know when it couldn't win and run off to fight another day. But no matter how they sound or how they look, those warriors are as earthbound and mortal as either of us. It'll do you good to keep that in mind. They have loved ones they care about waiting for them back home. They fear broken bones and infected wounds and catching a bullet in the belly, same as you and me. They freeze in the winter and roast in the summer, and they know the finality of death. It's up to us to remind them of their humanity if they're foolish enough to move against us now. Keep your rifle in hand and at the ready. Shoot only when you have something to shoot at and make sure your aim is true, for once that first brave drops beneath your gun, the mystique of what you think they are will lose all hold on you."

Private House's lips moved without making a sound before he said, "Is that what it's like, Colonel? In a fight, I mean."

"Always has been in my experience."

Private House swallowed hard. "What if I miss?"

"See to it that you don't. For all of our sakes."

McBride had been too taken with his own advice to notice Cobb's coach was already approaching his house. He went back inside as the stage pulled up and called for his niece.

"Tess! The coach is here. It's time to go."

He saw Tess Carlyle step into the hallway as Mrs. McBride followed close behind her. And much to the colonel's surprise, his wife was carrying something wrapped in brown paper bound by string.

Tess moved past him and accepted Butch's hand as he helped her up into the coach packed with supplies.

Mrs. McBride approached her husband and pressed the brown package against his chest. He knew from the heft of it that it was the Remington pistol he had used when still in uniform.

The colonel wanted to speak, but words failed him. "Martha, I—"

"You'd think that after thirty years of marriage, you'd finally get it into your head that you can't hide anything from me, Louis McBride. I knew you'd ride out with them as soon as that young private over there delivered Jack's letter to you. I knew there was no point in trying to talk you out of going, so I did my part to help you. Just as I've always done."

McBride took the bundled pistol in both hands and almost felt ashamed. He had not felt this embarrassed since his father had caught him sneaking out of school to fish back when he was a boy. "They need me, Martha. I can't just let them sit out there and rot."

"You can't do much from the back of a stagecoach, either, but I'm sure you'll find a way. Heavens know you always do."

He saw her mouth quiver as she placed her hand over his. "Make sure you bring it back when you're done. I'll expect you to bring it back personally."

"Yes, ma'am."

She gave him a kiss on the cheek and nudged him toward the waiting coach. "The sooner you get there, the sooner you'll be back, so you'd best be on your way. But if you get yourself killed out there, Louis McBride, I'll never forgive you for it. And there'll be no welcome for you in this house if you try to return to it after."

"Sounds like I'd better not get myself killed, then." He gave his wife a warm embrace, then quickly let her go. This was not farewell or even goodbye and he did not want her thinking otherwise.

Butch took the parcel from him and helped him around the other side of the coach. "You've got us too loaded down with supplies for you and Miss Tess to sit next to each other, but we managed to carve out a spot for you over here. It'll help spread out the weight a bit more evenly when we have to make a run for it." He winced, realizing he had said such a thing with Mrs. McBride listening, and quickly added, "That is, in the off chance we have to make a run for it, I mean. Why, I'll bet them warriors got bored looking at that fort and are off chasing buffalo somewhere right about now."

McBride did not see the point in telling Butch that his considerations were wasted on his wife. She had seen him ride off into danger many times before in their long marriage. He only hoped this would not be the last time.

Butch pointed at the rifle he had propped up against the bench for him before he shut the coach door and went to climb up next to Cobb in the wagon box.

The colonel heard Cobb say to House, "Private, you'd best ride point for us. Call out anything you see or just raise your hand if you spot trouble. They're bound to be waiting for us among the trees, so it'll pay to be vigilant."

"I'll be vigilant all right," McBride heard House say. "You two best be vigilant, too."

"You do your job, and we'll do ours, soldier boy," Butch answered. "The Frontier Overland Company ain't never missed a delivery yet, and we don't aim to start now on your account. Let's get going."

The springs of the stagecoach groaned as Cobb cracked the reins and got the team of horses underway.

McBride was glad Martha had not stepped out into the street to wave to them as the coach began to move. Seeing her standing alone and concerned might have broken his heart.

He closed his eyes and spoke quietly to her in his mind, as he often had before a great battle.

It's necessary, my darling. Not just for us. But for the Carlyles, too.

He opened his eyes and began to undo the string she had used to tie around the paper concealing his pistol. It was such a perfect job of packing that he hated to undo it, but it had to be done.

He picked up the Remington and the weight of it felt good in his hand. Reassuring, almost. It had served him well for many years. He was only sorry he might have use for it now. He opened the cylinder to check that it was loaded and was not surprised to see that it was. Mrs. McBride had always been a stickler for detail.

To his left, McBride noticed a gap in the pile of supplies between him and Tess Carlyle that allowed him to see his niece. She was as straight-backed and poised now as she would be during afternoon tea or at a dinner party. He admired the young woman's inner strength.

He said to her, "I believe your father once told me that he taught you how to use a firearm."

"He did," Tess said. "I even manage to keep in practice now and then. Why?"

He removed a cartridge from the cylinder before closing it and handing it across to her through the gap in the supplies. "You may find you have use for this before the day is through. It's loaded, so be careful."

She took the pistol and laid it flat on her lap. "Thank you, Uncle. You're very thoughtful."

"The bullets in that Colt are for anyone who tries to attack us." He pinched the last bullet between his fingers and handed it to her. "You should save this one for last. On the off chance they succeed."

He hoped his tone conveyed his true message as she took the bullet. He saw it had not when she opened the cylinder and slid the bullet inside it before closing it again. "Then let's make sure they don't succeed."

McBride smiled as she went back to looking out the window. Yes, she was John Carlyle's daughter all right.

Cobb had been encouraged by the quick time they were making as they drove on to Fort Washington. He had expected the heavy supplies they were hauling to slow them down some, but the horses were fresh and had no trouble keeping up with the brisk pace Private House had set as he rode in front of them.

He noticed that Butch had been quiet since leaving town, which Cobb took as a sign that his partner was keeping a sharp eye on the road. "Let's hope it stays this quiet all the way to the fort."

"Ain't no harm in hoping," Butch agreed, "but it ain't likely. That tree line starts just ahead and if them warriors haven't spotted us by now, they soon will."

Cobb pulled up on the reins to slow the horses when he saw House raise his right hand and made a fist. He watched the private turn to keep looking at the tree line as he rode back to the stagecoach. There was no mistaking the look in his eyes as anything less than concern.

"This is the same way I used when I snuck out of the fort to get to Laramie," House whispered to them. "I half expected them to come charging out after us by now. Maybe they don't see us?"

Butch kept watching the trees. "They see us fine. They're likely just taking our measure before they commit themselves. Probably looking to see how many we've got in the coach before they decide on how many men to send after us."

Butch's observation did little to calm Private House's nerves. "Are you two familiar with what's in these woods?"

Cobb did not think the stand of trees qualified as woods but saw no point in arguing that point now. "We've never had any reason to get close to the fort. We've always gone around them when we pass this way. Too many low branches for our coach to get through without scraping up the paint some. How straight is it between here and the fort?"

House turned his horse and pointed to a spot in the middle of the trees. "The boys from my fort cut through this exact spot all the time, so there's a line of dead earth straight through here. They hacked away at some of the greenery, so they can make it moving at a dead run without so much as a leaf or a branch grazing their hats. But since you're riding much higher up, I imagine you'll have a much tougher go of it."

Cobb knew they would. "Just our luck."

Private House continued, "Just keep your head down and your horses moving. The tribesmen are liable to start shooting at us as soon as they see us, but the trees should give us decent cover. But don't let your horses run flat out until you're in the clearing. It'll be open country from here to there, and that's when you'll need every ounce of speed you can squeeze out of them."

Butch asked, "And just where will you be in all this excitement, Private?"

"Right where I belong," House said, as he took his Winchester from the scabbard on his saddle. "You'll find me out in front leading the way. All you have to do is follow me."

Cobb gestured for Butch to stand up so he could get his double-barreled shotgun from where it was stowed beneath the bench, then handed it to Butch. "Hold on to this for me. I'll be too busy keeping the team in line as we're running through these trees, but once we reach that clearing, give it back to me before you climb on the coach roof to cover us."

Butch laid the coach gun across his lap next to his own Henry repeater. Cobb was glad he had placed the barrels facing away from him. There was less likelihood of him getting accidentally shot if they rumbled over a tree root.

The private heeled his horse forward. "Stay low and stay alive, gentlemen. I'll see you on the other side."

As they watched the soldier ride into the trees, Butch

said, "Am I seeing things, or has that boy grown up some since we left town? He was a squeaking little mouse back there."

Cobb knew there was nothing wrong with Butch's sight as he gathered up the reins for their next push. "Fear has that effect on some men."

"Guess you and me could use a dose of that fear right now, couldn't we?"

When House disappeared in the trees, Cobb cracked the reins and set the team moving. He was glad he did not have time to answer that question.

CHAPTER 4

Cobb just managed to duck his head before a thick tree limb almost decapitated him as they raced forward beneath the leafy canopy. By being forced to remain low with his feet spread wider than normal in the wagon box, Cobb had been able to avoid getting bounced out of his seat. His teeth rattled as the heavy coach bucked and jostled over the thick tree roots that crisscrossed the floor of the woods. Jagged branches of dead trees scraped the skin on the left side of his face, and he had almost lost his hat three times before he judged they were only halfway through to clear land.

The rumbling of the carriage drowned out the sounds of anyone who might be chasing them through the trees, but he was fairly certain no one had shot at them yet. He had been right in thinking the pines would provide decent cover as they made their way to the other side.

Up ahead, he watched House ride low in the saddle as his horse easily pulled away from the jostling coach. Cobb dared not look anywhere but at the back of the private's blue tunic out of fear he might steer the team into a tree.

And when he saw House break into the sunlight, he knew the first leg of their trek was coming to an end.

He expected the shooting to start at any moment.

The coach jumped as it ran over one final root before the first two horses of the team were bathed in sunlight. Cobb snapped the reins across the backs of his team, allowing as much slack in the leather straps as he dared in favor of more speed. Compared to the darkness of the wood, the sunlight was almost blinding as they reached the barren earth around the fort.

The difference from dark to light forced Cobb to squint to see even a few feet in front of him. For a few anxious moments, Private House was only a blurred blue spot on the edge of his vision.

Cobb moved his grip of the reins up in his left hand as he took the coach gun Butch handed to him with his right. He laid the shotgun across his lap, where it was within easy reach if he needed it.

Ahead, House remained low in the saddle as his horse kicked up a thin cloud of dust in its race onward. He was waving his rifle overhead to get the attention of whoever was watching from the high walls of the fort.

Butch had no sooner climbed onto the roof of the coach when Cobb spotted the first riders break from the tree line on both sides of them. He counted about twenty men in all. Ten on each side of the coach, yipping and shouting as they gave chase. He felt a stab of panic when he saw them begin to close in around them at a pointed angle like an arrowhead.

The chase was on and Cobb—his vision now clear—saw the fort was still a good distance away. But someone must have seen what was happening for the large gates began to open inward, revealing the relative safety that awaited them. If they managed to get there alive.

From behind him, Cobb heard Butch's Henry repeater

bark just after the lead rider on their right was knocked from his horse, only to be trampled under the hooves of the warrior behind him. That horse stumbled and spilled forward, hurtling its rider forward. Cobb saw the brave land hard at such an unnatural angle that it was clear he was already dead.

Cobb heard the sharp crack of a pistol echo from the right side of the coach and wondered if Tess Carlyle had thought to bring a weapon with her.

The remaining riders edged their mounts away from the fallen men, which cost them speed and distance. Cobb began to think they might have a chance after all.

But his hope was quickly dashed when a bullet splintered the wood on the left side of the wagon box. Fire burned at his elbow as Butch shifted his aim to the left side and began shooting. He heard the Henry rifle they had given Colonel McBride open up as well, though Cobb was too busy concentrating on his weakening grip of the reins to be certain. He felt the straps begin to slip from his hands as his left arm started to lose strength.

He was about to forget about the shotgun and take the reins in his right hand when a rider on his left raced forward and drew even with the coach. Cobb took the coach gun from his lap and squeezed both triggers. The painted warrior caught both barrels from less than twenty feet away and fell away from view.

Cobb dropped the empty gun into the footwell and kept his boot on it as he took the reins with both hands. The team was still running flat out as they followed Private House's horse to the open gates of the fort. Cobb judged that they were more than halfway across the open ground by then, but the tribesmen on either side of them had not given up the chase. Shots continued to ring out all around him as he heard the wounded men and horses of his pursuers cry out as the colonel and Butch's bullets found new targets.

They'll only come under more fire as they get closer to the fort, Cobb thought. *Why not break off now and escape?*

Cobb saw puffs of gun smoke rise from the top of the fort wall now that the stagecoach and their pursuers were within range. He almost cheered when he saw a cluster of ten cavalrymen on horseback ride through the gates toward the approaching coach. He wished they had sent more to fight off the enemy, but he was in no position to complain.

Cobb realized McBride and Butch had stopped shooting and took a quick glance behind him. The attacking warriors had broken off and were already racing back to the cover of the trees they had just cleared.

Butch called back to him, "You can start slowing them up now, Cobb. Our friends seem to have lost interest in us."

Cobb slowly began to pull back on the reins and brought the team out of their dead run as Private House stopped his mount in front of the cavalrymen who had ridden out from the fort. He brought the team to a stop beside them as House was giving his report to a young lieutenant.

"I delivered the colonel's message to Laramie as ordered, sir. I've also brought the colonel's daughter to see him, and these men have brought some supplies in their stagecoach, along with Colonel McBride."

"Good work, Private," the lieutenant said. "Get inside and get yourself a meal. You look like you could use one." The officer looked up at Cobb. "I'm Lieutenant Stanley. I'll be minding you while you're our guests here. Bring your coach and team inside the fort. We'll talk more in there. In case you haven't noticed, it's not safe out here."

Cobb looked down at his bloody left sleeve. "I noticed."

The men jumped when they heard the sound of a rifle shot echo across the flat and barren land. A bullet struck the ground a good fifty feet from where the horse soldiers had stopped.

Butch rose on the bench to look for himself but was careful to keep his head down. "Doesn't sound like they've given up on us just yet."

"The savages got hold of a buffalo gun," Lieutenant Stanley said. "They let off a shot every once in a while. Seems to me they might be trying to find its range. They get a little closer each time, but I'm not worried. Reinforcements will be here soon to drive them off. Our boys'll show them what real shooting's like then."

Cobb snapped the reins and steered the team inside the fort as Lieutenant Stanley, Private House, and the others trailed in behind them. Once inside, he saw two troopers pull the thick doors closed before they laid a heavy bar across it. He had a horrible suspicion that they would be there for much longer than the lieutenant might have thought.

Cobb winced as the fort's doctor cut away his shirt sleeve to get a look at his wounded arm.

"Did you really have to do that, Doc?" Cobb complained. "This was one of my good shirts."

"Hush now, Cobb," Butch chided him, as he looked on from the doorway. "Let the man do his work."

"Fashion's not much good to a dead man, Mr. Cobb," Doctor Earl Parson said, as he began to examine Cobb's wound. He looked to be about fifty or so and sported a full head of hair graying at the temples. His wire-rimmed spectacles were perched at the end of his long nose as he looked at the ugly gash in Cobb's left arm. "You're in better shape than I expected. That bullet took a good chunk out of your bicep just above the elbow. Nothing more than a nasty gash at this point, but if it were any lower, I'd be inclined to take the arm."

Cobb bristled at the thought. "You might've been inclined to take it, but I wouldn't have been inclined to let you."

"You'd change your mind about that once the fever sickness set in," Doc Parson told him, "but by then, you'd already be halfway to dying." He reached for a bottle and a bandage on the table beside him. "I have to clean out this wound, but it's going to burn something awful. I can give you something to bite down on for the pain if you want it. You'll get no points for stoicism from me."

Cobb was not sure what *stoicism* meant but could tell the doctor must have a low opinion of civilians. He had suffered through far worse injuries than this. "Do your worst, Doc. A one-armed coachman's not much good to—"

Cobb saw stars and yelped as the doctor poured liquid from the bottle on his wound. Parson began patting it with a bandage, which did little to tamp down the fire in it. "What is that stuff? Lightning water?"

"I wouldn't be wasting it on you if it was." Doc Parson set the bottle and bandage down and picked up a pair of small pincers. "The men in this fort haven't had a drop of whiskey in days. They'd kill for a sip of liquor right about now. You'd best look away while I pluck these splinters out of your arm. Many a man better than you has passed out at the sight of it."

Butch laughed from the doorway. "Lay it on him, Doc.

Old Cobb's tougher than one of them mules you've got in your stables."

"We no longer have any mules in our stables, Mr. Keeling." Parson began removing splinters. "We had to eat both of them a couple of days ago."

Cobb tried to focus on what the doctor had said instead of what he was doing. "I knew you boys had it pretty bad, but I didn't think it was *that* bad. I thought you'd only been under siege for a few days."

"A week would be closer to the mark," Parson said. "Those Indians hit us at just the wrong time. Or the right time, depending on how you look at it. Our food stores were low, and they ambushed our supply wagons as they were coming here. We sent out a patrol to look for them, and only one of them managed to make it back."

Cobb had already heard as much from Colonel McBride. "Guess you're lucky Private House was able to make it to Laramie alive."

The doctor did not look up from his work. "Luck had nothing to do with it. Those savages out there let him leave. I figure we'll know why they did it before long."

Cobb winced as the doctor pulled another wooden splinter from his wound. "Guess Butch and me are in the middle of it, right along with you."

Parson pulled another splinter. "If we make it through this, you boys'll never be able to buy another drink in Laramie when these troopers get leave. We needed those supplies you brought, and they'll be eternally grateful. Eating horse meat is hard on the morale in a place like this. Even mules have a purpose out here."

Parson squeezed Cobb's arm as he worked a large splinter free. "The men agreed to cut back on their own rations for the sake of Colonel Carlyle. They did without real food so he wouldn't have to."

Butch asked, "How is he, Doc? The colonel, I mean. We understand he's faring poorly."

"Poorer than you know." Parson plucked another splinter from Cobb's arm. "He died late last night. Just before midnight. Shame, too. The men liked him. So did the natives, come to think of it."

Butch said, "If that's true, they've sure got a funny way of showing their affection."

Parson paused to consider that as he found another splinter. "Well, I suppose they didn't actually like him, but they certainly respected him. He was always fair with them and gave them the benefit of the doubt whenever he could. Some called him an "Indian lover," but he didn't mind. He didn't lay into them like he'd been ordered to, either. It cost him a promotion to general, but such things didn't bother Jack much. He enjoyed being a colonel."

Cobb remembered the colonel's daughter, Tess, and was sad that she had endured so much only to arrive at the fort to find her father was already dead. He would have liked to have gotten her to the fort in time to pay her respects, but there was not much he could do about that now.

"We heard the colonel's been sick for quite a while now," Cobb said. "Colonel McBride told us it was cancer."

"It was." Parson smiled as he pulled a particularly long splinter from his arm and held it up for Cobb to see. "This one was hiding in there. You're lucky I kept prodding. You would've gotten an infection for sure if I'd missed it."

Cobb could not bring himself to look at it. "Who's been running things since the colonel was laid up?"

"Major Francis Aston." The doctor scowled as he spoke the name. "You won't find him as affable as Colonel Carlyle was. He's a bit of a bully, but maybe we need a bully right now if we hope to survive these attacks. But I wouldn't waste any time trying to get in his good graces if

I were you. I think he'd bleed army blue if it ever came to it. If it's not in the manual, it doesn't exist. And if a man's not in uniform, he doesn't count that much in the major's book."

"I'm familiar with the sort," Butch said. "Had a captain in the Texas Rangers who was like that. He gives old Cobb here a run for his money in being the most surly, disagreeable man I've ever met. He could fight, though, and we fought for him. Let's hope your Major Aston's cut from the same cloth."

The doctor placed his pincers in a solution of alcohol. "I'm going to sew up that wound for you now, Mr. Cobb. Then I'm going to bandage it with some moss from one of the trees outside. You'll think it's dirt, but it does wonders to stave off infection. That means it'll cut down the likelihood that I'll have to take your arm."

Cobb felt insulted. "I know what 'stave off' means, Doc. I ain't that ignorant."

"That remains to be seen," the doctor said, "because the smart part comes later. In addition to keeping it clean, you'll have to keep the moss on there for some time. Your wound will begin to itch something awful, but that's the sign of healing. If you remove it too early, you're almost assured of getting an infection. Do you understand?"

Cobb had never enjoyed the idea of needles but knew he had little choice in the matter. "Just get it over with before I change my mind."

Parson looked over at Butch. "You might want to step outside for this, Mr. Keeling. Some folks tend to get queasy right about now."

Butch went to a chair in the corner of the office and sat down. "Not me. I never miss the rare opportunity to see Cobb this helpless. Besides, I've got a gut tougher than a cast iron skillet."

The doctor shrugged. "Have it your way."

CHAPTER 5

Cobb helped Butch stand up straight after his partner got sick in the yard just outside Doc Parson's office.

Butch groaned. "Guess it's a good thing I skipped breakfast."

Cobb checked to see if any of the troopers atop the wall were watching the civilian get sick, but they were too busy looking for the enemy to notice. "I'm the one who got shot, and here I am tending to you. So much for that cast iron belly you claim to have."

Butch sagged against the wall as he wiped at his mouth with his sleeve. "I don't know what came over me. It's not like I haven't seen blood before."

Cobb was too tired from his ordeal to waste energy teasing his partner. "Who knows why these things happen? Who cares? Don't worry about it. Your secret is safe with me."

"Guess I kind of deserved it after the way I ribbed you back there in the doc's office."

Cobb grinned. "If you didn't rib me, we'd never have anything to talk about."

He turned when he saw a door to one of the buildings across the yard open. Colonel McBride escorted a weeping

Tess Carlyle outside. She held a handkerchief to her face and her eyes were swollen from crying. A tall officer appeared in the doorway. The buttons of his blue tunic gleamed as bright as his bald head in the afternoon sunshine. His posture was ramrod-straight and he used both hands to pull on a kepi that bore the crossed saber insignia of the cavalry. Cobb knew from Doc Parson's description that he had to be Major Francis Aston.

Cobb watched McBride lead Tess away from the building toward where he believed the mess hall was located. It did not take the major long to notice Cobb and Butch before marching over to them. Of course, he started out on his left foot and his boots struck a steady beat on the ground.

"You two must be the civilians the colonel mentioned," Major Aston said. "Which one of you is Keeling and which one is Cobb?"

"I'm Tucker Cobb." He nodded toward Butch, who was still trying to gather himself after being sick. "My ailing friend here is Butch Keeling."

Cobb almost flinched when the major shot out a gloved hand to him. "I'm Frank Aston, acting commanding officer of Fort Washington. Those supplies you brought us may have saved our lives, Mr. Cobb. On behalf of my men, I thank you for what you two have done. It would be an honor to shake your hand."

Cobb shook the officer's hand, as did Butch, who said, "Don't worry about me being sick, Major. Just something I saw didn't agree with me."

"Every man within these walls has had that same feeling," the major said. "I've seen a lot of things this past week that have turned my stomach."

Cobb had never been comfortable around soldiers, or men of authority in general, so he was not sure what he should say next. "We were sorry to hear about Colonel Carlyle's passing. We didn't know him personally, but Colonel McBride held him in high regard."

"We all did," the major said, "even when we didn't always agree. He's a great loss to this fort and the army." He looked up at the men standing guard and keeping watch on top of the wall. "But we can't allow our grief to overshadow our duty. The supplies you've delivered today should be enough to see us through until help arrives, but in the meantime, I'm afraid you're stuck in here with us. I doubt the Lakota or the Cheyenne will look kindly on allowing you to leave. Especially not after all of the losses they suffered under your rifles, Mr. Cobb. That was some mighty fine shooting out there."

Cobb said, "Only one of the dead was thanks to me. The rest were thanks to Colonel McBride and Butch. I'm fairly certain Miss Carlyle pitched in with a few choice shots of her own."

But Major Aston was unmoved. "Don't sell yourself short, Mr. Cobb. You had twenty hostiles on your tail as soon as you burst from the trees. My men report that you brought down five of them before they rode off. Those are five fewer red heathens out there waiting to take our scalps. I consider that a job well done, gentlemen."

Cobb had never seen killing men as a sign of progress, even when their death was justified. "How many do you think are left out there, major? Private House said he wasn't sure."

"We still don't have an accurate count," the major said. "Two Moons has proven himself to be a careful leader. He's never thrown his full force at us all at once, not even when he's attacked the fort directly. The lone survivor from that patrol they ambushed reported he saw about twenty or so warriors. My boys have gunned down ten of them when they've come at us during daylight. We've repelled a few night raids as well, but they always take their dead with them in the dark. There's never any sign of them in the morning. I'd like to think we've put a healthy dent in their numbers, but there's no way of knowing for certain. The Lakota and Cheyenne are a cunning breed, gentlemen, and not to be underestimated."

But Cobb remained fixated on the name Major Aston mentioned earlier. "You said Two Moons is out there?"

"That's what the lone survivor of our patrol told us," the major said. "He thinks he recognized Two Moons, but he can't be certain. And given our current situation, I don't think it matters. Whoever's out there leading this bunch knows what they're doing. I just hope whatever fort gets their men here first comes prepared. This lot won't be run off by a mere show of force."

But Cobb was still stuck on the name of the Indian leader in question. "Two Moons is a Cheyenne, ain't he?" A nod from Major Aston made Cobb ask, "And, from what Private House told Colonel McBride, you think there are some Lakota riding with him?"

"I don't think, Mr. Cobb. I know. I spotted Lakota warpaint during one of the attacks. I'd recognize it anywhere. I don't know what brought two warring peoples together to join against us, but they have."

Cobb knew the army had plenty of trouble trying to keep the various tribes in check as it was. If they got in the habit of fighting as one, they would have a long and bloody war on their hands. And, as in most wars, it would be the settlers and other civilians who would find themselves caught up in it.

Major Aston seemed to remember himself. "Here I am burdening you with the troubles of my command and I haven't had the decency to offer you a meal. Head over to the mess hall and get yourselves some biscuits. We've got a fair amount of flour now, thanks to you, and you should reap some of the bounty. Our way of showing our gratitude for your brave efforts."

Despite being sick to his stomach only a few minutes before, Butch was eager to take the major up on his offer, but Cobb held him back. "We know you and your men have had a rough time of it out here, Major. Butch and I would be more than happy to put in some time watching for attacks from up on the wall. It'll give us a chance to earn our supper."

"I'm more than fair with a rifle," Butch added, "and Cobb here can come along to keep me company. He can cut loose with that coach gun of his if they get close enough for him to hit."

"I know how to shoot a rifle, you ninny," Cobb said. "Don't make me out to be some kind of tenderfoot."

"Ain't nothing tender about you except your head," Butch said.

Major Aston was eager to put the matter to rest. "I'll have a sergeant come get you after you've gotten some food in your bellies. The men will be thankful for the relief. And the biscuits."

Major Aston offered them a curt nod before striding off to check the rest of his command.

Butch beckoned Cobb to follow him on the way to the mess hall. "Old Baldy was friendly enough. He doesn't seem nearly as bad as the doc made him out to be."

But Cobb knew it was difficult to tell much about a man from only a few minutes of conversation. "We'll see what you think of him after a couple of days cooped up in here."

"Guess that'll depend some on what Two Moons does next," Butch said.

"Yeah. That's what worries me."

* * *

As they sat together in the empty mess hall, Colonel McBride chose his next words to Tess carefully. He hated to risk upsetting his godchild further, but he did not have much of a choice.

"I know this might not be the best time to ask you about this, but you were alone with your father in his quarters for quite some time. Did you have the chance to search his belongings for that item we discussed?"

Tess pushed the plate of food away from her. "I didn't have to search, Uncle. Father had already written to me and told me where I could find his most important papers. He had a false bottom in one of the drawers of his wardrobe." She brought her handkerchief to her face again as more tears came. "I found what you were looking for there."

McBride was glad the young woman's mourning had not supplanted her subtle nature. "Did you bring it with you or did you leave it there?"

She gestured down at the bag on the bench at her side. "I took everything with me. His will. His letters to each of my brothers and sisters. And the agreement you've been asking for."

McBride hid his enthusiasm. He may have been deeply saddened by the loss of his friend, but bringing Tess to see her dying father had been only part of the reason why he had insisted on accompanying her to Fort Washington.

Colonel Carlyle had known he was dying for quite some time and feared that he would not have much of an estate to leave to his children after his passing. It was why he was grateful when his former commanding officer, Louis McBride, gave him a unique opportunity to change his fortunes considerably.

The geologists of the Wyoming Mining Company had reported that one of the largest coal and iron deposits in the territory was located close to Fort Washington. Unfortunately, it also happened to be on land deemed sacred by both the Cheyenne and Lakota people.

Carlyle spent his last months of life working on a pact that would not only allow the Wyoming Mining Company to purchase the land from the Cheyenne but also give them a percentage of the profits the company made from the deposit. The claim would also make the Carlyle children wealthy.

It was but a pittance of what the Wyoming Mining Company stood to make, of course. And money was not his sole goal. McBride took a great amount of joy in successfully snatching a prized parcel of land from the clutches of Charles Hagen, the ruthless land baron who believed himself to be the king of the Wyoming Territory. Mining iron and coal might not have been as exciting or as profitable as gold, but for a nation eager to resume its westward expansion using railroads, it was certainly significant.

The notion that renegades of the Cheyenne and Lakota peoples may be laying siege to the fort because of this agreement did not bother McBride in the slightest. The cavalry would rescue Fort Washington in a day or two. The matter would be forgotten and settled as soon as he was able to make it back to Laramie with the treaty. And John Carlyle could rest easy in the knowledge that one of his last acts of life had not only benefited his family, but his country, too.

McBride covered Tess's hand with his own as she began to weep again. "I know losing your father is a horrible blow, but you have to remember how long he suffered.

He's at peace now, which should be something of a comfort to you."

Tess used her kerchief to wipe away her tears. "You certainly hide your sadness well, Uncle. I'm sure the prospect of all the money you'll make from mining on Cheyenne land has eased your sorrow."

McBride could not blame her for being resentful so soon after losing her father. "None of this is about my aspirations. I already have more money than I can spend in this lifetime or the next, my dear. I've known your father for a great many years and was fortunate to consider him one of my dearest friends. I began to mourn him the day he told me he had cancer. But when he succeeded in getting the Cheyenne elders to sign that treaty, he knew it would benefit you and your siblings much more than it does me. And he'll rest easier knowing that one of his last acts in this life was to provide for his family." He squeezed her hand slightly. "He died well, Tess. About as well as any father could ever hope."

McBride heard Butch talking to Cobb out in the yard and knew they were probably on their way to the mess hall for something to eat. He told Tess, "It might be better if we keep any discussion of the treaty between us. No need for our friends to learn about it while we're trapped here in the fort."

Tess quietly lowered her head as more tears fell.

McBride stood to greet Cobb and Butch as they entered the mess hall. He decided it would be better if they left Tess alone in her grief. He noticed the left sleeve of Cobb's shirt had been cut away and his arm heavily bandaged. Some blood had already begun to seep through the packing. Butch looked paler than normal, but as he was talking up a storm, appeared to be his normal self.

McBride said to Cobb, "That arm looks worse than I expected."

"Doc Parson told me it ought to be as good as new in a few days if I don't take off this dirt he packed it with. They've sure got some peculiar notions about tending to injuries out here."

McBride recognized the moss. "Some of our surgeons did the same thing to wounds back during the war. I never saw it hurt any of the men who followed the doctor's directions. You should do the same."

Butch looked past McBride at Tess. "Looks like she's taking the loss of her father pretty hard."

"The poor girl is beside herself," McBride said. "Jack was a great man whose loss will take a long time to heal. I'm keeping her as comfortable as I can under the circumstances, but you boys might want to allow her to mourn quietly and in her own way. Perhaps you can make your condolences later after she's had a chance to calm down some."

Cobb readily agreed and gestured to a table by the door. "We'll take our food and eat it over here. If you need us later, you can find us standing guard up on the wall. Major Aston is going to let us give some of the troopers a break while we take over for them. Seems like the least we can do for them."

"Good thinking," McBride said. "And don't think I've forgotten what you two did out there today. I'll see to it that you're both rewarded handsomely for your bravery and your efforts."

Butch said, "And we'll be mighty glad to take it, provided we all get out of here alive."

McBride did not doubt they would survive. "Fort Washington was well-named, gentlemen. Jack Carlyle instilled a sense of resourcefulness in his men. The fort will hold no matter what the Cheyenne or the Lakota throw at us. In a couple of days, we'll all be back around my dining room table toasting our good fortune."

"I like the way you think, Colonel," Cobb said. "Now, if you'll excuse us, Butch here has his heart set on some biscuits. He gets a touch cranky on an empty stomach."

McBride was happy to leave the men to enjoy their meal. He stood alone and regarded Tess at a distance for a moment. The depth of her sorrow touched him. He knew he should have harbored some regret over asking about the treaty so soon after her father's passing, but progress waited for no man, living or dead. He only hoped he could find a way to console her until they could return to Laramie.

Not only for the sake of the Wyoming Mining Company, but for the sake of Tess and her family as well.

CHAPTER 6

Butch stifled a yawn as he stood atop the western wall of Fort Washington. The land between the fort and the trees was nothing but sun-scorched scrub grass with parched dirt thrown in. There was no wind to speak of and nothing moved, save for a thin mist of dirt that blew across the stark landscape.

He sometimes regretted not having served in the army, especially in the days following the War between the States. He had been haunted by the hollow looks in the eyes of some of the men who returned from the conflict, but he had also seen the pride many still had over their service. But it was only at a time like this that he remembered how much he disliked taking orders and performing menial tasks. And he saw guard duty as a menial task indeed.

"I feel sorry for the soldier boys who have to do this sort of thing all day long," he said to Cobb, who stood guard beside him. "No shade to speak of. No place to sit and enjoy a smoke or a chaw of tobacco." He cut loose with a stream that arced over the top of the wooden wall. "Nothing to look at or hold your attention for any length of time. It's just downright boring."

Cobb looked over the wall at the spot where Butch's tobacco had landed. "Boredom doesn't seem to have hurt your aim any. And as for staying watchful, the prospect of losing my hair is enough to keep me awake. I'm sure the soldiers think the same way about it."

Butch supposed that was true. "I wonder if they keep a man perched up here after dark. Can't see what good it would do since you can't see anything if the moon's not out."

"I imagine they listen for anything that sounds like it doesn't belong," Cobb said. "Don't believe everything you've heard about the Indians shying away from moving at night. They've been known to attack in the dark, too."

"I expect I know more about Indians than you know about rifles." Butch nodded down at the Henry repeater one of the troopers had given him to use on watch. It was almost as pristine as his own. "Just make sure you don't go forgetting which end you should point at the enemy. You've already got enough holes in you as it is to suit me for one day."

Cobb waved for him to be quiet as he pointed out at the tree line. "Shut your mouth and grab your rifle. Looks like we've got company calling."

Butch picked up his rifle as he followed where Cobb was pointing. A lone painted warrior, wearing a tall war bonnet bearing an impressive number of feathers, rode his horse out of the tree line and stood stock still in the distance.

Cobb turned his head and called out to any soldier within earshot, "Lone rider coming on this side!"

Butch shielded his eyes against the sun that had begun its gradual descent toward the western horizon. He imagined that was why the chief had chosen that direction for his approach. Keeping the sun in the eye of an enemy was a sound tactic. He noticed the chief was either holding a long rifle or a lance in his right hand.

Lieutenant Stanley climbed up the wooden steps to join them on the narrow ledge atop the wall. "What's he doing?"

"Just rode out and stood there," Butch told him. "He hasn't moved for a minute or so."

"He's waiting to make sure one of us noticed him," Cobb said. "He wouldn't be standing like that otherwise."

Stanley shielded his eyes against the sun as he squinted at the lone chief. "He's well out of range of our rifles. That means we're out of his range, too. You two better aim at him just in case." The lieutenant called over to one of the two troopers watching the south wall. "Dan, get over here and bring that Sharps with you."

Butch had been shot at many times in his life. The hairs on the back of his neck always stood up when he found himself under the sight of another man's rifle. Those same hairs were standing up now.

That was when he caught a glint of sunlight off something in the middle of the scrub grass. Something that did not belong.

"Get down!" Butch shouldered Cobb aside and tackled Stanley to the platform.

The loud, unmistakable boom of a Sharps rifle carried across the open land as Lieutenant Stanley's legs slid over the edge of the narrow platform.

Butch lunged and grabbed hold of the shoulder of the lieutenant's tunic just as Stanley lost his grip on the ledge. Butch felt the seams of the fabric begin to tear and took a firmer grip of Stanley's wrist with his other hand. "Help me, Cobb, or he's gonna fall!"

Cobb crawled over his partner and reached down to take hold of Stanley's left arm and struggled to help pull him back up to the platform.

As soon as he had been lifted out of danger, Stanley

slid around onto his backside with his back against the wall. Cobb and Butch did as well.

Stanley called out to the men, "Was anyone hit?"

"Dan's dead," a trooper responded from the yard below. "Look."

Butch joined Stanley in looking down at the body of Trooper Dan splayed out on the ground. The left side of his shoulder was a bloody pulp, and his eyes held the vacancy of death.

Stanley crawled to the steps and began to race down them as he told Butch and Cobb, "You two stay here and call out if you see anything. Eyes forward, men. This might be the big attack we've been waiting for."

Each trooper on the wall raised their rifles and kept their heads down as Butch chanced a quick glance over the top. He saw a green shape he might have taken for a tumbleweed moving across the ground between the fort and the tree line. But as he took a closer look, he realized it was a warrior with a patch of scrub grass on his back.

"That fella was laying out there in the open this whole time and no one knew it." Butch punched the wall in frustration. "I never even noticed him. He could've shot either one of us any time he wanted to."

"But he didn't want to," Cobb pointed out. "The chief's gone, too, but it looks like he left something behind."

Butch peered into the distance and saw a war lance sticking out of the ground. A white piece of cloth was billowing in the weak breeze at the top of it. "What'd he go and do that for?"

"He was most likely delivering a message," Cobb said. "Out there and in here, too. I'd wager that white cloth is something of a truce to their thinking. A Cheyenne or Lakota way of telling us it's safe to ride out and get it."

Butch looked down at the soldiers spilling out of the

barracks and the mess hall as they clustered around Trooper Dan's broken body. Stanley was still kneeling beside the dead soldier as Major Aston began barking orders to the troopers. He pointed up at Cobb and Butch. "You two come down off there. My men will replace you."

Butch could not speak for Cobb, but he welcomed the opportunity to be on solid ground. "That's about the best idea I've heard all day."

Cobb came down the steps behind him. "And the day's not over yet."

From a corner of the yard just outside the mess hall, Major Aston kept one eye on his mustering troops while Cobb finished telling him all he had seen while standing watch atop the wall.

"And you're sure this chief just stood there," Aston said. "He wasn't the one who fired the shot?"

"I'm certain of it, Major," Cobb confirmed. "He had one of his men hiding out among the scrub brush. He had scrub grass all over his back. It helped him blend in with the ground so none of us could see him. There's no way of knowing how long he'd been there, but he was there when Butch and I took over. We would've seen him, otherwise."

The major rubbed his clean-shaven chin as he thought it over. "He was probably there since before daybreak. Both the Cheyenne and the Lakota are known to be a patient lot. I warned you earlier about how cunning they could be." He quickly added, "I'm not blaming you gentlemen for what happened. I doubt it's anyone's fault except maybe mine for underestimating them."

Aston looked between the coach drivers as two of his men placed the dead trooper's body on a canvas stretcher and carried him into Doc Parson's office. "Shooting him was no accident. Trooper Dan was one of our Cheyenne scouts. They likely shot him as a message to us. He was the only one who spoke their language, so it likely means they're through trying to talk to us."

Cobb was not so certain about that. "Don't forget about that lance I mentioned, Major. That chief left it behind when he rode back into the trees. There's a bit of white fabric on the top of it. I think it's their way of delivering a message to us. I've heard it's been done that way in Nebraska with some Lakota who live out there."

"As have I, Mr. Cobb," Aston said. "As have I. But the Lakota we've got here are unlike any I've ever encountered before. Staking that lance in the ground could be their way of getting me to send another man out there to check. They'd like nothing better than to grab one of my troopers and make an example out of him. I can't risk their lives on a hunch, and I won't."

Cobb was not willing to give up that easily. "It could also be a way for us to get out of this alive. It's not just your soldiers you've got to worry about now. There's Miss Carlyle to consider, too. Her safety is worth the risk of being sure, especially if it doesn't cost you anything."

Major Aston lowered his hands and drew himself up to his full height. This was the first hint of a challenge the civilians had made to his authority, and he met it full-on. "I've already got two graves to dig, Mr. Cobb, not counting the patrol I lost out there at the hands of these devils. I'll not be burying another."

Cobb swallowed, knowing he was likely to regret what he said next, but there was no way to avoid it. "I'm not asking you to send one of your men out there, Major. I'm asking you to let me go."

"Me, too," Butch said right after him. "Cobb doesn't know Indian sign, but I do. I had a knack of dealing with the Apache back in Texas and, from what I've heard, these Lakota and Cheyenne use the same motions. Chances are they speak Spanish. I know a few words in that language, too."

Aston's eyes narrowed. "It's not a civilian's place to do a trooper's job. Either one of my men go or none of us go. And my word is final on the subject."

Colonel McBride cleared his throat as he stepped out of the mess hall and approached the group. "I don't mean to intrude, Major, but I've been following your conversation from in there and was wondering if you might be open to a suggestion from an old soldier like me."

Major Aston was flustered for a moment and pulled down his tunic. "Of course, Colonel. My apologies for disturbing you and Miss Carlyle, but we find ourselves in an extraordinary situation."

"That's why I decided to come out here to talk with you," McBride said. "Not because you disturbed us, but because this is, indeed, an extraordinary situation. I agree that it's wrong, almost insulting, to ask a civilian to do a soldier's job, but that's precisely what I recommend you do now."

Aston took a step back. "You can't be serious, Colonel."

"Cobb and Butch are capable men," McBride explained. "I wouldn't have hired them to bring those supplies—much less me and Miss Carlyle—out here otherwise. And you're right to be concerned that the sight of a trooper in uniform would be risky. Any one of those braves out there might take it upon himself to shoot, and Two Moons would be hard-pressed to stop him. It could be one of his Cheyenne who shoot first. It could be one of the Lakota. But Cobb and Butch? Two Moons won't be expecting that. It'll confuse them, perhaps enough for Two Moons to exert some authority over his men to hold their fire.

It's a risk, yes, but an acceptable one, and one these men are willing to take. The white cloth is a sign, Major. Let's see what it says. If we're wrong, it won't weaken your ranks any."

Major Aston looked into the mess hall before lowering his voice. "Are you prepared to hear the screams of these two men all night if Two Moons captures and tortures them? I know you performed with valor in the late war, Colonel, but you've never spent a sleepless night listening to the sounds of the Lakota working over a man. I have. Such agony ruins morale worse than dead bodies."

"We fight with the men we have at hand," Colonel McBride reminded him. "Not with the men we wish we had. Use these men to serve the greater good. Whatever happens, it'll help us know the mind of our enemy better. Besides, these two are mighty tough to kill."

Having said what he had come to say, Colonel McBride went back into the mess hall and left the three men to discuss it.

The major looked up into the clear blue sky as if he might find his answer there, then cast his eyes back down at the earth beneath his boots. "I won't be able to send any men after you if you're captured. No matter what they do to you, I won't lose more men to save you."

"We'll be careful," Cobb assured him. "All we need is a couple of horses to take us there and back."

"You'll get two of the best horses we have." The major flagged down one of his men and told him the names of two horses to bring from the stable. "They're both fast and sturdy. I'll make sure you're outfitted with rifles and pistols, too."

Cobb shook his head. "They won't do us any good out there, major. It's best if we go out unarmed. Less likely for us to have a misunderstanding that way."

Butch set his Henry against the wall and placed Cobb's shotgun beside it. "We'd appreciate it if you could mind these for us while we're out there." He unbuckled his gun belt and placed the rig on the floor next to it. "I know they don't look like much to you, but we're kind of partial to them."

Major Aston slowly shook his head. "I haven't decided if both of you are incredibly brave or completely insane."

Butch grinned. "Don't let it trouble you none, Major. Old Cobb and me ain't figured that out for ourselves quite yet."

Cobb and Butch rode out from Fort Washington on two borrowed army horses to meet an uncertain fate.

Cobb did not regret his decision to volunteer for such a dangerous duty, and he had not taken it lightly. But going up against the likes of Two Moons without so much as a blade tucked in his boot was beginning to feel like a poor choice.

He glanced at his partner, who rode beside him. "I half expected you to try to talk me out of this back there."

"I might've tried my luck if I hadn't seen that young trooper get himself blown off that wall like he did," Butch admitted. "I'd wager that's not the only warrior he's got stashed close to the fort. It showed me that Two Moons can kill us just as easily inside the fort as he can outside of it. I figured if I'm supposed to die today, I'd rather get it over with on my own terms."

Cobb had often taken comfort in Butch's observations on life and on any given situation at hand, but now was not one of those times. "Kinda makes me sorry I asked."

"Too late for either of us to do anything about it now." Butch pointed toward the lance in the distance that was still sticking out of the ground. "I can't see a warrior in sight, but I can feel them staring at us. I take them not riding out after us as a good sign. Makes me think this might not be a trap after all."

Cobb kept his eyes on the tree line. The branches were still and there was not a hint of a wind. He hoped things remained that way until they were back behind the relative safety of the fort's walls. "When we get a little more than halfway there, let's make sure we keep our hands up. Since we've gone to the trouble of riding out here unarmed, I'd like whoever's watching to be sure we didn't come out looking for a fight."

Butch agreed. "They'll probably send someone out to look us over when we get close to that lance. If they do, you stay quiet and let me do the talking. There's a good chance they'll know some Spanish. That'll be my way of putting them at their ease. You just sit there and hold your tongue."

Cobb remembered Butch had boasted about his language skills with Major Aston. "When was the last time you tried speaking Spanish to someone?"

"A couple of weeks back," Butch declared. "When we were in Cheyenne of all places. Seems like a coincidence now that we're facing a whole tribe of them."

Cobb remembered the incident clearly. "You mean that Mexican gal you were sweet on that night?"

"The very same," Butch said in a reverent tone. "I can still hear her name, too. Esmerelda Elegante. Ain't that just about the prettiest name you've ever heard in your life?"

"As I recall, she had a lazy eye."

"She surely did," Butch admitted, "but she had a warm heart and a fiery disposition. I remember how we spent the whole night whispering sweet nothings to each other while I charmed her. I sure hope you were paying attention,

Cobb. It would've taught you a thing or two about how you ought to talk to women."

Cobb had a different recollection of that evening. "She spat in your face and went for your eyes with that knife she kept in her apron."

Butch's face grew sour. "There you go again trying to spoil the memory of another pleasant encounter. It was just a lover's spat on account that she knew I'd have to be leaving early the next morning."

"She got mad when you started haggling over a price," Cobb reminded him. "And it took me and two other fellas to keep her from killing you."

But Butch stuck to his version of the story. "And I still say it was just a misunderstanding was all. The game of love isn't always a fair one."

Cobb minded the ground they had covered as he realized they were almost halfway toward the Cheyenne war lance. "I sure hope your Spanish has gotten better in the last two weeks. Two Moons will be a lot harder to stop than that señorita."

Butch grew quiet again as the two men closed in on the war lance. Both riders held up their hands and slowed their pace, so whoever was watching them from the trees would see they did not pose a threat.

The two men reined in their horses when they reached the lance. Cobb saw there was no letter or piece of paper on the lance head. The white fabric they had seen from the fort was a strip of torn lace, probably taken from the collar of a settler woman's dress. Cobb refused to think how they had come by it.

Cobb and Butch remained still when they heard the bushes rustle before a lone rider came out to greet them. And despite the great distance from earlier that day, Cobb recognized him as the same man who had driven the lance into the ground. The chief called Two Moons.

The Cheyenne cut an even more imposing figure in person. His long, thin nose was crooked, and his skin was darkened by a lifetime spent beneath the harsh prairie sun.

The two partners raised their arms slowly once again, to show him they were unarmed.

Butch asked the Cheyenne war chief, "Do you speak Spanish?"

Two Moons offered a curt nod.

Cobb could not speak the language himself, but had managed to pick up an ear for it by listening to the vaqueros with whom he had once ridden the cattle trails as a cook. He was able to follow the general gist of their conversation.

Butch spoke first. "My friend and I saw your lance from the fort. We came to see why you left it here."

Cobb held Two Moon's gaze as the war chief looked them over. It was impossible to tell what he was thinking until he said, "You are the men from the coach." He said the last word in English. "You killed five of my people."

"Only because they were trying to kill us," Butch answered. "We have ridden through Cheyenne lands many times and never sought trouble with your people. We do not seek it now."

"Yet you are there." Two Moons nodded at the fort. "With the blue coats who kill our people and steal our sacred land. You brought them food for their bellies and bullets for their rifles."

"We brought those things," Butch admitted, "but we also brought the colonel's daughter to see her father before he died. We were too late."

Two Moons narrowed his eyes. "You admit that you have a woman with you?"

"I admit only what you already know," Butch said. "Only a fool would think the chief did not know everyone and everything on his lands, especially when he is watching."

Cobb could not tell if Butch's attempt to flatter the Cheyenne had worked. The chief's face remained unreadable. "You speak of the woman, but not of the man who rode with her."

"I did not mention him," Butch said, "because he is fat and old. He means you and your people no harm. He was a friend of the dead colonel and came to help the woman. He is not in this fight."

"But you are?"

"There does not need to be a fight," Butch said. "Major Aston now controls the fort. He does not know why you attacked his supply wagon and his men. He thought your people had an agreement with the army."

"The Cheyenne had an agreement, but the blue coats always forget them when they wish. Tell this Major Aston to return our land to us. If he does this, we will let him live. If he does not, he and many blue coats like him will die." His chin rose a fraction of an inch. "You will die and so will the woman."

Cobb did not know what Two Moons was talking about. Neither did Butch. "What sacred land? This fort has been here for many years."

"The lands my father gave the blue coats. These lands were not my father's to give. They belong to my people, not to him."

Cobb saw Butch's confusion and did not know how Two Moons would take it. He might think they were arguing with him or lying to him if they continued to deny it. He hoped the chief would see they were being truthful.

"Butch, tell him we don't know about any lands being

taken from his people, but we don't doubt his word. Tell him that we will find out and will return as soon as we do."

Cobb let Butch's translation catch up before he said the rest of it. He glanced to the heavens and prayed he was not about to say too much. "Tell him we know the blue coats have lied to him many times before. Tell him you and I are telling him the truth now. Tell him I'll agree to remain here with him while you get answers. Tell him we hope this will be enough to show him we mean what we say."

Butch repeated Cobb's words without hesitation. He saw the chief glare at him when Butch finished relaying Cobb's offer to remain behind.

Cobb sensed his offer had not been well received.

Two Moons said, "Your offer is worthless. I can kill you whenever I choose. Out here or in there. You two can ride back to ask about returning our lands to us. My lance will remain in the ground until you do. If you do not come back, we will ride to that place where I will put my lance through your belly."

The war chief tugged on his horse's reins and backed into the tree line, where he was absorbed by the darkness of the greenery.

Cobb and Butch turned their horses and rode back to the fort at a steady clip.

"You know anything about this stolen land he was talking about?" Butch asked as their mounts began to pick up speed.

"No, but I sure as hell aim to find out." Cobb did not like the notion that was beginning to form in his mind. "But I'm starting to think that our friend McBride didn't come out here just to console Tess Carlyle in her hour of grief."

CHAPTER 7

Major Aston ordered the mess hall cleared of everyone except for the only four civilians in the fort. Not even the cook was allowed to remain in the kitchen. A trooper had been posted at each door with orders not to allow anyone in or out until he allowed it.

Cobb watched the major clasp his hands behind his back in an attempt to remain calm and official as he spoke to McBride. "Mr. Cobb and Mr. Keeling here had an interesting conversation with Two Moons. He claims that his people's land has been stolen from them."

Tess Carlyle kept looking down at her hands folded upon the table while Colonel McBride answered for her. "What of it? They're always mewling about some patch of land being stolen from them. They act as though they hadn't taken it from other tribes before them."

Major Aston said, "This sounds like a far more recent event. Two Moons said his father made a deal with a blue coat. And since I'm not aware of any such deal, I was hoping the two of you might be able to enlighten me."

Cobb watched Tess open and close her hands, but as it was not his place to speak, he kept his mouth shut.

The major looked at McBride. "Is there something

you'd like to say, Louis? I can ask Cobb and Butch to leave if you'd prefer."

"There's no reason for them to leave," McBride said, "just like there's no validity to what Two Moons is going on about. Yes, Colonel Carlyle helped broker a fair deal between the Wyoming Mining Company and the Cheyenne people. We believe there is a sizable deposit of coal and iron and other minerals on an unused piece of their territory, and we've agreed to pay them for the rights to explore it."

Major Aston stifled a curse as he walked away.

"It's not a formal acquisition yet," McBride went on. "We're paying them for the privilege of seeing if there's anything there. If there is, we've agreed to not only pay them for the land but give them a piece of the minerals we extract from it. It's quite a generous offer, Major. They stand to make quite a bit of money from it. Far more than they have now."

Cobb looked at Aston to see if he was ready to respond, but he was too busy trying to keep hold of his temper.

Cobb said, "Two Moons and his men don't have much use for our money, Colonel. That land means too much to them. They want it back and, if we have any hope of riding out of here alive, we'd better give it to them."

McBride held up his hands. "Gentlemen, please. Let's not do anything hasty."

Butch said, "A man can't be too hasty when it comes to saving his hide. Or his scalp."

McBride looked disappointed. "You're almost as dramatic as Leon Hunt. You remember how we dispatched those riders when they chased our coach on our way in here this morning? That was without the benefit of any cover or fortification. It was just the four of us then and there's five fewer of them now. They wouldn't dare attack us here. Not across such open ground."

Cobb noticed Major Aston no longer had his hands clasped behind him. Now they were balled into fists at his sides. "Not during the day, perhaps, but they'll come at night. They haven't come before because they never made their intentions clear until today. They've proven they know how to blend into their surroundings. I have a dead trooper in the storeroom who could attest to that." He pointed out the window. "I have men, good men, rotting out there somewhere right now because we're trapped in here and I cannot retrieve their bodies."

Major Aston slowly turned to face McBride. "Men have died for your parcel of land, Louis. Too many men for my taste. I don't care if it's a legal document. I don't care if you've found an entire mountain of gold that stands taller than Mount Olympus itself. You are going to hand over that deed, and you're going to hand it over to me this instant, or, by God, I'll have you thrown into the stockade."

McBride used his walking stick to steady him as he stood. "Is this the kind of officer they're turning out from West Point these days? Men who think you can barter with a savage like Two Moons? He didn't come here to negotiate. He only wants the land back because he knows it's worth something to us. He hasn't laid siege to this fort out of any sense of ancestral duty or tribal pride. He contacted us because we made him. Because he's lost too many men and can't risk losing any more."

Butch said, "That's a dangerous notion, Colonel. I've never known an Injun who could bluff worth a damn. They don't fight unless they think they can win, and he sure seemed confident when Cobb and me talked to him just now."

McBride shook his head. "After we killed five of his

men. I hold you in high regard, Butch, but I think I know a bit more about battlefield tactics than you do. Two Moons only agreed to talk because he's in trouble. And he's here because he wants what every man wants, no matter their race, creed, or color."

"And what would that be?" Cobb asked.

"He wants more. He thinks his father didn't get enough from us and maybe he's right. I had asked John to drive a mighty hard bargain with that old chief of theirs. In light of our current circumstances, I'm prepared to sweeten the pot now that he's made his intentions known to us. I currently gave them a quarter of whatever minerals we found on their land. I'm prepared to go as high as a third without consulting my board."

"Your board!" Cobb watched Aston's bald head grow scarlet and blocked him as he stepped toward McBride. "Two Moons doesn't want a third of anything. He wants one hundred percent of everything. And I'll not allow you to sweeten the pot with the blood of any more of my men. We're going to give that deed back to Two Moons and live to fight another day. And any further negotiations between your company and the Cheyenne will be conducted without any help from this army."

Aston pushed past Cobb and held out his hand at McBride. "I'll have that deed and I'll have it right now, Colonel. Your previous brave service to this nation is the only reason why I don't have you in chains right now."

McBride raised his chin at him. "That would be a tragic end to a promising career, Major. Don't do anything now you're sure to regret later."

Major Aston looked at the door of the mess hall and shouted, "Get Lieutenant Stanley in here on the double."

Tess Carlyle produced a document from somewhere

within the folds of her dress and placed it in the major's waiting hand.

McBride looked as if she had struck him with it. "Tess! What are you doing?"

"Something you should've done much earlier, Uncle. I hate to disappoint you, but it needs to be done." Tears streaked from her eyes as her voice broke. "I don't care about the money or the army or about how much money my family stands to lose. I've had enough death and I can't stand it any longer. I just can't!" She buried her face in her hands and finally succumbed to a fit of tears.

And although McBride did not move to comfort her, Butch did. The colonel was too busy watching Aston examine the deed.

McBride said, "If you give that document to Two Moons, you'll be placing a bounty on the head of every soldier in the territory. By God, on every soldier west of the Mississippi! Why, they'll be emboldened to pull this kind of tactic at every fort between here and the Pacific Ocean."

Aston's eyes continued to move over the deed. "I'm not the secretary of the army, Colonel. I'm the commanding officer of Fort Washington. Something has to be done to protect my men and I'm prepared to do it."

McBride stomped his walking stick on the floorboard in frustration. "Today it's a land deal. Tomorrow it's because of the land you've already allowed them to keep. After that, there'll be an uprising over their beef rations or the kinds of blankets you give them in the winter. Don't you understand basic military strategy? It's never about just one thing with an enemy. It's about the next challenge that faces us. You might save your skin today, but you'll pay for it with your heart tomorrow."

"Today is all I have," Aston said. "It's all any of us have." He folded the deed and handed it to Cobb. "I want you and Mr. Keeling back on your horses and delivering this to Two Moons as soon as possible. Tell him I expect him to accept this as a sign we mean him no harm. Tell him that I'm willing to pay for peace in ink, but if he doesn't withdraw his men immediately, I'll exact a price in blood."

Cobb placed the document in his back pocket. "We'll be happy to deliver the message, Major."

The door of the mess hall burst open, and Lieutenant Stanley stepped inside. "You sent for me, Major?"

"I certainly did," Aston said. "See to it that Mr. Cobb and Mr. Keeling are mounted as soon as possible. They have an important message to deliver."

"Yes, sir," the lieutenant said. "Will there be anything else?"

Aston looked at McBride, who matched his glare. "No. That will be all. For now."

Cobb wondered if Two Moons knew how to read as he watched the war chief look at the document Butch had handed to him. If he understood the lines and swirls on the paper, he did not show it.

"You white men are strange," Two Moons said. "You make marks on animal skin or wood and believe they hold great medicine."

"It depends on who makes the marks," Butch answered. "And if they can make other men believe in their medicine."

He held up the papers, allowing the weak breeze to buffet them in his fingers. "But without this, no medicine."

"The man who holds it has the medicine," Butch explained. "Right now, that means you have it."

Two Moons pinched the paper with the fingers of his left hand and tore the sheets down the middle. He opened his hand and let the air take the ruined document with it. "Now, no one has it, as it should be."

Cobb did not have to tell Butch to translate as he said, "The men who met with your father might want to talk to him again. It won't be one of the blue coats. We gave you what you wanted. The land is yours again. The blue coats ask you to leave this place so no one else has to die for it. Not blue coats. Not Cheyenne or Lakota, either."

"Or you," Two Moons said when Butch had finished translating it into Spanish.

"Or us," Cobb agreed. "You'll see our coach riding across your land. All we ask is that you leave us in peace as we'll leave you and your people in peace. I don't think that's too much to ask."

When Butch finished his translation, Two Moons surprised Cobb by smiling. He leaned forward on his horse and said, in English, "We'll see."

The Cheyenne sat upright on his horse before pulling his lance from the ground and riding back into the tree line as calmly and as quietly as he had emerged from it.

Cobb and Butch remained where they were as they heard a great cry leap up from the darkness of the trees before the ground shook with the thunder of many horses moving at once in the same direction.

Butch fought to bring his horse under control as the sound of the riders slowly disappeared. "I sure hope Colonel McBride was watching this. He was wrong about them not having many men left."

"He was wrong about a lot of things today," Cobb said. "Let's get out of here. I want to be back in Laramie before dark. This place gives me an ill feeling."

And as they rode back to the fort, he got no argument from Butch.

CHAPTER 8

Thanks to Tucker Cobb, Lucien Clay's jaw was swollen to twice its normal size and ached constantly. He grew dizzy whenever he opened his eyes—even though he was in bed—and preferred to keep them closed.

The same doctor who tended to the sporting ladies of the Longacre House had offered to give him laudanum to ease his suffering, but he refused. He had known Madam Peachtree would be sure to pay him a visit before long, and he wanted to have a clear head when she did. It was best for a man to have all his wits about him when faced with her wrath.

Clay could feel that wrath building now as Madam Peachtree glowered down at him from the foot of his bed.

"I can't believe you actually have the nerve to even think of yourself as a man," the older woman spat. "A disgrace is what you are. I've seen beaten dogs who have more pride than you."

Clay knew that Madam Peachtree may have come to America as a girl but had never entirely lost her French accent. It served to charm men when it suited her, but it also gave her words an even sharper edge when she was angry, as she was now. The black veil she wore only added to her menacing appearance.

"You're nothing short of an embarrassment," she continued. "Being found in the gutter like a dead rat. In front of the very house you run for me? I would have told them to leave you there had I been here."

"But you weren't here, were you?" Clay said. "You were up in Blackstone waiting for King Hagen to summon you." He was too tired and in too much pain to tolerate her insults any longer. "And you say I'm a dog. That's rich."

"I stayed in Blackstone," she said, "because I thought you had things here in Laramie well in hand. I see now that I was mistaken."

"You've never complained when you read my ledgers every week," he reminded her. "Longacre House has turned a nice profit ever since we opened our doors and business hasn't suffered any because of me."

She folded her arms. "It's been less than a day since it happened. Tonight will tell the tale. And you'd better pray that no one comes here thinking they can cause trouble and fight over payment. I pay you to run this place for me, not get into drunken brawls."

"I wasn't drunk and anyone who says different is a liar."

She scowled at him from behind the thin veil she always wore. "I wish you had been drunk. At least it would be an acceptable excuse. But this? Getting yourself beaten up by a common coachman? A lovelorn mule skinner? How could you have let this happen?"

Clay chose his words carefully for he knew each one would cost him dearly. Both in the pain it would cause to say them and in her already low opinion of him. "Cobb turned out to be much faster and stronger than he looks."

"You never should have tried to confront him by yourself. We pay thugs to take care of that kind of thing. You should've just let one of them talk to him."

"They were busy," Clay said. "I thought I could talk to him." He rubbed his jaw as it began to throb. "I see now that I was wrong."

Madam Peachtree went on. "And look at where thinking got you. You're not only stuck in this bed, but half the town thinks you're just another fool. I'm beginning to think I should put someone else in charge of this place. Maybe one of the other saloons. Your reputation is ruined beyond repair."

Clay knew Madam Peachtree had never feared striking a man at his weakest point. He had put in his time at the many saloons she controlled in Laramie, and he had no intention of going back to them. She knew how much his position meant to him and was using it against him.

"That took longer than I expected," Clay said. "You usually go for the throat much earlier in a fight. You're losing your touch, Amanda."

Even though the lamp on the bedside table offered weak light in his small room, he saw her recoil at the use of her given name. Few men in Wyoming or elsewhere knew she had been born Amanda Pinochet forty years before in the slums of Paris. The people of the Wyoming Territory had seen fit to Americanize her name to "Peachtree," and she had never bothered to correct them.

She rested a hand on the foot of his bed. "Careful, Lucien. You're too familiar for your own good."

Clay spoke through the sharp pain of his jaw. "I'm tired of always being the target of your scorn. I run this place for you, Amanda. I make you plenty of money, bring in plenty of customers, but it's not always as easy as it looks. Not all of our clients conduct themselves like gentlemen, and not all of our sporting ladies are exactly honest when I come to collect what they owe us."

"I don't need you to tell me what men are capable of." She brought a hand to the side of her face. Her looks had been ruined by a jealous beau long before Clay had met her, hence her insistence on appearing in public mostly at night and always with a veil. "I'm reminded of what men can do every time I look in a mirror."

Clay sensed a gap in her armor and hoped a bit of humility on his part might serve to widen it further. "I thought I could drive off Cobb and his friend alone, but I was wrong." He pointed at his swollen jaw. "I'd say I paid the price for my mistake, wouldn't you?"

He saw her raise an eyebrow behind her black veil. "If you hadn't gone after Cobb with a knife, I could believe he got in a lucky blow. But to throw you around twice? To do this to your face?" She shook her head. "That kind of embarrassment isn't easy for most men to live down. Not in our line of work. If you're not feared, or at least respected, you're worthless."

"I guess I'm lucky that I'm not most men. I never make the same mistake twice." He winced as a bolt of pain shot down his neck. "You know that."

"Just as you know I'm not one for offering second chances. They're too expensive and usually prove to be a poor investment."

Clay knew there was no sense in arguing with her on that point. But despite his recent failings, he still had one ace left to play. "We run a complicated business, you and I. It's not as clean as running a store or even a saloon. And not every man can run it as well as I do."

She laughed. "Taking money and keeping the girls in line doesn't require much skill. Jane Duprey does most of that for you."

"I'm not talking about just running a house." The idea of knocking her down a peg or two helped him deal with the growing pain in his jaw a bit better. "I'm talking about that dragon smoke we offer discerning customers in the basement."

He watched her look at the closed door as she waved for him to be quiet. "I told you to never speak of that within these walls. Not up here where anyone can hear you."

"I guess I'm not myself these days," Clay admitted. "That beating Cobb threw me might've scrambled my brains some. There's no telling who I might tell about your deal with the Chinese. How you help them pedal their opium all over this side of the territory."

"I'm not breaking any laws," she said. "It's not illegal."

"But it is unseemly." Clay grinned despite the pain it caused him. "So is prostitution, but that's an old vice as far back as the Bible. People don't like it, but it performs a service. Now, if the good people of Laramie learned that you were feeding foreign poison to good men, well, I don't have to tell you what would happen next, do I, Amanda?"

She charged the bed, her gloved hands like claws. "I should have you smothered to death for speaking to me this way."

"But you won't." Seeing the old gal riled up like this certainly did wonders for his spirit. "And not because I think you couldn't get someone to do my job. I'm sure you wouldn't have much trouble getting another man to run the girls for you. Like you said, Jane keeps them in line anyway, but your customers pay more for opium than for a woman's company, and opium's a tricky business. Dirty, too. Caring for the smokers while they float among the clouds. Keeping the Chinese in check so they don't raise too much suspicion in town, especially during the day.

And keeping a tight hold on who we allow to smoke. The good people of Laramie wouldn't stand for the sight of their husbands and sons passed out on Main Street, would they? It's a tiger that can get away from you awfully quick if you don't pay attention to the details. Details I already handle for you. Oh, I don't doubt you'd have men lined up for a mile to help you with the opium, but you won't know if they enjoy a trip on the dragon's back themselves until it's too late."

He watched her lower her hands to her sides. A small retreat, but a retreat just the same.

Clay continued. "We've all seen what happens when someone partakes too much in the services they provide. Drunks make bad bartenders. Satyrs make poor pimps. And opium smokers only care about their next trip to Elysium. That's not necessarily a bad thing, except they seek to remain there a bit longer each time they smoke. You don't have those concerns with me, Amanda. I like to keep my wits about me where money is involved. And there's still a great deal of money for both of us to make before that blessed day when we're finally through with each other."

Madam Peachtree rested her hand on one of the posts of Clay's bed. "You think too highly of yourself, Lucien. You always have."

"I know my worth," Clay said. "You can go on peddling smoke to every cowpuncher and dandy who comes to town. You'll make a lot of money before Sheriff Moran runs you out of town, but you and I have never seen wealth as its own victory. I can help you become much more than that. We've talked about how I can deliver more than just Laramie or even Blackstone to you. I can give you more than the Wyoming Territory."

Clay felt stronger the more he spoke. Talk of the future

was a wonderful tonic. "I can give you the lion's share of the opium trade from here to the Mississippi if you let me. As far north as Canada and as far south as Mexico."

He saw her thin smile behind her veil. "You've always been a dreamer, Lucien. Women like me know better than to trust dreamers like you. Tomorrow we'll conquer the world together, but today, we're just a couple of common vice peddlers in the wilderness. The cities back east and in Europe are full of such people."

Perhaps it was the pain or perhaps it was pride, but Clay felt now was the right time for him to reveal his intentions in full. "Remember how you had me keep a list of all Longacre House clients in a ledger for you?"

"I do," she said. "I hope you're not threatening to take them with you when I throw you out. Or take Jane with you. She's not the sort who likes to go out on her own. And she likes the protection I provide."

Clay put a finer point on it. "Protection like that which Charles Hagen provides you in exchange for a list of your customers. I know you're too modest to talk about having such a powerful friend, but a man in my position hears all sorts of things."

He gave her credit for not trying to deny it. "You spoke of the ledger. What of it?"

"It's not exactly as accurate as it could be," Clay said. "It's truthful as far as it goes. I've gone to great pains to write down who comes in and when. Even which girls they like in each visit. But I haven't included every customer who walks through the door. I've held some of those names back for myself in case I had a need to use them."

He could not see her very well in the weak lamplight of his room, but he sensed her grow still. "Ever the gambler, aren't you, Lucien? But you've overplayed your hand this time. I'll show the book to Jane. She'll be able to fill in any names you've missed."

"She won't be able to do that because the list of Jane's customers is accurate," Clay said. "But she never goes to the opium den in the basement. You wanted me to keep the operations separate and apart from each other, remember? I've done exactly what you wanted, though I didn't always record the men who decided to visit the opium den. In fact, I don't think I've written a single name in your book. Guess it must've slipped my mind."

He watched her gloved hand close around the bedpost as though it was his neck.

Clay felt good enough to push himself a bit higher in the bed. "The allure of opium is a strange thing. Men who would never dream of cheating on their wives will risk scandal to partake in a few moments of pleasure. They're hooked on it like trout on a fishing line, only they don't try to free themselves of it. It's always just one more smoke, and they promise to give it up forever. But they never do, do they? And so many of them are such important men, too, with such responsible positions."

"For instance?"

But Clay shook his head. "I've already been beaten bad enough for one day, Amanda. I'm not going to allow you to beat me, too. I'm not trying to threaten you, either. I'm trying to get you to see my worth. I'm reminding you of how valuable our partnership is."

"Ah, *mon dieu*," she said. "We're partners now, are we?"

"From this day forth as long as we both shall live," Clay said. "If you throw me out, I'll let you keep the girls, but I'll take the opium trade with me. I've saved enough to undercut your price by half. It'll be expensive in the short term, but worth it in the long run."

"The Chinese aren't fools. They wouldn't dare cross me."

"They know *of* you," Clay told her, "or should I say, what I've told them about you. But you've never dealt with them directly as I do. And don't bother threatening to have Sheriff Moran close me down because he knows we serve a purpose. I know how to keep it under control and contained. We also have some influential customers who'll be more than happy to blunt anything you do for the sake of a cheap fix."

He heard her choke off a curse as she moved away from the bed.

Clay knew he had pushed her as far as he dared. Now that he had presented the stick, it was time to show her the carrot. He slid his hand under his pillow while she was looking away. "None of that has to happen, Amanda. I'm not looking to be a full partner in all of your businesses. I'll go on running Longacre House and all the other houses you have in town like I've always done. But I want us to be equal partners in the opium trade. We're stronger together than we would be apart. I'm asking for a piece of the future, just like any dreamer would."

Clay watched her narrow shoulders straighten. "Too bad you don't have much of a future left."

She opened her bag as she turned to him. But before she could pull out the derringer he knew she kept there, he had his blade pointed at her belly.

Clay enjoyed her look of surprise as she dropped her purse. "I might've missed the mark with Cobb, but you're a different story. Give me your word that you'll agree to my terms, and it's settled. There's no reason why we can't make each other better."

Clay was glad to see her initial shock at her stomach disappear. "I suppose we'd both be fools if we thought we could completely trust each other, wouldn't we?"

Clay lowered the blade. "And I don't consider either of us foolish."

He watched her pick up her purse from the floor, but she made no effort to open it. "I agree to our new arrangement, but there's still the matter of your reputation to consider. You'll need to do something about Cobb and his friend soon before people begin to lose respect for you."

"Don't worry," Clay said. "I'm already taking care of it."

CHAPTER 9

It was only the late afternoon, but Cobb was bone-weary by the time he pulled the coach up to the McBride home.

He had wanted to spend the night at Fort Washington. He wanted to be certain that Two Moons had not left any warriors behind to ambush them on their way back to Laramie.

But Major Aston seemed just as anxious to send the civilians on their way as Colonel McBride had been to leave. Tess Carlyle was too lost in the emotions of her father's passing to care either way.

Cobb pulled the horses to a stop and threw the hand brake as Butch jumped down to help the passengers step down.

Mrs. McBride came to the door, relieved that her husband and Miss Carlyle had returned safely. "What happened out there? Is everyone all right?"

Butch said, "Everyone's alive and accounted for, ma'am. We brought them back in better condition than we found them."

Mrs. McBride tried to hug Tess, but the younger woman dashed past her and into the house.

Butch helped the colonel down and stood by while the

McBrides embraced. When Cobb and Butch had left the house earlier that morning, Cobb had been confident that the colonel was one of the most honorable men he had ever known.

But in light of the business with the mineral rights and the land—and all of the blood that had been spilled because of it—he was no longer certain of that opinion.

Mrs. McBride handed her husband an envelope and joined him as they approached the coach together.

"This is for you and your trouble, gentlemen." The colonel gave the envelope to Butch. "And I'm awfully sorry you two not only risked your lives but had to witness so much unpleasantness back there at the fort. I wish it could've been avoided, but I didn't have much say in the matter."

Butch climbed back into the wagon box beside Cobb. "Think nothing of it, Colonel. We know life's not always primroses and tea parties."

Cobb hoped McBride would let that be the final word on the matter, but he watched him struggle to say, "That deed Two Moons tore up was binding and legal and fair, boys. You'll have to take my word on that. It was the first agreement of its kind and might've changed things between how we deal with the Indians. I won't apologize for it. But I never would've done it if I'd thought it would turn out like this. John Carlyle would've prepared properly if he'd thought otherwise. I'm sure all of this may have changed your estimation of me, but don't let my shortcomings reflect on your impression of him. He was a good man and a brilliant officer. Nothing was more important to him than the safety of the men in his command."

Cobb did not enjoy seeing McBride humble himself like this and was anxious to bring it to a quick end. "Me and Butch haul folks for a living, Colonel. That's our business.

We've got no right to tell anyone how they should conduct their affairs. And, for as much as it's worth, I think things just got away from everyone. Regret won't change that now."

Colonel McBride began to speak but his voice cracked. He paused to compose himself before continuing. "I'd appreciate it if you boys could keep what happened out there to yourselves. I know word will get out about it in time, but I wouldn't want either of you to be tainted by that brush. You don't deserve it. The responsibility for what happened is mine and mine alone."

Cobb knew the proud man was not accustomed to asking favors of others, but he was asking one of them now. He wanted to put his mind at ease if he could. "What happened out there is nobody's business. You can count on Butch and me to keep it to ourselves."

Butch added, "You've nothing to worry about from me, Colonel. You know I've always been the shy, quiet type. Barely ever say a word."

McBride smiled as he patted Butch's leg. "Thank you, boys. I hope the contents of that envelope help you weather the current storm. You earned it and more this day."

Cobb and Butch watched the couple go back into the home they shared before the colonel closed the door.

Butch said, "I sure hope Tess will be all right. She's taking the loss of her father mighty hard."

But Cobb had other concerns. "I'm more worried about you. Did you really say 'primroses and tea parties?' Where'd you come up with that one?"

"Saw it in a book I read. Or maybe I overheard it some place. I was just trying to be eloquent and that was the first phrase that came to mind."

Cobb released the hand brake and got the team moving again. "Mercy. You sure do come up with them sometimes."

"Somebody had to say something," Butch said. "It wasn't like you were breaking the ice any. Sitting up here with that old stone face of yours. You're about as comforting as a mud slide."

Cobb began to feel better the further away he got from the McBride residence and all the troubles he had unloaded there. "After we get the team settled and the coach stored at the livery, I'm going over to get the barber to draw me a bath."

"That'll make it two in the same week," Butch noted. "You're getting accustomed to spoiling yourself. Could become a problem in leaner times."

"This week's an exception," Cobb said. "I feel the sudden urge to scrub this day off me."

"I wouldn't go scrubbing too hard if I were you," Butch said. "That was quite a thing we did today. Riding out to face Two Moons like we did. It's not the kind of thing I'd like to soon forget."

"You can do the remembering for both of us," Cobb said. "Me? I'm looking forward to that bath. You could use one too, you know."

"Not today," Butch said. "That's the smell of valor you're catching."

Cobb laughed. "It sure smells like something and it's not bravery."

Cobb was the last customer in the barbershop before it closed up shop for the night. He normally did not like to make trouble for folks, especially when they were getting ready to go home after a long day. But on that day, Cobb made an exception.

The fifty cents he had paid for a tub of fresh, hot bathwater was the best money he had spent in recent memory.

The water was just hot enough to be cleansing but not enough to be scalding. It was exactly the way he liked it.

Given that it was so close to closing time, the barber had run out of hand towels, so Cobb was forced to use a full towel to help him scrub away the dirt and grime from his skin. He was particularly careful to keep his wounded left arm over the side of the tub whenever possible. He remembered Doc Parson's warning about infection, and he wanted to keep it dry at all costs.

He could not remember the last time he had bathed twice in a single week, but he figured he had earned it. He hoped to cleanse himself of the haunting allure of Jane Duprey and of all that had happened at Fort Washington. He hoped to wash away his disappointment in Colonel McBride, too. And as he sank deeper into the cast iron tub, he began to think it was working.

He would make a point of rising early enough to return to the barber for a fresh shave and a haircut before he and Butch set off with new passengers bound for Cheyenne. He hoped they would be able to find more customers in the territorial capital looking to travel elsewhere in Wyoming. The further the better as far as Cobb was concerned. He had no plans to return to Laramie for a while.

He was glad he had gotten to the bank just before it closed so he could deposit the money from the envelope McBride had given him. The older man had been more than generous. It was more than he had expected his stage-coach to make for the rest of the year. Cobb was glad he had hidden the full amount from Butch. His partner was a good man, but he enjoyed the immediate luxuries that money could buy him. If he had known how much McBride had given them, Butch would have plenty of ideas about how they should spend it. Butch believed in living for today, not tomorrow.

Cobb was more practical. He wanted to keep the money in the bank, where it might see them through the tough times that surely lie ahead. They had survived Fort Washington and could count McBride as an ally, but King Charles Hagen still had them in his sights. It would not be long before he found another way to make Cobb and Butch pay for refusing his offer to buy their stagecoach line.

Cobb shut his eyes and allowed the warm water to seep into his pores. He forced the ugly memories he had of the past week from his mind. He tried to forget about Jane and how she had spurned his affections once again. Dwelling on it would not bring her back.

He could feel the fear he had felt in that mad dash to Fort Washington begin to leave him, but the memory of Trooper Dan's body splayed out in the yard would stay with him for a while yet. So would his encounter with Two Moons and his men.

Although he had scrubbed himself thoroughly, he felt the need to do it again. He placed the bar of soap in the long towel and began to rub it vigorously over his skin. The towel stopped the bar from escaping his grip and landing in the tub—or worse—on the floor.

He heard a knock at the back door of the barber shop and said, "The tub's taken. Go around front and talk to the barber if you want a bath."

"It's me, Tucker. I'd like to come in."

Cobb stopped scrubbing. He would have recognized that voice anywhere. It was Jane Duprey.

He began to look around for the newly laundered clothes he had brought with him, but they were out of reach. He would need to dry himself before he put them on, and he looked for another towel he could use for that purpose. "Just a minute. I'm still in the bath."

She opened the door and stepped inside anyway. "There's no reason to be bashful, Tucker. You don't have anything I haven't seen before."

He sank deeper into the soapy water, hoping it would be enough to hide himself. "You haven't seen anything I've got yet, and I wasn't counting on you seeing it now!"

She laughed as she quietly closed the door behind her. She was wearing his favorite dress—the dark blue one—and matching hat. She looked thinner than she had on that terrible night on the boardwalk. Her eyes had changed, too. Harder, maybe, but still lovely.

But those eyes widened when she saw the bandage on his left arm. "You're hurt? What happened? Did Lucien do that to you?"

Cobb had forgotten all about it. He did not know how many people in Laramie knew about Fort Washington's troubles, so he did not get specific. "No, Lucien never laid a hand on me. This was from something else. Little more than a scratch, really. I'll be fine."

She picked up the clean clothes he had put on a chair and sat down, keeping them on her lap. "I just hate seeing you hurt is all."

"And I didn't think you wanted to see me at all. I spent most of the week at—well—at your place hoping you'd come down, but you never did."

"I know. I saw Sheriff Moran take you away last night. Saw what you did to Lucien, too. I watched it all from my window upstairs."

Cobb had forgotten his run-in with Clay and the night he had spent in jail because of it. After the day he'd had, it felt like it had happened months ago. "I thought I saw the curtain in your window move. I was hoping you were watching. That's not why I did it, but . . ."

"I know why you did it, Tucker. You were sad and you

were hurt, same as me. Maybe it took seeing you act like that to make me realize how hard I've been on you. I never thought Lucien was good for much, but in this case, maybe he is."

Cobb felt his breath catch. "If I'd thought that's all it would take to get you to see me, I would've done it weeks ago."

He saw her mouth quiver as she looked away. "Am I still as pretty as you remember? I know I've changed some in the last few weeks. Be honest, not kind. I can take it."

The idea of saying anything other than what he felt did not enter his mind. "You're thinner than you were, not that you had any weight to lose. Looks like you haven't been sleeping much. I mean, you just look tired, but not in a bad way."

She brought a hand to her mouth to conceal her laughter. "You always know how to flatter a lady, Tucker. But you see quite a bit. I am tired. Awfully tired. Tired of being angry at you and tired of acting like I'm glad to see strangers who look at me like I'm nothing more than a side of beef. I guess you could say Laramie has been something of a disappointment to me. It isn't what I'd expected it would be. I guess my expectations for the future changed once I met you."

Cobb did not dare allow himself to think she meant anything by it. "I know how you feel. Are you thinking of leaving? Doing something else?"

"I've thought about it, but there aren't many places where a woman like me can go." She placed her hand on top of Cobb's clothes. "Maybe I can ask Mrs. Wagner to take me in as one of her converts? Help her save souls by sharing my sad story."

Cobb did not think she would have to resort to that. "I'm sure you've got some money of your own saved up.

Enough to help you start over in another town. In another line of work."

"Not in Wyoming," she said. "Madam Peachtree and Lucien know a lot of people. Who I am and what I've done will follow me wherever I go. They won't like it if I up and leave them with a house to run. And there's the other party to think about."

Cobb knew who she meant. "Charles Hagen casts a mighty long shadow, doesn't he?"

"Over the both of us," she agreed. "I don't spend all of my time hiding in my room from you, Tucker. He's made no secret that he wants to break you and Butch. He wants to drive you out of business and out of the territory entirely. Maybe even further than that. I haven't heard anything specific, but plenty of men have heard him say it."

Cobb knew men like Hagen were not given to making idle threats. But he shrugged it off for her sake. "People have tried to run me off before. It hasn't worked yet."

Before she could answer, the back door of the barbershop burst open and a tall man with a pistol aimed it down at Cobb.

The man said, "Lucien Clay says hello."

Jane screamed as Cobb grabbed the towel with the bar of soap and slung it at the intruder's gun hand. The pistol fired into the wall as Cobb leapt from the tub and at his attacker.

Cobb grabbed the man by the shirt and forced him hard back against the doorframe as he struggled for the pistol. The stranger tried to push Cobb back, but his soap-slicked body made it hard for him to get purchase.

Cobb pried the gun loose from his grip and brought the pistol across the man's face, causing his legs to buckle.

From the corner of his eye, Cobb saw a man in the alley behind the barbershop raise a rifle at him. Instinct caused

Cobb to bring his attacker down to the floor with him as the rifle fired. The bullet struck the ceiling, causing plaster dust to rain down upon them.

Cobb switched the pistol to his right hand as he saw the rifleman run off. Cobb got to his feet and ran outside. He snapped off three shots at the fleeing shooter, but none of the bullets hit their mark. The man kept his head low as he bolted around a corner and out of sight.

Cobb moved back inside the barbershop, where Jane was pressed against the wall, staring down at the man on the floor.

Cobb shook her by the arm. "Are you hurt?"

She shook her head quickly as the man on the floor started to recover and tried to get to his feet.

Cobb dropped to a knee and struck him again with the butt of the pistol, this time in the temple. The blow was hard enough to make his right arm give out, but he did not lose consciousness. A second blow did the trick.

Cobb found another towel and wrapped it around his middle as he pulled Jane close. "Everything's fine now. It's over."

From behind the closed door that led into his shop, Ken Hall called out, "What in tarnation is going on in there?"

Cobb motioned for Jane to be quiet as he said, "You'd better send someone to get the sheriff. Someone just tried to kill me."

"I knew I should've closed early," Hall grumbled. "I knew you were nothing but trouble."

Cobb waited until he heard Hall leave to fetch the sheriff before telling Jane, "You can't be here when the sheriff comes. Go back to Longacre House and don't tell anyone you were here. If anyone asks, you were out for a walk or shopping or something."

She tried to protest, but Cobb gently eased her toward

the back door. "I don't want you mixed up in this, Jane. Do like I told you and go back home. I'll send word for you as soon as I can."

She kissed him on the cheek. "I'll watch for you from my window. I'll find a reason to sneak out as soon as I see you. And be careful, Tucker. Please."

Cobb smiled for her benefit. "The thought of being any other way never crossed my mind."

He waited until she was well on her way before he finished drying off and began to get dressed. He did not want Sheriff Moran to find him wearing only a towel.

CHAPTER 10

Cobb watched Butch help Deputy Blake get his attacker to his feet before Blake led the prisoner off to jail.

Moran began questioning Cobb as soon as it was just the three of them. "You said you were taking a bath when this fella burst in here?"

"That's what I said because that's how it happened," Cobb told him. "He said Lucien Clay sent him."

Moran's shoulders sagged. "Don't try to gild the lily on this one, Cobb. The man who attacked you is already going to prison for a long time."

"'Lucien Clay says hello,'" Cobb repeated. "His very words. I'll be willing to swear to it in court. That ought to be enough for you to bring charges against him."

Moran took a moment to think about it. "Anyone else hear him say this to you? Maybe Ken Hall, the barber?"

Cobb knew Jane had heard him say it, but he wanted to keep her out of this. She still had to share a roof and a business with Clay. "Ken was up front cutting hair. The only other person who could've heard it was the rifleman who took a shot at me, but he didn't stick around very long."

Butch interrupted Moran. "What did he look like?"

"I couldn't tell you," Cobb admitted. "I didn't get a

good look at him. But he ran up the back street here and disappeared around a corner. I didn't want to chase him and risk losing the man I already had."

Moran looked at the tub still full of bathwater. "You likely weren't dressed for a chase. I'm glad you didn't chase him naked. The good people of Laramie don't deserve to see that."

Cobb was in no mood for humor. "Lucien Clay sent those two after me, Rob. I'm not lying about that."

"I didn't say you were," Moran assured him. "And I'll be asking that fella about that. I'll know if he's lying. I'll be sure to bring in Clay to talk with him, too. But I want your promise that you're not going to tear this town to pieces looking for that rifleman." He looked at Butch. "That goes for you, too. The law in Laramie is my concern, not yours. And unless you fancy spending another night behind bars, you'd do well to remember that."

Cobb was too tired to bother arguing with him. "I won't do anything. And neither will Butch. We're supposed to head out in the morning for Cheyenne, so we won't be around to cause you any trouble."

"I'm glad to hear it," Moran said. "Some time away from Laramie will likely do everyone some good, including you." He was about to leave but paused to impart a final word. "Just because I don't want you two looking for the rifle man doesn't mean I expect you to not defend yourselves. But if you see trouble brewing, send for me or my men, even if it means walking away."

Cobb assured him they would before Moran went into the barber shop to talk with Ken Hall about what had happened in his back room.

Cobb and Butch went out the back door and began walking back to the Laramie Hotel. The sun had already set, bringing a long day to a welcomed end.

After taking an alley to the main thoroughfare, Butch asked, "Who was in there with you?"

"Are you going deaf? You were standing right there when I told Moran I was alone."

"I heard what you said, but I was watching you while you were saying it," Butch said. "You've never been much good at lying. Moran doesn't know you well enough to notice it, but I did. Who was with you?"

Cobb hoped they could have this talk after they got back to their room. He did not want to risk anyone over-hearing them. But since there were few pedestrians on Main Street, he told him. "Jane came by to see me. She said she wants to make up."

Butch stopped walking. "She what?"

Cobb turned and walked back to him. "She came by to see me while I was taking my bath. I'll admit I was sur-prised at first, but at least it was a nice surprise."

Butch's eyes narrowed. "How did she know you were there?"

"I didn't have time to ask her," Cobb admitted. "Maybe she followed me from the hotel. Maybe she asked for me there."

Butch placed his hands on his hips. "You don't think it's strange that she decides to come see you only a bit before two guys try to take a shot at you?"

Cobb did not. "They probably already knew where I was. Or they followed her, thinking she'd lead them to me."

"Or the three of them were in on it together, and she was keeping you busy while the other two got ready to kill you."

If any other man had said that to him, Cobb would have knocked him flat. "She wouldn't do something like that, Butch. It's not in her nature."

"That so?" Butch went on. "How about I take a try at

guessing what you two talked about? You can bust me in the nose when I get something wrong."

Cobb was afraid of what he might do if Butch got everything right. "Don't do this to me."

"I'm doing it *for* you, not *to* you, Cobb." Butch went on. "I bet she told you how sorry she was, sorry about treating you so poorly. She said it hurt her every bit as much as it hurt you. Seeing you knock Clay flat on his back last night made her change her thinking and she wants to make things better. She told you everything you've been dying to hear for the past few weeks, didn't she?" He threw open his hands. "Since I'm still standing, I'd say I guessed pretty good, didn't I?"

Cobb did not dare admit he had been right. "You weren't there. You didn't see her. You didn't hear the way she said those things. She wants to give me another chance, Butch. I know she does. And don't forget she was right there in the room with me when they kicked the door in. She could've been shot right along with me."

"Was she standing between you and the door when they kicked it in?"

"No. She was sitting on the chair where I'd put my clean clothes."

"Just far enough out of the way," Butch pointed out. "Try thinking about this another way. Jane picked an odd time to mend fences. She could've sent for you any time she wanted, and you'd have come running. But she didn't. She came to you when you were all by yourself and nekkid, besides. If you weren't so damned ornery, you'd be dead right now."

Cobb's mind began to swim, and he held on to a porch post to keep from falling over. "It can't be like that. I know she was upset with me, but not enough to want me dead."

"Maybe it wasn't her idea," Butch said. "Maybe Clay forced her to do it. He runs the Longacre House, and maybe he didn't give her a choice. And maybe it's just happenstance, but I don't think it was. And deep down, now that you've had some time to think it over, you don't think so, either."

Cobb shut his eyes and tried to shake himself clear of the thoughts and emotions roiling inside him. Butch's doubts had made him doubt Jane and her intentions. He had been so happy before the shooting started. How could everything go so wrong so fast? "It can't be like you say, Butch. It just can't. I doubted her once and it cost me. If I doubt her now, she'll never want anything to do with me again."

Butch looked as though he felt his partner's pain. "I've got an idea about how we can put this thing to rest once and for all."

Cobb was desperate to try anything. How could he lose her after just getting her back? He needed to know if she had been telling the truth or had been lying to him. If she had tried to get him killed. "How?"

"When Hall went to fetch the sheriff," Butch said, "you had her clear out before Moran and his deputy got there. I'll bet you said you'd meet her somewhere later. Tell me where."

"She said she'll be watching for me at her window tonight. All I have to do is stand across the street, and she'll either come down or tell me where to meet her." Now that he had said the words, he realized how foolish he might have been. He might very well be giving Clay's men another chance to kill him. "We didn't pick an exact place and time."

"Then we have our answer." Butch looked up at the darkening sky. "It'll be pitch black in an hour or so. You're going to do what she said and follow her lead. Only this time, you won't be alone."

Cobb finally felt strong enough to stand on his own two

feet. He had to know the truth, even if it meant risking his life again. "Fine. We'll do it your way."

"That's the style." Butch clapped his partner on the back and they resumed walking toward the hotel. "Let's get ourselves something to eat. Say, did you really take on those two when you were nekkid?"

Cobb had not thought much about that detail. "I suppose I was."

Butch cut loose with a low whistle. "One afternoon spent with the Cheyenne, and you're already fighting like one of them. You'll be running around with face paint and a loin cloth next. If Hagen ever puts us out of business, you ought to look up old Two Moons. See if he's hiring on new braves. Sounds like you'd fit right in."

Cobb normally did not mind Butch's teasing, but he was too deep in thought to appreciate it now. "Thank you, Butch. Thanks for seeing what I couldn't."

"Nothing to thank me for yet. And I'll be happier than you if I'm wrong. Now, let's get something to eat. All this thinking has gone and given me quite the appetite."

Jane Duprey sat by the window and watched the candle she had placed there flicker in the darkness. She had not bothered to light any of the other lamps in her room. She had not been able to find the energy to rise from her chair since returning to her room.

She had not wiped away the tears that had streaked down her cheeks, either. She cried not for what she had done, but for what she had allowed herself to become.

She had never held the same affection for Tucker Cobb that he clearly had for her. She had grown fond of him, of course, and admired the bravery he had shown during the many trials they had faced on their long trek from North

Branch. He had saved her from Bart Hagen's advances and fought bravely at Delaware Station and later in Ennisville.

She supposed she had grown more than fond of him for a time, but true emotions for a man were dangerous for a woman like her. Cobb was good and kind-hearted, despite the rough exterior he showed the world. She had grown to like how she felt when she was with him; how his affection helped her forget about who and what she truly was, even if only for a little while.

But when Cobb learned that Charles Hagen had brought her to Laramie, he accused her of working for Hagen against him since North Branch. He thought that the affection she had shown him had been a lie.

Any feeling for him died in that moment. Not because Cobb was wrong, but because he had gotten closer to the truth than he knew.

Jane had not been working for Charles Hagen. Not directly. She had never even spoken to the man or corresponded with him. Madam Peachtree took care of that side of the Hagen business. Jane was just another cog in the cotton gin that was the growing Hagen empire. She doubted she was even an afterthought as far as the great man was concerned.

And on that terrible night on the boardwalk in front of the hotel, when Cobb accused her of being a Hagen spy, he saw her for what she truly was. Any bond between them crumbled to dust. Any spark they may have had was gone.

By refusing to see him in all the weeks since, she had been able to keep that truth at a comfortable distance. Paying attention to Longacre House had allowed her to forget about any romantic notions of a future with him. Of a life changed and reborn.

She had resisted Lucien Clay's idea when he had sent for her following the beating he had suffered at the hands of Cobb. She had never liked the cruel pimp but was glad he had allowed her to run Longacre House with minimal interference. As long as the house made money and the customers did not complain, he left her alone. So did Madam Peachtree and, ultimately, King Hagen himself.

When she first saw Clay in his bed the previous night—broken and swollen—she had expected to face his wrath. She had been the reason why Cobb had been in the Longacre House in the first place, and Clay would undoubtedly blame her for the beating and embarrassment he suffered.

He exacted his revenge, but in the most cunning way possible. He had threatened to make an example of her—to throw her out on her ear—if she did not help him get revenge on Tucker Cobb. He demanded for her to find a way to get back in his good graces and to keep Clay apprised of her progress.

Jane suspected Clay would use her to try to hurt Cobb, and she had hoped to warn him of it before it happened. When she had seen Cobb and Butch's coach ride past Longacre House that late afternoon, she decided now was the best time to speak to him. She had hoped to find him at his hotel, but when the clerk said Cobb was at the barber's shop, she went there instead.

She had every intention of telling Cobb that Clay was hunting him, but she could not bring herself to do it. Cobb had looked so happy to merely see her again that she found herself saying more than she had intended. So much between them had gone unsaid and she could not stop speaking her mind. Perhaps it was because, despite everything that she had told herself to the contrary, she felt the same way about Cobb.

Clay had not given her the chance to warn him. He'd most likely had those men follow her when she left Longacre

House to look for Cobb at his hotel, then finally to the barber shop where Cobb was taking a bath.

She had not dared go to Clay's room since the incident, though he was bound to know what had happened. She was sure that the man who had escaped had made a full report to Clay. Clay had not sent for her, and she prayed no one had seen her slip into her room from the back door of the house.

And now, as she sat alone in her room watching the flame of the candle in her window flicker, she prayed Cobb would not come. She prayed Butch or Sheriff Moran had made him question if she had been working with Clay's gunmen. She hoped he would not come to see her now. His love for her had already caused him so much pain. She did not think it should cost him his life.

Her stomach ached when she looked out her window and saw Tucker Cobb strolling by on the far side of the street. He stopped to lean against the wall of the bank building and casually looked around. He always appeared to be so at ease with himself. Confident, but not cocky, the way Lucien Clay and men like him tended to be. And when he saw none of the passersby were paying any notice, he raised his head toward her window to see if she was there.

She knew she should have blown out the candle. She should have pulled down the shade and remained in bed so he would not risk himself on her behalf any longer.

But she had not blown out the candle for the same reason why she went to the window now. She wanted to tell him everything.

She stood in the window and waved down to him. He acknowledged her with a curt nod before he checked the street again. No one else had seen her and, once more, he looked up toward her window.

She leaned outside and motioned for him to go down

the alley to the back of the house. Another nod confirmed he understood.

Despite the relatively warm evening, she felt a chill in the air. She pulled her shawl from her bed and pulled it tightly over her head and shoulders, hoping it would keep anyone from recognizing her.

She took the backstairs that led down to the alley behind Longacre House. The narrow street was lit only by whatever light bled out from the surrounding buildings. That was good. She would meet Cobb and quickly go somewhere else where they could talk. She had so much to say to him.

She stood in the middle of the alley and looked for any sign of Cobb in the darkness. Where was he? Had he not understood her gestures? Was he still waiting for her across the street?

She began to walk in that direction when a familiar voice from the darkness stopped her cold.

"That'll be far enough, Miss Jane. Just stay where you are and don't turn around."

"Butch?" He may not have been Cobb, but she was glad he was there. "Where's Tucker? I have to see him. It's important."

"Cobb ain't coming. Not until you and me get a few things straight."

She pulled the shawl tighter around her. His smooth Texas drawl was much colder than she remembered. "Please take me to him. I need to tell him about what happened today at the barbershop."

"I figured you would. He ain't coming, so you can tell it to me."

"Oh, please take me to him, Butch. I know you're his friend, but it won't sound the same coming from you."

"I'll tell it to him just as you tell it to me. Best get started. Time's wasting."

She tried to keep the emotion from her voice out of fear Butch might think she was acting. "Lucien told me to go to Tucker to try to win him back. I thought he might be using me as a way to get to him. I went to the barber shop to warn him. To tell him Clay was planning to move against him but . . ."

"Then why didn't you?" Butch asked from the darkness. "You were in there quite a while before those idiots busted in there. You could've started with that. Cobb would've been on his guard if you had, but you didn't. You were too busy turning him in circles while your friends got ready to jump him."

"I didn't know they were there." Her voice cracked. "Please, Butch. You have to believe me. I didn't know anyone was following me. I would've told him had I known. I would've led them anywhere far away from where he was."

"I don't believe you."

"Then believe what I'm doing now," she implored. "Clay wanted me to promise to meet Tucker somewhere later tonight. He wanted me to tell him where we'd meet so he'd have men waiting for him when he got there. But I haven't told him anything. I came down here to warn him, not have him hurt."

"You expect me to believe that?"

"No one else is here with us, are they? You must've checked. I know you did. You're careful that way. If I wanted to help Clay hurt him, he would've had his gunmen waiting here instead of me. But I don't want him hurt, Butch. Even when I was angry with him for what he said, I never wanted that. You know I'm telling you the truth. I told you that when you came to see me that time.

Remember? I was being honest then and I'm being honest now. I don't care if he doesn't want to see me. I just want him safe. I want him safe and far away from here where Clay's men can't get him. If I was lying, all I'd have to do is scream and men from the house would come running. But I haven't and I won't. You have to tell him that, Butch. He has to know I didn't want any of this to happen."

She felt something move behind her, and she might have screamed if a rough hand had not slipped over her mouth as she was slowly embraced. She did not need him to say anything for she remembered the touch so well.

"It's just me," Cobb said in her ear. "I didn't want you to scream and I'm not angry anymore."

She turned and threw her arms around his middle, burying her face in his chest. He smelled of bath soap and horse sweat but she would not have traded it for anything.

"I heard everything you said," he said, as she wept against him, "and everything's going to be just fine from here on in. I promise."

"I wasn't lying to you back there, Tucker. I meant every word I said. We need to get away from here. We need to leave tonight. Right now. I won't go back up to my room. I don't want anything that's back there. I don't need any of it as long as I have you."

He kept his arms around her as he led her through the alley. She did not know where they were going, and she did not much care.

She heard Butch following close behind them. "What are we doing, Cobb? We've got to talk this over."

"I'm done talking," Cobb said, as he spirited her through the alley. "I've never been much good at it anyway."

"Then I'll do the talking for you," Butch said. "If she doesn't go back up to her room tonight, Clay is likely to flood the town with men looking for her. The first place they'll go is to the hotel."

"We're not going back to the hotel," Cobb said. "At least I'm not. Jane can sleep in the coach tonight. I'll stay with her and keep watch. She'll ride out with you, me, and the rest of the passengers come morning."

But she knew Butch was far from happy. "He's liable to go to the sheriff. Tell Moran you took her against her will just to spite him. Haven't you spent enough time in jail to suit you?"

"Moran can look all he wants," Cobb said. "And if it comes to that, we'll tell him our plans."

"That's right." Jane held Cobb almost as tightly as he held her. "We'll tell him if we have to. We'll tell him together."

Butch grumbled to himself as they changed direction and headed toward the livery. "You sure have picked the worst time to go and become a romantic."

Cobb held her close. "Once I get her settled, I'll come back to the room to get my things. There's no reason for you to lug it all by yourself."

"With Clay's men looking for you, it ain't worth the risk," Butch said. "I'll come by the livery to help you hitch up the team in the morning. We can put our stuff on board when we go to the hotel to pick up the passengers."

For the first time in as long as she could remember, Jane was smiling. She had not allowed herself to feel hopeful since before she had come to North Branch, but everything was different now. She not only felt safe but loved. And it felt good to give love in return.

"I'll be early," Butch added. "*Real* early. The Frontier Overland Company doesn't stop for amorous pursuits."

"Don't worry," Cobb said. "The morning's a long way off."

CHAPTER 11

Lucien Clay, despite his swollen and sore face, raged at Moran as they stood in Jane Duprey's room. "Don't just stand there. I told you a woman has been taken, Sheriff. Why aren't you doing something about it?"

Moran was as calm as Clay was agitated. "On account that I already have. You said she was last seen in here, in her room. Look around. Do you see any sign of a struggle? Any overturned furniture or broken glass? I know I don't. There's not a single thing that's out of place in here. Everything she owns is still where it ought to be. A wardrobe full of clothes and all of her luggage. It looks like she's gone out for a while with every intention of coming back."

From where she stood in the darkened corner of the room, Madam Peachtree said, "Looks can be deceiving, Sheriff. Maybe the struggle didn't happen up here? Maybe it happened when she met a gentleman elsewhere?"

"She often do that kind of thing? I always figured she was a house gal."

Clay knew Cobb was behind this and saw his chance to get even with the man who had fractured his skull. "She's been acting strange the last few days, Sheriff. I finally got it out of her last night. She's afraid of some mule skinner who's been giving her trouble. His name is Tucker Cobb."

The sheriff's eyes narrowed. "That so?"

"It certainly is," Clay lied. "That's what led to our fight last night." He touched his swollen cheek. "That's why this happened. He and that friend of his have been hanging around the bar for a week, getting drunk and waiting for Miss Jane to come downstairs. I told them they had to quit coming around here and pestering that poor girl."

"Did she?" Moran asked. "Come down to see him, I mean."

"Never," Clay said. "She was too afraid to be anywhere near him, even in a place full of men who wouldn't hesitate to spring to her defense. Ask anyone who was here. They'll be happy to tell you the same."

Moran grinned. "I don't think your customers will be anxious to come forward and admit they've been in a place like this. That kind of means I'll just have to take your word for it, Lucien."

"And mine." Madam Peachtree stepped out of her corner and approached Moran. "The poor girl was absolutely terrified of him, Sheriff. She was so happy when she first came here, but I could see there was something haunting her. I didn't know what it could be until we realized she always grew troubled whenever Cobb's coach was in town. She wasn't supposed to meet anyone tonight, Sheriff. That means Cobb must have finally seen his chance to take her." She placed her hand on his arm. "You must bring her back to us before it's too late. He's due to leave town tomorrow."

Moran moved away and out of her reach. Lucien Clay watched him closely and could not tell if he believed their story. "I'll have my men look around town. I'll look for Cobb and Butch personally. If she's still in Laramie, I'll find her. And if she's left town, I'll know that, too. But I won't promise to bring her back. She's a grown woman and can go where she wants."

"No, she can't." Lucien Clay took a contract from the inside pocket of his jacket and handed it to Moran. "That there's a contract of employment. She agreed to stay here in Wyoming for three years and work for us." He pointed at the paper the sheriff was reading. "That contract is absolutely legal and enforceable in any court of law in the land."

Moran's expression soured as he read it. "I've seen this kind of document before." He handed it back to Clay. "It's modern slavery is what it is. We're just coming out of a war fighting that kind of thing. A judge might agree with you, but I don't." He looked at Clay, then at Madam Peachtree. "I'll look for Jane and make sure she's not in trouble. I'll bring her back and throw Cobb in jail if he's holding her against her will. But if she doesn't want to come back, I won't make her."

Clay was still suffering from the beating he had received from one man. He had no intention of taking another from Moran, even if he was the sheriff. "If you won't get the job done, Sheriff, my men will."

"Your men?" Moran walked closer to Lucien and stopped when there were only inches separating them. "Were those your men who tried to kill Cobb this afternoon?"

Clay feigned insult. "What a nasty thought. I'd never even consider doing such a thing."

"Well, you'd better consider this." He pointed at Clay, then at Madam Peachtree. "And this goes for the both of you. If Cobb took Jane, I'll throw him behind bars. And if I find any of your people causing trouble, I'll throw them in the cell right next to him. I've already got one of the men who tried to kill Cobb in jail, and I intend on asking him a lot of tough questions. And if he so much as hints that he was working for you, finding Jane will be the least of your worries."

"Careful, Sheriff," Madam Peachtree said from behind her veil. "Don't forget that Lucien and I have some powerful allies."

Clay saw the vein in Moran's neck bulge. "And if Charles Hagen gets in my way, he'll wind up in jail, too." Moran left the room and went downstairs without saying another word.

Clay could see the older woman had been taken down a peg or two by Moran's outburst. *Good.* "I hope you're happy. You pushed him too far, Amanda."

Madam Peachtree glared at the spot where Moran had been standing. "I haven't pushed him far enough. Not yet. Which of your idiots got arrested at the barbershop?"

"Johnny Standlee," he said. "Earl Panfil just managed to get away. He doesn't think Cobb got a good look at him."

"Standlee." She repeated the name as though it were a curse. "Can you trust him to keep his mouth shut?"

"I trust his greed," Clay said. "He wants the balance of his money, so he'll stay quiet. I've got a lawyer already working to get him out."

"How good is Panfil? How well does he know the land?"

"Good enough to keep from getting caught," Clay said. "I think he was born here, so he probably knows the area better than I do. I know he's capable enough and he runs with a dangerous crowd. Why do you ask?"

Madam Peachtree folded her hands in front of her. "Moran likes Cobb too much for my taste. I don't trust him to lean on Cobb too hard. That's why I want you to hire this Panfil and his friends to do a job for us. I want them to set up on the road to Cheyenne, wait for Cobb's coach to come by, and kill him if he isn't already dead first. With a rifle at a distance, if possible. They can leave the passengers alone or kill them. I'll leave that up to them."

This was one of those rare times that Clay wondered if the former sporting woman was beginning to lose her senses. "Why would Cobb be dead?"

She began to leave the room. Her long black gown made her look as if she were gliding above the floorboards. "Don't trouble yourself, Lucien. I've taken steps of my own to ensure this next trip is Cobb's last."

The next morning, Butch began work well before sunrise. He always liked to give himself a shave in the morning each time their stagecoach set out on a new trip. Each journey took about a week, which was just the right amount for the fair-haired man to grow any semblance of stubble.

His mind often wandered while he was doing such a mundane task. His thoughts went to Cobb and his concern for his partner now that Jane had come back into his life. It was not that Butch disliked Jane, but he could not fully trust her. Not yet. The notion that she had played a part in setting up Cobb to stop a bullet weighed heavily in his mind.

Butch could not remember a time when he had truly disagreed with his partner's decisions. He may not have liked those decisions, but he knew Cobb had made them with a clear mind. Cobb could not think clearly when it came to Jane, and he never would. Butch would have to do the thinking for him.

Butch shaved, wiped the soap from his face, and placed the razor in his bag. Since the coach would be picking up their passengers here at the hotel, he decided to leave their things in the room. It would save him the effort of lugging them to the livery.

He dressed quickly and strapped on his gun belt. As was his custom, he opened the cylinder to make sure the gun was loaded. He usually preferred to keep the chamber under the hammer empty to avoid an accidental shot. He placed a bullet in it now and flicked it shut. Lucien Clay had likely noticed Jane's absence from Longacre House by now. He probably had men out looking for her, and Butch wanted to be fully armed if they did.

He took his Henry from beside his bed and locked the door behind him. He paused at the top of the stairs to look and listen for any sign that one of Clay's men might be waiting for him. It was going on six o'clock in the morning, and early risers like him were only beginning to start their day. When it looked and sounded like no one was waiting for him, he went downstairs.

He was about to walk through the lobby and straight on for the livery when the sight of a woman sitting in one of the chairs by the door caught his eye.

Tess Carlyle's face and eyes were swollen from hours of constant crying. He thought she was wearing a different dress from the day before but could not be certain of it.

Butch doubled back and approached her. "Morning, Miss Carlyle. Are you feeling all right?"

She looked at him as if she had just woken from a dream. "Mr. Keeling. No need for formality. You may call me Tess."

"I will as long as you call me Butch." He set his rifle against the wall beside her chair and took a knee in front of her. "What are you doing here?"

"I couldn't sleep last night, so I went for a walk. I'd hoped the night air would be good for me. Then I remembered I hadn't thanked you and Mr. Cobb properly, so I came here."

Butch had thought that was the case. "It's not safe for you to be walking alone around here, Tess." He looked around for the clerk, but the front desk was unattended. "Why don't you let me walk you back home so Mrs. McBride can take care of you?"

She looked down. "I suppose I look quite mad, sitting alone in a hotel lobby by myself like this. I'm sure my aunt will find it scandalous."

Butch could see her inner turmoil. "You don't look crazy, but I hope you won't mind me telling you that you don't look quite like yourself."

"Only the wicked are insulted by the truth when they hear it." She looked out the front of the hotel and at the brightening day beyond. "Am I wicked, Butch? For the role I played in what happened yesterday, I mean. All those fine soldiers who got killed for my father's greed."

Butch had to get to the livery to help Cobb hitch up the team, but he could not leave Tess alone in such a condition.

"What happened wasn't your fault, Tess. It wasn't your father's fault or even Colonel McBride's, neither. Your father was doing what he could to help his family, and he did it fair and square. The colonel didn't cheat them, but many other white men have. Two Moons and some of his braves didn't like handing over the land and tried to do something about it. Sometimes it's not about who's right and who's wrong. It's about how people handle disappointment."

Tess's eyebrows raised a bit. "You should be a philosopher, not a gunman for a stagecoach."

Butch was glad to see her mood brighten a bit. "I'm a gunman for my very own stagecoach, Miss Carlyle. And

Cobb's the only one who benefits from hearing me talk. Well, he would if he ever took the time to listen."

"Is Mr. Cobb here? I'd like to thank both of you for what you did. For being brave enough to save us all."

"We're taking some passengers over to Cheyenne this morning, so he's at the livery getting the team ready to travel. I'll be going over to help him after I see you get back home safe. And there's no need to thank us. Your uncle did that for you yesterday."

"Money." Her eyes got a far-off look again. "It seems all the world's problems can be traced back to the desire for gold and silver."

"If it wasn't money, folks would find something else to kill each other, be it for food or trinkets or something else." He stood up and held out his hand to help her up. "Let's get you back home where you can rest some. You've been through quite an ordeal."

She placed her hand in his and slowly stood. "You and Mr. Cobb had a much tougher time of it than I did, yet you seem none the worse for it."

He took his rifle and walked her outside. "That's on account of me and Cobb are used to this sort of thing. Why, we wouldn't know what to do with ourselves if someone wasn't trying to kill us. We'd probably die from the pure shock of it."

The sun was still low in the sky, but the air was growing muggy. It was shaping up to be an uncomfortable day in Laramie, and Butch was happy he would soon be out on the road.

As they began walking back to the McBride residence, Butch was concerned that she had grown quiet. He did not want her to withdraw again, so he tried to keep her talking. "How long were you fixing to stay here in Laramie?"

"I didn't know how long my father would need me by

his side, so I didn't pick an exact date to leave. My aunt and uncle have told me I'm welcome to stay for as long as I wish. My father wanted to be buried here close to the fort, and I had been thinking about going back home right after the funeral. But I don't have much reason to rush home right away. I may accept my aunt and uncle on their offer to let me stay here for a while."

Butch knew his next question might test the boundaries of polite conversation, but he asked it anyway. "Don't have anyone waiting for you back there?"

She smiled thinly. "I'm quite unattached if that's what you're asking. Independent-minded women aren't exactly popular back in Baltimore. In fact, they're outright frowned upon."

"Well, they're in short supply out here where a little independence is best. You might find Laramie more to your liking."

She looked up at him as they walked. "Yes, I'm beginning to see that. I take it you and Mr. Cobb are leaving town this morning."

"We'll be ferrying a bunch of passengers over to Cheyenne," Butch said. "Cobb hates it when I call it 'ferrying,' but I like it. Has more flair to it than just saying we're driving a coach."

She made him happy by laughing. "I can tell you're quite a talker, but I was wondering if you were much of a writer."

Other than being able to write his name, Butch had gotten through life without the benefit of knowing how to read, much less write. He had never been ashamed of it until that moment. "I've been known to put pen to paper when I had a good reason."

"Well, if you think I'm a good enough reason, I'd enjoy hearing from you while you're gone."

"I'd be glad to if you didn't think you'd be too bored by it. There's not much to write about except long hours sitting next to Cobb, who ain't all that interesting. He's a brooder, but I do my best to keep him occupied."

"I imagine you do. And I'd appreciate the effort. It doesn't have to be anything thrilling. Just a note now and then when you think of it."

Butch doubted he would be thinking of much else. "As long as you're not expecting fancy prose, I'll be happy to oblige."

He was glad he could see a visible change in her by the time they reached the McBride residence. She did not look as sad as she had back in the lobby, and some of the color had returned to her face. He felt bad about his first impression of her appearance the previous day. She was actually quite pretty if a man took long enough to look at her.

She offered him her gloved hand. "I'll look forward to reading your letters, Butch. I'll happily reply if you want. They can be waiting for you at each spot you make on your return trip back here to Laramie."

He found himself wondering what his old friend Leon Hunt would do in a situation like this. The old actor would probably quote Shakespeare or do something fancy and theatrical.

Butch kissed her hand, then tipped his hat as he backed away. "I wish you a good morning, Tess."

As he walked toward the livery, he remembered how he had spent much of the previous night fretting about how the new day would begin. He only hoped his new acquaintance with Tess was a harbinger of better things to come on the road ahead.

CHAPTER 12

Butch was disappointed that Cobb had not made much progress in hitching up the team to the coach.

"I figured you'd have this done by now," Butch said, as he placed the collar on one of the lead horses. "Guess you must've slept in a bit this morning."

"Knock it off," Cobb said, as he led the Wheelers to the coach. "I've lost track of all the mornings I had to do all the work because you were off somewhere with one of your señoritas."

Butch knew Cobb might be right, but that was no excuse to prevent him from having some fun at his partner's expense. "Where is her ladyship this morning, anyway? I hope she ain't up and changed her mind on coming along."

"She's over at the general store buying some clothes and things for the road," Cobb said. "And no, I didn't give her any money. She wouldn't take it. Said she had plenty of her own."

Butch imagined she probably had more money than the both of them put together but decided to keep that observation to himself. "You think it was a good idea to let her go alone?"

"She insisted," Cobb said. "No one came looking for

her last night, and I wouldn't be surprised if they haven't missed her yet at Longacre House. I told her to be careful, and she said she'd go in the back way and get one of the clerks to help her. I think you'll find her a mighty resourceful young lady."

Butch wisely changed what he was going to say and said, "I'm sure I will. I just hope she doesn't buy too much. We'll need to save room for the luggage of our paying passengers."

Cobb began his final check of the braces and straps that secured the teams in place. "How many are we taking on this run anyway?"

"Four, according to the hotel clerk last night," Butch said. "We'll know the final number this morning."

Cobb frowned as he gave one of the straps a firm tug. "That's fewer than I was hoping."

"That's a decent number considering King Hagen has put out the word against us," Butch reminded him. "I asked the clerk if he knew what they were like, but he wasn't much use. Seemed more interested in dozing off than helping me."

"I guess we should be grateful that they spoke to you at all," Cobb said. "I doubt the hotel will even give us the time of day when we swing back here in a week's time."

Butch knew Cobb might be right, but it did not mean he had to agree with him. "That's why we get along so well, Cobb. We're a pair of optimists."

Cobb stopped checking the straps on his side of the team and took a close look at his partner. "You're not usually this chatty this early in the morning. Why the change?"

Butch was pleased there was just enough give in the straps to allow the horses some room. "Let's just say you're not the only one in this outfit who benefited from some female company. I had a conversation with a pretty young lady this morning."

"Uh-oh," Cobb said. "You'd better hope her husband doesn't find out."

"She ain't married," Butch told him. "It's Tess Carlyle."

Cobb looked impressed. "Was she lost or something?"

"You could say that. And I was happy to help her find her way. And unlike you, she's a good judge of character. She thinks I'm interesting. She even wants me to write to her while we're on the road, and I have half a mind to do it."

"I hope you find someone to help write those letters for you," Cobb said. "She won't be able to read your chicken scratch, and you don't know many words."

"I'll find a way to make do," Butch said with confidence. "Love has a habit of finding a way."

"It certainly does," Jane Duprey said, as she swept into the livery. Butch noticed she was wearing a new dress that was much plainer than the fancy kind she usually wore. And she was only carrying one large carpetbag that did not appear quite full.

She held up the bag as if it was a trophy. "See? I told you I could travel light. I only bought the essentials for a week on the road. Bet you didn't think I could manage with such a small bag, did you, Tucker?"

Cobb was beaming. "No. I can't say that I did, but I'm glad I was wrong."

Butch kept busy with the horses while they greeted each other. He had a lot of questions about Jane's involvement in their enterprise. He had not had the chance to ask Cobb about the particulars, and Cobb had not offered any. Would she remain with them on the trip back to Laramie, or would she stay in Cheyenne? Would they work out of the territorial capital from now on, or would they remain in Laramie? Did Cobb still have an appetite for this line of work, or would a future with Jane change his plans?

Butch imagined there would be plenty of time for questions once they got underway, but for the moment, they had passengers to pick up at the hotel.

Cobb surprised him by putting Jane's bag in the rear boot himself. "Now, remember what I told you about what we have to do."

"I've got it all right up here." Jane tapped her temple. "I'll sit in the back quietly with the shade drawn while the passengers board. I won't say a word until we're well out of town, and even then, I won't say much."

Butch, now finished checking the horses, leaned against the coach. "You're sure no one saw you going into that general store just now? There's lots of people on the streets this time of morning."

"No one saw me, I promise. They may not even know I'm gone yet, which is fine by me."

"Let's keep it that way." Cobb opened the coach door for her and undid the strap that kept the shade rolled up and in place. "This'll make it good and dark inside. Just do what we talked about, and we'll be out of here before they know it."

She squeezed his arm as she climbed inside, and he closed the door for her.

Cobb and Butch climbed up into the driver's box together, with Butch resting the butt of his Henry on his leg. "I hope you know what you're doing, Cobb, because I sure don't."

"Don't trouble yourself any, Butch. My thinking's always been good enough for both of us so far."

Butch had never suffered from Cobb's thinking. It was his emotions that he was worried about.

Cobb released the hand brake and snapped the straps

that set the team moving out of the livery yard and onto the Laramie Hotel where their passengers awaited.

As Cobb steered the team onto Main Street, his heart sank over what he saw waiting for them in front of the Laramie Hotel.

Sheriff Rob Moran and two of his deputies were on horseback and facing in the coach's direction. There was no doubt they were waiting for him.

"How do you want to do this?" Butch asked him. "It sure doesn't look like they're here to give us a send-off."

"I'll worry about Moran," Cobb said. "You just see to it that the passengers get loaded. I'll want to be on our way as soon as we can."

"If Moran lets us, that is."

Cobb ignored his partner's pessimism.

He drew rein in front of the hotel and threw the hand brake, locking the team in place. Butch jumped down and began talking to the customers who were already lined up with the luggage on the boardwalk.

Moran moved his horse next to the coach. "You know why I'm here, Tucker. Where is she?" He pointed at him. "And if you play cute, I'll throw you in jail for a week."

Cobb knew the lawman would not hesitate to do so. "She's right behind me with the shade drawn. She's here on her own free will, Rob. I'm not making her go and she can stay if she wants."

Moran frowned as he edged his horse over to the door and rapped on it with his knuckles. "It's Sheriff Moran, Jane. Pull up the shade so I can get a good look at you."

Cobb twisted in his seat and saw her pull back the leather just enough to reveal her face. "Good morning,

Sheriff. And before you ask, Tucker's not making me go anywhere. If anything, he's saving me."

Moran looked up the street. "Lucien's mighty concerned about you. It took a good deal of talking on my part to keep him from sending men out to look for you. I thought you liked it over at Longacre House."

"I liked it just fine," she admitted, "but I love the idea of leaving with Tucker and Butch. There's a whole lot of nothing waiting for me back there, but a whole lot of something with Tucker."

Moran leaned over in the saddle to get a closer look at her. "I figure I already know the answer, but I have to ask. He's not making you leave with him? I've got two men with me right now who'll keep him away from you if you want. Just tell me and it's done."

"It would take more men than that to get me to leave," she said. "And if you do, you'd better have someone watch me day and night. I'll steal a horse and ride after him if I have to. And you can tell Lucien Clay and Madam Peachtree where they can go if they don't like it."

"Yeah," Moran said. "I figured it was something like that. The problem is that you've got a contract to stay on with them for almost three years more years. It's legal. I read it over myself."

"Tell him he can sue me if he wants," Jane said. "I left enough back in my room to cover that much and more. Tell him he can keep it all if he'll just let me be."

Moran scratched his cheek with a thumbnail. "I guess I'll just have to pass that message on to him. You can pull the shade down again if you want. Have a pleasant journey."

Cobb felt a strange combination of pride and love when he heard the shade flop into place as Moran moved his horse toward him again.

"I don't think I've ever met a man who loves to make life as hard on himself as much as you, Tucker."

"She loves me, Sheriff. And I love her, too."

Moran looked like he wanted to say more but held his tongue. "You know I only have a say over what happens here in Laramie. Out there, you'll be on your own, and Clay is apt to want to try to get her back."

Cobb had expected as much. "He tell you what he's fixing to do?"

The sheriff shook his head. "He knows I like you, so he kept that much to himself. He won't let it rest, though. It might take him a month or a year, but he won't let it slide. And even if he did, Madam Peachtree won't. That is one vindictive woman."

"They're welcome to try, but I've never been one to back down."

"No. You're not. Sometimes, I wish you were. It'd be easier on the peace if you were. Easier on you, too. You know Clay and the madam are tied to Charles Hagen, don't you?"

"Yeah. I've heard that."

"Hagen already hates you and this won't make him look any kinder on you."

"I don't expect it will."

Moran looked like he had hoped that would make a dent and was disappointed when it failed to do so. "I just hope you're not expecting much help from your passengers. Me and the boys had a chance to give them a good look over before you got here. Three drunks with the shakes and a lady with the coldest eyes I've ever seen. I know you and Butch can fight, but you'll be hauling a lot of dead weight if Clay's men start causing trouble out there."

"We'll manage," Cobb said. "We always have."

Moran held out his hand to him. "Then I wish you luck, Tucker. I hope you'll be back real soon. I mean it."

Cobb knew he did and shook his hand.

Moran gestured for his two deputies to follow him. "Let's go give Lucien the bad news, boys. It promises to make for an interesting morning."

Cobb sat alone in the wagon box as one of the porters from the hotel helped Butch stack the luggage on top of the coach. It was mostly flat ground between Laramie and Cheyenne with a few stations in between to offer food and fresh horses. Hagen probably controlled most of the stations, but he was certain that even his reach weakened the further away from Laramie.

The coach swayed a bit as the last passenger climbed aboard and Butch shut the door. "That's it, Cobb. All passengers present and ready to ride." He patted his shirt pocket where he kept the money. "All paid up in advance, too."

Cobb released the hand brake and snapped the reins, causing the team to start moving forward along Main Street.

Butch was in the middle of recounting the money when he noticed something. "You can turn them around any time you want. There's no other wagons on the street and Cheyenne's in the other direction."

"So is Longacre House," Cobb said. "I figure this way's less likely to draw attention."

Butch went back to counting their money. "Tucker Cobb, going out of his way to avoid a confrontation. That's a first."

"It's a day of all kinds of firsts," Cobb said. "Let's hope it's no one's last."

CHAPTER 13

The ride out from Laramie was as calm as he had hoped, but Butch's silence was troubling. He normally could not get his partner to quit talking. "Why are you so quiet?"

"Just watching and waiting." Butch had his Henry flat across his lap. "Making sure there are no surprises waiting for us out there. I thought Clay would've kicked up more of a fuss about Jane. The fact that he didn't has me thinking he might be fixing to do something on his own."

That had been Cobb's concern, too. But as he could not do much about it, he decided to concentrate on the task at hand. "What did you make of the passengers? I'm sorry I didn't have the chance to greet them before they boarded, but Moran waiting for us like he was kind of threw me."

Butch looked at him. "Jane sure must be having an effect on you. I can't imagine you admitting such a thing a week ago."

"A lot's changed since then," Cobb said. "Some for the good. Some isn't so good."

"Sounds like a good way to describe these passengers we're hauling," Butch said.

Cobb doubted the passengers could hear them talking, but he motioned for Butch to keep his voice down anyway.

The shotgun rider obliged. "Ned Vetrano, Dick Matthews, Parker Renfro, and a lady by the name of Miss Cassie Hyde. She bought her ticket last night according to the clerk."

"And what do you make of them?" Cobb asked. "Moran wasn't impressed."

"My estimation's not much better than his," Butch admitted. "A couple of those boys looked like they were either still drunk or working on a powerful hangover. One of them, Vetrano, already had the shakes. I'd place even money that we might have use for an old mop and bucket by the time we switch teams at Wingate Station."

Cobb hoped, for the sake of the women, that would not be necessary. "I was hoping there might be another Leon Hunt in the bunch. A man of his skills would be a pleasant surprise."

"Not with this group. They're about as twitchy as a tree full of squirrels."

"What about the woman? That Miss Hyde you mentioned."

"She doesn't look like a gunfighter, either," Butch mused. "Not much to say about her. Quiet. Buttoned up. Polite but not as friendly as Jane." He held up his hand to head off any argument. "That's meant as a compliment, not a complaint. I just meant she's closer to Tess than Jane if that reference is helpful."

Cobb kept his eyes on the road ahead as the coach continued on. It was a warmer day than he had expected, and the horses were beginning to labor. He thought they would be able to make Wingate Station if they did not have to make a run for it.

"There's a stream about a mile away from here," Cobb said. "The horses look like they could use a drink and a rest. It'll give me a chance to look over the passengers for myself while we're at it."

"I know that tone, Cobb. Something gnawing at you again. What is it?"

Cobb saw no reason to hide his concerns from his partner. "That crack you made about Clay earlier. About him letting us leave Laramie too easy."

It took a moment for Butch to catch on. "I was figuring he'd have some men waiting to jump us out here on the road. You think he might've snuck one of his men on here with us as a passenger?"

Cobb was beginning to wonder if that was possible. "A man that slight in a business like his can't fight. You saw what happened to him when he tried. He has to find other ways to cut a man down to size. I don't know him well, but I wouldn't put anything past him." He nodded at the road ahead. "But you and me will have plenty of chances to look them over when we stop. Don't just go by appearances. Study them all and study them close, Butch. Use your ears as much as your eyes. It could be important."

"I will." Butch shifted in his seat as he let out a heavy sigh. "I wish we could have one journey without having to worry about getting killed."

"That would be nice, wouldn't it?"

As Cobb allowed the horses to drink from the creek, he made a point of being the first one to help the passengers step down off the stage. It was time to start glad-handing his customers.

"Sorry I couldn't make everyone's acquaintance earlier, but Sheriff Moran was anxious to talk to me."

After helping Jane down, Miss Hyde was next. Butch usually had a good eye for describing people and his description of the woman had been true. She had a prim and proper manner to her, much like Tess Carlyle had. She had clear blue eyes that looked right through him as he offered his hand to her.

"Tucker Cobb, co-owner and operator of the stage, ma'am. Thank you for traveling with us."

She smiled as she said, "Is there a problem we should know about, Mr. Cobb?"

"Just some thirsty horses," Cobb said, as he turned his attention to the men. "Nothing more to it than that. We'll be on our way before you know it."

The first man off bore a dark complexion and a thread-bare suitcoat. His shirt had once been white, but now was closer to gray. "Ned Vetrano, Cobb." The smell of whiskey was still on him. "Hope you're right about getting us to civilization. I'm not much of an outdoorsman."

Cobb imagined he was more comfortable in saloons than in nature. "Just a quick stop for the sake of the horses. Nothing to worry about."

The next man off the coach bore the swollen, red-veined nose of an accomplished drinker, but he had more of a spark to him than Vetrano. "Dick Matthews, Mr. Cobb. Glad to be able to put a face to the driver. Say, how long before we hit Cheyenne?"

"I'd say we'll be there by late morning tomorrow," Cobb told him. "We'll be swapping out teams at Wingate Station first. You'll find it a clean, quiet place to lay your head, I promise you."

The last man off the coach kept his head down as he moved by Cobb. He barely offered a nod as he pulled on a slouch hat that looked as though it had seen all sorts of weather through many seasons. Since he knew the names of the other passengers, he took this one to be Parker Renfro.

Jane had remained by his side as he greeted the passengers, and he turned to see her smiling up at him.

Cobb could not avoid smiling back. "How's the ride been so far?"

"Quiet, but I'm not complaining. How's your arm?"

He rubbed the bandage beneath his sleeve. It ached some, but not enough for him to notice. "Quiet, but I'm not complaining."

She joined him in watching the customers who had spread out along the creek bed.

"Well?" he asked her. "What do you make of them?"

"That Miss Hyde seems to be a nice sort, but she doesn't like talking about herself much. I think she's on her way to Cheyenne to be a schoolteacher, but she's too reserved to give out with much more than that."

"Don't take it personally," he said. "She seems to be the prim type. What about Vetrano and the others? They pay you any notice?"

She looked down at her new shoes. "Mr. Vetrano slept most of the way here. I don't think he's feeling very well. I think Mr. Matthews recognized me. I certainly remember him." She answered Cobb's question before he could ask it. "No, not in that way, Tucker. He always had Lucien's ear. He's something of a huckster. Always had a new scheme about how they could make money together. He wanted to run the card games, but Lucien wouldn't hear of it. He already had people he trusted to do that."

Cobb eyed the roundish man in a new light. "He's close with Clay, is he?"

"I wouldn't say they were friendly," Jane said. "Lucien always seemed to just tolerate him. He's very conversational and he makes people laugh. The better they feel, the more they drink. I think he's going to Cheyenne to try his luck there. I think he's harmless."

But Cobb knew anyone close with Lucien Clay could possibly be trouble. "What about that cowpuncher over there? I think Butch told me his name is Renfro or something like that."

"Do you mean Parker Renfro?" She giggled. "Is that the name he gave? That ragamuffin isn't Renfro. Parker's a banker, not a cowhand."

Cobb watched the man with renewed interest. He saw him lean against a tree as he looked down at the water flowing by. "Is that so?"

"Renfro's one of Lucien's best customers downstairs." A curious look from Cobb made her explain further. "The opium den. We're not supposed to know about it, much less talk about it, but we all know what goes on down there. A lot of Lucien's customers quit coming upstairs, so they could spend more time smoking the stuff."

Cobb had heard rumors about such places in Laramie, but he never paid them any mind. "I bet Clay doesn't like that."

"He loves it," she told him. "They pay more to smoke than they do for us. And the Chinese run it all on their own. They pay Lucien to use the cellar and give him a cut of their take, but no one complains. They all seem to be profiting quite nicely from it."

But Cobb did not care about that. "If he's not Renfro, who is he? And what's he doing using another man's name?"

Jane's smile slowly faded. "Oh, no. Tucker, you don't think Lucien could've sent him here in Parker's place, do you?"

"I don't know, but I aim to find out."

Butch jumped down from the wagon box to block his path. "I've been listening to you two talk this whole time, and I think I've got a better way."

Cobb tried to keep his voice down for the benefit of the passengers. "It was you who planted that idea in my head about Clay sending someone with us. Now you're telling me to let him go. This coach isn't moving until I know who he really is and why he lied."

"He'll just lie or try to talk his way out of it if you do," Butch said. "I've got a better suggestion. You keep Jane up in the wagon box with you while I take her place inside. Try to get to know our passengers better on the way to Wingate Station."

Cobb did not think much of Butch's idea. "I need you up top looking for trouble, not back there running your mouth."

"There might be trouble out there," Butch allowed, "but I reckon they would've hit us by now if there was. I know that's what I would've done if I were them. And if you spot trouble, I can hop out and help you take care of it."

Cobb knew his partner had a point, but he still did not like it. "You might be trapping yourself in there with a man who's come to kill us."

"That's one way of looking at it," Butch said. "The other is that they'll be trapped in there with me. And I ain't so easy to kill in case you haven't noticed."

"I noticed." He could tell Butch had made up his mind, and once an idea took root, there was no budging him. He asked Jane, "You mind sitting up in the wagon box with me? I won't tell you it's comfortable, but I can promise it's a better view than the one you have in there."

She stroked his right arm. "You're always such a romantic, Mr. Cobb."

Butch handed her his Henry. "I won't have much use for this in there, but I'll have my pistol handy. You just hold onto this for me while I try to figure out if one of them is trying to kill us."

CHAPTER 14

Phil Bengston peered through his field glasses, watching the team of horses drink water from the stream while passengers spread out along the creek bed.

Earl Panfil was crouched to his left. "This is the time to do it, Phil. Let's hit them now while they're afoot. You could peg both of them with your Sharps before they heard the first shot. I've seen you do it lots of times."

Bengston ignored him and kept watching the creek. "Cobb and Keeling are standing too close to Jane. Clay doesn't want her hurt, remember?"

"All this waiting around just doesn't make sense to me."

"Don't rush me because you lost your nerve yesterday. You should've killed him while he was in that tub, but you flubbed it. We're doing this my way this time. Not yours."

Panfil had always been slow to think and quick to rile. "Don't go forgetting who hired you on for this here expedition, mister. Why, Lucien didn't even know who you were before I told him about you."

Bengston refused to be lured into another one of Panfil's pointless, petty arguments. Clay had not hired him because of Panfil. He hired him because he had done this kind of work before.

Bengston focused his field glasses on Cobb, Butch, and the passengers instead.

Panfil was still pouting when he asked, "Did I hear you right just now? Miss Jane is down there with them?"

"She's there," Bengston confirmed. "And so is our other friend." He was hoping he could judge the mood of the group by the looks on their faces as they spoke to each other. "Everyone seems to be at ease. Cobb and Butch are talking to Jane, but they don't look troubled. That's a good sign. I think we're still in business. They probably don't suspect a thing."

Panfil pulled off his hat and slapped it on the ground in frustration. "When's the shooting gonna start? This is the time to do it, while they're on foot and easy targets. They'd never even know it was coming. Why doesn't Renfro just kill 'em right now and get it over with? It's a short ride back to Laramie from here, and we've got an extra horse."

Bengston knew that, unlike Panfil, Conner was smart. Shooting Cobb and Butch now would mean killing the others. They would be witnesses and could not be allowed to live. It was better to wait for the best time to strike. He imagined they were headed to Wingate Station for some fresh horses to continue on to Cheyenne. He could tell by the position of the sun that it would be dark before they reached the capital. And knowing Cobb was a cautious man, he would not risk traveling at night. They would take their time getting to Wingate Station and likely stay the night. That was where Conner would most likely kill them.

Bengston got to his feet and slid the field glasses back in their pouch. "They'll be there for a while yet. If we move now, we can reach Wingate Station long before they do. We'll figure out what to do next when we get there."

He helped pull the older and heavier Panfil to his feet but held on to him as he got his balance. "You're sure

Cobb didn't get a good look at you in the alley yesterday? You'd best tell me now if he did so I can be ready for it if he recognizes you later."

"I shot at him while he was struggling with the other fella," Panfil said. "He only saw the back of me as I ducked down a side alley. I'm not even wearing the same clothes."

Bengston was not sure he believed him. Killing Cobb and Keeling would have been much easier if he left Panfil here with a bullet in his head. He was loud, stupid, and petty. Add in the cowardice he displayed in the alley the previous day, and he was a grave liability. He had failed to kill a man taking a bath. He doubted he would do anything different if that same man and his partner were shooting back.

But Clay's orders had left no room for doubt. If Panfil did not make it back, Bengston and Conner would not be paid. For once in his life, Panfil was worth more alive than dead.

"Let's get going," Bengston said, as he began walking back to their horses. "I want to get to Wingate Station in time to look the place over."

As he rode in the back with the passengers, Butch decided he and Cobb should have spent more on the cushions. His backside was already beginning to ache even though they were less than a mile from watering the team. He seemed to feel every bump and divot in the road and wished he was back up top with Cobb.

Mr. Matthews, who was sitting across from him and next to Miss Hyde, was the first among them to ask the obvious question. "I'm curious as to why you're in here with us instead of the other lady. I'm sorry, but I don't remember her name."

"That's because she didn't offer it," Miss Hyde said. "As if we already didn't know who and what she was."

Butch was glad Jane had kept that much to herself, but wanted to know how Miss Hyde had come by that assumption. "And just what do you suspect her of being, ma'am?"

The woman harrumphed as she looked out the window. "It's obvious, isn't it? A soiled dove. A sporting lady? Why, I can still smell the stench of the cheap perfume from her pores. Her kind can change their clothes and appearance, but never what they really are."

Butch hoped she would leave it at that. The more she talked, the longer it would take for him to discover the intentions of the rest of the passengers. Mr. Vetrano was opposite Miss Hyde and the constant jostling of the coach did not appear to affect his dozing.

But Butch was more interested in the man crammed into the seat next to him. Parker Renfro. He would get to him in time.

"To answer your question," Butch said to Mr. Matthews, "I'll only be down here for a short while. Cobb and me like to judge the comfort of our coach for ourselves from time to time. The Frontier Overland Company always wants to provide its passengers with the best ride possible."

"Like the wings of angels," Mr. Matthews said. "I read that on your poster the clerk at the hotel showed me. Quite a catchy title to be sure."

"That was all my idea," Butch boasted. "Cobb takes care of the business aspect of things and leaves the more creative side of the business to me." He remembered what Jane had said about Matthews being close to Lucien Clay. He certainly did not look like a killer, but men had been known to do all sorts of things if they were threatened. "What's waiting for you in Cheyenne, Mr. Matthews? If memory serves, you've been in Laramie since before Cobb and me started this line."

"Your memory serves you well." The man's graying eyebrows rose. "I'm going to Cheyenne searching for opportunity, sir. The promise of a better future. Laramie's a fine place, but not always the best fit for a man of my talents."

"And what might those talents be?" Butch asked.

"Intuition. Conversation. Understanding a man's true nature and wants when he may not even know it himself."

Butch had heard that line before. "You're a salesman."

Mr. Matthews smiled wide and easily. "A huckster would be closer to the mark. I imagine I've sold everything under the sun at some point in my life. Started with insurance back in Philadelphia and I've been doing it ever since. Haberdashery, mining tools, farming tools, livestock, and liquor." He looked at Miss Hyde. "Why, I even dabbled in ladies' fashions for a time. I still keep up on the latest fashions. I'm sure I could help you get a whole new wardrobe when we reach Cheyenne. For a modest fee, of course."

"Of course." Miss Hyde dismissed him as she looked out the window again. "I have no need for fashion of any kind. The clothes I have will suit me fine, thank you."

Mr. Matthews took the rejection in stride and turned his attention back to Butch. "I'm usually far more convincing than that. I hope I haven't begun to lose my touch."

But Butch was interested in more than just his skills as a salesman. "Kind of risky leaving all your friends in Laramie for something different in Cheyenne."

"I make friends wherever I go, Mr. Keeling," Matthews said. "Affability has always come natural to me."

Butch decided to push a bit. "True, but friends like Lucien Clay are hard to come by."

Matthews's smile slowly faded. "Lucien is a shrewd

businessman. Had he taken a different path, he might have given Charles Hagen himself a run for his money. He still might, if he keeps on like he is. I understand you and Mr. Cobb learned that first-hand a couple of nights ago at a place we won't mention here in mixed company."

Miss Hyde shifted in her seat and looked out the window in earnest.

"I'd say it was Clay who learned something from Cobb." Butch narrowed his gaze. "Funny. I don't remember seeing you around when it happened."

"Word travels fast in a town of Laramie's rather limited size," Matthews explained. "I'm sure everyone has heard about it by now. I paid Lucien a visit to say goodbye last night. He's doing remarkably well."

Butch smiled. "How's his jaw?"

Matthews did not smile. "It's much better than it looks."

Butch felt he had prodded Matthews enough and decided it was time to give the stranger next to him—the one posing as Parker Renfro—a try. They were sitting close together in the cramped coach. If he tensed or went for a gun, Butch was sure he would sense it. "What about you, Mr. Renfro? Did you stop in to pay your respects to poor old Lucien on his sickbed? I understand you two are close."

The cowboy fiddled with the brim of the hat on his lap. "I . . . I wouldn't say that. I imagine we're friendly enough, but I wouldn't call him a friend."

"You don't have to play it small for our sake," Butch said. "I hear you give him advice on all sorts of things, what with you being a banker and all."

The man stopped fiddling with his hat brim but did not look up from it. "It ain't like that."

"And you ain't Parker Renfro." Butch could feel the

cowboy's tension radiating off the man like heat. Butch was ready to grab him if he so much as flinched. "What's your real name and what are you doing on my coach?"

The impostor shut his eyes as if that would be enough to make the accusation go away.

Matthews leaned forward to intervene. "Now, see here, Keeling. You have no right to—"

Butch glared at him until he sat back. "This is my coach, and I've got every right to do anything I want. This fella lied about who he was, and I intend on finding out why."

The impostor swallowed hard. "I ain't Parker Renfro."

"I already knew that much," Butch said. "Who are you? And no more lies because I ain't in a forgiving kind of mood."

"My name's Nick Fisk, not that it means anything to you."

"It'll mean more to me once you tell me why you took Renfro's ticket."

"I don't even hardly know the man," Fisk said. "I only came to Laramie last week when the Lazy T let me go. I took what money I had and started spending it at the den below Longacre House."

Butch noticed Miss Hyde shift in her seat but kept looking out the window.

"Go on," Butch prodded.

"I saw Renfro there a couple of times, and we got to talking some while we waited for the smoke to reach us. He was always talking big, about how his daddy was sending him to Cheyenne to work at his bank there. It didn't seem fair that he had all these chances to go wherever he wanted, and I had nothing. We wound up in Clay's place last night and, come this morning, he was still asleep. The girls told me he'd paid for an extra bowl. I knew he'd never make it to the coach before it left, and I didn't see why I should let a good ticket go to waste. I figured Cheyenne's a better place to be broke than Laramie, so when the Chinese girls who tended to us weren't looking, I took the ticket from his pocket and here I am."

When he finally looked at Butch, he was close to tears. "You can kick me off if you want to, but I'm not sorry for what I did. And if I had to do it all over again, I'd do it the same way."

Butch wanted to believe he was telling the truth, but he had to be sure. "You sure you didn't hurt him? If you did, best tell me now because I'll find out once we get to Cheyenne."

Fisk slowly shook his head. "I just took the ticket from his coat, which was hanging on a hook. If he's dead, it ain't because of anything I did. I swear it."

Matthews cleared his throat. "I can't exactly vouch for his story, Mr. Keeling, but I know Parker Renfro. He's a careless young man who has allowed his curious appetites to get the better of him. Everything he has just told you seems perfectly plausible to me."

He looked at Matthews. "You heard me call out the names of the passengers in the hotel lobby this morning. You knew this fella wasn't Renfro, but you kept your mouth shut. Why?"

"Why should I get involved?" Matthews asked. "He wasn't hurting anyone. Besides, I figured Renfro could've just as easily lost his ticket in a card game or on another game of chance. Parker isn't known for always making wise decisions with his father's money."

Butch sat back, defeated. He could tell Fisk was being truthful, but that did not necessarily eliminate him as one of Clay's men. Butch had never even heard of anyone named

Parker Renfro before that morning and, for all he knew, this was a scheme Clay had cooked up with Matthews and Fisk.

He felt a sharp coldness spread in his belly as another thought came to him. He realized Jane was the one who had told him and Cobb about Renfro. What if Clay had brought all three of them into his scheme? What if Jane had fed him and Cobb the lie, Fisk copped to it, and Matthews vouched for it? Having caught Fisk in such a big lie might be enough to make Cobb and Butch believe that was the end of it. They might let down their guard, believing there was nothing more to uncover.

Butch would not let that happen.

CHAPTER 15

It was still a few hours away from sunset when Cobb saw Wingate Station further down the road.

Still sitting beside him, Jane did not hide her disappointment. "Is that where we'll be staying for the night?"

Cobb could not blame her for having reservations about the place. The station did not have high walls around it, only a weathered split rail fence on the perimeter that looked about ready to collapse. The station building itself was not much to look at, but it had withstood many Wyoming winters and summers. The sloped roof was still crooked and looked like it had been added as an afterthought.

"I know it doesn't look like much from here, but that's part of its charm. Charlie Smith ain't one for outward appearances, but it's nice enough inside. There'll be plenty of room for us to bed down, and the food's not half bad. Charlie prides himself on his breakfasts. I think it's the only thing he knows how to cook. It's not like the fine dining at the Laramie Hotel, but it'll see us through until tomorrow."

She put her arm through his. "I don't care as long as I'm with you."

Cobb knew his next point might be a touchy one. "About that. We're going to have different sleeping arrangements than last night. Being out here alone for so long has turned Charlie into something of a zealot. Women sleep in one part of the building and men in the other. He likes to keep watch by the door all night to make sure it stays that way."

Jane clearly did not like that. "Sounds like a prude."

"His station, his rules." Cobb kept the rest of his concerns to himself. He had heard that Charlie Smith had sold out to Hagen a few weeks back. He only hoped he did not deny them room and board and a team of fresh horses for the push to Cheyenne.

He saw Smith come out of the station building and hobble over to the gate. His leg had been crushed beneath a horse some years back, costing him his left leg below the knee. He got around with the use of a crutch, which never failed to impress Cobb. Keeping a station running alone would be tough for a man with two good legs, but Charlie was a resilient man.

He watched the figure rest by the gate as the stagecoach drew closer. The few hairs he still had on his head had gone gray and appeared to be holding on for dear life, just like the rest of the place.

Cobb threw the hand brake after reining in the horses. Charlie beckoned for him to come down and talk to him, so he did.

Cobb tried the friendly approach. "Good to see you again, Charlie. It's been a while."

"It surely has," the station master said. "A lot's changed since you were last here. I signed on with the Hagen outfit. You know what that means."

Cobb looked down at his boots and played it humble.

"I'd heard something about that back in Laramie. I was hoping it wasn't true."

"It's true," Charlie said. "And he pays good money. More than I figured he would. On time, too. His paymaster rolls through here on the first of the month as regular as the setting of the sun. I could set my watch by him."

"I'm glad you've got that kind assurance, Charlie. I mean it. You've worked hard for a long time. You deserve a break."

Charlie ran his hand over his clean-shaven face as he looked over the horses. "They look about done in. You been pushing them hard?"

"No, but this warm weather's taken something out of them. I had to water them halfway here. They could go a few more miles, but we can't make it all the way to Cheyenne. I'm hauling almost a full coach of passengers who could use some watering and feeding of their own."

Charlie rested his hand on the fence. "I'd like to help you, Tucker. I really would. But Hagen pays me, and he made it clear that I'd be in trouble if I did business with you. You really must've done something that got under his skin for him to hate you like he does."

"I committed the worst sin imaginable in his eyes," Cobb said. "I told him no."

"Tough break all around, I guess."

Cobb did not know Charlie Smith well, but he knew him a little. He had told them about Hagen's command, but he had not told them to leave. "I know you said he pays you well. I'd be happy to pay extra if you'll let us in." He looked beyond him at the corral and did not see any extra horses beyond those fit for hauling coaches. "It looks like you don't have any guests at the moment. We'll be out of here at first light. Hagen would never know you helped us."

Smith shifted his weight. "I don't know, Tucker. Someone could come along soon. I'm not expecting another coach until tomorrow, but you never know if stragglers come by."

Cobb took out the wad of bills he had placed in his shirt pocket for this purpose. "The wonderful thing about money is that there's no such thing as too much of it. Not for the likes of you and me."

The station master licked his lips as he snatched the bills from Cobb and quickly pocketed them. "As long as you promise to be gone first thing in the morning."

Cobb was glad Charlie Smith was not a man of principles. "Head on in and start fixing some food for these folks. Butch and I will take care of the horses for you."

Cobb undid the latch and pushed the gate open before climbing back into the wagon box and releasing the hand brake.

"What was all that about?" Jane asked.

"Just a bit of haggling," Cobb said, as he snapped the reins. "Don't give it another thought."

It was already dark and well after dinner by the time Cobb and Butch got the chance to move away from the others and head outside for their nightly conversation. They walked over to the corral fence together, where Cobb filled his pipe as Butch bit off a chaw of tobacco from the wad he had stashed in his pocket.

"I reckon it'll be too hot to sleep in there this evening," Butch said. "Even with all the windows and doors open, it's still unbearable. I think I might just bed down out here for the night."

"It's too hot in there for a lot of reasons," Cobb said. "I guess you didn't learn much from all of that time back in the coach, or you'd have told me by now."

Butch worked the plug of tobacco around the inside of his mouth. "Jane was right about Renfro not being Renfro. He's a cowpuncher named Fisk who took Renfro's ticket in an opium den. The same den Lucien Clay runs out of the basement of Longacre House."

Cobb had heard rumors about Clay's involvement in Laramie's opium trade but had not paid it much mind. "Did you believe him? Fisk I mean."

"I did as far as it goes, but that's not very far," Butch admitted. "That Matthews fella knew Fisk wasn't Renfro and didn't say anything to us about it. He said it was none of his business, but it still doesn't sit right with me. They've all got some kind of link to Clay, and that's not good."

Cobb was beginning to think he had been wrong for thinking Clay might have gone to the trouble of sneaking someone on board as one of the passengers with the intent to kill them. Now that he'd had most of the day to think about it, it began to sound foolish.

"I'm starting to feel like an idiot for even talking about it," Cobb admitted. "If Clay had sent someone to kill us, they would've tried something back when we stopped to water the horses. Or after we pulled in here." He hooked his boot heel on the lowest rail on the fence as he puffed on his pipe. "Guess I'm just getting fretful in my old age."

Butch flinched when he heard a birdsong in the darkness.

Cobb was amused by his friend's reaction. "Relax. It's

just a night bird. I might be getting fretful, but you're downright jumpy."

Butch kept looking around through the darkness, but the only light was that which bled outside from the open windows of the station building. "The Apache used to call to each other like that at night down in Texas. Comanche, too. It was their way of telling where everyone was at night."

Cobb had heard the calls, too. "We're a long way from Texas, Butch. And both the Cheyenne and the Lakota are way back there behind us."

Butch relaxed a little, but not much. "And that's enough talk out of you about getting old. You ain't old. You're careful and you're right to be that way. I don't think your idea was a bad one. Clay let us leave Laramie a might too easy for my taste. You happen to see any sign of riders on our back trail after we watered the horses?"

"I turned around a couple of times, but didn't see anyone," Cobb said. "But if they were coming for us, I doubt they'd stick to the road."

Another birdsong caught their attention.

"That settles it." Butch pulled his revolver and kept it flat against his side. "You stay here. I'm gonna go take a look."

But Cobb stopped him. "You're staying right here and acting calm, like we're just out here enjoying the night air and some tobacco. Not even you can see much in this darkness. If we hear anything, we drop to the ground." He cursed himself for leaving his coach gun inside with the rest of his belongings. "I ain't armed, but shoot at anything you hear."

"I can feel someone watching us." Butch leaned against the railing as he continued to look around. "It might be a good idea for you to head inside and grab your shotgun.

It'll come in handy. But don't run. Make it look like you forgot something."

Cobb began to make a show of patting his pockets and spoke louder for the benefit of anyone who might be listening. "Looks like I'm all out of matches. I'll go back inside and see if I can find some."

Cobb started walking back toward the station building when he heard the unmistakable sound of a hammer being pulled back.

Butch knocked him flat from behind and hit the ground with his pistol ready. The impact caused the wound on Cobb's left arm to burn while he watched his partner fire into the darkness at the corner of the station building to his right. A shotgun blast erupted in the darkness, but the shot was much higher than where they had landed.

Another barrage of shots erupted from somewhere beyond the station fence. Bullets struck the wooden posts of the corral where they had just been standing only moments before. Butch reached over Cobb's prone body and answered with three shots of his own.

The gunfire stopped as quickly as it had started.

Cobb remained flat on the ground. "Did you hit any of them?"

"I think I got the first one by the station, but the others out there are a different story. At least they stopped shooting at us."

Cobb knew they were probably still out there adjusting their aim. He was grateful the shooters were as blind as they were.

Charlie Smith appeared in the doorway of his station with a rifle in hand. "What's all the shooting about?"

Butch told him, "Blow out all them lamps, Charlie. Someone's trying to kill us out here."

"And watch yourself," Cobb added. "Butch wounded a shooter to your left."

Cobb was relieved to see the light from the oil lamps dim as the passengers inside heard Butch's order.

Now that they were all enveloped in complete darkness, Cobb and Butch got to their feet. The fire in his left arm began to die down as they felt their way toward the building. Cobb hit the front step with his boot but managed to prevent himself from falling over.

"I'm still here, boys," Charlie said, barely above a whisper. "What do you want me to do?"

Butch whispered, "Follow me but be quiet about it. That fella I shot was right over here. But don't make a sound because he's still got that shotgun."

Charlie used his crutch to step down from the porch and join them on the ground as they crept forward, following Butch's lead.

Cobb and Charlie stopped when they heard Butch stumble over something, followed by a high-pitched yelp.

The sound of boots scraping dirt was followed by Butch saying, "Light a match, Cobb. Let's see who was trying to kill us."

Cobb made sure he and Charlie were around the corner of the building when he thumbed a match alive. He almost dropped it when the burning sulfur revealed Butch was holding their shooter fast in a headlock.

It was Miss Cassie Hyde, one of the passengers.

Cobb saw the left side of her dress was dark with blood from her hip and growing darker.

Charlie hobbled over to the building and leaned against it. "Well, I'll be damned."

Cobb was more angry than surprised when he saw his coach gun on the ground beside her. He picked it up and cracked it open. Both barrels had been spent.

"Shooting at a man with his own gun is mighty low, Miss Hyde." The match flame began to singe his fingers and he flicked it away. "Let's you and me get her inside, Butch. Looks like we've got a lot to talk about."

She hurled a stream of curses at them as Butch hauled her to her feet. He took one arm while Cobb took the other. She tried to go deadweight on them, but their grip on her was too strong and she ultimately limped along.

Charlie said, "I'll close all the shutters and keep the lamp light to a minimum when we get her inside. I'll keep watch out here while you tend to her wounds. I ain't no doctor and wouldn't know the first thing to do for her."

"Don't trouble yourself, Charlie," Butch said. "I know exactly what this lady needs."

CHAPTER 16

Cobb was glad the rest of the passengers did not complain much when Charlie Smith closed the shutters and only lit one lamp in the women's section of the sleeping area. Cobb stood guard while Butch worked on Miss Hyde's wound by lamplight.

Cobb found himself admiring the woman's toughness. She did not make a sound when Butch poured liquor over the wound on her hip to clean it or when he brought the lamp close to examine it.

Jane busied herself by tending to the bandage on Cobb's left shoulder. Despite all that had happened, it felt good to be fussed over by a pretty lady.

Cobb waited for her to finish retying his bandage before asking Jane, "You ever see this lady before?"

"Never," Jane said, "but it explains why she wasn't too talkative on the coach. She was probably afraid she might say something that would give her away."

"I'm not afraid of you," Miss Hyde hissed while Butch examined her wound, "nor of these two mule skinners either. You're all nothing but trash. Common, lowdown—"

She drew in a deep, jagged breath as Butch pushed

down on her wound. "You keep a civil tongue in your head when you talk to us, and I won't do that again."

Cobb figured it would take a lot more than that to keep her quiet. "How bad does it look, Butch?"

"My bullet hit a bone and went out the side. I can't tell if there are any fragments in there, but it looks clean enough to me. She's gonna have a limp for a while, though. Maybe the rest of her life. It's still bleeding pretty bad, so I'll have to burn it shut. It's the only way to be sure."

"Let it bleed," she seethed. "I'd rather be dead than owe my life to the likes of you."

Butch set the lamp back on the table as he stood. "Whether you live or die is up to Cobb here and Mr. Smith. I'm gonna go heat my knife in case they decide to save you."

As Butch moved toward the kitchen, Jane pulled up a chair and sat beside her. Despite her pain, the presence of the younger woman seemed to give her renewed energy. "Get away from me, you wretched cur. I can't stand the sight of you."

"Then close your eyes because I'm not leaving your side until Butch gets back."

Cobb glanced toward the front door where Charlie Smith was standing guard. He was sitting on the ground just outside the door frame with his rifle flat across his lap. His crutch was against the wall. "You see anything moving out there, Charlie?"

"Nope. Not even the wind."

"Want us to try to save this lady? It's your station. Your rules."

"I don't care what you do with her as long as you don't plan on leaving her here. I don't want her and I ain't no jailer."

Cobb looked back down at Miss Hyde. "Looks like

your life's in my hands, lady. Seeing as how you tried to cut me down with my own shotgun, I'm inclined to let you suffer, but maybe there's a way you can help me change my mind. You can start by telling me about your friends out there. And don't bother denying it. We heard you whistling back and forth to each other. How many of them are we up against?"

Sweat broke out across her forehead as she sneered up at them. "Ten? Fifty? Maybe it's only one. What difference does it make? You won't believe me no matter what I tell you."

Cobb knew she had a point, but as long as he kept her talking, she might give away something he could use. "Clay sent you, didn't he?"

"That miserable pimp?" She laughed, but her wound made her immediately regret it. "He wouldn't have the brains or the nerve for something like this."

Jane's face brightened. "It must've been Madam Peachtree, then." Cobb saw Miss Hyde's expression change just enough for him to notice. "She's certainly capable of it, Tucker."

Cobb put the question to her. "That true, Miss Hyde? Was it her who sent you to try to kill us?"

"Madam Peachtree." She sniffed. "You sound like a couple of children when you speak her name. That woman is Amanda Pinochet, and she has more guts in her little finger than any of you have in your entire body put together."

Cobb was glad Jane had been right. It might help them save a lot of time. "She's that sore about Jane leaving her, is she?"

Miss Hyde weakly raised a finger and pointed it at Jane. "This little mouse? She can be replaced in a month. But reputations are harder to come by out here and almost as valuable as gold. She couldn't stand the thought of anyone finding out you got the better of her and her people. What did you expect her to do? First, you beat up Lucien, then, you take her best girl? She can't have you strutting around Cheyenne telling the world how weak she is. How easy it was for you to walk away from her." She lowered her hand and sank her head deeper into the pillow. "But she won't have to worry about that. You'll never make it to Cheyenne alive."

"I wouldn't be too sure of that," Cobb said. "Your friends out there didn't come within a country mile of hitting us. They'll wind up in worse shape than you if they try anything."

Her head shot up and she seethed through the pain. "My Phil's twice the man you'll ever be. And when he finally catches up to you, he'll make you pay for what you've done to me. He'll have you begging for death."

Cobb crossed his arms and looked down at her. "Phil who?"

She closed her mouth and slowly lowered her head again. She had already said too much and knew it. He asked Jane, "Any idea on who this 'Phil' might be?"

Jane shook her head. "No. Not anyone who could do something like this, anyway."

"No one you saw talking to Clay? Maybe hanging around Longacre House? Maybe a friend of Madam . . . whatever her name is?"

"She only came during the day and only spoke to Lucien," Jane said. "She never stayed around long. She always seemed in a hurry to get back up to her place in Blackstone."

Cobb turned the name of the town over in his mind. Blackstone. Hagen's ranch was in Blackstone. Why did everything wrong in his life seem to come from there?

Since it was clear that Miss Hyde was done talking for the moment, Cobb went to speak with Butch. He found him at the station's fireplace, which also served as the place where Charlie Smith cooked food.

Mr. Matthews and Mr. Vetrano rose from their cots and immediately started asking him questions. Fisk, the cowboy, remained on his cot with his feet crossed. This was not his fight and did not seem to concern him.

Cobb spoke over the curious passengers. "Save your questions, gentlemen." He nodded toward the blanket that separated the women's quarters from the rest of the sleeping area. "You've heard as much as I have. Now, I'd appreciate it if you could leave so my partner and I can discuss a few things in private. I promise I'll tell you how this affects our journey to Cheyenne as soon as I know."

Matthews and Vetrano did not like to be dismissed, but they offered no protest as they moved off to the dining room together.

From his cot, Fisk asked, "Do I need to go, too?"

"Not if you keep your mouth shut and don't repeat what me and Cobb say to each other," Butch said.

The cowboy folded his hands behind his head and stretched his limbs.

Cobb watched Butch turn his knife blade over the hot coals of Charlie's fire. The steel was beginning to glow red. "You hear what that lady had to say?"

"Like you just told the others, that blanket doesn't offer much in the way of privacy."

"What do you make of it?"

"You managed to get under her skin like I figured you would," Butch said. "You've got a knack for annoying people."

"Thanks. How many of her friends do you think are

out there? I wasn't able to look around to count muzzle flashes."

"I was." Butch turned the knife on the coals. "I only counted two at a time and from the same place. They've probably been dogging us all the way from Laramie, just like you figured."

Cobb did not always enjoy being right. "You know any gunmen named Phil? Anyone who might work with a lady like Miss Hyde, if that's even her name."

"Can't say as I have," Butch admitted. "It might be easy enough to figure who he was if it was Clay who'd put them up to it, but this Madam Whatever-Her-Name-Is puts a new wrinkle in things entirely. And since she spends so much of her time up in Blackstone, 'Phil' could be a man Hagen uses. That means he's probably good, which is bad news for us. Sometimes I wonder if we didn't have bad luck, we wouldn't have any luck at all."

Something Butch said stuck out in his mind. "Have."

Butch looked up from tending to his knife blade. "What was that?"

"Have," Cobb repeated. "Possession. Mine. My."

Butch's eyes narrowed. "Did you hit your head when I knocked you over out there? You're babbling. Talking nonsense."

Cobb slapped Butch on the shoulder. "It's not what I said, dummy. It's what Miss Hyde just said. 'My Phil.' She's not just working with whoever's out there. She's in love with one of them. Her Phil."

Butch pushed his blade deeper into the coals. "You sure do pick an odd time to be a romantic."

But Cobb was not thinking like that. "Don't you see? It explains why they didn't start shooting at us on the ride here. Phil didn't want to risk his woman getting hurt. And that birdsong we heard outside before was their way of talking to each other. Signaling that it was time to start shooting at us."

His blade now glowing, Butch pulled it free. "I know what happened, Cobb. I was there, remember? Now step aside and let me lay this along her wound."

But Cobb made his friend stay where he was while he continued his thought. "Whoever shot at us tonight is liable to be out there waiting to shoot us tomorrow morning, won't they?"

"It's likely."

"And if they didn't attack us while Miss Hyde was in back, they probably won't risk it if she's riding up in the wagon box with me, will they?"

"That'll depend on how this 'Phil' feels about the lady," Butch said. "If she treats him like she's treated us, he might not care about what happens to her."

"He cares." The more Cobb thought about it, the more he was convinced he was right. "He cares plenty. He would've shot at us before now if he felt otherwise."

"If you're fixing to prop her up next to you, I'd better get to working." Butch moved past him, holding the hot blade before him like it was a torch. "You'd best clear out of there, Jane, and hold your nose. What comes next won't be pretty."

Jane scrambled out from behind the blanket and buried her face in Cobb's chest. "I know he has to do it, but I hate this part."

Cobb gently placed his hand over her ear. "Normally, so does he. But not tonight."

He heard Miss Hyde begin to protest as Butch closed in on her. "I'd offer to give you something to bite down on, but you seem like a tough old gal. I'm sure you can take a little discomfort."

And, to her credit, Miss Hyde did not make a sound as

the hot knife seared her wounds closed. The smell that followed after was enough to make Jane gag.

Cobb noticed that, through it all, Fisk had barely stirred. "Are you one of those shiftless cowboys, or are you up for earning that free seat you're filling on my coach?"

Fisk examined his stubby fingernails. "That would depend on what it is."

"Keeping an eye out for the people looking to kill us," Cobb said. "With a gun in your hand."

"I reckon I could do that easy enough."

Cobb rested his chin atop Jane's head as she held her nose against the stench.

He reckoned they would all have to do more than just keep an eye out come the morning.

After first light the following morning, Cobb brought his coffee with him as he spoke to Charlie, who had been keeping watch from his seat by the window of the dining room.

"See anything out there?"

"No, but this ain't an ideal spot to see things from," Smith said. "I still don't know why you had to go and park that wagon of yours right in front of my door early this morning. It wasn't even light out yet."

"That's why I did it." Cobb sipped his coffee. "Bringing the coach closer to the station gives whoever's out there a tougher shot at us. They'd be able to pick off me and Butch if we tried moving it in the light of day."

"They'll be able to pick off them horses easy enough if they wanted," Smith said. "And keeping them hitched up for so long is just plain wrong, Cobb."

"But necessary. And they won't shoot the horses. That would force them to come in here and try to finish us off.

They would've done that last night if they had enough men with them. They'll try something now or later on the road."

Charlie grumbled to himself. "I knew I never should've allowed you boys to stay here. Nothing but trouble."

Cobb finished his coffee and left the mug on a table. "You got well paid for it, Charlie. And you'll get more of the same each time we pass this way."

Charlie remained at the window while Cobb went back to check on Butch and the passengers. Matthews, Fisk, and Vetrano were ready to go while Butch and Jane were still at Miss Hyde's cot, trying to convince her to get up.

"If you don't go on your own, we'll have to carry you," Butch told her. "We ain't leaving you behind because Charlie don't want you."

"And I won't help you hurt Phil." She held onto the edges of the cot with both hands. "You don't think I overheard your schemes? I won't allow myself to be trussed up and stuck on top of the wagon like an old scarecrow. I've been shot—by you, I might add—and I need time to let my wounds heal properly."

Cobb motioned for Butch and Jane to step away from her. "The coach is close enough to the door that you all can begin boarding. Fisk, you get in first so you can watch the left side of the coach."

He held up the pistol Butch had given him. "Got it."

"The rest of you file inside how you please as long as Butch ends up on the right side of the coach, facing forward. That'll give us the cover we need if those fellas try to hit us."

None of them complained.

Butch began to help them board the coach, leaving Cobb alone with Miss Hyde.

"Get up and on your feet," Cobb told her. "I want to make it to Cheyenne by the afternoon."

"Then you'll just have to go on without me." She gripped the edges of her cot tight enough to turn her hands white. "You'll have to pry me out of this bed if you expect me to go."

"I'll do it if I have to, but I don't think it'll come to that," Cobb said. "What's this 'Phil' fella to you anyhow? Your beau? Your husband?"

Her face turned bitter. "I never should have mentioned his name."

"But you did. It's because he means something to you. I can't say that I care why he matters because it doesn't make any difference. It's clear you care about him, which is why you're going to get on top of that wagon and sit right beside me. You're not going to do it for me. You're going to do it for him."

She slowly shook her head. "Give me one good reason why I should."

"Because he won't shoot at me if he sees you. And I won't have to shoot back at him. You don't have to worry about me so much. I'll be busy driving the horses. It's Butch who ought to concern you. He's a crack shot and doesn't miss often with a pistol. He's even deadlier with a rifle. There are a few dead Cheyenne and Lakota back at Fort Washington who could attest to that. So, if you care for him as much as I think you do, you'll come with me. It's the only way to make sure no further harm comes to him."

Her small eyes narrowed. "Amanda Pinochet warned me about you. She said she'd heard you're not as dumb as you look. I see now she heard right."

"I reckon I'm as smart as I need to be." He held out his hand to her. "Now get up so we can both do what needs doing."

Her hands did not move from the edge of the cot. "And what happens once we reach Cheyenne? You'll hand me over to the sheriff, won't you?"

"That's for certain," Cobb told her, "but if I tell him how you helped us out when I asked, he might be inclined to go easier on you." He held out his hand to her. "Let's get going."

She ignored his hand and edged her way out of the bed. Her face twisted in pain as she began to sit up, but she still did not make a sound. "That burn your friend gave me stings something awful."

Cobb had already planned for that. "I've got a jug of whiskey for you to pull on to help ease the pain a bit. You can drink your fill as far as I'm concerned."

As soon as her feet touched the floor, Cobb took her by both arms and helped her stand. He kept hold of her as she hobbled over to the door.

She braced herself in the doorway where Butch stood waiting.

"I don't know how in the world you two fools expect me to climb up there in this condition."

Butch said, "Don't give it a second thought. Cobb and me will get you up there like we were loading a sack of flour."

Butch climbed up on the wheel as Cobb lifted her by the waist. Butch held on, wrapped his arm around her middle, and placed her on the bench. He was gentler than Cobb had expected him to be.

Butch jumped down and took up the Henry rifle he had laid against the coach. "You really think this'll be enough to keep Phil from shooting at us?"

Cobb motioned for his partner to get inside the coach. "Ask me when we get to Cheyenne."

CHAPTER 17

Phil Bengston cursed as he threw his Sharps rifle aside and looked through his field glasses. "Those dirty snakes!"

Earl Panfil had never seen his partner betray such emotion. "What's wrong?"

"They've got Cassie propped up in the driver's seat. I can't get a clear shot of Cobb or Keeling now."

Panfil squinted at Bengston's target. He could make out the station building, and the stagecoach parked in front of it, but the people were just a blur. He had never been gifted with good eyesight. He could have asked Bengston to borrow the field glasses, but he was not in a generous mood.

"But Cobb will still be right next to her, won't he? I've seen you make tougher shots than this."

"That's when I didn't care about who I hit. That's Cassie up there beside him. I can't risk it." He pounded the ground in frustration. "This whole night wasted. We could've gotten ahead of them and hit them when they stopped to water their horses. Now we'll spend half the day just trying to keep up with them."

Panfil did not see the problem. "Those horses are

pulling a heavy coach. We aren't. We can still get ahead of them and take them then."

Bengston pushed himself off the ground and gathered up his rifle. "Get ready to move. We won't get a clear shot at them until we're in Cheyenne. I'll take care of them there."

Panfil got to his feet and trailed behind him. "But that's not what Madam and Clay wanted, Phil. They didn't want them to reach Cheyenne, remember?"

"They wanted a lot of things, but they're not here." Bengston shoved the Sharps in the saddle scabbard below his Remington. "I'm the one they paid to do this job, and I'll do it my way."

Panfil had always respected Phil, but he feared the wrath of the Madam and Lucien Clay much more. "But Cobb and Keeling are bound to know she tried to kill them. If we let them reach Cheyenne, they'll turn her over to the sheriff the first chance they get."

Bengston placed his foot in the stirrup and climbed up into the saddle. "Then we'll just have to find a way to get her out of there, won't we? But only after I take care of those two mule skinners first! Now get on your horse. We've got a day's worth of hard riding ahead of us."

Panfil went to his horse, wondering if Bengston may not have lost his mind.

Cobb watched Miss Hyde take another swig from the whiskey jug as the coach rumbled along the road to Cheyenne. They were making better time than Cobb had expected, and the fresh team of horses was not laboring as much as the previous team had. At this pace, they might even make it to Cheyenne just after noontime.

He saw Miss Hyde spill some of the whiskey on her

dress, but she was well beyond the point of caring about her appearance.

Her words slurred together as she said, "I suppose you're expecting me to thank you."

Cobb kept his eyes forward and on the team. "The thought never crossed my mind."

"Well, you've got some thanks coming whether you want it or not. Thank you for not tying my hands in front of me."

Cobb had dedicated a significant amount of thought to how he would transport his prisoner the previous night. "I figured you were already infirmed enough as it was, what with that hole in your hip and all. Besides, I didn't fancy the notion of you tumbling over the side from a loss of balance."

Miss Hyde managed to suppress a belch. "What's stopping me from jumping clear right now? Giving Phil a clear shot at you?"

"It'd be a wasted effort," Cobb said. "Your beau was probably waiting to pick off me and Butch back at the station. And when that didn't work out for him, I figure he's either behind us or ahead of us by now. Most likely ahead. Might even be staked out at a watering hole up ahead. I'll be happy to disappoint him by not stopping. This new team is a lot more fit than my old one."

She looked out at the horses that were moving at a good clip. "What's keeping me from belting you with this jug? Amanda wants you dead. She won't care much how it happens."

Cobb grinned at the intoxicated woman. "You couldn't hit the broad side of a barn if you were standing in front of it right now. And you'd pay a terrible price in the bargain. With the whiskey gone, you'd be feeling the pain from that bullet hole in your hip before long, with a mighty powerful hangover besides."

She took another long sip before putting the cork back in the jug and setting it on the narrow floor between them. "You really must love her. Jane, I mean. You really must love her to go through all this trouble for her."

Cobb did not see it that way. "I was already in a mess of trouble with Hagen just by being me. Me and Butch didn't sell out to him like he wanted us to. Jane didn't have anything to do with my reasoning, nor with this spate of problems I've got now, either. I would've slugged Clay for talking to me that way even if she'd been on my arm when he said it. I don't take kindly to pimps with big mouths."

"Pimps." She did not bother stopping the next belch that rose from her. "We've all got pimps of one kind or another. Every man who draws a wage is for sale, even you. You just don't want to think of it like that."

"I get paid to provide a service," Cobb said. "There's a difference."

"I never thought you were stupid until now," she slurred. "Dangerous and annoying, yes, but not stupid."

She reached for the jug, but Cobb reached it first and moved it between his feet. "You've had enough as it is. If you keep drinking like this, you're liable to get sick. Let what you've already got in you go to work."

She placed both hands on the bench and tried to remain upright as the wagon bounced over a series of divots in the road.

"You're wrong about Phil," she said without prompting.

He wanted to keep her talking. He doubted he had seen the last of the man and wanted to know more about him. "How do you figure?"

"He's not my beau," she slurred. "He's my boy. My son."

Cobb found that much more interesting, though he

thought it might be the whiskey talking. "You don't look near old enough to have a boy of an age to hunt a man."

"I had him young," she said. "Had a devil of a time giving birth to him, too." A boozy smile spread across her face. "He came out kicking and screaming like he was mad at the world. He was a fighter from the start. He was always that way, even as a little guy." She sniffed. "The war made whatever he was worse. He came home to me, though. Those rebels never could put a mark on him. Other men, yes, but not my Philip."

Now that Cobb understood the connection, it changed things. "From what I've seen, he got a lot of his spirit from you."

She drew herself up in a drunkard's dignity. "I always did whatever I had to do to keep him alive. Sometimes it meant doing what your woman did. Sometimes it meant killing. Pretty soon, killing for money was better than earning it other ways. Amanda saw I was more than just a saloon girl. Folks always expect a strange man in town to be a killer, but never a lady. A lot found out how wrong they were too late."

Cobb did not know if that was true or just the whiskey talking for her. He had covered a fair piece of the Wyoming Territory and had never heard anyone talking about a murderess and her son. That did not mean it was not possible, though. And he was glad Jane had searched her thoroughly for any weapons or knives the night before. A woman did not need to be sober to plunge a blade in him, especially while driving a coach.

She nodded off for a moment before snapping back awake. "You'd do well to turn me loose, Cobb. Leave me right here on the side of the road."

"I wouldn't think of it," Cobb said. "I'm beginning to enjoy your charming company."

"You can joke about it now, but no one'll be laughing if you hand me over to the sheriff. Phil will make you pay for it, and a lot of people will get hurt when he tries to get me out of there."

Cobb had been to Cheyenne several times and doubted her son or even ten men could get her out of their jail. "Don't think about such things now. You just let yourself fall asleep and leave the worrying to me and Butch."

She wanted to continue the argument but slumped over to her left and fell asleep against him.

And as the miles toward Cheyenne rolled on, he found himself hoping that she had only been bragging about the skills of her son as a killer of men.

Cobb had to keep a tight rein on his horses as the team reached Cheyenne. The constant stream of people and wagons of every description moving in all directions was enough to spook the animals. The constant sound of hammering and cutting wood only added to their discomfort. It might have been enough to bother Cobb if he had not known what to expect.

He and Butch had brought passengers to the territorial capital a few weeks before, soon after the railroad had set up their headquarters in town. There had been rumors that train service would begin in the fall, and the people of Cheyenne intended to be ready when it did. The place was almost unrecognizable now as men and women in the latest fashions from back east strolled its streets as the coach rolled by.

After several near misses with carriages and wagons and distracted pedestrians, Cobb managed to steer the coach over to the left side of the thoroughfare where the Frontier Hotel stood. It had been covered in wooden scaffolding the last time he was in town. Now it boasted a stone facade with marble columns holding up the balcony over the front door.

The still-unconscious Miss Hyde slumped to the bench as Cobb threw the hand brake, locking the coach's wheels in place. She had begun to snore a few miles before town and was still at it.

"We're here, everyone," Butch announced, as he hopped out and scrambled up the roof to begin handing the luggage down to their owners. "Welcome to Cheyenne. The Magic City of the Plains. This place sure did go and get itself fixed up, didn't it, Cobb?"

Cobb looked across the street where the town marshal's office used to be, but any hint of the building was gone. There was a new structure rising in its place, one that looked to be larger in every aspect than its predecessor. "Looks that way."

He spotted Deputy Bobby Toneff in the middle of the street, trying in vain to bring some order to the unending tide of people and goods moving to and fro along the thoroughfare.

Cobb cupped his hands and called out to him. It took him three tries before he caught a lull in the din of noise on the street and the deputy heard him and came to the coach.

"Sorry about that, Cobb," Bobby said, when he reached the coach. He was a man of medium size and appearance who had been a lawman in town for a year or so. "Hugh's got me out here trying to keep things in order, but no one listens to me. Everyone just goes wherever they please. A lady and her kid almost got run over last week, and the people are starting to complain."

Butch tossed one of the bags down to Mr. Matthews. "Sounds to me like you're the one who's complaining,

Bobby. First, you griped about how quiet everything was, now you're griping about how busy you are."

Deputy Toneff smiled at Cobb's partner. "Hey ya, Butch. Glad to see you haven't changed any."

Cobb said, "And you'll be glad I've got something better for you to do." Cobb gestured down at the sleeping Miss Hyde. "I need you to help me bring her over to your jail. This woman tried to kill me and Butch last night, and she needs to be locked up."

Toneff climbed up to take a look and immediately backed down. "Smells like she needs to sleep it off."

"That was just my way of keeping her quiet until we got here," Cobb told him. "She's wounded besides, so you'll probably want to have a doctor check her over once you find a cell for her. Where'd you put the jail?" He tossed a thumb over his shoulder. "Looks like they knocked down the old one."

"They stuck us over in an old barn on Court Street," Toneff said. "Well, that's what it's going to be named anyway after they get around to building the courthouse. It's going to have a jail, court rooms, and everything."

Cobb had always liked Toneff, but the younger man had never been accused of being bright. "Courthouses usually have those kinds of things. How can I find it?"

"I'll be glad to take us there if you slide over," Toneff offered. "The traffic can be pretty tricky to figure out this close to lunchtime."

"I'm the only one who drives my coach," Cobb said. "Just tell me where to go and I'll get us there."

"Go up to the corner, make a left, and it's two—no, three—streets that way, then make a right. Are you sure you don't just want me to do it for you? It'll be easier if I do it."

"Easy isn't my way," Cobb reminded him, "but you can hop in once Butch finishes unloading those bags."

Toneff pitched in to help Butch with the luggage. Neither Matthews, Vetrano, nor Fisk bid them farewell, and the coachmen had not expected them to. They had paid their fare and they had been brought to Cheyenne. Unless they intended on taking the coach elsewhere, their business was at an end. Matthews and Vetrano entered the hotel. Fisk wandered away from the coach. He did not have anywhere particular he needed to be.

Butch reached down from the roof and helped Cobb pull Miss Hyde upright. "This one's just about pickled, Cobb. Why'd you let her drink so much?"

"It kept her from trying to kill us, didn't it?" He sat down and looked back to see the deputy pause before he entered the coach. He took off his hat and smiled at Jane. "Hello! Are you under arrest, too?"

He heard Jane laugh. "No, but you could say I'm in Tucker Cobb's custody."

"She's with me, Toneff. Now get in before I leave you here."

The deputy got inside and pulled the door shut behind him.

As he remained sprawled on the roof, Butch cautioned, "Take it nice and slow, Cobb. I've lived through too much to get thrown off my own coach."

Cobb released the hand brake and snapped the reins. The team lurched forward, cutting off a buggy as it pulled away from the hotel. Maybe he would get a knack for city driving after all.

CHAPTER 18

The temporary home of the town marshal and town jail was an old barn on what had once been the outskirts of town. Now, it was smack dab in the middle of the city that was growing up around it.

A local blacksmith had worked to piece together a row of bars where horse stalls had once been. Cobb thought the cells looked about ready to topple over onto each other, but it was sturdier than it looked.

Town Marshal Hugh Perry helped Cobb, Butch, and Toneff carry the passed-out Miss Hyde into the cell at the far end of the convicts. She continued to snore away as Perry locked the cell door.

"This is the fifth woman prisoner I've had this week," Perry said. "If this trend keeps up, I'll need a whole other barn to house them all."

"Everything has its price I guess," Butch observed. "All this modernity has to cost something."

Perry grunted his agreement as he walked back to his desk, which sat in the middle of the cavernous building. "I don't like the bother, but there's something to be said about having the jail here. The odor of horses kills the stench of the prisoners."

Cobb had always enjoyed Hugh Perry's company. He had been the law in Cheyenne since the days when it was just a small sentiment. He imagined that now that the railroad was coming to town, that people would want another, younger man to enforce the peace. But for now, the job was his.

Perry ran his hands through his sandy, graying hair as he lowered himself into his chair. He beckoned for Cobb and Butch to make themselves comfortable in the chairs on the opposite side of the desk.

"You've done your part," the marshal said to his deputy. "You'd best get back out there and try to keep those wagons from running anyone over."

Toneff frowned at the assignment. "Don't you need me here to help you tend to the prisoners, Hugh?"

"Sure I do, but I need the mayor and all the busybodies who have his ear to see you out there trying to maintain some order on the streets. Do it for another hour, then come back in. I'll see if I can't get someone else to do it after that."

Cobb turned in his chair to watch Toneff leave. He looked like a kid who had been sent to bed without his supper. "Things sure have changed over the last couple of weeks."

"Change is one thing," the town marshal said. "This is closer to an invasion. The railroad coming here has gone and stirred things up. It'll be good for the town when it's over, but until then, it's a mess." A thought came to him. "You boys came here from Laramie, didn't you?"

"We did," Cobb said. "Stopped off at Wingate Station last night to sleep and eat. We also got a new team of horses. That's when our lady friend back there tried to kill us."

Perry found a toothpick in his shirt pocket and stuck it

in his mouth. "She unhappy with your level of service, was she?"

"She was unhappy with us in general," Butch answered. "She was paid to do it. Paid by Madam Peachtree and Lucien Clay."

Perry almost swallowed his toothpick. "You don't say? You boys really know how to pick your enemies. First Hagen, now them."

"They're one and the same," Cobb told him. "They're all lumped in together some way. And if you're not careful, they'll get their hooks into you, too."

"I hate to break it to you boys," the town marshal said, "but they've already started. Hagen sent his son, Bart, out here to open up an office for their mining concern last week. Brand new building, too, from the base to the eaves. Has his own private saloon in there and everything. From what I've heard, it's supposed to serve as a club for all the other mining companies in the area, but that's probably just hogwash."

Cobb closed his eyes. He had already had one run-in with Bart Hagen back in North Branch. And it had been over Jane, too. "That boy's got a bad habit of being in the wrong place at the wrong time."

"Or the right one, depending on how you look at it. But let's handle one problem at a time. You sure you want to swear out a complaint against this woman? If she's really working for Madam and Clay like you said she is, you might get back in their good graces by letting her go. It might make your lives easier if you did."

Butch sat forward in his chair. "You mean you want us to let the woman who tried to kill us go? She shot at us with Cobb's own shotgun."

Perry held up his hands. "I'm not trying to talk you into it. Just trying to help you out is all. You've finally got something to trade, and I wanted you to have the chance to make the most of it. There's a wire up between here and Laramie now. I'll be happy to hold on to her for you if you want to send a telegram. See what they have in mind."

"Thanks, but no thanks," Cobb said. "It wouldn't do us any good anyway. She's only about a half of our troubles."

Perry took the toothpick from his mouth. "How do you figure?"

"She wasn't the only one who tried to kill us last night," Cobb explained. "Her son and at least one other fella tried to help her. She said his name is Phil."

"Phil Bengston? The shootist?"

Cobb and Butch traded glances, with Butch saying, "She didn't give a last name, just that he'd kill us if we didn't let her go."

"Who's Phil Bengston?" Cobb asked.

The town marshal rested his elbows on his desk. "He came to town with the railroad boys when they set up shop here. I could tell he was trouble, so I asked about him. They said he takes care of things for them. Things they don't ask me to do and don't seem to want me knowing about. From what I've seen, they trot him out to keep the workers in line, but I figure he does just about everything they need him for. He's a bad one, boys."

Butch did not look encouraged. "That sounds awfully vague, Hugh. Can't you give us something else to go on? What he looks like? Who he runs with?"

"That's the trouble with a fella like Bengston," the town marshal said. "He doesn't look like a killer. He's not particularly tall or tough-looking. If anything, he's kind of short and forgettable, except that he doesn't sport a beard or mustache of any kind. He wears his brown hair short and wears a pistol on his right hip. He's the sort you would pass on the street without noticing him even if you met him a dozen times."

Cobb knew that was probably the reason why he was so dangerous.

"He blends in well," Perry went on. "He doesn't talk big or brag. He doesn't square up to a man or threaten. But he doesn't forget anything, either. He has a gun on his hip, but I've never heard of him reaching for it, even when some of those drunk railroad boys called him out. But anyone who's ever shown him up always meets with a bad end while they're out working on the track. They get dropped like a buffalo without anyone knowing where the shot came from. Well, not that they could swear to in court, anyway."

Perry glanced back at the cells. "And if he'll kill a laborer over something he said when he was drunk, I don't want to think about what he'd do in this instance. If that woman we've got locked up back there is really his mother, then you really ought to think about swearing out that complaint against her."

Cobb had never heard Hugh Perry talk this way. "You sound like you're afraid of him."

"You're damned right I am," Perry confirmed. "People who run afoul of Phil Bengston don't live long, and I don't aim to wind up on his bad side. But you boys have a card to play." He inclined his head toward Miss Hyde's cell. "You've got the Queen of Hearts back there, and I suggest you put it to some use. Send a wire to Clay and the madam. Tell them you won't press charges if they call off Phil."

Butch sagged in his chair. "We were counting on you having a bit more backbone than this."

Perry took the toothpick from his mouth and pointed it at him. "I've got plenty of backbone to do this job, but

I'm not going to get myself killed on account of your pride. I didn't say I wouldn't charge her. I'm asking you to think about it long and hard before you ask, because I'm stretched thin enough as it is. More people come here every day and my men are run ragged."

Butch looked like he wanted to continue the argument, but Cobb gestured for him to stay quiet. They would not gain anything by attacking the town marshal. "If we make our complaint official, how long before she appears before a judge?"

"The one thing we've got plenty of around here are judges and lawyers," Perry said. "We're practically tripping over them. They all want to get in good with the railroad, so they're thicker than flies in town. I can get her charged in about an hour, day or night. That'll make it legal, but it won't settle anything as far as Bengston's concerned. In fact, it might complicate matters. His friends at the railroad have a lot of influence in this town. If the judge sets bail, they'll likely pay it to make Bengston happy. Then, they'll try to get the judge to throw out the case. They'll probably succeed, too, seeing as how you don't sound like you have any witnesses to back your claim."

Perry ignored Butch and focused on Cobb. "Do yourself a favor, Tucker. Play the high card while you've got it because that Queen of Hearts back there is going to turn into a Two of Clubs if you don't. Send a wire to Clay and try to do yourself some good."

"Because you're not sure you can do your job if we don't."

Perry sat back in his chair and tucked the toothpick in the corner of his mouth. He did not admit Cobb was right, but he did not have to. The expression on his face said it all.

Cobb knew Perry was right to ask them to cut a deal. And if he thought there was a chance it might work, he might consider it. But even if he got Butch to agree to let her go, there was no way of making sure Clay could get Bengston to live up to his side of the deal. In fact, with Miss Hyde free, there would be no reason for Bengston or Clay to allow them to live. There was no way to avoid trouble. It was already upon them. And Cobb did not want to give up what little leverage he had for the hope of something better tomorrow.

"I'll make a deal with you, Hugh," Cobb said. "Seeing as how you're short-handed, Butch and me will agree to be your deputies for the duration of Miss Hyde's stay with you. You won't even have to pay us. You can call us volunteers. We'll help out where and when you say, so you can make sure someone else stays here to help you keep an eye on the prisoners."

The prospect of more deputies did not change Perry's mood. "I've got plenty of money to hire deputies but no takers. Besides, I don't need more guns in town, Cobb. I need fewer prisoners. Every cell I've got is occupied, and I've already got three women locked up back there and no regular matron to look in on them. I've got a nurse from one of the doctor's offices who's supposed to come in every day to check on them, but sometimes she gets busy and doesn't show up."

Cobb already had a replacement in mind. "I know someone who might be willing to tend to your lady prisoners for you. Jane Duprey."

Perry clearly recognized the name. "Jane Duprey? You mean that . . ."

Cobb held up a hand to stop him from saying too much. "Careful, Hugh. She's a friend."

The town marshal swallowed his words while he thought of something else to say. "It's just that I don't know why a gal like her would want a job like that. Her chosen profession pays much more than I ever could."

Butch answered before Cobb. "She's turning over a new leaf, Perry. She's looking to make a fresh start of things. She's got no means of employment at present and wouldn't turn down the notion of working here. In fact, she's outside in our coach right now as we speak. This way, you get yourself two deputies and a matron. That sounds like a fair bargain to me."

Cobb did not like Butch speaking for him, but in this case, he was glad he had. He made the case for Jane better than he could.

Marshal Perry scratched behind his right ear as he thought it over. "A woman who ought to be in jail tending to the women who are. A peculiar notion to be sure, but these are mighty peculiar times in Cheyenne."

Cobb could not tell if Perry was trying to make up his mind or talk himself out of going along with the idea, but knew the longer he thought about it, the less likely he was to be in favor of it. "How about this? You go outside and present the idea to Jane alone. See if she wants to do it. See if you want her to do it. We'll stay right here so you don't think we're influencing you either way."

Perry stopped scratching and looked at the two coachmen in turn. "I feel like you boys are trying to sell me a bill of goods, but I'll be hard-pressed to figure out how." He pushed himself up from his seat and began walking outside. "You two stay right here while I go have a word with her."

Cobb waited until Perry was out of earshot before

speaking to Butch. "Thanks for speaking up for Jane just now."

"I didn't do it for her," Butch admitted. "I know how much she means to you."

"I'll feel a whole lot better about being a deputy if we can get him to make Jane the matron. I won't worry about her as much as I might have otherwise."

"I'm all for it if it buys us some good will with Perry," Butch said. "He could help water down some of that ill feeling that King Hagen's been spreading about us."

"Don't call him that," Cobb said. "He's no king, just a common man. All that money doesn't make him royalty."

"I guess rich folks are as close to royalty as we can get in this country." Butch nodded over toward Miss Hyde. "Our friend has woken up. She doesn't seem to enjoy her new accommodations."

Cobb looked over to see the woman glaring back at them as she gripped the bars of her cell door. She was still unsteady on her feet, but not nearly as drunk as she had been. She was in that twilight time between sobriety and an epic hangover which would only feel worse now that she was in jail.

"She's where she belongs," Cobb said. "And she's going to stay there if I have anything to say about it."

"It's not just up to you and me," Butch reminded him. "Her boy gets a say, too, and I don't expect our deputy badges will be enough to change his mind any."

"The badges might not, but we will."

Cobb turned in his chair when he heard Marshal Perry and Jane talking as they entered the temporary jail together. And just as Cobb had expected, she seemed to have the lawman already eating out of her hand. Perry had taken off his hat and allowed her to enter before him.

"Why, Tucker," Jane beamed, "you didn't tell me how much of a charming gentleman the marshal is. He's not nearly as sinister as you made him out to be. To hear you talk about him, I was expecting to see some fire-breathing dragon."

Cobb was encouraged when he saw Perry blush. "That's because you seem to have caught him on a good day. You'd think differently if you saw him facing down a criminal."

Perry grew downright bashful. "There's no sense in you two trying to talk me up. I already offered her the job and she accepted. We'll be glad to have her, too, though I warned her some of these women can be a bit rough. Even rougher than our menfolk inmates."

She rested a hand on Perry's arm. "And I promise to steer clear of them and limit myself to tending to the ladies whenever possible. Don't worry about me, Hugh. I've been with Tucker and Butch long enough to know how to handle tough customers."

"You!" A low growl from Miss Hyde's cell drew their attention. She might have fallen over if she had not been holding on to the bars tight enough to turn her fingers white. "You traitorous slut! You'd better talk some sense into your man about turning me loose and be quick about it, or my Phil will save you for last."

Jane stepped past Perry and walked over to a bucket on the floor that was well out of reach of the cells. Without checking to see what was inside it, she picked it up and hurled the contents at Miss Hyde. The prisoner shrieked as she fell back onto her cot.

Cobb could tell that there was more than just water in that bucket.

Jane raised her chin at Miss Hyde as she lowered the

bucket to her side. "Any more nasty comments from you, and you'll get more of the same from me."

Perry joined Cobb and Butch in laughing at the sight of Miss Hyde as she tried in vain to wipe the muck from her body.

Perry said, "Looks like she's taken to the role of matron just fine."

Cobb had never been prouder of her. "Seems that way. And it looks like you've got yourselves two deputies if the offer still stands."

Perry dug two deputy stars from the top drawer and tossed them on the desk. "And I've got four more of them just like it and looking for takers if you find anyone eager enough for the job."

Cobb handed one star to Butch and kept the other one for himself. He regarded it for a moment. It looked small in his calloused hand. "Me being a lawman. I never thought the day would come."

Perry was not moved by the sentiment. "I can let you borrow my handkerchief if you're about to cry. Now pin them on so I can swear you in. There's plenty of work for you boys to do once you boys stow your coach and get yourselves settled in."

CHAPTER 19

The Cheyenne Grand was nothing like its name. The entrance of the hotel appeared to be nothing more than a shack cobbled together with whatever bits of wood the builder had been able to find from various construction sites around town. It was dark and stank of damp wood and tobacco juice. The warped floorboards creaked under- foot, and Cobb thought he heard rats scurrying in the many shadows just out of sight.

"We've slept in worse," Butch observed.

"Not often." Cobb walked toward a heavyset manager sleeping against the wall behind a crooked desk. He hoped the man would agree to give them a room, or whatever passed for a room in such a place. Every livery in town turned their coach away, even after they produced the badges Hugh Perry had given them. Only a small feed store on the edge of town reluctantly agreed to let them keep their coach and team of horses there, provided they did not tell anyone about their arrangement.

Finding a place to stay had proven equally as challeng- ing. They had already tried five other hotels in Cheyenne and, upon hearing their names, all of them claimed to have no vacancies. They did not say Charles Hagen had put out the word against them. The frightened looks on the faces of the clerks told him everything he needed to know.

"If this place doesn't work out," Cobb told Butch, "we might be better off sleeping in the jail."

"Might be safer," Butch agreed.

Cobb dropped his satchel down on the desk hard enough to jolt the clerk awake. His jowls waggled as he shook himself awake before glaring up at Cobb for disturbing his slumber. If the coach driver's size did not make him think twice, the star pinned to his shirt did.

He cleared his throat as he slowly got to his feet. "What can I do for you boys?"

"We're looking for rooms," Butch said. "Two of them if you've got them."

His small eyes narrowed as he looked them over. He pointed at the star on Butch's shirt. "You two join up with Perry's bunch?"

"He swore us in a couple of hours ago," Cobb said. "What about those rooms?"

"That depends on how long you want them," the clerk said. "We rent by the half day or the week around here. And we get paid in advance."

Cobb took some coins from his pocket and let them drop on the desk. The clerk moved quickly to keep a couple of them from rolling off the edge. He took one of the coins and bit into it, clearly pleased to find it was genuine.

"I'd say this ought to be enough to give you boys two weeks of lodging. Give you real fine treatment, too. Clean sheets and everything."

Cobb picked up his satchel. "Show us where they are."

"I'll be happy to right after you sign your names." The clerk fumbled to open the closed ledger on the desk. "I normally don't like being so formal, but the marshal insists on knowing who's staying on the property."

Cobb took the book from him and laid it flat on the desk. "The marshal won't give you any trouble about that. The rooms. Now."

The clerk offered a nervous laugh as he fished two keys from his pocket. "Follow me. I'll give you a tour of the place."

Cobb exchanged glances before following the heavy man as he parted a curtain leading to a hallway. Butch went first as the clerk waddled away.

"The name's Clark," their host told them, "which ought to be easy enough for you boys to remember since I'm also the clerk. What can I call you two boys?"

"Deputy will do," Butch said.

"I guess it'll have to." Clark led them through a door that led out to an open alley behind one of the liveries that had refused to take their coach or their horses. The Cheyenne Grand looked like it had once been some kind of storehouse and Clark had erected thin walls and flimsy doors to create rooms that were closer to cribs. Someone had thought to stretch canvas between the two buildings, but years of harsh Wyoming weather had caused it to sag. The only thing that stunk worse than the horses in the livery was the stale water that had accumulated atop the canvas.

"I know it doesn't look like much, but if it's privacy you want, we have that in abundance. The people who stay here aren't particular about their neighbors and like to keep to themselves. They're laborers from the railroad, mostly. They're usually quiet except around payday when they like to cut loose. I try to keep it down to a dull roar, but these boys can be rowdy when the spirits take them. You two being lawmen probably know the type."

Cobb and Butch let that go unanswered. They passed a half-opened door where two men who looked like laborers were passed out on the floor. Two more had fallen across the bed and were snoring loudly.

Clark asked, "Where'd you boys say you were from?"

"Wyoming," Cobb said, hoping he had run out of questions.

Clark got the hint and continued on in silence until they reached the end of the alley where a sturdy door was closed. "I like to call this our Presidential Suite. It used to be the manager's office back when this was a storeroom." He placed his key in the lock and opened it to reveal two windowless rooms inside separated by a low pony wall. "The walls here are thicker than any of the other rooms and a mule could kick that door all day without putting a dent in it. Stays cool in the summer, too. Some folks don't like that there's no view to speak of, but I think of it as cozy."

Butch took the key from Clark before he had the chance to hand it to him. "We'll take it. And this is the last time we expect to see you back here."

"You've no fear of that." Clark held up his hands as he began to back up. "I've never been one to ask too many questions. I'm here day and night, so if you boys need anything, you can always find me up front."

Cobb blocked his way before he could leave. "We don't want anyone knowing we're here. So, if anyone besides Hugh Perry comes looking for us, you tell them you haven't seen us. That clear?"

"Clear as a bell," Clark said. "Like I told you, I'm not the curious type."

Cobb still was not satisfied. "And I'll expect you to tell us if anyone *does* come around asking about us."

Clark licked his thick lips as sweat broke out across his upper lip. "Anyone I should be mindful of?"

Cobb leaned closer to him. "Anyone and everyone."

Clark quickly nodded and Cobb stepped aside to let him go.

Butch closed the door behind him and worked the lock with the key. "The rest of this place looks like it's about to fall down, but at least the lock works." He tugged on the door and found it did not give. "Seems solid. I just wish there was more of a wall separating us on account of your frightful snoring."

Cobb tossed his satchel on the bed on the left side of the wall. "We won't be spending much time here anyway. This place is more of a distraction than anything."

"A distraction?" Butch asked. "What do you mean?"

"A distraction for Phil Bengston." Cobb tossed a thumb over his shoulder as he sat down on the bed. "That fat idiot won't waste any time telling anyone who'll listen about the two deputies he's got staying here. It won't take him long to figure out who we really are. I'm counting on word spreading until it reaches Bengston and whoever he's got riding with him. We'll do most of our sleeping over at the jail, but having a place to stow our stuff will give Phil more than one place to watch. That's good for us."

Cobb did not like to talk much about his plans, not even with Butch. He felt that the more air he gave a thought, the more likely it was to fail. He had learned that announcing one's intentions was a good way to hear God laugh.

"Stow your stuff and let's get started on patrol," Cobb told his partner. "Hugh's not paying us to be idle."

As he and Butch began their patrol on the streets of Cheyenne, Tucker Cobb realized he had lost count of how many wild towns he had visited in his life. He imagined it must have been at least a dozen between Texas and Wyoming. Many of them had names, but some did not. A few had been south of the border in Mexico now that he thought of it.

But Cheyenne was not one of those places, not even now. It was a busy place to be sure—the railroad coming to town had seen to that—but it was not exactly dangerous. The people who lived there seemed to be too busy to get themselves into much trouble.

All the men he saw were either working on one of the many buildings being erected all over town, or they were hauling goods by wagon or on their shoulders. The long summer days meant the crews worked from sunup to sundown without many breaks in between. He doubted any man complained since he knew he would likely be replaced easily enough. New arrivals to Cheyenne milled around the many job sites around town hoping a foreman would need a man for a paying task. Cobb recognized Fisk as one of them and pointed him out to Butch.

"There's your friend from the coach," Cobb told his partner when they stopped at a corner. "Fisk or Renfro or whatever his name is."

Butch saw him, too. "He said his name is Fisk and he's no friend of mine. We're liable to be locking him up at some point before we leave this place. I hope he doesn't think being a customer of ours will cut him any favors."

Cobb watched the man as Fisk looked up at the busy workmen as intently as if he was watching a horse race. He had worked with many cowboys over the years, and there was something about Fisk that made Cobb think he had been a decent hand not too long ago. "What do you make of him? As a cowpuncher, I mean. You worked that side of things longer than I did."

"I don't think anything of him." Butch spat a stream of tobacco juice into the street. "Any man who smokes opium can't be relied on. Not now and not ever. That stuff tends to ruin a man for life. Once you get that itch, there's only one thing that can scratch it."

But Cobb was not as sure as his partner. "Getting drunk doesn't make a man a drunk. Life doesn't always cut so clean."

Butch used his sleeve to wipe the tobacco juice from his mouth. "When did you become a shepherd?"

Before Cobb had a chance to answer him, several male voices cried out from the building site across the street. Cobb looked up in time to see a man tumble from a wooden beam he judged to be about fifty feet above the ground.

Another cry went up from the unemployed men on the street as they rushed forward, each man raising his hand in the air as he shouted for the foreman's attention. No one knew if the worker was dead or alive. None of them cared. All they knew was that his day was done, and he would need to be replaced.

Cobb and Butch bolted between two heavy wagons that had stopped in the middle of the thoroughfare to watch the scene unfold. The drivers struggled to maintain control of their teams frightened by the sudden loud noise of shouting, desperate men.

Butch knifed his way through the crowd first, quickly followed by Cobb. They had to struggle to push their way through the men, not caring who they knocked over as they did it. Cobb looked over the heads of the men pushing forward to see only a few up at the front pushing back. One of those men holding the line was Fisk.

"Get back!" the cowhand hollered above the many

shouts and threats hurled at him. "Clear out of the way so the doctor can get through."

Cobb saw Butch stumble into the clearing at the front as Cobb himself was almost knocked aside by the jostling crowd. None of them had seen the star pinned to his shirt, and none of them cared, either.

He had almost made it to the front when Butch drew his pistol and fired it into the air. The first shot quieted them. The second shot caused them to take a step back, which allowed Cobb to get through to where his partner stood with his smoking pistol still in the air.

"You all heard what this man said," Butch yelled, "now get moving. A man's been hurt and needs tending to. Move away so a doctor can get by."

The men all held their ground until Cobb rested the butt of his coach gun on his hip. "Make a path or I'll cut one for you."

Cobb was not sure if it was the shotgun on his hip or the star pinned to his shirt that brought the crowd to its senses. But the knot of humanity began to loosen a bit as the stragglers in the back moved away. They grumbled to themselves as they moved, but none stood in their way.

Cobb told Butch, "I'll keep an eye on things up here while you go back and check on that fella who fell."

His partner disappeared into the skeleton of the building, leaving Cobb and Fisk alone at the front.

Fisk glanced at Cobb's star as he kept his eyes on the street. "You didn't tell me you were the law when I was riding in your coach."

"I wasn't the law then." Cobb lowered the shotgun to his side. "That happened after we dropped off you and the others. A long story."

"I reckon it must be."

"Why'd you go and do that just now?" Cobb asked

him. "Hold those men back, I mean. I'd have expected you to join in with them. You need a job as much as any of them."

"I didn't think of it that way at the time," Fisk said. "I can't say I thought of it at all. It just didn't seem right, especially since we don't know if that man's alive or dead. A few minutes wouldn't make much of a difference."

Cobb had not paid the man much mind when he had been riding in his coach, but he had a chance to look him over now. He was taller than Butch, but not quite as tall as Cobb. He might have been as tall, if not taller than Cobb if his legs did not have a slight bow to them. He imagined he had gotten that way from so much time spent in the saddle. He had a lean build and calloused hands like his own. Holding on to reins for hours on end tended to do that to a man.

Cobb asked him, "Have any luck finding a job yet?"

"Sure. That's why I was standing here. Figured I had some time on my hands before I had lunch with the bank president."

Cobb liked his attitude. "I was only asking because I was thinking I might have a job for you if you were interested."

"No, thanks. You might be ready to take up waxing a wagon bench with your behind but not me. I'd rather swing a hammer or ride a horse than look at the back of a horse for the rest of my life."

"I was thinking of something different than that." One of the men to his right started to get loud, but a stern look from Cobb quieted him down. "You ever been a lawman before?"

"I reckon that I've spent enough time in jail that I could be," Fisk said. "But I've never been on your side of the law before."

"Then maybe now's a good time for you to consider it. Hugh Perry's the town marshal here and he's sort of a friend of mine. He's got a bunch of stars just like this one in his desk and no takers. I thought you might be interested in the job."

"How's the pay?"

"Money's not a concern," Cobb said. "You can come over to the jail with me and Butch after things quiet down here. I can introduce you to Perry and see if he wants to hire you on."

Fisk looked at the men at the right, who had moved a good bit away from them by then. "I don't think your partner would like that."

"It's not his decision. It's mine and Perry's. But there's one condition you'll need to keep in mind if you take it."

"Here it comes." Fisk kicked at the dirt with the toe of his heel. "This is about me stealing that ticket from Renfro. Well, you can save your breath. I'm not proud of it but I ain't ashamed of it, either. It just would've gone to waste in his pocket if I hadn't taken it. I'm not a thief, but I'm not a fool. I saw a chance to better myself and I took it."

"It's not about stealing the ticket," Cobb told him. "It's about where you were when you stole it. If I put in a good word with the marshal about you, then I'll expect you to lay down the pipe for as long as you're working for him. I don't know how deep the dragon's got its claws in you, and I don't care to know. It's none of my business, and it'll stay that way if you live up to your end of the bargain." He offered his hand to him. "Do we have a bargain?"

Fisk looked Cobb in the eye as they shook hands. "That sounds fair enough to me, Mr. Cobb."

"I'll remember you said that." Both men went back to watching the men around them as more shouts came from the workers behind them on the site. "Just keep this between you and me until all this is over. I'll have to find the right time to explain this to Butch. He doesn't like you much, and I don't think I have to tell you why."

"Guess it'll be up to me to prove him wrong."

"I guess so."

CHAPTER 20

Butch pushed his way through the workmen who had clustered around the spot where their comrade had landed when he fell from the building. "Make way. Let me see to him."

The men begrudgingly parted enough to reveal the crumpled form of the man on the ground. He was groaning, which Butch took as a hopeful sign.

One of the men who had been kneeling beside the worker looked at Butch as he pushed him away. "Are you a doctor?"

Butch began to move his hands over the wounded man to check for broken bones. "No, but I'm closer to one than any other man here. Give me room so I can check to see what's broken. What's his name?"

"Sid," the concerned man said. "Sid Gillman. He's my friend."

Butch spoke directly to the man by name. "Sid, I know you're hurting, but I'm going to need you to stay as still as you can. If you move, you might hurt yourself even worse than you already are. Can you tell me where it hurts the worst?"

"Everywhere," Sid groaned. "I feel worse than when I was kicked by a mule."

"I know what that's like." His legs and knees did not feel broken, which Butch took to mean that he had landed exactly as he was laying now—on his left side. "Been kicked by one a time or two myself. Could you feel me when I was checking your legs just now?"

"I did but it's my middle that's paining me."

Butch ran his hands along Sid's left arm, and it felt like it was solid. But when he placed a hand on his ribs, Sid howled in agony.

"I was expecting that," Butch said to the concerned friend. Sid would be lucky if he had only busted some ribs. "Check his mouth. See if there's any foam coming out of him there."

The man leaned closer to look. "Can't see any. Does it hurt when you breathe, Sid?"

Sid cursed him for asking a foolish question as Butch moved his hands to check Sid's neck. He gently felt around the back of his head without any protest from the man. Another good sign.

But when he touched the man's skull, he felt the broken bones, which caused Sid to cry out again.

Butch's hand came away bloody. He looked at the concerned friend. "What's your name?"

"Jack Thomas. Why?"

"Jack, I'm gonna need you to go get something I can use to bind his head. Some smaller pieces of wood, too. His head's busted and I think his right arm is, too. We'll need to set it before we can bring him to a doctor."

"Stay where you are, Jack," a man at the front of the group said. Since he was holding a clipboard, Butch took him to be the foreman. "My name is Reeves and Sid's one of my men. I already sent someone to fetch a doctor. I don't think you ought to touch him until the doctor gets here."

Butch stood up and pulled Reeves aside. He kept his voice low as he said, "Sid's in a bad way, mister. He's got some broken ribs and a busted skull." He held up his bloody hand for the foreman to see. "He's bleeding, and I've got to patch up that wound before he loses too much blood. I won't move him until the doc gets here, but there's plenty we need to do before then."

Reeves scowled at Jack and offered a curt nod.

As Butch knelt back beside Sid, Butch began to cough from the dirt Jack had accidentally kicked up as he went to find some cloth and wood for a splint.

Butch rested a hand on Sid's shoulder. "We're gonna get you fixed up in no time, amigo. You just stay as you are and let us tend to you. The doc will be here before you know it."

"I heard what you told Reeves," Sid said. "I'm bleeding bad."

Butch cursed himself for not speaking low enough. "Not bad enough for you to worry about. Just stay still and we'll patch you back together."

Butch looked up when he heard a great commotion from outside where he had left Cobb and Fisk on the street. Three men on horseback rode into the site, dismounting only when they got close to where Sid had fallen.

The first man to reach the ground was hatless, had wire-rimmed spectacles, and carried a black medical bag. Butch took him to be the doctor as he rushed to Sid's side.

The second man down had a roundish shape and had not shaved for several days. His clothes were dusty and stained by sweat.

The third man to drop from the saddle was leaner and younger than the other two and was just as dusty as the roundish man. His eyes were shielded from the afternoon sun by the flat brim of his black hat. He wore his pistol low on his right leg, but within easy reach of his hand.

Butch had never seen this man before but knew the type. The only kind of men who wore their rig that way were the types who fancied themselves as shootists.

He stepped toward Butch as if he knew him. "What are you doing in here, Keeling? This is railroad property and you're trespassing."

Butch remembered how Marshal Perry had described Phil Bengston and, given what he had just said, imagined this must be him. "It's railroad property in the town of Cheyenne." He touched the star on his shirt without taking his eyes off Bengston. "I got hired on as a deputy earlier today. I was on patrol when I saw this man fall, and I ran over here to see if I could help him. Figured a man's life was more important than some boundaries on a deed."

"The railroad doesn't need any help from the likes of you." Bengston looked at the foreman. "Ain't that right, Reeves?"

But the foreman refused to make eye contact with him as he watched the doctor begin his examination of Sid.

Bengston moved his eyes back to Butch. "You'd best clear out of here before I run you off."

The roundish man, who had remained back with the horses, said, "Careful now, Phil. He's one of Perry's deputies and he's got cause to be here."

Bengston did not look like he had heard his friend. "I'm the only one who decides who can and who can't be on railroad property. I told you to move, mister, so move and be quick about it!"

Butch remained where he was. "Be careful what you wish for, because when I move, it might be faster than you'd like."

Butch watched Bengston's right hand flex near his pistol as the doctor called out, "Someone get me some wood and some cloth. This man's got a broken skull and a broken arm. I need to fix him up before I try to move . . ."

"I've got it right here for you, Doc," Jack said, as he ran toward him. He was carrying wooden strips of several different sizes and remnants of canvas bags in both hands. "The deputy already told me to fetch this stuff."

The doctor glanced up at Butch before sifting through what Jack had brought him. "You just might've helped save this man's life, Deputy."

Butch grinned at Bengston. "You hear that? The doc said I'm helpful."

Bengston's hand remained near his pistol. It was clear he was working himself up to pulling, but the men around them were watching. "It doesn't matter what he says, only what I say, and I told you to leave. This is your last chance."

Butch heard the hammers of Cobb's shotgun being pulled back as he moved closer to Bengston. "And this is your last chance, too, mister. Your last chance to listen to reason, because if you pull, so will I. Get your hand away from that hogleg and rest it on your belt buckle. Do it real slow."

Butch waited until Bengston did as he had been ordered before approaching his new enemy. He stopped alongside him and said, "How'd you know my name was Keeling?"

Bengston did not make a move and did not make a sound. He just kept looking in the direction where Butch had been standing.

Butch had not expected him to answer. "You know who I am, and now I know who you are. I know who we've got locked up over in the jail right now and what she means to you. Keep your distance from us, and things might turn out your way. But if you give us any trouble, you'll have some of your own to worry about. You'd do well to keep that in mind before you do something stupid."

Bengston looked at the workers who were watching him as much as they were watching the doctor work on Sid.

"Funny thing about jail. People get held there while waiting to be tried for something. Trials ain't much good without witnesses and evidence. Cheyenne's a dangerous place. New people come in and out of here every single day. Anything could happen to you while you and Cobb are on one of your patrols." He slowly turned his head and locked eyes with Butch. "You'd do well to keep that in mind yourself."

Under other circumstances, Butch might have enjoyed the younger man's confidence. He might've even admired it. "Guess we'll all have to be careful, won't we? I'll be seeing you around, boy."

Butch joined Cobb as his partner backed away from Bengston, keeping both barrels of his shotgun trained on him as he did.

Cobb said, "So that's Phil Bengston. Not much to him, is there?"

Butch kept walking. "There's more to him than you think. But at least now we know what he looks like."

Back at the jail, Marshal Perry was absorbed in his paperwork while Jane began to organize the supplies for the prisoners. She had gone out back and refilled each of the water buckets for the three female prisoners on this side of the jail. Marshal Perry had told her not to bother with worrying about the male prisoners because one of his deputies was already taking care of them. She was happy to oblige. The vulgar comments and catcalls they had thrown her way earlier had taught her to stay away from them. Perry had put a blanket in the cell of a woman waiting for trial for murdering her husband so Jane could stay out of their sight.

She arranged the blankets and bedclothes on the near wall of the barn. Perry and his deputies had been content to leave everything in a mess in several burlap sacks against the wall, which made it harder to know how much they had. She decided to use a couple of shelves against the wall of the old barn to lay everything in plain sight where it was easier to see what was needed. She created one pile for the male prisoners and one for the female prisoners.

The sheets, blankets, and pillows were not the only objects in plain sight. Jane was conscious that Miss Hyde had been watching her the entire time.

"Look at you," the female prisoner said from the cot of her cell. "Keeping yourself busy by tidying up the place. You'll make Cobb a fine wife someday. That is, if he can ever bring himself to forget what you really are."

Jane continued with her organizing. The black-and-white-striped garb she had given Hyde to wear after she had cleaned up from the slop bucket mess made her look small. The clothes had been made for much larger male prisoners. "You sound almost as ridiculous as you look. Remember what happened the last time you decided to get nasty with me." She looked over the small pile of striped garb she had folded. "We won't be able to spare another outfit for you next time, so you'll be forced to keep a blanket wrapped around you. Assuming I let you keep one."

Hyde crossed her arms in front of her. "You really think you've got everything figured out, don't you? You think you're safe just because you got that idiot mule skinner and his friend to sneak you out of Laramie. You think Amanda and Clay will just let you go as easy as all that? You thought you signed a contract with them in ink, but as far as they're concerned, you might as well have signed it in blood. You may be done with them, dear girl, but they're not done with you, yet. Not by a country mile. And when my Phil comes to get me, I wouldn't count on that old fool Perry to stop him. He knows who butters his bread and it's not you."

Jane faced her and placed a hand on her hip. "You and I are going to be spending a long time together in here. We can either make it pleasant or nasty. It's the same amount of effort for me either way, but no matter what you think, I'll always win."

Hyde's thin mouth turned into a smile. "I won't be here for as long as you might think. And as soon as I get out of here, I'll show you what happens to traitors like you."

Jane thought about dousing her with a bucket of water but quickly remembered how heavy it had been to bring in from the pump outside. Hyde simply was not worth the effort.

She saw a man in a brown uniform with an odd badge pinned to it as he entered the jail. He had a hat that looked like the kind Union soldiers had worn during the war. He wore a wide, droopy mustache that matched the saggy countenance of his face.

He stopped at Marshal Perry's desk and whispered something to him, which caused the law man to get to his feet as he took the ring of keys and hand shackles from his desk. The man in the brown uniform followed him. "That's enough grousing out of you, Hyde. On your feet and turn around with your back to your cell door."

Jane watched Hyde remain cross-armed on her cot. "And what if I refuse?"

"You won't like what happens next." Perry shook the shackles, making them rattle. "Do like I told you, and let's get this over with so me and Court Officer Childs here can run you over to the courthouse. Judge Waller is ready to hear your plea."

Hyde swore to herself as she got up from her cot and followed Perry's orders. The deputy reached through the bars to secure the manacles to her wrists before Perry unlocked the door and led her outside.

Perry asked the court deputy, "You think you can run her over to the judge on your own? I'd be glad to go with you, but someone's got to stay here with the prisoners, and all my men are either out on patrol or making sure those wagons don't crash into each other."

Jane was glad, in more ways than one, when Cobb, Butch, and Fisk entered the makeshift jail. "Not all of them are out there, Marshal. You've got two right here with you and a promising young man eager to join up with you."

Miss Hyde cursed at them, causing Officer Childs to pull hard on her arm.

Marshal Perry told Childs, "Those two up front there are my new deputies. Tucker Cobb and Butch Keeling." To them, he said, "What are you two doing back so soon? You're not due back for another few hours or more."

While Jane ran to Cobb to embrace him, Butch said, "I guess you could say that old Cobb and me managed to cram a whole day's worth of deputy duty into a short while. We were keeping an eye on the town when one of the fellas working at a building site must've gotten careless and fell. The two of us rushed in to restore order before the men looking for work in front of the place stormed the site in hopes of finding a job. It was dangerous work, Marshal, but we held them off. You would've been mighty proud of us, Perry. Kinda felt like we were Davy Crockett and Jim Bowie at the Alamo for a moment."

Perry rolled his eyes. "You Texans and your tall tales. What's the injured man's name?"

Butch said, "When he wasn't caterwauling from his injuries, he told me his name was Sid."

Perry's concern turned into a frown as he trudged back toward his desk. "I know him. I'd place good money that he was probably hungover. That man hasn't drawn a sober breath since he came to town a few weeks ago. I'm surprised Reeves has kept him on as long as he has, given how he's a stickler about such things."

"Sid's always been harmless enough." Officer Childs steered a grumbling Miss Hyde toward the others. "I like that old codger. He never lets life get him down and can make a man laugh about just about anything." He asked Butch, "Does it look like he'll pull through?"

"He broke a few bones when he landed," Butch said, "but the doctor thinks he'll make it. We watched them cart Sid out on a wagon a little while ago."

Marshal Perry said, "I'll have to remember to stop by and see him later tonight if he's up to it. Which doctor took him?"

"He didn't introduce himself," Cobb said, "but I heard some men in the crowd call him Doc Fry."

Perry looked at Officer Childs. "Bob Fry wouldn't have been my first choice. Wonder why they picked him?"

Childs shrugged. "He's the railroad's doctor and that hotel Sid's building is a railroad hotel. It only makes sense they'd get Fry." Childs asked Cobb, "Did Doc Fry come alone?"

Jane felt Cobb's muscles tense a little. "He showed up with Phil Bengston and some other fella."

"Swarthy?" Perry asked. "Kinda round, but not exactly fat?"

Cobb nodded. "Sounds like you know him."

"Earl Panfil," the marshal said. "His real name is Morales, but he thinks Panfil makes it sound more American. He's Bengston's shadow."

The chains of Miss Hyde's shackles rattled as she said, "My boy stands on his own two feet. He doesn't need any shadow."

Officer Childs pulled on the prisoner's shoulder. "That's enough of that out of you."

Perry ignored her outburst and pointed at the man with his two deputies. "And what's your story? Were you playing Jim Bridger during all this Alamo business?"

Cobb answered before Butch could manage it. "This man's name is Nick Fisk. He helped us keep order out on the street after Sid's accident. He just pitched in without us asking him to do it. He just so happens to be in need of a job, and since you're in need of deputies, I figured you two ought to meet."

Perry looked over the taller, younger man from the top of his hat to the tips of his boots. "You vouch for this man, Cobb?"

Jane felt Cobb tense up a little further before saying, "I do."

"What about you, Butch?"

"If Tucker vouches for him, so do I."

Perry kept his eyes on Fisk. "Cowpuncher?"

Fisk stepped out from behind the two deputies. "I've punched cows, horses, and men in my time, Marshal. I don't cause trouble, but I know how to handle it if it happens. I'd be happy to handle it for you if you give me half a chance. I could sure use the money."

Perry gestured at the gun holstered on his right hip. "You know how to use that thing?"

Fisk nodded. "And I know when to not use it, too."

Perry grunted in approval as he opened the top drawer of his desk, took out a deputy's star, and tossed it over to Fisk, who easily caught it in his right hand. "Consider yourself hired. I'll swear you in later. Right now, I've already got something you can do. Accompany Officer Childs and the prisoner here over to the courthouse. If you don't screw that up, come back, and I'll have more work for you to do." He pointed over at a cabinet against the wall where Jane had been organizing things. "Take a Winchester with you. People are more apt to get out of the way when they see that in your hand and the star on your shirt."

"No need for that," a man said from the street behind him. "She's not going anywhere except with me."

Jane and the others turned to see a tall young man with a shorter, swarthy man enter the jail. She may not have seen the men before, but she knew who they were.

"There's my boy!" Miss Hyde cried out at the sight of her son. "I knew you'd come for me, Phil."

Marshal Perry slammed his desk drawer shut as he stepped around it to confront Bengston. "I don't know what you're trying to pull here, Phil, but it won't work. The judge wants the prisoner in his court, and not you or anyone else is going to change that."

Phil produced a paper from his back pocket and handed it to Panfil. "Give this to the marshal before he makes a fool of himself."

Panfil took the paper and scurried over to Marshal Perry, who snatched the paper from him.

And as Panfil went back to join his partner in the doorway, Bengston said, "It's all right there in writing. It's from Judge Waller himself. He's agreed to release my mother to my care until the trial." He offered a flat grin. "Assuming there's ever going to be a trial."

Childs looked on as Perry read the document. "That's the judge's handwriting all right. His signature, too. I've seen it so many times, I'd recognize it anywhere. That's his seal and everything."

Jane watched Perry's face redden as he refolded the document. "I won't believe it until I hear it from the judge himself." He pointed at Cobb, Butch, and Fisk. "You three stay right here until I get back. We're taking this prisoner to court to get this straightened out."

Bengston and Panfil spread themselves out across the wide entrance of the makeshift jail. "You're not taking her anywhere, Perry. That's not just me talking. That's not just Judge Waller talking. That's the railroad talking. You don't want to run afoul of them."

Jane watched Perry slowly draw himself up straight. He looked like he might have been quite a formidable man once upon a time. He was summoning some of that old strength now. "Are you challenging me, boy?"

"I'm not your boy," Bengston said. "I'm her's. She's my mother."

"And she's my prisoner." Perry's face was beginning to redden. "And if you two don't step aside right now, this is going to go bad for you and right quick."

Butch and Fisk rested their hands on the butts of their pistols. Cobb pushed Jane behind him as he took a better grip on his shotgun. "You'd better listen to the marshal, Bengston. Your hand so much as twitches toward your gun, and we'll cut you down where you stand."

Jane expected Panfil to lose his nerve, but he surprised her by being as calm as his partner.

She saw Bengston's Adam's apple rise and fall in his throat before he said, "The least you can do is take those chains off her. Allow her some dignity when you're leading her through the streets."

But Perry would not budge. "Those shackles come off if and when Judge Waller tells me to take them off. Until then, they stay on." He stepped closer to Bengston. "You two had best step aside. Right now."

Jane watched Bengston's top lip quiver and, for a moment, thought he might try to shoot it out. But he gestured to Panfil to move out of the way. "We'll be right behind you, Perry. And we won't forget this."

Perry looked back at Childs and the prisoner. "Let's get this over with." To Fisk, he said, "You come, too. Escort these *gentlemen* while they're escorting us. And if they make a play for their guns, shoot them."

Fisk nodded. "It'll be my pleasure."

Perry led Officer Childs and Miss Hyde from the jail. Fisk paused at the entry and allowed Bengston and Panfil to move first before falling in behind them.

Cobb and Butch slowly walked to the front and watched the small contingent as they took the prisoner to the court. No one on the busy street seemed to pay them any mind.

Jane sighed as she rested her head on Cobb's shoulder. It felt like the first breath she had taken in minutes. "That was a close one."

Butch spat a stream of tobacco into the street. "It's not over yet."

Cobb agreed. "If anything, it's just beginning."

CHAPTER 21

While Cobb began reading over some of the paperwork that Perry had left behind, Butch contented himself by standing watch at the door. A man could learn a lot about a place just by watching how it went about its business. He wanted to feel the rhythms of the town that would serve as his home for the next few weeks. Where people went and where they were coming back from. He had to understand it if he hoped to stay alive, especially now that the railroad and all its considerable influence in Cheyenne would likely be against them.

It was late afternoon, and many of the saloons that had been closed during the day had begun to open. He could hear the rough sounds of tinny pianos being played over the din of foot traffic along the thoroughfare. The workday was coming to an end for some folks, and the saloons would begin to fill with tired men with sore muscles and stories to tell.

Sid's misfortune from earlier that afternoon was bound to be the favorite topic of conversation. He was sure that, by the time last call rolled around in the wee hours of the morning, reports of Sid's condition would change for the worse. Butch made a mental note to stop by Doc Fry's place to see how the injured man was doing. He doubted any of his comrades would think to do the same.

He turned when he heard Jane approach him. She had kept herself busy by tending to the female prisoners and organizing goods against the wall of the old barn. She had succeeded in making herself look busy but he had not paid enough attention to her work to know if she had accomplished much of anything.

He spat a long stream of tobacco into the street, hoping he would not have to do it in front of her.

She leaned against the other end of the open door as she joined him in looking out at the citizens. "Our first day in Cheyenne has certainly been an eventful one, hasn't it?"

"You can say that again," Butch said. "This place sure has changed since the last time me and Cobb were here. It was just a sleepy town back then. Looks like the railroad's pouring plenty of money into the town. That'll change things forever and not necessarily for the better."

Jane used her hand to fan herself. "It ought to bode well for you and Tucker's coach business, though. There's bound to be plenty of travelers who won't care that King Hagen has put a word against you."

"There'll always be plenty of people who won't care about that. It's the ones who care that bother me because there's a lot more of them. We had a tough time finding a place that would let us stay there. Every hotel in town was closed to us. We were lucky to get some rooms in a hovel behind a livery two streets over from here." He had not given thought to Jane's accommodations until that very moment. "We got two beds with a thick door and a good lock on it." He dug his hand into his pocket and handed her the key. "It's not much, but it's better than sleeping in here. I think you'll like it."

Jane regarded the key for a moment. "You said you got two rooms. Where will you sleep?"

Butch knew that much did not matter. "Don't worry about me. I've spent so much of my life under the stars; I've never gotten the knack of sleeping under a roof. It always feels like I'm missing out on something. I'll find a place for me. Maybe one of those old cots in an empty cell back there if it's raining." Watching Jane fanning herself reminded him of how warm it was. "It's too hot to sleep anyway."

She tried to hand the key back to him. "I don't mean to put you out, Butch. I'm sure I can find a rooming house somewhere in town that has a space for me. One that caters to only women. I'm pretty good at finding such places."

Butch laughed in spite of himself. He may not have trusted her or her intentions toward Cobb, but there was no denying that she was a difficult woman to dislike. She could be mighty charming when she put her mind to it. "If you happen to find such a place, I'll take that key back from you. But until then, I'll rest easier knowing you've got a place to lay your head. Cobb won't complain."

She slowly slipped the key into the pocket of her apron and looked back at Cobb, who was still pouring over papers at Marshal Perry's desk. "He's a lucky man to have so many people concerned about him, isn't he? I don't think he's gotten quite used to it yet. He's been alone for so long. I know he's had you, but . . ."

"But I'm not as pleasant company as you," Butch said. "I already knew that."

She stopped fanning herself and rested her head against the sliding barn door. "You know, I'd like to think you've begun to warm to me, but you're a tough man to figure out."

Butch felt antsy. "I haven't used it in so long, I've kind

of forgotten it myself. But if you promise not to tell anyone, not even Cobb, I'll tell it to you."

She smiled in a conspiratorial manner. "You have yourself a deal. I'll take it with me to my grave. What is it?"

"It's Aloysius."

Jane failed to suppress a giggle. "I see why you use Butch."

"I had no choice because I don't know how to spell it," he admitted. "It's too long a name anyway, so Butch suits me just fine."

"Your secret is safe with me."

Butch did not think it was much of a secret. "I'm more concerned about Cobb being safe with you than my secret." He had not intended to say that, but now that he had, he did not regret it.

He watched her smile dim a little. She was not angry. She was not even hurt. "You mean you still doubt me? Even after all of this?"

"Don't take it personally. The only one in the world I don't doubt is Cobb. You see, all the kin I have are either dead or might as well be. And that big lug over at that desk might not be much, but he's the closest thing I have to family."

"You're right," she agreed. "He may not be much, but as much as he means to you, he means even more to me. He means everything."

But Butch was not sure that was the case. "I haven't forgotten how poorly you treated him back in Laramie. He did everything but call for you from the street, and he didn't do that because I wouldn't let him. I know how pigheaded he can be, especially when he's certain he's right. He can be a surly cuss, too, when the mood strikes him. But you can't just shut him out like you did. You hurt him more than you realize. More than he'll ever admit to you. I don't want to see him go through that again."

He watched a tear run down her cheek. She was not crying like she had in the alley back in Laramie. These were real tears, yet they had no effect on him.

"Folks can't always control what they feel for each other," he told her. "And in your old line of work, I imagine emotions for a man are tough to conjure up. But even if you don't love him as much as you say you do or as much as Cobb loves you, I'm pretty sure you like him for the kind of man he is. If you can't treat him well out of love, then do it out of gratitude for saving your life. I like you, Jane, but if you hurt him like that again, I won't be happy about it."

She wiped her tears away with the heel of her hand. "There are bound to be arguments in every relationship, Butch. I'm not the kind of woman who cottons to a man's mood."

"I'm not asking you to. This is different and you know it. You know what I'm saying."

She blinked her reddened eyes clear. "I know better than you think. And I thank you for being clear with me. At least now I know where you stand."

"As long as you stand by him, I'll never stand against you. And if you don't want him, it's best to tell him now before he gets even more attached to you. It won't be pleasant, but I'll respect you for it. So will Cobb in the long run."

She tried to muster something of a smile. "That's just it, Butch. I really do love him, even though I know I have no right to do so."

Butch hated awkward talks like these, especially with a lady, so he was almost relieved to see Hugh Perry storming toward the jail with Fisk at a good distance behind him. Fisk caught Butch's eye and slowly shook his head. It was clear things had not gone well with the judge.

Butch told Jane, "You'd best get back inside and put some cotton in your ears. Ol' Hugh is coming back with a full head of steam and is liable to curse up a blue streak when he gets here."

She took a quick glance in Perry's direction before hurrying back inside. "He looks fit to be tied. Don't worry about me. It won't be anything I haven't heard before."

But given the look on Perry's face, Butch was not too certain about that.

Hugh Perry stomped around the jail like a mad bull as he repeated what Judge Waller had said in court. "The defendant is hereby released on her own recognizance to the care of her son, Philip Bengston of the Pacific Railroad Company."

He kicked his wooden chair away from his desk, causing it to bang against the bars. The prisoners cheered on the excitement.

Perry marched toward the cells. "I hear so much as a peep from any of you sorry mongrels, I won't feed you for a week."

Cobb was glad the men grew silent, for Hugh Perry rarely said what he did not mean, not even when he was angry.

He came back to where he had left Cobb, Butch, and Fisk at his desk. "Can you believe that? A woman with an attempted murder charge hanging over her head released. I never expected something like that from a man like Judge Waller. I'm almost embarrassed for him."

Cobb saw it as much simpler than that. "I don't like it any more than you do, but I understand it. The judge lives in Cheyenne. The railroad has a lot of pull in Cheyenne, and it only gets stronger every day. Bengston has a lot of influence with the railroad, and I'm sure he got them to put in a good word for his mother with the judge."

Perry slammed the palm of his hand down on the desktop. "I told you to cut a deal with Madam Peachtree and Clay while you had the chance. Now you've got nothing."

Butch said, "She got cut loose before a telegram would've reached Laramie. They wouldn't have called off Bengston because they didn't have to call him off. Cobb and me are used to being at the whims of our betters."

"The railroad's not better than us," Cobb said. "They're just bigger."

Perry wheeled his chair back to his desk and plopped himself down in it. "You two have bigger troubles than the railroad when it comes to Miss Hyde. I hope you weren't counting on any of the men who were staying at the stage station to testify against her. I can all but guarantee they've either been paid off or told to say they didn't see her try to kill you boys." He pointed at Fisk. "And since you had me make him into a deputy, the court won't accept his testimony."

"None of them would've testified anyway." Cobb sat on the edge of Perry's desk. "No one else saw her do it except me and Butch. That's how she got wounded. That's got to count for something, doesn't it?"

"It comes down to your word against hers," Perry explained. "She could say she was looking for the outhouse and got lost in the dark. She could say the gun you found on her wasn't even hers. There are all sorts of ways her lawyers could get her out of this now, and I bet they know them all. Bengston's probably got every lawyer on the railroad's payroll doing that as we speak." He shook his head in disgust. "I'm sorry about this, boys. I really am.

I wouldn't hold out much hope for a conviction if I were you."

Butch spat a stream of tobacco juice into the cuspidor on the floor beside the marshal's desk. "Makes me regret I only winged her."

But Cobb knew they did not have the luxury of regrets at the moment. "How many men does Bengston have working for him? On the railroad, I mean. He can't be the only gun they've hired. It's a long way between here and the next station."

"I've known him to have as many as ten with him," Perry said, "but most of them follow the track gangs. They move along with the workers. I haven't seen any of them in town since work started. And I don't think the railroad will let him pull them in from the field on account of this. They'd lose more than half their laborers if they did, and if there are two things that matter to a railroad, it's time and money. I wouldn't count on any trouble coming from them."

Fisk said, "There were plenty of men who were standing with me out in front of that building site. If Bengston was looking to hire on some men, he'd have no trouble finding them."

"That's not Phil's style," Perry assured them. "He knows better than to hire a mob to go after these two. He likes to be in control of things and a mob is hard to control. Word would be bound to get out, and it might make him look bad to his bosses. He won't risk that, especially now that he got them to spring his ma loose. Any trouble we'll have will come from him and him alone. That is unless he sends a wire for some men outside of Cheyenne to come help him. That's always a possibility."

"We'll be ready for anything he does," Butch said. "You can count on that."

Perry said, "And I wish I could tell you boys that you could count on me and my men to back you, but I can't make that kind of promise. Toneff's about the only man I have who I can depend on as long as I don't ask much of him. Him and the others I have are having a devil of a time keeping the streets clear. They won't stand up in the face of hired gunmen, assuming that's the way Bengston tries to take this."

Cobb had been expecting as much. "What about you, Hugh? Will you stand with us?"

"Against a bully like Bengston, yes. But against the railroad? Against the mayor who hired me?" He slowly shook his head. "I can't make that kind of promise, boys. I'm too old to find another town to settle, and my gun-fighting days are well behind me. You boys knew that already just by looking at me." He wiped his hand across his mouth. "That's why I've decided to release you from your promise about staying on here a couple of weeks. I didn't hold up my end of the bargain by keeping Bengston's mother as a prisoner. I think it might be better for everyone if you two got out of Cheyenne while the getting is still good."

Cobb remained perched on the edge of Perry's desk. "Are you ordering us out of town, Hugh?"

"I'm strongly suggesting it," the marshal admitted. "Because I have a feeling you two boys are about to cause me no end of trouble. The kind of trouble I can't handle as I am now or with the men I've got working for me. It pains me to no end to admit that to you, but I'm afraid that's the way it is. I'm sorry. I truly am."

Cobb winced at the cold feeling he felt course from his heart to his stomach and back again. If men like Hugh Perry could not be counted on to uphold law and order in a town like Cheyenne, then the likes of King Hagen and his people had already won.

He looked at Butch, who—judging by his expression—had come to the same conclusion. "Looks like we've overstayed our welcome yet again, partner."

But Butch stood firm. "I'm not ready to pull out until you tell me we're pulling out. I'm for staying and fighting if you are."

Cobb wished it was that simple, but the longer they stayed, the more danger the town faced from Bengston's vengeance. The only thing that might keep Phil from coming after them was the open court case against his mother. Judge Waller would not look kindly on the two main witnesses dying before the matter had been resolved properly. He might hold Bengston responsible, and his friends at the railroad would not be there to back him again.

Cobb was counting on Bengston to be as smart as he appeared to be, but not for his sake. "Can Jane stay on here at the jail for a while? I'll rest easier knowing she's safe."

Perry's mood brightened a bit. "Of course, she can stay. And you have my word that no harm will come to her. I don't give my word lightly."

But Cobb already knew that. It was why he had not given them his word that he would stand by them against Bengston.

He aimed his thumb in Fisk's direction. "I hope you'll keep Fisk here on, too. I have a feeling he'll turn out to be a decent deputy if you give him half a chance."

"I intend on giving him more than just half a chance." Perry looked down at his hands, unable to meet Cobb's eyes. "I'm sorry about this, Cobb. I really am."

Cobb and Butch unpinned their stars at the same time. Butch handed his to Cobb, who placed them on the desk. He patted Perry on the shoulder and could feel the disappointment from him like the heat of a fever. "Don't trouble yourself on our account. We'll get by. We always do."

They both shook hands with Fisk, who could not seem to find any words to say in parting, then went to the rifle rack where Cobb had stowed his shotgun. Butch had left his Henry back at their rooms behind the livery. "Mind if I take Jane here to see where she'll be staying? She won't be gone for long."

"Take all the time you need," Perry said, without looking up. "And be sure to stop by the Fiddler's Elbow before you bring her back. The owner's expecting you. His name is Hans Hock. German fella. He's got a proposition for you. A way you might not have to go back to Laramie empty-handed."

Butch, as was his custom, tried to take some of the bitterness out of the moment. "As long as he doesn't ask us to tote any drunks for him. I've had my fill of drunks for a while."

Perry finally smiled at them. "I have a feeling you boys won't object to the kind of passengers he has in mind."

CHAPTER 22

As they returned from showing Jane her room, Jane held tightly onto Tucker's middle, while Butch went ahead to cut through the crowd of the bustling boardwalk. She feared she might be carried away if she did not. "I don't want you to go without me, Tucker. You can't just leave me here. Please take me with you."

"I wish I could, but I can't do that," Cobb said. "It'll be bad for Butch and me and even worse for you. We might have to make for some hard riding once we leave town. I can't do that if I'm worried about my passengers and you at the same time. We got lucky on our last leg from Cheyenne because I had Bengston's mother right next to me to keep Phil from shooting at us. But she's free, and there's nothing to keep him from coming after us now. I wouldn't be surprised if he already had a spot picked out where he plans to kill us."

"I know all those spots better than he does," Butch called back to them. "I'll be ready for him when we pass every one of them."

Jane tried to change his mind. "I'm not helpless, Tucker. I can fight alongside you. I can handle a rifle well enough. Maybe better than that Carlyle girl you took with you to the fort."

Cobb laughed. "So, you heard about that back at the Longacre, did you? I was wondering if the gossip had carried that far."

She did not think this was the right time for jokes. "Three guns are better than two."

"Not if you're holding one of them," Cobb said. "I'd only be worried about you the entire time. I know you want to help, and the best thing you can do is stay here with Perry in the jail. I don't think Bengston, or his mother, will risk crossing him because of you."

"But—"

Cobb did not let her speak. "I know the room we got might not be much, but it's safe enough. At least you don't have to worry about anyone trying to jump you in the alley."

"I'd rather be crouching behind a rock somewhere with you than being left here alone." She only wished she could come up with a way to make him listen to her. "We spent so much time apart because of me, and I don't want to feel that distant from you again. I know you want to keep me safe, but life's not much to look forward to if you're not with me."

Cobb held her closer as they kept walking. "I don't like this any more than you do. I kind of liked the idea of being here with you for a couple of weeks, even if it was as one of Perry's deputies. But there's no telling what Butch and me will come up against out there. At least let us make a couple of runs by ourselves. Maybe Bengston will let up on us by then. He's bound to lose interest once his mother's cleared of all charges."

But Jane knew the type of man Phil Bengston was. Maybe even better than Cobb or Butch. "He won't forget.

His kind never forgets. And even if he wanted to, that evil witch he has for a mother won't let him. She'll come for me the second she thinks she can get away with it."

"Which is all the more reason why you should stay close to Perry and his deputies at the jail. Have one of them walk you back to your rooms if it'll make you feel any better. They won't mind."

She knew there was no point in arguing with him any further. Doing so would only risk making him angry, and she did not want that. She only wished they could spend more time together now. "Are you sure you have to leave tonight?"

"It'll be safer if we do," Cobb said. "By now, the word about us not being deputies anymore has spread all over town. For all I know, the railroad pressured Perry into letting us go. We'll fare better out in the open in the dark than being cooped up here in town. I'll send you a telegram as soon as we reach Laramie. It's not that far and we can make good time, even at night."

"We'll have the moon in our favor," Butch said from the front. "It'll make easier going for us. The horses will like it, too, because it's cooler for them at night."

Jane stopped walking when they reached the corner in front of the Fiddler's Elbow Saloon. It was only two short blocks to the jail, and she did not want him to walk her there. She did not trust herself to not make a scene in front of Marshal Perry and the others, so it was best to say her goodbyes here.

"This is as close to the jail I can risk, and you have business here with Mr. Hock." She took his face in both of her hands. "You've been fighting me all afternoon, Tucker Cobb, but I won't let you fight me on this." She pulled his face down to hers and kissed him deeply. Perhaps deeper than she had ever kissed anyone, for it had never meant as much as it did now.

She released him and turned away from him, almost walking into Butch as she did. She took a firm grip of his arm as she said, "Bring him back to me, Butch. Promise me you'll bring him back alive and in one piece."

Butch touched the brim of his hat. "I'll bring him back to you better than you left him, ma'am."

She popped up on her toes and gave him a quick kiss on the cheek before walking away from them as quickly as she could manage. She did not look back. She did not dare.

But over the noise of the busy street, she thought she heard Butch say, "That's quite a woman you've got there, Cobb."

And she heard her lover say, "She certainly is."

She smiled through her flowing tears. At least she had finally gotten him to admit it.

Cobb looked curiously at the mug of brown liquid that had been placed on the bar in front of him. "You're telling me that's beer?"

"Looks closer to whiskey to me," Butch said. "I've never seen beer that dark."

Hans Hock, the owner of the Fiddler's Elbow, stood proudly behind the bar as he looked down at the mugs that held his latest creation. "I assure you it's beer. Observe the thick head of froth at the top of it. See the richness of it in the mug." His brown hair and beard were trimmed, and his bar apron was spotless. His German accent was distinctive, but clear. "Please, gentlemen. Enjoy and let me know what you think."

Cobb figured he had done more dangerous things than sampling a glass of beer, so he brought it to his lips and drank a deep swallow. As he set the mug back on the bar, his first reaction was that it was certainly beer. But the pleasant, rich taste of it did not reach him until he finished swallowing it.

Mr. Hock enjoyed the look on the coachman's face. "You like it, don't you?"

"That's good." There was certainly an aftertaste, but it was smooth. "That's very good."

Butch took two swallows and wiped the froth from his mouth with the back of his hand. "I like it. It's got substance to it. Feels almost like I'm drinking bread if that makes any sense. Never had beer like it."

"That's because there hasn't been a beer like this," Hock said. "Not in this territory. I've created it myself using my family's recipe and methods. You think your friends will like it?"

Butch put his mug on the bar. "Cobb and me don't have many friends. But both of us like it, for as far as that'll take you. I've always been more of a whiskey man myself, but I'd sure drink this stuff."

"My customers agree with you," Hock said. "That is why I plan on bringing it to other customers in other saloons in the territory. Marshal Perry tells me you men have a coach. I would like to hire it so you can bring three barrels of this beer to Laramie for me. I call it 'Hock's Bock.'"

"Catchy name," Cobb said. "Easy to remember. But I hate to disappoint you, Mr. Hock. Butch and me haul people, not goods."

Butch cleared his throat. "Don't be so hasty, Cobb. Let's hear the man out. Why don't you just pay a freight wagon to bring it to Laramie? There's bound to be plenty of reliable outfits here in Cheyenne who could do it for you. And cheaper than what Cobb and I would charge you to haul it."

Mr. Hock's face soured. "I tried that. One shipment failed to make it there. Three whole barrels just disappeared. I think the freighter must have sold it and left the territory with the money. I've never seen or heard of him again. A second freighter took too much time bringing my beer to Laramie. He allowed it to sit in the sun for days despite my strict orders to keep the beer covered. The batch was spoiled, and the bar owner refused to buy it. This is why I believe your coach is the best way to bring my creation to Laramie."

Mr. Hock's reasoning made sense to Cobb. "Now that we know they 'why' of it, there's the question of how much you're willing to pay."

"If you agree to bring my barrels to Laramie without passengers," Mr. Hock said, "I am prepared to compensate you the same you would make if you were carrying six passengers. It would be a round trip, too, because I need the barrels back. I've cured them myself."

Butch leaned forward, his eyes wide. "You mean you'll buy out our whole run just to bring your beer to town? Round trip?"

Mr. Hock closed his eyes and nodded once. "Yes. This is that important to me. And if you return with orders for my bock, I will be happy to pay you again under the same agreement. It will never be more than three barrels as the fermenting process takes time. I already have a saloon in Laramie that is willing to accept the barrels now."

Cobb closed his eyes and prayed it was not one of Lucien Clay's places. "Which one is that?"

"The Abbey Saloon."

Cobb opened his eyes and asked Butch, "I've never heard of it. You know that one?"

"It's just a small place opened around the corner from City Hall," Butch said. "No cards, no women. Just drinking and fraternizing. It appeals to a toney crowd."

Mr. Hock said, "That's because my beer is an experience, gentlemen. It's not to be swilled by miners and cowhands looking to slake their thirst. Though, if such places wish to carry my bock, I will consider it. That will mean less quality, of course, but my special brew won't suffer." He bowed at the waist as he began to step away. "I must check on my other customers. I'll give you gentlemen a few minutes to think over my proposal."

Butch waited until Mr. Hock had moved down the bar before telling Cobb, "He's got good manners, and this dark beer of his ain't half bad."

But Cobb was already thinking of something more. "You really think men will buy this stuff? Beer drinkers are a frugal bunch."

Butch thought about it. "Hock knows his customers. A cowboy won't pay extra for it, but I can see it selling in places like the Abbey Saloon and the Longacre House. What do you care? He's buying out our whole rig just to move three barrels. No cranky passengers griping about how hot or cramped or how bumpy it is. No feeding them or stopping for water breaks every hour or so. Could be a whole new way of making some money for ourselves. Makes me feel kinda foolish for spending all that money on having the inside of it outfitted with good cushions and such. But at least we won't have to wash it out after some old drunk—"

But Cobb did not care about that. "What if we stay in the coach business, but get ourselves a piece of Hock's beer business? Not his saloon, just a piece of every barrel sold. He brews it, we haul it. Even if King Hagen keeps putting out the word against us, Mr. Hock won't care, and we'll have a steady stream of money coming in whether we have passengers or not."

Butch did some math in his head. "One of those barrels is about a hundred pounds. Three of them will still be lighter than six passengers. If we took our time, we might even be able to make it to Laramie with one team of horses. That'd mean we wouldn't have to stop at Wingate Station or pay off that old horse thief Charlie Smith to let us stay there."

Cobb had another thought. "And if we don't have to stop at the station, we don't have to worry about anyone seeing what we're hauling. It'll just look like we're traveling back each way empty."

Butch said, "You've always handled the business end of things, so if you're for it, so am I." He caught Mr. Hock's eye and beckoned him to come back.

He listened politely to Cobb's proposition about receiving a percentage of the barrels sold. And when Cobb was done, the brewmaster said, "If you can guarantee delivery of my beer as I've asked, you gentlemen have yourselves an agreement."

After the three men shook hands, Cobb said, "We'll go hitch up our team and bring our coach around back of this place. We'll load up your barrels and be on our way as soon as we can." He looked through the thick glass of the saloon's front window. "The sun's about to go down, which'll make it cooler for the horses. We might be able to make it to Laramie without stopping. We'll be back with your money tomorrow afternoon."

Mr. Hock pledged to help them load the beer when they returned before Cobb and Butch left. They were leaving the saloon with brighter prospects than when they had entered the place.

Butch kept pace with his partner as he strode through

the pedestrians toward the place where they kept their coach and team. "That was real fancy talking you did back there, Cobb, but I think we're forgetting about Phil Bengston. He's still liable to be out there gunning for us whether we're carrying suds or southerners."

Cobb had nearly allowed himself to forget about their Bengston problem, but not quite. "Just once I'd like to have some good news that wasn't quickly spoiled by bad news."

"That's usually how it is out here in the territories."

Cobb knew that, but wished it was not so. "We'll be traveling mostly in the dark by moonlight. Even if Phil's as good a shot as they say, we won't give him an easy target. I still like our chances."

For once, he did not get an argument from Butch.

CHAPTER 23

Cobb and Butch got the last two horses hitched up to the coach and began to check the rigging of each horse.

And as was his custom, Butch finished first. "I've got to tell you, Cobb, the more I think about this beer business, the more I like it. Just might be the best idea you've come up with since I've known you."

Cobb was glad Butch was beginning to warm to the idea, but his happiness had not been his reason for coming up with it. He hoped that, by getting in early on a good thing, he might be able to have enough money to properly provide for Jane. They had not had the chance to talk about how she would make a living here in Cheyenne, and while he did not think she wanted to go back to her old life, he did not want her even considering it. A piece of Mr. Hock's business might just be a way to make her feel comfortable. That was his hope, anyway.

Butch cinched up the reins and brought them up to the wagon box with him. "You sure you don't want to stop by the jail and say goodbye to Jane? I'm sure she'd be happy to hear the good news."

"You should do that, Cobb," a man said from behind

him. "For all you know, it might be your last chance to see her alive."

Cobb whipped around as Butch drew his pistol from his hip.

Phil Bengston was leaning against the wall of the feed store behind which they had stowed their horse and team. He held up his hands to show they were empty. He was not wearing a coat, so it was evident he did not have a gun on him.

"Careful, Butch. You wouldn't want to wind up in jail for shooting an unarmed man." He smiled. "Though it'd give you more time with the lovely Jane Duprey."

Cobb had already stowed his coach gun in the bench of the wagon box, so he was also unarmed. "What are you doing here, Bengston?"

"Just checking to see how you boys are faring. I know seeing my mother go free must've ruined your day. I wanted to make sure it did."

"Haven't given it a moment's thought since Perry gave us the bad news," Butch said. "How's the old gal doing? That was a mighty big hole I put in her hip."

Cobb knew what Butch was doing. He was trying to bait Bengston into doing something stupid. But the railroad's hired gun did not bite. "She's doing just fine. Thanks for asking. Doc Fry patched her up. Gave her something to dull the pain. She's almost as good as new."

"We're sorry to hear it," Butch said. "I knew I should've aimed higher."

Bengston slowly shook his head. "Don't be ungrateful. You two never would've made it out of Wingate Station alive if you hadn't perched her right next to you. But don't worry. I'll have my chance again. And soon. Real soon."

"You forget who you're talking to." Cobb took a step

toward him. "We're not like those poor old Chinamen you shoot for the railroad. We shoot back."

Bengston's cold smile held. "That's when you have something to shoot at. I won't give you the chance." He inclined his head to the left. "There's a whole lot of open country between here and Laramie. Lots of other places along the road, too. You'll never happen upon a rocky outcropping or a stand of trees without worrying if I'm up there somewhere just waiting for my chance to pick you off. Most of the time, I won't be. But one day, I will. And I promise I won't miss. I rarely do."

Butch said, "You've been killing half-starved men for too long, Bengston. We've heard that kind of big talk from better men than you and, in case you haven't noticed, we're still here. Cobb and me ain't that easy to kill."

Bengston pushed himself off the wall and stood on his own two feet. Even Cobb had to admit the killer cut quite a figure. His flat-brimmed hat gave him a sinister look. "I guess we'll all be finding out if that's true soon enough. Just wanted to stop by and give you boys fair warning. I'm not going to kill you because Madam Peachtree or Lucien Clay want you killed. I'll be killing you for me."

Cobb took another step toward him. There were only a few feet between them now. "Why put it off? You're not toting a gun, and neither am I. I'm the one who decided to stick your old lady up in the wagon box at Wingate Station. Your fight is with me. Let's settle this the old-fashioned way. No iron. No knives." He put up his fists. "Right here. Right now."

But Bengston did not budge. "I would if my fight was just with you, but it's not. I intend on making both of you pay for what you did to my mother." He looked up at Butch. "Don't worry. I plan on shooting you first." His eyes moved back to Cobb. "I'm going to save you for last.

It'll be nice and quiet. No distractions from that crow up there while I take my time." He touched the brim of his hat with two fingers. "Now that I've given you boys plenty to think about, I'll be on my way. I might stop by the jail a little later tonight. Thank your woman for taking such good care of my mother."

Cobb lowered his fists as he watched Bengston walk back up the alley. He felt sweat burst upon his brow as the edges of his vision faded until all he could see was the back of the man who had just threatened Jane—*his Jane*—walking away.

He could not just let him go after that.

Cobb heard Butch call out his name as Cobb began to storm after Bengston. He felt Butch try to grab at him, but he shook his partner off. Bengston had just taken their feud a step too far, and he had to pay for it.

Bengston slowed as he reached the mouth of the alley, and Cobb began to speed up. He was standing there, back to him, practically daring him to strike. And that same cold, crooked smile was still etched on his face.

Cobb lurched forward to grab him when he was knocked flat on his stomach from behind. He struggled to get up, but Butch had a firm hold on him now as he yelled, "Don't do it, Cobb! He's not alone. He's got men with him. Look!"

Cobb strained his neck to see five men wearing tweed suits and bowler hats looking down at him as though he was a butterfly under glass. One of them was puffing away on a pipe while the other four held cigars.

Bengston stood in front of the men and joined them as they looked down at Cobb. "Sorry to have pulled you away from your desks for nothing, gentlemen. I thought I could goad that idiot into doing something stupid. In front of witnesses, no less." He shrugged. "I wasn't counting on the smaller one to be able to stop him."

"A shame," sighed the man with the pipe. "I had my heart set on witnessing a spectacle."

"Would've been nice to see Marshal Perry throw his miserable carcass in jail," said one of the men with a cigar. "Well, the show's over, gentlemen. I don't know about the rest of you, but I'm famished. I hear we brought in some fine steak and lobster on the wagon train today. Eat hearty and drink your fill because Phil is buying."

The men laughed as one as they turned and walked off together. Not even Bengston bothered to take a last look at the two men on the ground.

Butch got off Cobb and held a hand down to help him up. "I hated to knock you down like that, but you were too angry to see those fancy men with him. If you'd so much as touched Bengston, they would've locked you up for certain. I didn't want that. I didn't think you wanted it, either."

Cobb ignored Butch's hand and got to his feet on his own. His temper slowly began to subside as his vision returned. "I can't believe I was stupid enough to fall for that trick. You were baiting him, but I was the one he hooked."

"You'd have done the same for me," Butch said. "And have. More than once."

Cobb wiped the dirt of the alley floor off his shirt and cleaned his hands on the legs of his pants. "You think he meant what he said about threatening Jane? Maybe it's a bad idea to leave her here."

"You heard what Bengston's friend said. They'll be too drunk to harm anyone except themselves. His fight's with us, not her. I was listening to what he said better than you were. He won't harm her if only because we won't be around to see it."

Butch's words chilled him worse than Bengston's cold expression had. They chilled him because he knew his partner was right.

"Come on. Let's get moving. The sooner we get Hock's beer to Laramie, the sooner we can start making some money."

Jane was too tired to argue with Marshal Perry about walking her back to her rooms at the livery. "You really don't have to do this, Marshal. I'll be fine walking back alone."

"Cheyenne's become an unpredictable place to live," Perry said. "Besides, I promised Cobb I'd take care of you while you were in town, and that's what I aim to do. I wanted the chance to thank you for what you did at the jail today. I was never comfortable taking care of those women prisoners, even if I think we're one lighter than we should be. You've been a great help."

"I didn't really do much," Jane said. "All I did was organize some things and feed the ladies. Give them new clothes and send the others out to be laundered. They're not anything like Miss Hyde was. They're nice in their own, rough way."

"They're violent prisoners," Perry reminded her. "One killed her husband and the other beat her own sister half to death. You keep that in mind when you're dealing with them. The threat of violence is always there."

She did not bother to remind the marshal that she had seen the uglier side of human nature her entire life. The greed and lust of her male customers. The calculating cunning of a whore who would cut a girl's throat for a better room. Other things that she did not like to think about, not even if it might take her mind off Tucker leaving her behind.

"Everything happened so fast today," she said, "that I never got the chance to ask you or Tucker about how long you've known each other. Has it been long?"

"A couple of years or so," Perry said, as they rounded the corner toward the Cheyenne Grand. "And to prove it to you, I'll admit I didn't know his first name was Tucker until you said it just now."

"Oh." She did not take that as a sign of encouragement. "I thought you were old friends."

"We might not have been acquainted long," the marshal said, "but we know each other. He and Butch aren't altogether different than me. You could say we understand each other. We know where the lines are or at least where they should be. I guess that might sound like a bunch of foolishness to you, but it makes sense to me."

"I understand it. In a way."

They passed a dining hall where the raucous laughter from a group of men having dinner carried out into the street. All of them were wearing suits that did little to hide their growing bellies. A shudder went through her as she recognized one of them as Phil Bengston. His friend Panfil was nowhere in sight. And neither was his mother, Miss Hyde.

Perry pointed back at them as they walked by. "Take their kind, for instance. They're city men and they're accustomed to city ways. They're railroad men who aren't used to being refused by fellas like me. They work for an important concern and think that makes them important because of it. They won't realize until they're too old that the only one who has any true power is the man who signs the checks that pay their wages. But men like me and Cobb and Butch? We know life is fickle and can change forever in the blink of an eye. That's what I meant when I said we understood each other. There's more men like us than like those city boys back there for now, but that'll change some day. Pretty soon, everyone'll dress like them, sound like them, and think like them. I'm sure glad I'll long gone before that happens."

Jane did not want to think about such things. Not with Tucker being away from her in Laramie. "That's just crazy talk, Marshal. You're still in your prime and have a good long life left ahead of you."

Marshal Perry laughed as he rubbed his left shoulder. "These old joints of mind don't seem to agree with you."

They had finally reached the ramshackle edifice of the Cheyenne Grand. "Thank you for walking me this far, Marshal. What time do you want me back at the jail in the morning?"

Perry's face dropped as he looked the place over. "You mean this is where Cobb has you staying? In this garbage dump? I knew King Hagen wouldn't let them get rooms in a decent place, but you can do better than this."

Jane did not care about how it looked. It had a clean bed, which was all she wanted now. "It's not quite as bad as it looks. Most of it is rundown, sure, but my rooms are in the back where the manager's office used to be. It's got good walls and a solid door. Tucker and Butch showed it to me right before they left for Laramie. I'll be just fine."

But Hugh Perry would not hear of it. "It's a flophouse for drunks and reprobates. Why don't you come back to my house? Mary and I have plenty of room. And I'd rest much easier knowing you were safe. I made a promise to Cobb, remember?"

But there were other reasons besides her weariness why she did not want to accept the marshal's generous offer.

"I'm sure you know how I made my living, Marshal. I wouldn't want you or your wife being embarrassed by me."

"I didn't exactly find Mary in a convent when I met her," Perry said, "and we'd be happy to have you. It would be nice to have someone else around instead of just hearing our old bones creak all the time."

Jane might have taken him up on it if she had not been so tired. "Since Tucker's already paid up for a couple of weeks, let me at least try it for tonight. If it's too loud or too noisy or too dangerous, I'll accept your invitation. I promise."

Perry clearly did not like her rejection of his offer but did not force the issue. "At least let me walk you back to your room. This place caters to a rough crowd."

But Jane would not hear of it. "You've gone out of your way enough on my account already. Now, when would you like me back at the jail in the morning?"

Perry shrugged. "The place is always open and there's no fixed schedule on things. Get a good night's sleep and come around whenever you like. We'll be there and so will those lady prisoners. Let's just hope they don't get any more company. Are you sure you won't let me walk you back to your room?"

She rested a hand on his arm and smiled up at him. "I'll be fine. You go on home, and I'll see you bright and early tomorrow. Thank you, Marshal. Thank you for taking me in and keeping me safe. It's quite a comfort. People haven't always been so nice to me."

Perry tipped the brim of his hat to her and remained in the street as he watched her enter the dilapidated entrance of the Cheyenne Grand.

Jane thought the marshal was a sweet old bird but was glad to finally be alone. Much of what she had done that day had been busy work, but it was more than she was accustomed to doing.

She found the cool darkness of the entrance comforting as she began to walk back to her room. Mr. Clark was asleep, face down on his desk. She obviously was not the only tired person on the premises.

She was careful not to disturb him as she stepped past him and through the heavy curtains that led back to the rooms.

She had just entered the alley when someone grabbed her left arm and wrenched her around. Cassie Hyde's face was twisted in anger as she brought a knife back, ready to stab at her.

Jane brought up her free arm to block her thrust and pushed the hobbled woman back against the wall.

Now free from her grip, Jane tried to escape through the curtain, but a wicked slash of Hyde's blade forced her to jump backward.

As her attacker limped over to block her path, Jane saw the blade she was holding was silver and already stained with blood.

"Don't look for that fat fool at the front desk to come help you." Hyde seethed as she held the knife edge toward her. "I took care of him a while ago. It's just you and me and my sharp friend here."

Jane wished she had a shawl or a bag with her, anything that she might be able to use as a weapon against this mad woman. "You don't have to do this, Cassie. You already got what you wanted. You're free!"

"With a hole in my hip and a judge's gavel hanging over my head?" She slashed again and, once more, Jane narrowly avoided it by jumping backward. "Just because I'm out of jail doesn't mean I'm free. I'll never be free of you or those two mule skinners."

She thrust the knife at Jane's middle as she backed away, cutting her dress at the stomach.

Hyde recovered quickly and prepared for another strike. "The doctor said I'll have a limp for the rest of my life. I'll never know a day without pain unless I take laudanum. Laudanum!"

She slashed at Jane twice more. Her second attempt caught the flesh of her arm.

"You've seen what happens to girls on that stuff," Hyde growled. "Dead, pitiful things trapped inside their own minds." Her knuckles whitened as she gripped the handle tighter. "I can stand the pain from my leg, but not the pain of knowing you and Cobb and that other one got away unharmed. You'll still be young and pretty while I toddle around like a cripple."

Jane saw her eyes narrow and knew she was preparing herself for another strike.

"I'll kill two birds with one stone when I kill you." The madwoman winced as she shifted her weight from her bad leg. "When you're dead, a piece of Cobb will die, too. He'll live just long enough to rue what he did to me before my boy cuts him down for good, you miserable—"

Hyde lunged forward, swiping the blade from left to right. Her next sweep was leveled at Jane's neck, but the younger woman ducked it and threw herself against Hyde's middle. She easily knocked the hobbled woman onto her back as Jane fell with her.

She landed on top of her attacker and slid to the side off onto Hyde's right arm. The woman screamed in frustration and pain as she tried in vain to pull her knife out from under Jane's weight. She used her free hand to grab a thick handful of Jane's hair at the root and wrench her head back with all the strength she could muster.

Jane flailed with her arms and legs to keep herself from

being pulled onto her back, knowing the woman would be able to finish her then.

She managed to grab hold of Hyde's wrist and tried to slam it down on the cobblestones of the alley floor, hoping it would break her grip on the knife. But Hyde's hold on her hair was too strong, and she felt herself being pulled backward.

She kept her left hand on Hyde's right as she brought her right elbow across the attacker's jaw. The first blow rocked her head to the side but did not weaken her. A second elbow barely grazed her cheek and made Hyde pull back on her hair even more. She felt herself losing, her strength weakening as she kicked her legs to maintain some kind of leverage.

Amid her struggles, her elbow found Hyde's throat. Instinct caused her to bring her elbow down hard on it. The impact weakened her grip on Jane's hair just enough for Jane to get more leverage for a second blow that freed her entirely.

She rolled to her side, pried the knife from the woman's fingers, and plunged the blade down into her chest.

She rolled off the woman and found herself between the wall and Hyde, panting and exhausted from the struggle. The dying woman looked down at the handle of the blade now protruding from her chest but made no attempt to remove it.

Instead, the fingers of her left hand reached out for Jane's face. She pulled away but Hyde's bony fingers found Jane's throat and she began to press them against it. Jane tried to pull them away, but her death grip was too strong.

Jane tried to get her arm beneath her as she felt her windpipe begin to close.

But the madwoman's grip weakened as a great rattle went through her body, allowing Jane to finally get free of her. She bolted through the curtains and into the street, screaming for someone to help her as if anyone on the street could.

CHAPTER 24

Cobb's good mood quickly disappeared as they stood in front of the Mulholland Hotel. He threw down his bag on the boardwalk in disgust. The hotel was the last place in Laramie where they had hoped to get a decent room for the night. Every other hotel in town had turned them away. No vacancies, they had said. What they did not say was that it was courtesy of King Charles Hagen.

Butch set his bag on the boardwalk and removed a wad of tobacco from his pouch. "Don't let it spoil your evening, Cobb." He placed it between his cheek and jaw. "We knew this was bound to happen. We're just lucky the livery agreed to take our rig."

Cobb did not see that as much of a victory. "That's only because Hagen's men tried to burn him out a while back. We got lucky."

"Nothing wrong with relying on a little luck every once in a while," Butch said. "You're not used to it is all. Give it time." He nudged his partner's shoulder. "Look on the bright side of it. You got that fella in the Abbey to buy that beer above what he was asking for it, which will please Hock to no end. We'll pick up the barrels in the morning and drive back to Cheyenne with a fair amount of money in our pocket. Some might call that a good day, even if we might need to spend it in the livery."

But Cobb was not willing to look at it that way. "Good enough is never good enough for us, is it? We always take one step ahead only to get pushed back another. How long is that lunatic Hagen going to keep giving us the boot? We didn't do anything to him except refuse to sell out to him."

"Sometimes that's enough to set a man like that against a man," Butch said. "I give it about a year or so before he loses interest or people forget. Don't let it get you riled. He wins if you do."

"Just once I'd like to sleep in a nice bed after having a good day."

"Colonel McBride's place is just down the street here." Butch looked in that direction. "I can see a light in the window, so someone's bound to be up. He's always telling us he's willing to help us if we need it. What do you say about us going over there and knocking on the door? Ask him to put us up for the night. We know he's got room."

But Cobb knew what his partner was really driving at. "He's got that pretty niece of his you're sweet on, too. Miss Carlyle."

"There's nothing wrong with the sight of a pretty woman before turning in for the night," Butch observed. "In fact, the only thing better is if she's still there in the morning."

"As if you'd know how that feels. Your kind of women always pay attention to the clock."

"True." Butch spat some tobacco juice into the street. "But maybe she can reform me. Anyway, it's either the McBride place or the coach. Just make up your mind, so I know where I'll be bedding down for the night."

Cobb picked up his bag and started walking toward the McBride place. "Everyone else in town has slammed a door in our face. It's only fair that we give the colonel a chance to do the same."

Butch picked up his bag and followed him. "He's probably inclined to help us, seeing as how we did him a good turn at the fort and all."

Cobb knew that should be the case, but it was no guarantee. "I never put much faith in the goodwill of folks. Like my mother used to say, 'Eaten bread is soon forgotten.'"

Butch laughed. "I like that one. Think I might adopt it as my own. Say, in the two years I've known you, this is the first time I've ever heard you mention your mother. I was beginning to think you didn't have one."

Cobb stopped at the McBride's door and began to knock. "I'm full of surprises. In another couple of years, I might mention my pappy."

Cobb took a step back and waited. He heard the floorboards inside creak as the lock was turned before Colonel McBride opened the door. His spectacles were perched atop his head and a book was in his hand.

"Hello, boys," the colonel said, as he stepped aside and beckoned them in. "This is a pleasant surprise. I didn't think you'd be back in town so soon."

"Neither did we," Cobb said, as Butch followed him into the house. "We hate to bother you like this, but we find ourselves in a bad way."

The colonel closed the door and already seemed to know why they were there. "No hotel in town will give you a room, eh? King Hagen's orders?"

Cobb hated referring to the man like that, but it happened to be the truth. "I guess you could say something like that. I know it's an imposition, but we were kind of hoping we might be able to sleep here for the night. We'll be back on the road early in the morning well before breakfast, so we won't be a bother to you or Mrs. McBride."

"It'd be no bother at all if you stay on through dinner," the colonel said. "We're glad to have you. There's a room off behind the kitchen you can use. Mrs. McBride hasn't gotten around to hiring a maid yet, so you're welcome to it. There's only one bed, though, so one of you will draw the short straw and sleep on the floor. You're welcome to the sofa in the parlor if you wish, but I wouldn't recommend it. I've had to spend a few nights on it over the years, and my back has always made me pay for it in the morning."

They stepped lightly, careful not to creak any of the floorboards as they followed the colonel to the back room. "I can dig around for some blankets if you wish, though you probably won't need them on a warm night such as this. Where's your lady friend? Miss Jane. You all raised quite a stir when you left town like you did."

"She's back in Cheyenne with—"

The three men stopped when they heard a loud series of knocks at the front door.

Cobb and Butch traded looks as the colonel limped his way back up the hall. "This place is turning into a regular train depot. I wonder who it could be at this hour."

Butch placed his hand on the butt of his pistol as he moved in front of Cobb and headed for the door. It was a bit too late for the visitor to be a coincidence. Cobb only hoped they had not succeeded in bringing trouble to the colonel's door.

McBride opened the door to reveal Sheriff Rob Moran standing outside. Cobb could tell by the concerned look on the lawman's face that it was serious.

"Sorry about the hour," Moran said, "but I've got something important to tell Cobb and Butch. Mind if I come in?"

"Certainly," McBride said, as he allowed the sheriff into his home. "Just try to keep your voice down. The women of the house are asleep upstairs."

Cobb and Butch met him in the parlor and saw he was holding a telegram envelope.

Butch asked, "How'd you know we'd be here, Rob?"

"I checked all the hotels first," Moran said, "and when I didn't find you there, figured you'd probably come here. I just wish I had better news for you boys."

Cobb knew Rob Moran did not rattle easily and he was rattled now. "What is it? That envelope have something to do with it?"

"It's from Hugh Perry in Cheyenne," the sheriff said, as he handed the envelope to him. "Jane's killed a woman named Cassie Hyde."

"What?" Butch exclaimed, as Cobb opened the envelope. "That just can't be, Sheriff. That old witch was lame when we left Cheyenne earlier this afternoon. Her hip was all shot to pieces. I ought to know because I'm the one who shot her."

Moran waved down the useless information. "The telegram doesn't explain how it happened or why, just that Jane killed her. And if it's the Cassie Hyde I've heard about, I'm sure it was in self-defense."

Cobb read and re-read the telegram, hoping he might find something in the terse message that Moran had missed. "It doesn't say if Jane's hurt or not."

"Hugh would've mentioned it if she was," Moran said. "He's bound to have a lot to do right now, so just be glad he got any word to you at all."

Cobb almost allowed the telegram to slip from his fingers when Butch took it from him and handed it back to the sheriff.

Cobb ran his hands over his face. "Poor Jane must be scared out of her mind right now. I knew I shouldn't have left her like that. Left her alone."

"Don't do that to yourself." Butch pulled his partner's hands away from his face. "Perry so much as ordered us to leave, and we didn't have any choice. I didn't think that old bird would've been in any shape to cause Jane trouble. If anything, I'd have expected it from Bengston."

"Phil Bengston?" Moran asked. "The shootist for the railroad? What's he got to do with all this?"

But Cobb was too worried about Jane to answer his question. "Bengston will be looking to lynch her for this. The moon's still up and we can ride back there tonight. Perry's men aren't enough to stop Bengston."

"We can't do that, Cobb," Butch said. "The team's all played out from the trip here and so are we. We won't do her any good if we drop out of the saddles on the way there."

"I know you care for her, Cobb," Moran said, "but don't let your emotions get the better of you. Things aren't as bleak as they seem. I'm the sheriff of Laramie County which includes Cheyenne. This happened in my jurisdiction so, technically, Jane is my prisoner."

Cobb was growing frustrated with all this talk while there was work to be done. "I don't care about jurisdictions, Rob, and neither will Bengston. You're here in Laramie, and she's there in Cheyenne with only a scared old man and a couple of dimwitted deputies to protect her."

"Fisk is there," Butch reminded him. "He's capable. You've said as much yourself."

"What good will one man do against the numbers Bengston is likely to bring with him to get her? Jane's just killed his mother for God's sake. Do you expect me to stay here and sleep while she's in danger?"

He took a step toward the door, but Moran was in his way and did not move. "Listen to reason, Cobb."

"I'm reasonable, but Bengston isn't. He's promised to kill us for his mother getting shot. What do you think he'll do to the woman who killed his mother?"

Colonel McBride slowly lowered himself into a chair. "Dead mothers. Vengeful sons. What's going on up in Cheyenne these days?"

Moran let out a long breath as he hung his head and thought it over. He looked at Butch. "You think it's really that serious?"

"Cobb ain't exactly impartial where Jane's involved," Butch said, "but he ain't wrong, either. I reckon Phil Bengston's capable of just about anything, and I don't know that Hugh Perry and his boys are enough to stop them."

Moran rubbed the back of his own neck. "You boys are bound and determined to ride back there tonight, aren't you?"

Cobb felt his vision begin to close in again, just as it had in the alley when Bengston had threatened Jane. "The only way you can stop me is to arrest me, Rob. And given my mood, I wouldn't recommend you try."

Moran stood upright. His mind was made up. "Fine. We'll do it your way, but we'll do it together." He turned to leave the house with Cobb and Butch right behind him. "You two head over to the livery and see if they'll let you use two horses. Make sure they're fast. I'll saddle one of mine and we'll ride out at the same time. We ought to get there before dawn if we push hard. I just hope you two are fresher than you look because I don't aim to prop you up the whole ride back."

Cobb's vision began to clear. "Make sure you pick out

a fast one for yourself, Rob. I'd hate to have to leave you behind because you couldn't keep up."

They were halfway to the livery before he realized he had not thought to apologize to Colonel McBride for the intrusion. But he imagined the old soldier knew something about protecting the people he loved.

The sky had begun to brighten when the three travelers from Laramie arrived in Cheyenne. They had only been forced to stop and rest their horses twice on the journey, but even those brief, necessary pauses were almost too much for Cobb to bear.

Cobb ignored Moran's order to wait as he dug his heels into his mount and sped toward the old barn that now served as the jail. Butch and Moran were forced to do the same. Cobb was not thinking rationally. He never had when Jane was involved.

Cobb brought his horse to a skidding halt as he dropped from the saddle and ran inside. Moran followed while Butch grabbed the reins and secured the animals to the hitching rail.

"Where is she?" Cobb asked the deputy manning the desk. "Where's Jane?"

Butch watched the young man rise with his hand on his pistol. "And just who might you be, mister?"

"I'm Tucker Cobb. Where's Jane Duprey?"

Moran moved in front of Cobb and spoke to the concerned young deputy. "Don't worry about him, Putnam. He's with me. Where's Prisoner Duprey?"

Putnam looked less concerned when he saw Sheriff Moran. "The marshal told me you might be coming by, though he wasn't expecting you so soon."

Butch saw Cobb's hands ball into fists at his sides. "Why isn't she here?"

"The marshal didn't think it was safe enough," Putnam told them. "We had a whole slew of railroad men gathering in front calling for her head since it happened. We think Phil Bengston got them stirred up. His man, Panfil, was right in the middle of them."

Cobb brought his fist down on the desk. "I don't care about that. Where is she?"

Putnam looked at Moran, who encouraged him to answer the question. "The marshal brought her over to his place right after it happened. Said it would be safer to have her there where folks might not go looking for her. Toneff and that new guy, Fisk, are there with him, guarding her now."

Cobb began to leave when Moran gripped his arm. "Hold on for a minute." He asked Putnam, "They posted out front or inside."

"Inside," Putnam said. "The marshal figured it would draw less attention. I wouldn't go barging in there if I were you. It might make people think she's in there."

"He's right," Moran told Cobb. "I know where his house is. It's not far from here. We should leave the horses here and walk over there nice and quiet. Follow me and we'll use the back door. He's got lots of neighbors close by who are bound to be looking out their windows. I'll go in first, then you and Butch can follow a little while later. We'll draw less attention that way."

Butch asked Putnam, "You sure there's only two in the house with Perry. Just Fisk and Toneff. No one on the street?"

Putnam shrugged. "I know they've been over there since it happened. The marshal said he'd keep them inside and off the street, but I don't know if that's still the case. All the other deputies we've got are in some cells over there sleeping. Like I told you, it's been a busy night. The workers had torches outside, calling Miss Duprey by name and demanding we hand her over to them. We thought they might've stormed the place, and we're lucky they didn't try. The last of them just left about an hour ago."

Moran let go of Cobb's arm but held up a finger in front of his face. "You'd better calm yourself down. Running over there will only put her in more danger. Tell me you understand."

Butch saw Cobb tremble a bit as he struggled to keep hold of his emotions. "I understand."

Moran looked at Butch. "See to it that he does. Now, follow me."

Moran left the jail at his usual brisk pace while Butch and Cobb hung back. Butch tilted his hat lower to hide his face and did the same for Cobb.

"Moran's right about this," Butch said to his partner. "You remember the trouble you almost had by letting Bengston get to you. Same rules apply now."

Cobb said nothing but walked along quietly.

The streets of Cheyenne were deserted and quiet despite the close approach of day. Butch spotted a man lingering at the corner on the opposite side of the street and thought he saw one at the corner beyond. They had an expectant look, reminding him of coyotes lingering around a dead steer, waiting to see if the humans would shoot them before they fed.

He kept his voice low as he told Cobb, "You see that fella over there? I think he might be keeping watch for Bengston."

Cobb kept his head down as they continued to move.

"There's no sense in telling me something if you won't let me do anything about it."

Butch decided to keep any further observations to himself. They rounded the corner in time to see Moran cross the thoroughfare, but they did not do the same. Following the sheriff so close would only tip their hand.

Butch saw a man standing in a doorway on their side of the street step back and out of view. He clearly did not want to be seen.

"Just keep walking, Cobb. Pass by him without any notice."

But when they reached the doorway, Cobb stopped and fired a straight left hand into the shadows, followed by a right hook to the gut.

Butch tried to grab Cobb, but he already had the man by the throat and pinned against the door. His partner could be faster than he looked when he wanted to be.

"Who sent you here?" Cobb pushed him harder against the door. "Tell me."

The man gagged. "The railroad told me to do it, I swear."

Cobb pulled the man away from the door. "Well, you can tell them this from me." Cobb leveled him with a hard shot to the jaw, knocking him cold.

Cobb left the man slumped in the doorway as Butch looked around to see where Moran had gone. The sheriff paused at the far corner, looked around, then proceeded to walk in that direction. Butch led Cobb to the corner before crossing the thoroughfare and doing the same.

Butch could tell this was not a well-traveled road. The backyards of houses met there, and there were few places where a man could hide without being spotted.

Moran was halfway down the street when he stopped at

a gate in a low wooden fence. He opened it and stepped into the backyard.

Butch could not contain Cobb any further and watched his partner run to follow the sheriff. Butch had no choice but to follow, peering into the shadows to see if they were still being watched. If the railroad had thought to put any men back there, they were well hidden.

There were no lights visible inside the house as Moran lightly rapped at the door. He kept his voice low as he said, "It's Sheriff Moran. I've got Cobb and Butch with me. Open up."

The lace curtain on the window parted, revealing the dark interior. Butch heard something heavy being pulled away from the door just before it opened, and Deputy Toneff let them in.

"Keep quiet," the deputy whispered to them, as they filed into the house. "Nothing above a whisper. The marshal doesn't want to draw attention."

Butch followed them into the house and helped Toneff move a heavy kitchen table back against the door.

"How'd you boys know to come here?" Toneff asked him in a whisper.

Butch responded in kind. "We stopped off at the jail and Putnam told us you were here. I heard you had quite a night."

"Not so much here as back at the jail." Toneff turned up the light of an oil lamp and led him through the small kitchen. "Hugh was right to bring her here. No one's bothered us all night. I'm sure glad you're here. We're gonna have quite a time bringing her before the judge in the morning. We sure could use your help."

"It's already morning," Butch said. "And I don't think you could refuse Cobb's help if you tried."

Toneff placed the lamp on the mantel above a fireplace

to reveal Cobb and Jane in a warm embrace. Butch could see her forearm was bandaged as she held Cobb around the middle and quietly wept into his chest.

"Everything's going to be just fine," he soothed her. "I'm here now."

Moran motioned for Butch to follow him and Marshal Perry out of the room and into the hallway that led to the stairs. The sheriff closed the door to the parlor, so they could not be heard inside. Fisk was standing by the front window. He held a Winchester repeater at his side.

"I'm sure glad to see you here," Perry said. "We've got quite a mess on our hands."

"Best way to clean up a mess is to know what's spilled," Moran answered. "Tell me what happened. Start at the beginning."

"Not much to tell," Perry began. "I walked Jane to the Cheyenne Grand where she was staying."

Moran glared at Butch. "You mean you and Cobb let her stay in that pit?"

"It was the only place in town that would give us a room," Butch said. "We weren't planning on letting Jane stay there when we picked it. Things just kind of happened that way."

Moran told Perry to continue with his tale, which he did. "I was almost home when I heard a great commotion back on the street. I rushed back and saw Jane in the middle of the thoroughfare. Her dress was covered in blood, and she had a nasty cut on her arm. I grabbed hold of her and brought her straight back here where she's been ever since. When I got her to calm down, she told me Cassie Hyde stabbed the hotel clerk to death and tried to do the same to her, too. They struggled for the knife, and it wound up in Cassie's chest. By the time I got back to the

Grand, a crowd had already started to gather there, but Fisk and Toneff helped me clear them out. From what I saw, everything happened exactly as how Jane said it did."

Perry sat on one of the stairs and rubbed the heels of his hands into his tired eyes. "Cassie Hyde killed the clerk and tried to kill Jane. Came close to doing it, too. My poor Mary had quite a time stitching up that cut on her arm."

"Mary?" Moran said. "Why didn't a doctor do it?"

"I couldn't risk bringing any of them here," Perry said. "And they wouldn't even come to the jail. They knew who Cassie was. They were all too afraid of crossing Bengston and the railroad."

"Where's Bengston now?" Butch asked.

"I saw him having dinner with some of his friends up the street from where the killing happened, but I haven't seen him since. He's got the workers riled up, though. Panfil's been stoking the fires while he stays out of sight."

Moran thought that over. "He probably doesn't want to be blamed if something happens. And this Cassie Hyde was his mother?"

"That's what she told us," Butch confirmed. "And he tried to claim her when Perry was bringing her over to see Judge Waller. He managed to talk the judge into letting her go, even though she was facing an attempted murder charge. She'd tried to kill me and Cobb at Wingate Station. I winged her for her trouble. She and Bengston had been hired by Clay and Madam Peachtree to kill me and Cobb on account of us spiriting Jane away from them."

Moran crossed his arms in front of his chest. "Sounds like a real mess. How could Hyde have been up and about with that hole in her hip?"

Perry sighed. "I asked Doc Fry that very question. He gave her an injection for the pain after he bandaged her up. Since he's the railroad's doctor, he's got medicines other doctors just don't have. Guess it dulled her pain a bit too much. Said the stuff is called 'morphine.' Bengston brought her to him as soon as the judge let her go. Fry said he treated her wound and left her to rest while he tended to a worker who fell from a building site. When he came back later to check on her, she was gone. Guess the medicine worked too well for her own good. She was likely out of her mind on the stuff when it happened. That would answer a lot of questions."

Butch watched Moran as he took in everything Perry had said. "Are you going to be charging Jane with murder?"

Perry shook his head. "It's just about as clear a case of self-defense as I've ever seen. The town solicitor sees it the same way. I still have to bring her before Judge Waller this morning, though. There'll have to be a hearing, seeing as how there was a death involved. I don't think Jane's got anything to worry about on that score. It's what happens to her afterward that troubles me. She can't stay cooped up in here forever, and Bengston's not going to allow a judge's ruling to stop him from making her pay for killing his ma."

Butch knew they could worry about Bengston later. "I know I speak for Cobb when I tell you we'll do everything we can to help."

"I figured you'd say something like that." Perry dug two deputy stars from his shirt pocket and handed them to Butch. "You and Cobb can help by putting these back on. Your oath is still binding, which makes anything you do from here on in legal."

Moran watched as Butch pinned the star on his shirt. "You mean you deputized these two?"

"I needed the help to keep Bengston at bay," Perry explained. "I still need them for that."

Moran slowly shook his head. "You two as lawmen. I never thought I'd see the day. Just make sure you don't stray too far from what we tell you. That star comes with authority and a fair amount of responsibility, too."

Butch palmed Cobb's star. "No need to tell me twice. Cobb, on the other hand, could stand to use some re-minding."

CHAPTER 25

Phil Bengston sat beside the bed where his mother's body lay. He had lost track of how long he had been sitting there. It had been dark outside when Doc Fry allowed him to see her. It was growing light outside now. A whole night passed in the blink of an eye.

He vaguely remembered someone talking to him. Panfil, maybe, and him yelling something back. Or perhaps he had dreamed it? It was tough to know what was real and what he had imagined. It was not worth the effort anyway, not with his mother's body in a bed only a few feet away from him.

He heard a knock at the door but did not have the strength to respond. Panfil entered and tried to catch his attention.

"Sorry to bother you like this, Phil, but the men from the mortician are here. They say it's time to get your ma ready."

"Time," Bengston heard himself say. "It's such a foolish idea, isn't it? We think we have enough of it until it's too late." He could not bring himself to look upon her this way, even though Doc Fry had been kind enough to cover her with a clean sheet. "She thought she had all the time in the world. She'd thought that when she sent me away all those years ago. 'It's only for a few weeks' she'd told me then. It was more than ten years before I'd see her again."

"Phil," Panfil tried again. "They want to—"

"Want." He was not angered by the interruption. Panfil was a simpleton and did not know any better. He did not know anything, really, except for what Bengston told him to do. If he had to live by his wits, he would probably starve to death.

A distant memory came back to him now. Or maybe it was not so distant. He remembered telling Panfil what to do in this very room when it was still dark outside. "What about what I wanted you to do? Did you do it?"

"I rounded up some boys and had them march over to the jail just like you said," Panfil told him. "We stayed out there all night and most of the morning, but I don't think she's in there. I managed to get close enough to take a good look inside, and I didn't see her."

Bengston felt something stir deep within him. It was not sadness, though he was sure that would come in time. It was something else. An emotion that had a much sharper edge to it.

"That whore killed my mother. I want her dead, Panfil. Every breath she's taken since my mother died has been an insult to her very memory."

"I know that, Phil," Panfil stammered. "But we don't know where the marshal's hiding her. I had men posted all over town. One of them got beaten pretty bad just before sunup. From the fella he described, it sounds a lot like Cobb."

Bengston closed his eyes. *Yes, Tucker Cobb. And his friend, Butch Keeling.* He remembered them now. How Clay and Madam Pinochet had wanted them dead and how he had failed to make them so. How that failure had cost him his mother. This began and ended with the two of them. The whore had only played a small part in it all, though a deadly one.

"Where was our man attacked?"

"In a doorway just off Main Street. Right by Stanton Way."

Keeping his eyes closed, Bengston brought the image of that part of town to mind. Stanton Way was a quiet back street with nothing on it except for fences that led to the backyards of the houses on Elston Street.

Of course. Elston Street. That made sense. It fit.

"Marshal Perry lives on Elston Street. Send the men there. Pull them off the work gangs if you have to. Give them rifles from our office. I don't care what it takes. Write down the name of any man who refuses to go. I'll deal with them later. And if a foreman gives you any trouble, write his name down, too. Tell any man who kills her that I'll give them five hundred dollars."

"Phil," Panfil tried. "We can't do that. Sheriff Moran's in town. He's going to bring Jane Duprey to his courtroom personally."

"Then make it a thousand dollars!" Bengston roared, as he stood. "Tell them whoever kills her will have the best lawyer in the territory if they do. They won't spend a day in prison. Tell them, Panfil. Tell them because I can't tell them myself, though, by God, I wish I could. I wish I could be there to see the life slip away from her, just as she watched the life slip from my mother when she plunged that knife into her."

"Didn't you hear what I said? It's not just Hugh Perry they'd be going against. It's Rob Moran out of Laramie. He's here. I saw him going in to see Judge Waller a little while ago. You can't expect any of our boys to go up against the likes of him."

Bengston had not expected anything. He had ordered it to be done, which should be enough. "One man, even Moran, isn't enough to stop twenty men armed with rifles."

"But these boys ain't the kind who—"

Bengston was on him in two steps. Panfil backed up against the wall without being touched. "What time is the hearing?"

"Nine o'clock unless there's been a change. I wouldn't know because I've been here with you."

Panfil was even more of a fool when frightened. "What time is it now?"

"Just after eight."

Panfil flinched when Bengston stuck a finger in his face. "I'm going outside to stand in front of that courthouse. If I see Jane Duprey is still alive when she gets there, you'd better climb on the fastest horse you can find and get as far away from here as you can manage."

Bengston pulled open the door and pushed his way through the morticians waiting in Doc Fry's office. He had his own appointment with death. Either Jane Duprey's or his own.

Rob Moran was not accustomed to failing, but he had failed in making Judge Waller listen to reason.

"Justice delayed is justice denied," Moran could still hear him say as he walked out of the old bank building that now served as the temporary courthouse for the town. "If the Duprey woman's life is in jeopardy, I expect you to deputize as many men as you require to assure she arrives here safely. I was foolish enough to allow Perry to give her special treatment by keeping her in his home. I'll not bend the rules for her even further. 'Let justice be done, though the heavens fall,'" the fat old bulldog had barked at him in his chambers. "If she dies, it will be on your head, not mine."

Judge Waller had always been full of himself, but he could usually be counted on to be reasonable. But this time was different.

"I hope the deceased's relations with the railroad don't have something to do with your decision, Your Honor." Moran had been careful to add the "Your Honor" part in the hope it might water down his inference.

Waller had threatened to throw a law book at him before he ordered him to leave his chambers immediately. Moran normally did not try the patience of judges, but there was nothing normal about this.

If they were in Laramie, Moran would be confident he could keep Jane Duprey alive. The jail and the court were in the same building. But here in Cheyenne, he was alone except for a lovestruck coachman, his friend, and a couple of green deputies. Hugh Perry could be counted to stick, but not for much else. He had trouble standing up, much less quelling an angry mob of railroad workers. Panfil had whipped them up into a frenzy outside the jail the previous night. There was no reason to expect he would not do the same today.

Moran paused at the entrance to the bank building to look over the street with a more critical eye. He still did not like what he saw. The thoroughfares were still being constructed and were impossibly wide. The harsh summer sun had baked the dirt hard, which would only encourage spectators and those with more devious plans in mind to gather in front of the building to watch the excitement.

He could not bring Jane here on foot. They would have to ride if they had any chance of making it. She could double up with Cobb. The rest of them could form a square around her with Cobb's horse in the middle. She would be an easy target, of course, with speed her only hope of survival.

He wished he could do more for her. The poor girl was not a saint, but she did not deserve to die for defending her own life.

Moran opened the door and walked down the stone steps to the street. He saw a lone figure standing in front of a half-built building across the way. The site was still, which Moran thought was odd, given that it was past eight o'clock. But when he recognized the man, he knew no work would be done that way.

Moran slowly walked over to Phil Bengston, careful to not get too close. "Morning, Phil. Sorry about your mother."

"Nothing for you to be sorry for, Sheriff. You didn't help her kill my ma. You weren't even in town when it happened."

"That's right, but I'm here now. I'm here to make sure justice is done."

"Fancy that," Bengston said. "So am I."

"That isn't the way, Bengston. That's revenge and I won't allow it. Your mother was half out of her mind on morphine when she attacked that girl. All Jane did was defend herself. I know you're grieving, but even you must be able to see that."

"All I see is my mother under a sheet in Doc Fry's office. I see it every time I close my eyes. Even when I just blink. You can't expect me to let the woman who put her there just go."

"You're not letting her go, son. You're letting justice work."

"Some laws ain't written down in books, Sheriff. I had you figured for the kind of man who knows that."

Moran could see there was no point in reasoning with him, so perhaps another tactic might work. "I know I'm responsible for keeping the peace. I know that I'll be bringing Jane Duprey to stand before Judge Waller in a little while. And I know any man who gets in my way is going to find himself in a world of trouble."

"You've got nothing to worry about from me, Sheriff," Bengston said. "I'm content to stand right here and watch the wheels of justice turn."

"It's not just you I'm worried about." Moran pointed up at the half-built building. "Call your men out of the street and put them back to work before someone gets their head busted."

"We already had a man fall and bust his head yesterday," Bengston said. "Trouble can always find a man no matter where he is. Up there. On the street. Anywhere."

Moran decided to put a finer point on it. "Any trouble starts this morning, and I mean anything, I'm going to hold you personally responsible."

Bengston's eyes remained vacant. "I hold myself responsible for enough."

Moran could see that he did. And as he walked back to the temporary jail to gather up his and the other horses, Moran checked behind him a few times to see if Bengston was still there. He had not moved since Moran had left him there.

The small front parlor of the Perry home seemed even smaller given how many people were in it. Mary Perry refilled everyone's coffee mugs while Cobb was on the couch with Jane, who had not let go of him since the moment they had seen each other. Cobb was not complaining.

Marshal Perry was in one of the chairs, and Butch and

Fisk remained standing while Moran told them how the rest of the morning would unfold.

Moran looked comfortable standing in front of a room full of people. "I just came back from Judge Waller's chambers. I tried to get him to postpone Jane's hearing until things quieted down, but he refused. He's agreed to keep the public out of the courtroom, so at least we've got that in our favor. Fewer people to worry about that way."

Butch pointed out the window. "There's a fair number of people gathered right now. I've seen a couple of them with Winchesters. I'm pretty sure I know where they got them, too."

"And who from," Moran added. "I ran into Bengston as I was leaving the courthouse. He says he'll be standing there for the duration. I thought about locking him up, but that would just stir up the mob even worse. We've got few enough hands as it is."

Marshal Perry said, "That was good thinking on your part, Rob. How many do you figure are out on the street now, Butch?"

He allowed Fisk to answer for him. "About forty here in front of the house. I checked out the side window and saw a bunch more scattered around the street. Those horses you brought back with you, Sheriff, will help us to get there fast enough. We might be all right if we keep our heads down."

But Cobb was not content to allow things to happen and hope for the best. "We ought to go and clear them off the street before we risk bringing Jane out there. We've got enough men with us here to do it."

Moran shook his head. "If it was just us we were talking about, I might chance it. But I don't want to start a dustup with Mary and Jane in the way. That's why the rest of us will go out first and get mounted. Perry and I will go out first. Then the rest of you. Together, we'll push the crowd back so that Cobb and Jane take the last horse. We'll proceed to the courthouse in a square." He traced the shape in the air in front of him. "Perry and I will be at the front. Butch and Toneff will ride along each side while Fisk brings up the rear. Cobb and Jane will be in the middle of the square. I'm sure it won't be as neat as all that when we get started, but I want you all to do your best to stick to that formation."

Moran grew quiet as he looked at each of the men in turn. "I don't want anyone to think this will go smoothly. Bengston and Panfil have those workers out there pretty riled up. I wouldn't be surprised if they're offering some kind of reward for hurting Jane."

She stifled a sob by burying her face in Cobb's arm.

Moran winced. "I'm sorry to say it like that, but it's the truth. The only thing we have going for us is that none of them have anything against Jane personally. I'm hoping they'll only go so far in risking their lives for a few dollars."

Cobb consoled Jane with his free hand. "There's bound to be at least one fool among them willing to take a shot at us."

"I'm sure there will be. There are a lot of armed men out there, so if anyone aims at you, shoot them. If any of them tries to grab your horse or pull you from the saddle, shoot them. More of them will run than stick if the lead starts flying."

The clock on the mantel sounded the half-hour. Thirty minutes before they were due to appear in court.

Moran did not ask them if they were ready. They had no choice but to be ready.

"Perry," Moran said, "let's get out there. The rest of you follow. Cobb and Jane, stay by the door until we call for you to come out. When you do, get on the horse as fast as you can and keep up with the rest of us."

Hugh Perry refused Moran's help to get up from the chair and followed the sheriff outside. Toneff and Fisk went next, with Butch remaining behind with Cobb and Jane.

"You don't worry about a thing except holding onto Cobb nice and tight," Butch said. "And not for your benefit either, but his. He can steer a coach like nobody I've ever seen, but he's lousy on horseback."

Butch did not wait for Cobb to respond as he ran out to join the others.

Cobb felt Jane begin to shake and held her even tighter. "Stick as close to me as you can, and we'll get you there and back. Everything will be fine. I know it will."

Jane's teeth began to chatter despite it being warm in the Perry home. "How can you know something like that?"

"Because I remember what it was like without you," Cobb said. "And this doesn't feel nearly as bad."

He stroked her hair as he craned his neck to look outside. Moran, Perry, and the deputies were all on horseback and had moved the crowd back and out of the street.

He heard Moran say, "Any of you men who are armed, had better take notice. If any of us see those barrels pointed anywhere other than the sky, we'll shoot the man holding it. Don't test us, boys. We're not in a forgiving mood this morning."

Perry, whose horse was next to Moran's, beckoned them to come outside.

Jane grew rigid with fear, so Cobb had no choice but to pick her up into his arms and carry her.

Cobb felt the world begin to slow down as he moved from the house into the bright morning sunshine. He had spent so much time in the darkened house that he had to squint to see the horse, which was still tied to the Perry fencepost.

He tried to look at the crowd, but none of them could see over the top of the deputies' horses that blocked their view.

Cobb lifted Jane high enough so that she could pull herself onto the back of the waiting horse. Cobb stepped into the stirrup and climbed into the saddle, careful not to allow his filthy boot to graze her dress.

He pulled his coach gun from the saddle holster as Moran began to lead them up the street. He motioned for Cobb to ride slower until they were in the middle of the line of horses, which he did.

Jane gripped him tightly around the middle, pressing the side of her head flat against his back. He imagined her eyes were probably shut.

Cobb silently willed her to be brave. *Just a little while longer. We'll be at the courthouse before you know it.*

With the right side of the street blocked by the lawmen, Cobb looked back to see Fisk had remained behind to keep any of the spectators from closing in behind them. That was good. There were only a few people scattered along the left side of the street, and from what Cobb could see, none of them appeared to be holding rifles.

Cobb began to allow himself to think that Bengston's threat against Jane might have been an empty one. The railroad workers had not come in the same numbers he had heard had been at the jail the previous night. And no one had fired a shot yet.

But as they passed the first corner, Cobb heard a bullet pass overhead as the sound of a shot rang out from his left. Jane buried her head under his right arm as Cobb raised his coach gun in the direction from where the shot had come.

He saw Earl Panfil charging toward them on horseback as he levered a fresh round into his Winchester.

Cobb cut loose with both barrels before heeling his horse into a gallop. He saw Moran cut over in front of him into the middle of the street before he, too, raced up the street. Pistol fire erupted behind him as the few people on this part of the street either ducked or ran away.

Jane shrieked as she clung to him so hard that Cobb had difficulty breathing.

Butch and his horse darted past them on the left just before Butch fired at a man with a rifle on the boardwalk less than twenty yards away. Cobb saw the man stagger backward but he held on to the weapon. Butch's second shot put him down for good as Cobb and Jane sped by.

Moran's horse reared up as two men tossed heavy buckets, sending liquid into the street as they tumbled. At first, Cobb thought it was just water, but when he saw a third man rush forward with a lamp, he knew it must be something else.

Moran shot the man before he could throw the lamp, but his momentum carried him forward into the street and, when he fell, the lamp was crushed beneath him. A thick stream of flame quickly spread out from under his body and across the thoroughfare, igniting the flammable liquid.

Cobb's horse tensed and may have reared up, too, if Cobb had not leaned forward in the saddle and slammed his heels hard into the animal's flanks. The frightened horse kept on through the rising flames.

More gunfire rang out as Butch and Fisk brought their horses through the right edge of the fire—the flames were not as high there—and flanked Cobb's horse in the mad dash onward toward the courthouse.

Cobb felt like a fool for riding with an empty shotgun, but he had not had time to reload it. He had six more shells in his vest pocket but did not dare try to reach them now. It took all of his skill to keep the horse running flat out and in a straight line.

On the street in front of him, he saw something writhe across the surface of the thoroughfare that looked like rattlesnakes. This time, he could not keep the animal from sliding in its tracks and bucking away from a mortal enemy. Jane dug her nails into him as he tried to bring the frightened horse under control.

Butch and Fisk began to shoot at men on either side of the street. Cobb saw it had not been a snake, but a rope that had been pulled taut across the thoroughfare to trip their horses.

Cobb had just gotten the horse to calm as Fisk dropped from the saddle and cut the rope with a knife.

"Go on!" the deputy shouted. "You're almost there!"

Cobb leaned forward in the saddle once again and heeled the horse to get moving as Butch rode ahead, keeping his pistol trained on any man that might be a target.

Cobb was glad to see the brown uniform of Officer Childs and some of his men up ahead. They had blocked off the street with wagons, creating a cordon for them to reach the courthouse safely.

They had made it after all.

CHAPTER 26

Butch reached the old bank building first and was already off his horse to help Jane get down to safe ground. Officer Childs and his men closed in around them, though no one was on the street in front of the building.

One of the officers took hold of the horses as Jane latched onto Cobb again. He held on to his coach gun as Childs led them into the courthouse. Butch followed.

"Where's Bengston?" Butch asked, as they moved up the steps.

"He's already inside with the others," Childs told them. "I saw what you went through on the way here, so I'll let you bring the guns in the building, but not the courtroom. That'll go for Moran and Perry, too. Judge Waller only wants his court officers to have guns when he's on the bench.

"Mine's empty, anyway." Cobb did not like any of this. "We haven't even had enough time to get Jane a lawyer."

"She's already got one," Childs said, as another court officer let them inside. "A pretty good one, too. Les Richter."

Butch said, "You say that name like it's supposed to mean something to us."

"You'll be finding out for yourselves soon enough," Childs said. "And I don't think you'll be unhappy about it."

He led them to the left side of the building where some chairs had been put out for the occasion. Two tables had been placed in front of either side of the aisle and a table on top of a wooden platform lorded over them all.

But it was not the way the furniture was arranged that made Cobb and Jane stop in the middle of the aisle. It was the two people sitting up at the front talking to a man in an expensive tweed suit.

Madam Peachtree and Lucien Clay were sitting next to Phil Bengston.

Jane regained some of her strength and composure now that they were finally inside. "What are those two doing here?"

Officer Childs began to tell them. "The fella they're talking to is Ron Quinlan. That's Mr. Bengston's attorney. He sent word for them to come here last night. They got here about an hour ago. That's all I know."

Cobb did not know much about how courts worked, but Butch did from his time as a Texas Ranger. "Why is he allowed to bring his own lawyer here in the first place? The town attorney ought to be standing up against Jane instead of him. That's the law."

"Don't ask me because I just work here," Childs said. "The judge said it was going to work this way, so that's the way it is." To Jane, he said, "Mr. Richter is over there at the other table, ma'am. You ought to take a few moments to acquaint yourself with him." To Cobb and Butch, he said, "I'm gonna need your guns, boys. Don't worry about Bengston. His rig is right over there. I searched him close, and he's got nothing but lint in his pockets."

Cobb handed Childs his empty coach gun and Butch handed over his gun belt.

The officer carried them away. "They'll be waiting for you out here when you're done."

Cobb eyed Bengston and Clay as he escorted Jane to the front of the room where Mr. Richter stood to greet her. He was a tall man with a long fleshy face and gray hair. His pale skin spoke of a life spent more indoors than outside.

Butch kept his voice low as he spoke to Cobb. "Why do you think the judge wanted them here?"

"I don't think it was the judge." Cobb hoped Bengston would look his way, but the railroad's hired killer kept looking straight ahead. "This was his doing and he's got a reason."

Jane's mood had brightened considerably after her brief conversation with her new lawyer. "Tucker, this is Mr. Richter. He said I shouldn't have anything to worry about."

"Pleased to meet you, Mr. Cobb. And Mr. Keeling." He shook hands with them both. "Our mutual acquaintance speaks very highly of you two. Can't say enough about you, actually."

Cobb knew when he was being shined on and did not like it. "I doubt Jane could've told you that much about us in such a short time."

"I wasn't talking about Jane," Richter said. "I was talking about our other mutual acquaintance. Colonel McBride. He wired me last night and asked me to take on Jane's case. I'll be representing her for the duration."

Cobb had not been expecting that. "That was awfully nice of him, but you just give me your bill after this is over, and I'll be happy to pay it."

"It's already been taken care of," Richter said. "And I'm glad to report saving Miss Duprey won't take much effort on my part. It's perhaps the most clear-cut case of self-defense I've ever seen in thirty years as a lawyer."

Butch inclined his head toward Bengston's side of the court. "It sure doesn't look like they see it that way. He didn't bring Madam Peachtree and Clay here because he missed their company."

"Yes," Richter said, as he looked over at them. "That concerns me, too. Ron Quinlan is Bengston's lawyer. He's very good, but not as good as me. He can pull all the tricks he wants here today. Judge Waller is a fair man, though I must admit that I don't know what he's up to."

Cobb did not like the sound of that. "Meaning?"

"Meaning the town attorney isn't here and he should be, even if it's to say that he won't be bringing charges against her." Richter shrugged off his doubts. "I doubt we have anything to worry about. Our case is solid, as we'll soon prove."

Cobb turned when he heard more people enter the courtroom. Perry, Fisk, Toneff, and Moran were placing their gun belts on Childs's table before walking up to join them.

Moran noticed Peachtree. "What the devil are they doing here?"

"That's the same question we've been asking ourselves," Butch said.

From his spot at the back of the courtroom, Officer Childs called out, "All rise! This court will come to order. The Honorable Judge William Waller presiding."

Cobb saw a man who looked more like a blacksmith than a judge in a black robe trudging up the aisle. "Sit down, everybody. There's no need for such ceremony in this instance."

Cobb studied the man as he stepped up on the platform. He had jowls like a bulldog and wire-rimmed spectacles perched on the end of a piggish nose. The thick mustache he wore was blondish-gray and, upon sitting, he folded his stubby fingers on the table in front of him.

He looked over everyone in the court before he began to speak. "Mr. Richter, you're representing Miss Jane Duprey? And Mr. Quinlan, you're here on behalf of the Hyde woman, is that it?"

Both attorneys answered that was true.

"Good. I'll expect the rest of you to remain quiet during these proceedings. Anyone who talks out of turn will get themselves thrown in jail. It's not exactly a nice jail, so I wouldn't recommend it." He paused to push his spectacles further back on his nose. "I'm aware that there's a lot of tension in town over this case. People seem to feel strongly about it, and I think Mr. Bengston is the cause of a lot of it."

Mr. Quinlan got to his feet. "Objection, Your Honor."

"Sit down, Ron. You've got no call to object to anything yet because, while we may be in a courtroom, this isn't exactly an official hearing." Judge Waller pointed at Moran. "My clerk told me how you and your men had quite a time bringing Miss Duprey here this morning. He was able to watch it from one of the windows in my chambers. Looks to me like everyone made it."

"We're alive, Your Honor," Moran said. "Not everyone who tried to stop us can say the same."

"Folks who try to stop you usually can't say much after the effort, Sheriff," Judge Waller observed. "We can get around to talking about that later. But the reason why I called you all here today is that, despite all the evidence to the contrary, Mr. Quinlan here tells me this case is far more complicated than it looks. He has asked me to give him a chance to change my mind. And, since he often represents the interests of the railroad, I figured the least

I could do is give him a fair chance to make his case. These informal proceedings are a way for me to figure out what this case is all about before I determine if there's even a case at all. He's got a mighty steep hill to climb because not even the town prosecutor thinks Miss Duprey did anything wrong. So, while this gathering isn't legally binding, it's not illegal, either. Let's just say it's what you might call 'extra-legal' and get on with it."

This time, Mr. Richter stood. "Objection, Your Honor. My client hasn't even been afforded the opportunity to enter a plea."

"Sit down, Les. There's been no venue for her to enter a plea yet, and I'm not sure we'll even get that far. Your client is still presumed innocent. The burden is on Mr. Quinlan over there to convince me we ought to have a trial. He's brought a couple of people with him who've got some things to say about Miss Duprey that he thinks might help me look at this case in a different light. I'm going to hear them out. You'll be allowed to ask them questions after Quinlan calls them. Ron, call your first witness."

Quinlan cleared his throat. "I call Miss Amanda Pinochet to the stand."

Cobb waited until Richter sat down before he leaned forward and asked him, "Can he really do this?"

The lawyer whispered back, "I don't know, but he's doing it. We have no choice but to go along with it. Don't worry. I'm proceeding as if it's a legitimate hearing."

As Miss Pinochet began to walk to the witness stand, Judge Waller said, "No need for that. Just stand where you are and speak from there. You can remain seated if you want, so long as you speak up so the rest of us can hear you."

The woman dressed in all black remained where she was as Quinlan began to question her.

"Miss Pinochet, please tell us how you came to know the defendant."

"Don't test my patience, Quinlan," the judge cautioned. "She's not a defendant because she hasn't been accused of anything yet. You'll refer to her as Miss Duprey."

Quinlan repeated the question, referring to Jane as Miss Duprey.

Pinochet kept her expression flat as she answered, "I had hired her to be a hostess at the Longacre House in Laramie."

Quinlan took a sheet of paper from his table. "How did you come to hire her?"

"Laramie is a growing town, and I came to know of her from her work in North Branch," Pinochet said. "She had a solid reputation, and I thought she would be a wonderful addition to my establishment."

Quinlan handed her the paper. "Have you seen this document before?"

Richter rose to object, but the judge waved him to sit down.

"I have," Pinochet said. "It's the contract Miss Duprey signed when she agreed to come work for me."

"And what is the term of that contract?"

"Five years. It's standard for an agreement such as this."

"And did she fulfill that contract?"

Pinochet handed the document back to Quinlan. "She barely lasted two months."

"And why was that?"

"I learned that her reputation was a false one. She was abusive to the other women, aloof with the customers, and refused to take direction from Mr. Clay, the manager, and myself."

Jane pulled Richter close and whispered to him that Pinochet was lying.

Quinlan placed the contract on the table. "Did you tell Miss Duprey that you were not satisfied with her work?"

"Several times," Pinochet said. "She only grew more uncooperative after each time. She began to refuse to leave her room. When things took a violent turn, we had no choice but to throw her out on her ear."

"Beatings?" Quinlan asked. "Who did she beat?"

"Her?" The madam smirked. "She didn't hit anyone. She didn't have to. She had one of her many male admirers do it for her."

"And do you see that male admirer here today?"

Pinochet pointed a long finger at Cobb. "He's sitting right there. Tucker Cobb."

Quinlan barely bothered to glance back at Cobb. "And who did Mr. Cobb attack?"

"The house manager, Mr. Lucien Clay. He assaulted him one night after Mr. Clay asked him to leave Longacre House. And although I didn't see it happen, I saw the results."

Quinlan looked over at the bandaged man huddled against the wall. Cobb could tell the pimp was playacting for the benefit of the judge. He had looked fine before the judge had walked in.

Judge Waller said, "That's all for now, Quinlan. Give Mr. Richter a chance to ask her a question."

Richter got up and slowly walked toward Miss Pinochet. "You said you threw Miss Duprey out on her ear. Is that true?"

The madam sat upright. "It certainly is. I have no reason to lie."

"You have no reason to tell the truth, either, since you weren't sworn in," Richter pointed out. "That's why I want you to be clear that it was you who threw Miss Duprey out. You're sure she didn't leave Longacre House on her own? Against your wishes."

"Why would she want to leave on her own? She had everything she could want. Fine clothes. Free meals. A clean place to stay."

"From where you expected her to, let's say, 'entertain' the gentlemen customers of your establishment. Isn't that right?"

"My customers spend quite a bit of money for the company of beautiful women," Pinochet explained. "When she refused to leave her room, she hurt our business and we explained that to her. She didn't like it and grew violent."

"With you?" Richter asked. "With the other women in your employ?"

Pinochet's mouth became a colorless line. "If she had raised a hand to me, we wouldn't be here."

Richter grinned. "Sounds like you've got a violent streak yourself."

Quinlan was on his feet. "Objection, Your Honor."

"Sit down," Judge Waller told him. "Get to the point, Richter."

Richter took the rebuke in stride. "I noticed you and Mr. Clay took the time to travel here today, but none of the other women who work for you did."

"They're busy," she said. "It didn't seem right to deprive them of the chance of earning a living. Miss Duprey had already done that."

"Yes, you've said that. But I'm sure you must've brought signed statements from the abused. An affidavit? Sworn testimony of some kind."

"All I brought was my own word," she said. "But we can get statements from them if you want."

"All we have is your word," Richter noted. "And if

Miss Duprey left Longacre House on her own volition, then it stands to reason that you weren't happy about it. You might be looking to make her pay for breaking her contract. Isn't that why you hired Miss Hyde and her son in the first place?"

Again, Quinlan was on his feet. "Objection, Your Honor. There's no proof that any such contract exists."

Richter did not wait for Waller to comment. "Then why was Miss Hyde on the stagecoach in the first place?"

"To visit her son, Phil Bengston, who works here in Cheyenne."

"Perhaps," Richter allowed, "but that doesn't explain why she tried to shoot down Mr. Cobb and Mr. Keeling at Wingate Station a few nights ago."

"Another objection, Your Honor," Quinlan implored the judge. "That's slanderous hearsay. There's not a shred of proof that the late Miss Hyde tried to kill these men."

Butch cursed under his breath before saying, "She wouldn't have had a hole in her hip if she was just going to the privy."

Judge Waller glared down at Butch from behind his desk. "That's enough commentary from the gallery. One more outburst like that and I'll have Officer Childs remove you." He looked at Quinlan. "Your objection is denied. All we've got is hearsay, so you can keep any future objections on that score to yourself. Mr. Richter, you have any more questions for Miss Pinochet, or can we move along?"

Richter went to sit down. "I've got nothing further at this time, Your Honor, but reserve the right to ask her additional questions later."

Judge Waller gestured at Quinlan. "Call your next witness."

"I ask Mr. Clay to speak, if he's able."

Cobb watched Clay make a show of struggling to lift his head. "I think I can speak through the pain for a little while."

Cobb shifted in his seat. He was playing this to the hilt.

Quinlan began. "You seem to be in considerable pain, Mr. Clay. Could you please tell us what is ailing you?"

"My head's cracked like an egg." Clay barely managed to speak above a whisper. "I'm in constant pain. My vision is blurry and I'm constantly dizzy, which makes me sick to my stomach so much that I'm not able to eat."

"And how did you get these injuries?" Quinlan asked. "Were you thrown from a horse?"

"No. I was hit by an ox. A great big ox who was angry at me for telling his lady friend she had to live up to her contract. A legal contract, I might add."

"And is that big ox you just mentioned here in this courtroom today?"

Clay feebly raised a hand and pointed to the left. "He's sitting right over there. His name is Tucker Cobb."

"Tell us what happened the night he did this to you."

Clay rubbed his bandaged head. "The details are a little fuzzy now. But as I remember it, Cobb and Keeling were drunk and out of order. They stood most of the night at the bar, sullen and giving the bartenders a tough time of it. That's why, when they were ready to leave, I asked them to not come back. We prefer a certain clientele at Longacre House, and there are plenty of other places in Laramie that serve their kind. The rough-hewn type."

Quinlan continued. "You told them they were no longer welcome in your establishment. What happened then?"

"Cobb flew into a drunken rage," Clay struggled to remember. "He grabbed me and began tearing at my clothes. He's much bigger than me and threw me an awful beating. I wish I could remember all the details, but I can't. The only thing I remember, before I was helped up to my room, was that Sheriff Moran arrested him for what he'd done to me. The next morning, when I finally woke up, I learned that the sheriff had let him go in the morning. I never got an answer why, only that he did. I'll admit I was in no condition to ask him any questions."

Quinlan concluded, "Because of the effects of the beating you received at the hands of Mr. Cobb?"

Clay nodded, then quickly winced from the effort.

Quinlan sat down as Richter stood. "You seem to be in a great deal of discomfort, Mr. Clay. Are you still nauseous and in pain?"

"Constantly," Clay told him. "I haven't known a moment's peace since I woke up. I've been forced to stay in bed under doctor's orders."

"Yet here you are," Richter said. "Despite all of your numerous injuries, you managed to ride through the night to be here."

"Some things are worth the effort," Clay said. "Doing right is one of those things."

"Doing right here in Cheyenne, but not in Laramie," Richter stated.

Clay's eyes narrowed as he remained silent.

"I see that the statement confused you," Richter pointed out, "so I'll put a finer point on it. You could've pressed charges against Mr. Cobb in Laramie for assaulting you, but you didn't."

"I was bedridden."

"But I doubt you were alone the entire time. You live in Longacre House. You could've sent someone to get the sheriff so he or one of his deputies could've taken down your complaint, but you didn't do that, did you?" Richter pointed back at Moran. "The sheriff is sitting right back there, Mr. Clay. I can ask him directly if you'd prefer. So please clarify this point for us. You didn't send anyone for him, did you?"

"No."

"And no one who works for you thought to bring him on your behalf, did they? Miss Pinochet, perhaps?"

"No," Clay said.

Richter folded his hands in front of him. "That was because you were thinking about justice of another sort. You didn't think to charge Mr. Cobb because you already had a way to punish him for what he had done to you. You had already hired Miss Hyde and her son for that purpose. That's why she was on that stagecoach, wasn't she? She had been hired by you to kill Mr. Cobb and Mr. Keeling and bring Miss Duprey back to Longacre House."

"I was in no condition to hire anyone," Clay said. "I was bedridden."

"But well enough to travel through the night to get here by this morning," Richter concluded. "How convenient."

"That's enough," Judge Waller said. "You've made your point. You have anyone else you'd like to question, Mr. Quinlan?"

"Only one more, Your Honor. Mr. Phil Bengston."

CHAPTER 27

While Jane whispered quickly into her attorney's ear, Cobb watched Bengston stand from his seat. His black, flat-brimmed hat was in his hand and his brown hair fell over his forehead. Cobb thought he looked incredibly young, perhaps even young enough to be his son. *How could a boy of such tender years become such a man?*

Quinlan began. "I know you're still mourning the loss of your mother, Mr. Bengston. I hope you'll accept my condolences at such a difficult time."

Bengston offered a curt nod, but nothing more.

"Miss Cassie Hyde was your mother, was she not?"

"She was."

"And one could conclude that she had a rather sordid past, did she not?"

"Depending on who you ask."

"She was known to be a violent woman at times. She'd been arrested and tried for killing a man in Ogalala and other places."

"And was freed by a jury each time. They said it was self-defense."

Cobb watched Quinlan pause just long enough to allow

that fact to take root in the judge's mind. "Why was she in this part of the territory, Mr. Bengston?"

"She'd written me to tell me she was turning over a new leaf. Said she wanted to start over. Since I have a good job with the railroad, I thought this would be a good place for her to try." Bengston looked down at his hat. "Now I wish I hadn't. She might still be alive."

"You were here in court when Miss Duprey's attorney claimed that you and your mother were hired to kill Mr. Cobb and Mr. Keeling. What do you make of that?"

"My mother was on that stage to come live here with me," Bengston said. "I don't know about anyone hiring her to do anything."

"It's possible, isn't it?" Quinlan asked. "Given her violent past and all."

"That was a long time ago. I'd expect most folks would've forgotten about all that by now."

"What was your reaction when you learned that your mother had been arrested by Marshal Perry for attempted murder?"

"I was angry about it," Bengston admitted. "You could say I lost my temper. Made threats. I'm not proud of it, but it's not every day I learn my mother's been locked up for something she didn't do."

"Mr. Keeling's outburst earlier claims he shot her in self-defense that night at Wingate Station. What do you make of that?"

Bengston glared across the courtroom at Butch, and Butch glared right back. "I don't doubt he shot her, just his reasons why."

Quinlan threw open his hands. "What other reason might he have? Cobb and Keeling make their living by their stagecoach. Shooting customers isn't good for business."

"That's why they had every reason to lie about it," Bengston said. "They might've gotten spooked while they were standing outside. Heard something in the dark and shot my mother while she was going to the privy. Maybe she couldn't sleep and went for a walk. They realized their mistake and cooked up that story about her being hired by Miss Pinochet and Clay."

Quinlan frowned. "But they claim to have witnesses. Mr. Fisk, currently serving as one of Marshal Perry's deputies, backs their claim. He was there when they found the shotgun by your mother's side after she was shot."

"Cobb's shotgun," Bengston said. "He could've placed it there after he saw what he'd done. And Fisk wasn't there when they shot her. He came afterward."

"Sounds like you know a lot about what happened that night," Quinlan said.

"Only what my mother told me after Judge Waller there had her released. We talked about it before Doc Fry worked on her."

Quinlan looked at the judge. "I'd be happy to call Doctor Fry to support his statement, Your Honor."

"I imagine he's pretty busy with other things right now," Judge Waller said. "Any other questions for Mr. Bengston?"

"I do. Was Mr. Fisk one of Marshal Perry's deputies at the time your mother was shot?"

"No. That happened after he got to town."

"That sounds strange. Does Marshal Perry often hire random men to serve as his deputies?"

"Not from what I've seen," Bengston admitted. "I heard he got the job after Cobb spoke up for him."

"He did? Sounds awfully convenient that the only

other witness to your mother's shooting should become employed by the same man holding her for trial."

Bengston's glare shifted to Perry. "I thought the same thing."

Quinlan moved on to another question. "Where were you when your mother was fatally wounded?"

"I was having dinner with some friends from the railroad when I got word about it. I rushed to where they said she was, but I was too late. She was gone."

"Did anyone say who had done it?" Quinlan asked.

"They didn't need to. Miss Duprey was running through the street, saying she'd killed her. She kept on doing that until Marshal Perry came and got her."

"Would you have brought her to the marshal if you'd gotten to her first?"

"Can't say that I would. What would you do if you'd just found your mother stabbed to death?"

Quinlan threw open his hands again and sat down.

"Mr. Richter, I imagine you have some questions."

"A few," the lawyer said, as he stood. "Mr. Bengston, you seem to know quite a bit about what happened at Wingate Station the night she was shot. One might be forgiven for thinking you were there, too."

"Except I wasn't there. I was working for the railroad at the time."

"In what capacity?"

"Policing the workers. Making sure they weren't getting up to any trouble once the workday ended. I like to show up unannounced, so I can catch them if they're doing something they shouldn't."

"And what happens to them when they break your rules?"

"They're the railroad's rules, not mine. And when they break them, I discipline them for it."

"How?"

"How I see fit, given the circumstances. The railroad pays me to keep their people in line. I know how they like things done."

"Ever shoot them for running away?"

Bengston paused. "Sometimes."

"So, you're a killer," Richter stated.

"When I have to be."

"So, if Miss Pinochet and Mr. Clay were looking to hire someone to kill Mr. Cobb and Mr. Keeling for helping Miss Duprey escape from Laramie, you'd be the sort of man they'd hire to do it. Isn't that so?"

"There's no shortage of men like me out here, mister."

"No, there aren't," Richter admitted. "Even I could attest to that. But I'm curious about something. Where were you in the hours before your mother was killed?"

"Having dinner with some friends from the railroad," Bengston said. "I already told you that. Every one of them will be willing to tell you so."

"I have no doubt they would," Richter said. "But I'm more interested in your whereabouts immediately before that dinner occurred. Where were you then? Did you all leave the railroad offices and go straight to dinner?"

Cobb felt a spark in his belly. Richter was leading Bengston somewhere he did not want to go.

"I'd stopped by the offices after spending most of the day tending to my mother at Doc Fry's office. I later had a run-in with Cobb and Keeling behind the feed store where they kept their coach and horses."

"How? Did you just happen to be passing by when you noticed they were getting ready to leave town?"

"I was."

"Did you and your friends from the railroad chastise them?" Richter asked. "Give them a rough time of it?"

"They saw Cobb try to attack me," Bengston said. "It happened out on the street as plain as day. I'm sure a lot of other people saw it, too. He made quite a fool of himself."

"After you baited him," Richter said. "After you threatened his life and Miss Duprey's life, too."

"We barked a lot of things at each other. I don't remember everything I said. The two of them shot my mother and were getting away with it. No one was bringing them to account."

"But you were going to bring them to account, weren't you? You're not the kind of man to allow something so personal go unanswered."

Bengston's left eye twitched. "He came after me in front of witnesses. Keeling tackled him before he got his hands on me. I'm sorry he didn't let him go. We might not be here if he had. And my mother might still be alive."

"Perhaps." Richter stuck his hands in his pockets. "I do have one final question for you. We know where you were when your mother was killed. I'm sure every man there will be glad to tell us you never left their sight. But how did your mother know where she could find Miss Duprey?"

Bengston grew still.

Richter leaned forward to press his point. "It's a fairly important question, Mr. Bengston. Your mother was led from the jail, where Miss Duprey worked, then here to this very courtroom, then spirited away from here by you to Doc Fry's office for treatment. You said you were with her all day until you returned to the railroad office, met your friends, and had a run-in with Mr. Cobb and Mr. Keeling on your way to dinner. How did your mother know where Miss Duprey was staying?"

Cobb watched Bengston's lips move, but no sound came out until he said, "They must've said something about it in front of her while she was at the jail."

"But Miss Duprey didn't know where she'd be staying until well after your mother was being treated by Doctor Fry. How could she have overheard that if Miss Duprey herself didn't even know where her rooms were?"

"I . . . I don't know."

Cobb and Butch moved to the edge of their seats. Cobb placed his hand on Jane's shoulder, and she squeezed it, unable to take her eyes off Richter.

"Did you have people watching where Mr. Cobb and Mr. Keeling went, Mr. Bengston? Like you had men watching the town last night?"

"No. When the men aren't working, they're free to move around town. They weren't working for me."

"Then how else did your mother know exactly where Miss Duprey would be? Someone must've told her where she could be found. Perhaps she overheard one of your men telling you."

"No."

"Perhaps it wasn't as simple as that," Richter pressed. "Perhaps you two planned it out that way. Perhaps you already knew where Miss Duprey would be that night and agreed to help your mother kill her."

"No."

"It's certainly possible, isn't it, Mr. Bengston? Miss Duprey didn't attack your mother at Doctor Fry's office. Or do you expect us to believe that she dragged your mother halfway across town only to kill her and the clerk at the Cheyenne Grand?"

"I never said that," Bengston yelled. "She was full of medicine that made her do it."

"And I suppose it's the medicine that made an injured woman wander the streets alone, aimlessly until she just happened upon the very place where Miss Duprey was staying. And isn't it convenient that, despite your mother's condition, you just happened to be at dinner with a table full of witnesses while your mother killed a hotel clerk and laid in wait for Miss Duprey to arrive?"

Bengston stammered while Richter thundered home his point. "There's only one way Cassie Hyde could have known where to find Miss Duprey. Either you mentioned it in front of her, or the two of you cooked up a scheme to kill her for all the trouble she had caused both of you."

"No."

"It was a good plan. People get knifed in that part of town all the time, don't they, Mr. Bengston? No one would've doubted it was just a random act of violence. It almost would've been the perfect crime if she'd gotten away with it, but she didn't, did she?"

Bengston's eyes grew wide. "She killed my mother."

"In defense of her own life." Mr. Richter faced Judge Waller. "Your Honor, let us assume everything you've heard in this courtroom today is true. Let us assume that Miss Duprey was dismissed from Longacre House because of a cruel, even violent disposition. Let us further assume that Mr. Keeling panicked and shot Miss Hyde by accident and concocted a story with Mr. Cobb. Assume it all to be true and we are still left with one final, immutable fact. Cassie Hyde left Doctor Fry's office with a knife, intent on killing Miss Jane Duprey. If she had been successful, she would be in this courtroom right now facing a charge of premeditated murder. But she's not because Miss Duprey killed her while struggling for the knife Cassie Hyde brought with her. Nothing you've heard changes that fact, which is why I ask you to allow my client to leave."

Bengston punched the wall with the side of his fist. "It's lies, judge. It's all lies."

Quinlan rose to calm him down, but Bengston shoved him aside. "They're lying about hired killers and revenge.

They're doing it just to save that woman from a noose. My mother was killed by a common, two-bit whore, and she has to answer for that. You have to make her answer for that, or this town won't be fit to live in."

Judge Waller ran his hands over his bald head. "Officer Childs, remove Mr. Bengston from the court. Don't give him his guns back until he's outside. If he gives you any trouble, lock him up for contempt of court."

Childs brought his rifle with him as he strode up the aisle and beckoned Bengston to come out.

Cobb and Butch stood in front of Jane, blocking her from any outburst from the gunman.

Bengston left without a word as Childs marched him outside.

Judge Waller scratched at his scalp as the court returned to order. "That turned out pretty much as I expected it would." He looked at Quinlan. "You gave it a good run, Ron. I heard you out and you offered a compelling view of the case. It might even prove that Miss Duprey had a reason and the disposition to kill Miss Hyde in cold blood. But it still doesn't prove how she wound up in that place with that knife at that time."

The judge shifted to Richter. "Your client has it in her to kill someone, Les. The fact that she's still alive is proof of that. But being able to defend yourself doesn't make her a killer. I've got no choice but to rule in Miss Duprey's favor. That means you're free to go."

Judge Waller beckoned one of the court officers to step forward. "Seeing as how tempers ran pretty hot here today, I think it's best if Mr. Quinlan and his people leave first. And when you leave this building, I want you all the way gone. Anyone found hanging around out front or harassing this young lady will be held in contempt. I'm holding you personally responsible for them, Quinlan. I want them out of town and on their way back to Laramie within the hour."

He banged the gavel and got up from the desk. Jane threw her arms around Cobb, who held her close.

"See?" he told her. "I knew you had nothing to worry about."

Marshal Perry, Fisk, and Toneff helped herd Quinlan and his friends down the aisle and outside.

Madam Pinochet popped up on her toes and managed to spit in Jane's direction before hurling curses at her in her native French. Perry moved her forward as Toneff and Fisk waited for the shuffling Lucien Clay.

Clay shoved himself between the deputies and said to Cobb, "This isn't over, boys. Not by a long shot. We'll see you in Laramie. We'll see you real soon."

Fisk took him by the arm and kept him moving. "Get going before you get your head busted again for your trouble."

Moran and Butch remained behind as Judge Waller went to move past them. Richter offered his hand to him.

"Thank you for giving us a fair hearing, Your Honor. I appreciate it."

The judge ignored Richter's hand. "No need to thank me for doing my job, Les. And just because I didn't hold her over for a trial doesn't mean she's free. Phil Bengston's not the kind who's just going to let this go. His mother's still dead and he holds your client responsible. Maybe even more responsible than Cobb and Keeling here."

The judge looked past Richter and at Jane. "I'd enjoy myself while you can, little lady, then I'd do everything I could to get myself out of the territory. That goes for you boys, too. Bengston's a dangerous man, but you might have a chance if he can't find you."

"If he's stupid enough to try," Moran said, "he'll pay for it."

"I hope you're right, Sheriff. For all your sakes."

CHAPTER 28

Jane buried her head against Cobb's chest as the others watched the jurist trudge out of the makeshift courtroom.

"I'm afraid the judge is right," Butch said. "Bengston's probably out there right now whipping up his men into a fighting mood."

"I half hope he is," Moran admitted. "He'll be easier to catch that way. You three stay here for a bit while I make sure it's safe for you to go outside."

"I'll go with you," Butch said. "I imagine these two want to be alone for a bit."

Cobb knew they could not stay in the courtroom forever and began to slowly move her along.

Her grip around his middle did not weaken. "I can't believe it's over. It all happened so fast. I've hardly had time to get myself to understand that I killed a woman."

Cobb knew that nothing was over. Not really. "Judge Waller was right about Bengston. We can't stay here, and I can't keep bringing you with me whenever me and Butch make a run. We've got to get you out of town today. The sooner the better. There's nothing keeping us in Wyoming, so there's no reason why we shouldn't leave."

"I can't let you do that," Jane said. "You and Butch have your stagecoach line here."

"The wonderful thing about horses is that they don't care where they are as long as there's grain to eat and water to drink. We can make a living almost anywhere. I'm thinking Colorado is closest. Charles Hagen hasn't sunk his fangs into them yet. Maybe me and Butch can run folks between Fort Collins and Denver."

"We just can't turn tail and run on account of Phil Bengston," Jane argued. "We can't let his kind drive people like us out of the places where we want to live."

Cobb wished she would hurry up. "You think that way because you're a good person, honey. Men like Bengston don't see things that way. They live on making people afraid of them. Me and Butch are used to tangling with his kind, but not you." She began to argue but he pulled her along with him. "I know you don't like the notion of giving up, but sometimes holding on to something just because someone else wants it is foolish. Wyoming's not fit for us anymore. It's time to put roots down in a place where a madman like him isn't looking to settle a score."

She stopped resisting him and walked with him. "I don't care where we live as long as we're there together."

His coach gun was the only weapon left on the table and he picked it up. They moved into the lobby of the old bank, and he heard their footsteps echo among the marble. He looked down the row of teller's windows to the entrance and saw Moran and Butch standing just outside.

He felt a shudder go through her as they went that way. "It's nice looking, but so cold and empty when it's just the two of us in here."

The closer they got to the entrance, the more Cobb could see of the street outside. He was expecting to see

Bengston's railroad workers gathered on the street, but aside from Childs and the other court officers, the area in front of the bank was empty.

He paused to open his shotgun, remove the spent shells, and replace them with fresh shells from his vest pocket.

"Do we have to leave town right away?" Jane asked, as she watched him finish reloading.

"It's safer if we do, honey. I'd like to be well into Colorado before Bengston has a chance to cook up something against us. Plenty of hills between here and Fort Collins where we'll be able to hide. Our coach is still back in Laramie, so we'll have an easier time hiding ourselves. Butch and me will go back to get it once I know you're safe." He gently eased her behind him. "Might be a good idea if you let me go first. Stick close behind me and do what I say once we get outside."

Cobb pushed open the door as they reached the first step. Jane remained right behind him.

Butch beckoned them to hurry up. "There's no one out here, which ain't good. And there's no sign of Bengston, which is even worse. Childs has our horses here. We'd best climb aboard and make ourselves scarce."

Moran was already in the saddle. His Winchester in hand as he continued to look over the street. "We'll head down this street, which leads south. I'll ride with you for a while until I'm sure you're clear. Jane, get on your horse."

Jane stepped out from behind Cobb and allowed Butch to help her step into the saddle. She swung her leg over the top and beamed down at Cobb.

"See that, Tucker. You'll make a horsewoman out of me—"

Cobb saw her buck forward before he heard the shot ring out in the street. The horse reared up as she spilled from the far side of the saddle before Butch could grab her.

Cobb ignored the raised hooves of the frightened animal as he dove past it to rush to Jane's side.

He slid on the dirt and mess of the thoroughfare and saw the dark patch of blood spread along the back of her dress.

Moran began shouting and Butch moved around the other side as Childs pulled the scared horse away.

Cobb's hands shook as he called her name and tried to roll her onto her back. She offered no resistance. She'd always been so light.

And as he took her in his arms, her head lolled back. He saw the hole burned through the left side of her dress front, then the vacant look in her half-closed eyes.

Cobb knew she was in shock. She must have hit her head when she fell from such a height. Why hadn't Childs kept a better hold on the animal?

"Jane," Cobb said, as he lightly patted her face. "It's me, honey. Tucker." Another shot boomed along the street, but Moran and the others could handle it. Jane was hurt and needed him. "It's all right, honey. Everything'll be all right. Just look at me and we'll get you to a doctor."

Butch was crouched beside them with his pistol in hand. "Cobb."

Cobb ignored him. Ignored another shot and the blood and that horrible blank look on her face as he continued to try to bring her around. "It's all right, honey. Doc Fry will patch you right up as good as new. Don't you worry."

Cobb moved to his knees and wished Butch was paying attention instead of looking for someone to shoot at. "Help me here, Butch. We've got to get her to a doctor."

Moran pointed somewhere and took off in that direction. Perry and Toneff ran behind him on foot while Fisk stayed behind.

He recognized the look on the young deputy's face

but dared not consider it. "Help me get her up, will you? We've got to get her to a doctor and fast!"

Cobb had not been expecting Butch to grab him by the collar and yank him as violently as he did. "She's beyond a doctor's care now, Cobb. She's gone, do you hear me? She's gone."

Cobb wondered if his friend had lost his senses and tried to break free of him. "She's not gone, damn it. She's lying right there, and she needs my help."

Butch shook him harder. "She doesn't need any help. She's dead. Bengston did it with that rifle of his."

Cobb heard the words but could not accept them. She was just hurt was all. Doc Fry could help her, just like he had helped Cassie Hyde. And that workman who fell from the building.

"No. She—"

But as his eyes fell upon her, he saw that Butch was right. Not because of anything he saw, but because of what he did not see. That spark in her eyes she always had when she looked at him. The way she looked at him now was flat, as though he was not even there.

"No." Cobb heard his voice begin to crack. "No. Not her. Not now."

He reached for her but Butch would not allow him. "She's dead and so are we if we stay out here like this. Bengston's up high somewhere and he's picking us off. He just shot Toneff through the head. Look!"

Cobb looked in the direction where Butch was pointing and saw Toneff lying face-down in the packed dirt.

Butch's words began to mean something to him then. Words he did not want to understand.

Cobb did not move as a bullet passed between him and Butch, striking the dirt near Jane's head. When she did not flinch or cry out in surprise, he knew what Butch had told him was true.

The love of his life was dead.

Butch grabbed Cobb and dragged him back beside the stone stairs where Fisk had already taken cover.

"I hear the shots," Fisk said, "but I can't see where they're coming from."

"That's because he's moving around up on the roofs of those buildings over there." Butch thumped Cobb on the chest. "Snap out of it, partner. We need you."

But Cobb could not take his eyes off Jane. He had never seen her so still before. Even when she slept, her chest rose and fell with every breath. But there was nothing now. Nothing except the sound of the shot that had taken her from him echoing in his mind.

The shot that killed her had come from behind. The other buildings around the bank were wooden skeletons still under construction. If Bengston was shooting from a roof, there was only one place he could be.

The Cheyenne Hotel on the other side of the thoroughfare. One of the many places that had turned him and Butch away when they had been looking for a room.

"Cobb!" Butch thumped his friend's chest again. "Are you listening?"

Cobb pitched forward and grabbed his shotgun from the street as he ran toward the hotel. He heard Butch and Fisk running right behind him.

As he reached the corner, Cobb saw Moran and Perry going in the grand entrance at the front of the building, so he continued straight ahead, looking for a back way in. Bengston would not have walked through the lobby with a rifle in his hand.

Cobb rounded to the back of the building and saw a cook hauling a crate of rubbish from the kitchen. He bolted past the man and into the kitchen. One of the cook's helpers began to yell at him until he saw the shotgun in Cobb's hand.

"Back stairs," Cobb said. "Where are they?"

The helper pointed in the direction from which Cobb had just come. "It's off the hallway. The maids use it to—"

Cobb ran back in that direction, only to find Fisk and Butch already running ahead of him up the back staircase. The hotel was only four stories tall, but the stairs were narrow and tight.

One flight above him, Cobb heard Fisk call out. "He's here! I found him!"

Cobb heard a pistol shot, followed by a great commotion. He hoped they had not killed Bengston before Cobb got a chance.

On the next flight up, he found Butch tending to an unconscious Fisk.

"He belted him with his rifle butt," Butch said. "Knocked him cold."

Cobb pushed past them and kept climbing without breaking his stride. The doors from the stairwell leading to the long hallways had small windows in them. He looked through the second-floor window and saw no one in the hall. The same at the third and fourth.

That meant Bengston must have run all the way back up to the roof, probably looking for another way down.

Cobb felt a rush of energy course through him as he now took the stairs two at a time. He burst through the door leading to the roof and saw Bengston running toward the stair shed on the opposite side of the hotel.

"Bengston!" Cobb called out, as he charged toward the man.

The killer turned, dropping his rifle as he went for the gun on his hip.

Bengston jumped out of the way as Cobb cut loose with both barrels of his coach gun. He had managed to dive clear of the blast as Cobb quickly closed in on him.

Bengston was flat on the ground as he rushed several shots at the charging coachman.

Cobb kept gripping his coach gun by the barrels as he closed in on Bengston. The murderer got to his feet and raised his left arm in time to absorb the blow as Cobb swung the stock of his gun down with all his strength.

The blow missed Bengston's left arm, but connected with his gun hand, knocking the weapon from his grip. Cobb swung the shotgun again and struck Bengston in the side of the jaw, rocking him backward against the stair shed.

Cobb brought the butt of the coach gun hard into Bengston's middle, doubling him over. A well-timed knee caught him under the chin and shot his head upward.

And with a mighty roar that came from somewhere deep within him, Cobb drove the stock hard into Bengston's throat and sent him reeling backward. His legs hit the raised ledge along the edge of the roof before he tumbled over the side. He managed only a brief scream before he landed in the alley below.

Cobb looked down at the broken body of the man who had taken everything from him with only one squeeze of the trigger. He remembered he had fired both barrels at Bengston and his gun was empty. He doubted the man had survived a fall from such a great height, but he needed to be sure.

Cobb cracked open his coach gun and dumped out the spent shells. He fumbled for fresh cartridges in his pocket, but his fingers had grown numb.

He ignored the sound of someone calling his name as

he willed his fingers to work. He tried to shake some blood into his hand, but his arm did not respond.

It was only then that he saw the blood beginning to spread on the right side of the front of his shirt. Bengston's bullets had found him after all.

He dropped to his knees as the gun fell from his grip. Butch slid to his side and eased his partner down to the roof floor.

"Kill him," Cobb whispered, as he felt the iron taste of blood in his mouth. "Kill him for me. Kill him for her."

"Moran!" Butch yelled, as Cobb felt himself grow tired. So very tired. "Get a doctor! Cobb's hit bad!"

Cobb's eyes found the blue sky above him and behind the look of concern on Butch's face and he found himself wondering if Jane would be waiting for him up there. He hoped she would be. He hoped he would see her soon.

CHAPTER 29

Cobb lifted his head and immediately regretted it. A web of pain spiked through the middle of him, and he slowly let his head sink back.

His vision blurred, but as he opened his eyes again, he saw Butch and Doc Fry looking down at him.

"I'm not dead."

He felt Butch grab his left hand. "No, but you were mighty close to it for a long time, partner. We didn't think you'd make it, but it looks like you have."

Doc Fry had taken hold of his right wrist. "Don't try to move, Mr. Cobb. You'll be in pain for a while yet. You've been through quite an ordeal."

Cobb tried to speak, but his throat felt like barbed wire. It hurt when he tried to breathe, but he managed to croak out, "What happened?"

Butch spoke over Doc Fry. "You got shot four times in the chest. Four times and you still managed to knock Bengston off the roof. By God, I've never seen anything like it and doubt I ever will again."

Doc Fry let go of Cobb's wrist and pulled his right eyelid open, then his left. "We thought we had lost you when we were pulling those bullets out of you, but by some miracle, you survived. You'll find it hard to breathe because pneumonia has set in, but you seem to have made it through that trial, too. I wouldn't have given a plug nickel for your chances, but you survived. I've never been so happy to be wrong in my life."

Cobb had never had pneumonia before. It felt like he was breathing through a wet cloth. He barely got enough air in his lungs to ask, "How long?"

"That doesn't matter much now." Butch patted his hand. "You just stay still like the doctor told you and get better."

Cobb jerked his hand back. "How long?"

Butch looked away, so the doctor spoke for him. "A month."

The words landed on him with great impact. "That long?"

"A weaker man would've died," Doc Fry told him. "You have a remarkable constitution, Mr. Cobb. You should be grateful. You've been running a high fever for almost a week, but it finally broke this morning, just before you woke up."

But Cobb did not care about that. He only had one thing on his mind. Despite the pain, he had to know. "Bengston?"

Doctor Fry said, "It sounds like you two have quite a bit to talk about. I'll be back in a while."

Cobb kept his head still as he turned his attention to Butch. "Bengston."

"He's dead," Butch told him. "But it took him about a week to get that way. The beating you threw him didn't kill him right away and neither did the fall. He hung on for as long as he could and longer than he should have, but he died. If it makes you feel any better, he was in pain the whole time."

But the news did not make him feel any better. Only

one thing in the world could do that and he knew it was impossible. "Jane."

Butch pulled up a chair and sat beside his partner's bed. "We laid her to rest in a beautiful spot just outside of town here. She's got a great big tree there to give her plenty of shade in the summer. I think she'd like it. I truly do. I'll be glad to take you to visit her as soon as you're able. They've got one of them fancy chairs with wheels on it. I can roll you up there myself. You've lost so much weight in here that it won't be much trouble at all."

But Cobb knew he would never visit her grave. There was nothing to see except a hole in the ground where all his life's hopes were buried under six feet of dirt. He could not think of her as gone, just not there anymore.

"Fisk?"

"Bengston hit him pretty good, but he's fine. He took Toneff's place. Perry thinks he has the makings of a good sheriff one day. Fisk came by to see you every day. He'll be happy to know you've snapped out of it."

Cobb was glad to hear it. At least one good thing had come out of so much misery.

But something Butch had said earlier stuck out in his muddled mind. "You saw me hit Bengston." He labored for another breath. "You were there."

"I would've shot him, too, if you hadn't been in the way." Butch looked down. "If I'd have shot him, he wouldn't have done this to you."

But Cobb was not thinking about that. "You . . . let me kill him. Why?"

"I guess you could blame this old Cheyenne war chief I met once. He told me there's more than just the law written down on paper. Sometimes, doing what's right and doing what's legal ain't the same thing."

Cobb closed his eyes, wishing news of Bengston's suffering might have helped ease his own, but it did not. "The whole time I was asleep, I never saw her, Butch. She didn't come visit me, not even once. She wasn't here."

"That's on account of you didn't die. You were too ornery and stubborn to let go and for once, I'm glad for it."

But that was not what Cobb meant. "She wasn't here, but you were."

"I was, but don't worry about me. I put my time to good use. I've been trading letters with Colonel McBride's niece, Miss Carlyle. One of the nurses helped me. I don't like to brag, but I'm getting the hang of it. I—"

Cobb grabbed his friend's hand. "You stayed."

"Of course, I did." Butch smiled. "Where else would I be? We're partners, ain't we?"

Cobb might not have had the love of his Jane, but he had something that was almost as rare. He had a true friend. "You're damned right we are."

It starts with a jailbreak.
Frank Thorson and his gang ride into Wolfwater
to bust Frank's brother out of the slammer.
First, they slaughter the deputy. Then, the town marshal.
Finally, they run off with the marshal's daughter and no
one's sure if she's dead or alive. The townsfolk are
terrified—and desperate. Desperate enough to ask
"Catfish" Charlie to put down his fishing pole, pick up
his Colt Army .44, and go after the bloodthirsty gang.
Sure, Charlie may be a bit rusty after all these years.
But when it comes to serving up justice,
no one is quicker, faster—or deadlier . . .

Once a lawman, always a lawman.
Especially a lawman like Catfish Charlie.

**National Bestselling Authors
William W. Johnstone
and J.A. Johnstone**

CATFISH CHARLIE

On sale now, wherever Pinnacle Books are sold.

Live Free. Read Hard.

www.williamjohnstone.net

Visit us at www.kensingtonbooks.com

CHAPTER 1

May 2, 1891

"Bushwhack" Wilbur Aimes, Deputy Town Marshal of Wolfwater, in West Texas, looked up from the report he'd been scribbling, sounding out the words semi-aloud as he'd written them and pressing his tongue down hard against his bottom lip in concentration. He knew his letters and numbers well enough, but that didn't mean he had an easy time stringing them together. He almost welcomed the sudden, uneasy feeling climbing his spine, stealthy as a brown recluse spider. He frowned at the brick wall before him, below the flour sack–curtained window, the drawn curtains still bearing the words PIONEER FLOUR MILLS, SAN ANTONIO, TX, though the Texas sun angling through the window every day had badly faded them.

The sound came again—distant hoof thuds, a horse's whicker.

Silence.

A bridle chain rattled.

Bushwhack, a big, broad-shouldered, rawboned man, and former bushwhacker from Missouri's backwoods, rose from his chair. The creaky Windsor was mostly Marshal Abel Wilkes's chair, but Bushwhack got to sit in it when he was on duty—usually night duty as he was on tonight—and the marshal was off, home in bed sleeping within only a few feet of the marshal's pretty schoolteacher daughter, Miss Bethany.

Bushwhack shook his head as though to rid it of thoughts of the pretty girl. Thinking about her always made his cheeks warm and his throat grow tight. Prettiest girl in Wolfwater, for sure. If only he could work up the courage to ask the marshal if he could . . .

Oh, stop thinking about that, you damn fool! Bushwhack castigated himself. The marshal's holding off on letting any man step out with his daughter until the right one came along. And that sure as holy blazes wasn't going to be the big, awkward, bearded, former defender of the ol' Stars an' Bars, as well as a horse-breaker-until-a-wild-stallion-had-broken-him—his left hip, at least. No, Miss Bethany Wilkes wasn't for him, Bushwhack thought, half pouting as he grabbed his old Remington and cartridge belt off the wall peg, right of the door, the uneasy feeling staying with him even beneath his forbidden thoughts of the marshal's daughter.

He glanced at his lone prisoner in the second of the four cells lined up along the office's back wall.

"Skinny" Thorson was sound asleep on his cot, legs crossed at the ankles, funnel-brimmed, weatherbeaten hat pulled down over his eyes.

Skinny was the leader of a local outlaw gang, though he didn't look like much. Just a kid on the downhill side of twenty, but not by much. Skinny wore his clothes next to rags. His boots were so worn that Bushwhack could see his socks through the soles. The deputy chuffed his distaste as he encircled his waist with the belt and soft leather holster from which his old, walnut-gripped Remington jutted, its butt scratched from all the times it had been used to pulverize coffee beans around remote Texas campfires during the years—a good dozen. Bushwhack had punched cattle around the Red River country and into the Panhandle—when he hadn't been fighting Injuns or bluebellies and minding his topknot, of course.

You always had to mind your scalp in Comanche country.

Or breaking broncs for Johnny Sturges, until that one particularly nasty blue roan had bucked him off onto the point of his left hip, then rolled on him and gave him a stomp to punctuate the "ride" and to settle finally the argument over who was boss.

That had ended Bushwhack's punching and breaking days.

Fortunately, Abel Wilkes had needed a deputy and hadn't minded overmuch that Bushwhack had lost the giddy-up in his step. Bushwhack was still sturdy, albeit with a bit of a paunch these days, and he was right handy with a hide-wrapped bung starter, a sawed-off twelve gauge, and his old Remington. Now he grabbed the battered Stetson off the peg to the right of the one his gun had been hanging from, set it on his head, slid the Remington from its holster and, holding the long-barreled popper straight down against his right leg, opened the door and poked his head out, taking a cautious look around.

As he did, he felt his heart quicken. He wasn't sure why, but he was nervous. He worried the old Remy's hammer with his right thumb, ready to draw it back to full cock if needed.

Not seeing anything amiss out front of the marshal's office and the jailhouse, he glanced over his shoulder at Skinny Thorson once more. The outlaw was still sawing logs beneath his hat. Bushwhack swung his scowling gaze back to the street, then stepped out onto the jailhouse's rickety front stoop to take a better look around.

The night was dark, the sky sprinkled with clear, pointed stars. Around Bushwhack, Wolfwater slouched, quiet and dark in these early-morning hours—one thirty, if the marshal's banjo clock on the wall over the large, framed map of western Texas could be trusted. The clock seemed to lose about three minutes every week, so Bushwhack or Wilkes or Maggie Cruz, who cleaned the place once a week, had to consult their pocket watches and turn it ahead.

Bushwhack trailed his gaze around the broad, pale street to his left; it was abutted on both sides by mud brick, Spanish-style adobe, or wood frame, false-fronted business buildings, all slouching with age and the relentless Texas heat and hot, dry wind. He continued shuttling his scrutinizing gaze along the broad street to his right, another block of which remained before the sotol-stippled, bone-dry, cactus-carpeted desert continued unabated dang near all the way to the Rawhide Buttes and Wichita Falls beyond.

The relatively recently laid railroad tracks of the Brazos, San Antonio & Rio Grande Line ran right through the middle of the main drag, gleaming faintly now in the starlight. Most businessmen and cattlemen in the area had welcomed the railroad for connecting San Antonio, in the southeast, with El Paso, in the northwest, and parts beyond.

Celebrated by some, maligned by others, including Marshal Abel Wilkes.

The San Antonio & Rio Grande Line might have brought so-called progress and a means for local cattlemen to ship their beef-on-the-hoof out from Wolfwater, but it had also brought trouble in the forms of men and even some women—oh, its share of troublesome women, as well, don't kid yourself!—in all shapes, sizes, colors, and creeds. However, it being a weeknight, the town was dark and quiet. On weekends, several saloons, hurdy-gurdies, and gambling parlors remained open, as long as they had customers, or until Marshal Wilkes, backed by Bushwhack himself, tired of breaking up fights and even some shootouts right out on the main drag, Wolfwater Street. Marshal and deputy would shut them down and would send the cowboys, vaqueros, sodbusters, and prospectors back to their ranches, haciendas, soddies, and diggings, respectively.

The road ranches stippling the desert outside of Abel Wilkes's jurisdiction stayed open all night, however. There was nothing Wilkes and Bushwhack could do about them. What perditions they were, too! When he'd heard all the trouble that took place out there, Bushwhack was secretly glad his and the marshal's jurisdiction stopped just outside of Wolfwater. Too many lawmen—deputy U.S. marshals, deputy sheriffs from the county seat over in Heraklion, and even some Texas Rangers and Pinkertons—had ridden into such places, between town and the Rawhide Buttes, to the west, or between town and the Stalwart Mountains, to the south, never to be seen or heard from again.

In fact, only last year, Sheriff Ed Wilcox from Heraklion had sent two deputies out to the road ranch on Jawbone Creek. Only part of them had returned home—their heads in gunnysacks tied to their saddle horns!

As far as Bushwhack knew, no one had ever learned what had become of the rest of their bodies. He didn't care to know, and he had a suspicion that Sheriff Ed Wilcox didn't, either. The road ranch on Jawbone Creek continued to this day, unmolested—at least by the law, ha-ha. (That was the joke going around.)

Bushwhack shoved his hat down on his forehead to scratch the back of his head with his left index finger. All was quiet, save the snores sounding from Skinny Thorson's cell in the office behind him. No sign of anyone out and about. Not even a cat. Not even a coyote, in from the desert, hunting cats.

So, who or what had made the sounds Bushwhack had heard just a minute ago?

He yawned. He was tired. Trouble in town had kept him from getting his nap earlier. His beauty sleep, the marshal liked to joke. Maybe he'd nodded off without realizing it and had only dreamt of the hoof thud and the bridle chain rattle.

Bushwhack yawned again, turned, stepped back inside the office, and closed the door. Just then, he realized that the snores had stopped. He swung his head around to see Skinny Thorson lying as before, only he'd poked his hat brim up on his forehead and was gazing at Bushwhack, grinning, blue eyes twinkling.

"What's the matter, Bushwhack?" the kid said. "A mite nervous, are we?"

Bushwhack sauntered across the office and stood at the door of Skinny's cell, scowling beneath the brim of his own Stetson. He poked the Remington's barrel through the bars and said, "Shut up, you little rat-faced tinhorn, or I'll pulverize your head."

Skinny turned his head to one side and a jeeringly warning light came to his eyes. "My big brother, Frank, wouldn't like that—now, would he?"

"No, the hangman wouldn't like it, neither. He gets twenty dollars for every neck he stretches. He's probably halfway between Heraklion an' here, and he wouldn't like it if he got here an' didn't have a job to do, money to make." Bushwhack grinned. "Of course, he'd likely get one of Miss Claire's girls to soothe his disappointment. And every man around knows how good Miss Claire's girls are at soothing disappointments."

It was true. Miss Julia Claire's sporting parlor was one of the best around—some said the best hurdy-gurdy house between El Paso and San Antonio, along the San Antonio, and Rio Grande Line. And Miss Julia Claire herself was quite the lady. A fella could listen to her speak English in that beguiling British accent of hers all day long.

All *night* long, for that matter.

Only, Miss Claire herself didn't work the line. That

fact—her chasteness and accent and the obscurity of her past, which she'd remained tight-lipped about for all of the five years she'd lived and worked here in Wolfwater— gave her an alluring air of mystery.

Skinny Thorson now pressed his face up close to the bars, squeezing a bar to either side of his face in his hands, until his knuckles turned white, and said, "'The Reaper' ain't gonna have no job to do once he gets here, because by the time he gets here, I won't be here anymore. You got it, Bushwhack?"

The Reaper was what everyone around called the executioner from the county seat, Lorenzo Snow.

The prisoner widened his eyes and slackened his lower jaws and made a hideous face of mockery, sticking his long tongue out at Bushwhack.

Bushwhack was about to grab that tongue with his fingers and pull it through the bars, pull it all the way out of the kid's mouth—by God!—but stopped when he heard something out in the street again.

"What was that?" asked Skinny with mock trepidation, cocking an ear to listen. "Think that was Frank, Bushwhack?" He grinned sidelong through the bars once more. "You know what? I think it was!"

Outside, a horse whinnied shrilly.

Outside, men spoke, but it was too soft for Bushwhack to make out what they were saying.

The hooves of several horses thudded and then the thuds dwindled away to silence.

Bushwhack turned to face the door, scowling angrily. "What in holy blazes is going on out there?"

"It's Frank, Bushwhack. My big brother, Frank, is here, just like I knew he would be! He got the word I sent him!" Skinny tipped his head back and whooped loudly.

Squeezing the cell bars, he yelled, "I'm here, Frank. Come an' fetch me out of here, big brother!"

Bushwhack had holstered the Remington, but he had not snapped the keeper thong home over the hammer. He grabbed his sawed-off twelve gauge off a peg in the wall to his left and looped the lanyard over his head and right shoulder. He broke open the gun to make sure it was loaded, then snapped it closed and whipped around to Skinny and said tightly, "One more peep out of you, you little scoundrel, an' I'll blast you all over that wall behind you. If Frank came to fetch you, he'd best've brought a bucket an' a mop!"

Skinny narrowed his eyes in warning and returned in his own tight voice, "Frank won't like it, Bushwhack. You know Frank. Everybody around the whole county knows Frank. You an' they know how Frank can be when he's riled!"

Bushwhack strode quickly up to the cell, clicking the twelve gauge's hammers back to full cock. "You don't hear too good, Skinny. Liable to get you killed. Best dig the dirt out'n your ears."

Skinny looked down at the heavy, cocked hammers of the savage-looking gut shredder. He took two halting steps back away from the cell door, raising his hands, palms out, in supplication. "All . . . all right, now, Bushwhack," he trilled. "Calm down. Just funnin' you's all." He smiled suddenly with mock equanimity. "Prob'ly not Frank out there at all. Nah. Prob'ly just some thirty-a-month-and-found cow nurses lookin' fer some coffin varnish to cut the day's dust with. Yeah, that's prob'ly who it is."

His smile turned wolfish.

Grimacing, anger burning through him, Bushwhack swung around to the door. Holding the twelve gauge straight out from his right side, right index finger curled over both eyelash triggers, he pulled the door open wide.

His big frame filled the doorway as he stared out into the night.

Again, the dark street was empty.

"All right—who's there?" he said, trying to ignore the insistent beating of his heart against his breastbone.

Silence, save for crickets and the distant cry of a wildcat on the hunt out in the desert in the direction of the Stalwarts.

He called again, louder: "Who's there?" A pause. "That you, Frank?"

Bushwhack and Marshal Wilkes had known there was the possibility that Skinny's older brother, Frank, might journey to Wolfwater to bust his brother out. But they'd heard Frank had been last seen up in the Indian Nations, and they didn't think that even if Frank got word that Wilkes and Bushwhack had jailed his younger brother for killing a half-breed whore in one of the lesser parlor houses in Wolfwater, he'd make it here before the hangman would. There were a total of six houses of ill repute in Wolfwater—not bad for a population of sixty-five hundred, though that didn't include all of the cowboys, vaqueros, miners, and sodbusters who frequented the town nearly every night and on weekends, and the mostly unseemly visitors, including gamblers, confidence men and women, which the railroad brought to town. It was in one of these lesser houses, only identified as GIRLS by the big gaudy sign over its front door, that Skinny had gone loco on busthead and thrown the girl out a second-story window.

The girl, a half-Comanche known as "Raven," had lived a few days before succumbing to her injuries caused when she'd landed on a hitchrack, which had busted all her ribs and cracked her spine. Infection had been the final cause of death, as reported by the lone local medico, Doc Overholser.

Anger at being toyed with was growing in Bushwhack. Fear, too, he had to admit. He stepped out onto the stoop, swinging his gaze from right to left, and back again, and yelled, "Who's out there? If it's you, Frank—show yourself, now!"

Bushwhack heard the sudden thud of hooves to his right and his left.

Riders were moving up around him now, booting their horses ahead at slow, casual walks, coming out from around the two front corners of the jailhouse flanking him on his right and left. They were ominous silhouettes in the starlight. As Bushwhack turned to his left, where three riders were just then swinging their horses around the right front corner of the jailhouse stoop and into the street in front of it, a gun flashed.

At the same time the gun's loud bark slammed against Bushwhack's ears, the bullet plundered his left leg, just above the knee. The bullet burned like a branding iron laid against his flesh.

Bushwhack yelped and shuffled to his right, clutching the bloody wound in misery. He released the twelve gauge to hang free against his belly and struck the porch floor in a grunting, agonized heap. He cursed through gritted teeth, feeling warm blood ooze out of his leg from beneath his fingers. As he did, slow hoof clomps sounded ahead of him. He peered up to see a tall, rangy man in a black vest, black hat, and black denim trousers ride out of the street's darkness on a tall gray horse and into the light from the window and the open door behind Bushwhack.

The guttering lamplight shone in cold gray eyes above a long, slender nose and thick blond mustache. The lips beneath the mustache quirked a wry grin as Frank Thorson said, "Hello, there, Bushwhack. Been a while. You miss me?"

The smile grew. But the gray eyes remained flat and hard and filled with malicious portent.

CHAPTER 2

Marshal Abel Wilkes snapped his eyes open, instantly awake. "Oh, fer Pete's sake!"

Almost as quickly, though not as quickly as it used to be, the Colt hanging from the bedpost to his right was in his hand. Aiming the barrel up at the ceiling, Abel clicked the hammer back and lay his head back against his pillow, listening.

What he'd heard before, he heard again. A man outside breathing hard. Running in a shambling fashion. The sounds were growing louder as Wilkes—fifty-six years old, bald but with a strap of steel-gray hair running in a band around his large head, above his ears, and with a poorly trimmed, soup-strainer gray mustache—lay there listening.

What in blazes . . . ?

Abel tossed his covers back and dropped his pajama-clad legs over the side of the bed. He'd grabbed his ratty, old plaid robe off a wall peg and shrugged into it and was sliding his feet into his wool-lined slippers, as ratty as the robe, when his daughter's voice rose from the lower story. "Dad? Dad? You'd better come down he—"

She stopped abruptly when Abel heard muffled thuds on the floor of the porch beneath his room, here in the second story of the house he owned and in which he lived with his daughter, Bethany. The muffled thuds were followed by a loud hammering on the house's front door.

"Marshal Wilkes!" a man yelled.

More thundering knocks, then Bushwhack Aimes's plaintive wail: *"Marshal Wilkes!"*

What in tarnation is going on now? Wilkes wondered.

Probably had to do with the railroad. That damned railroad . . . bringin' vermin of every stripe into—

"Dad, do you hear that?" Beth's voice came again from the first story.

"Coming, honey!" Abel said as he opened his bedroom door and strode quickly into the hall, a little breathless and dizzy from rising so fast. He wasn't as young as he used to be, and he had to admit his gut wasn't as flat as it used to be, either. Too many roast beef platters at Grace Hasting's café for noon lunch, followed up by steak and potatoes cooked by Beth for supper.

Holding the Colt down low against his right leg, Abel hurried as quickly as he could, without stumbling down the stairs, just as Beth opened the front door at the bottom of the stairs and slightly right, in the parlor part of the house. The willowy brunette was as pretty as her mother had been, but she was on the borderline of being considered an old maid, since she was not yet married at twenty-four. The young woman gasped and stepped back quickly as a big man tumbled inside the Wilkes parlor, striking the floor with a loud *bang*.

Not normally a screaming girl, Beth stepped back quickly, shrieked, and closed her hands over her mouth as she stared down in horror at her father's deputy, who lay just inside the front door, gasping like a landed fish.

Abel knew it was Bushwhack Aimes because he'd recognized his deputy's voice. The face of the man, however, only vaguely resembled Bushwhack. He'd been beaten bad, mouth smashed, both eyes swelling, various sundry scrapes and bruises further disfiguring the big man's face. He wore only long-handles, and the top hung from his nearly bare shoulders in tattered rags.

"Oh, my God!" Beth exclaimed, turning to her father as Abel brushed past her.

Like Abel, she was clad in a robe and slippers. Lamps burned in the parlor, as well as in the kitchen, indicating she'd been up late grading papers again or preparing lessons for tomorrow.

"Good God," Abel said, dropping to a knee beside his bloody deputy, who lay clutching his left leg with both hands and groaning loudly against the pain that must be hammering all through him. "What the hell happened, Bushwhack? Who did this to you?"

He couldn't imagine the tenacity it had taken for Bushwhack in his condition to have made it here from the jailhouse—a good four-block trek, blood pouring out of him. The man already had a bum hip, to boot!

"Marshal!" Aimes grated out, spitting blood from his lips.

Abel turned to his daughter, who stood crouched forward over Aimes, looking horrified. "Beth, heat some water and fetch some cloths, will you?"

As Beth wheeled and hurried across the parlor and into the kitchen, Abel placed a placating hand on his deputy's right shoulder. "Easy, Bushwhack. Easy. I'll fetch the sawbones in a minute. What happened? Who did this to you?"

Aimes shifted his gaze from his bloody leg to the marshal. "Thor . . . Thorson. Frank Thorson . . . an' his men! Shot me. Beat me. Stripped me. Left me in the street . . . laughin' at me!" The deputy sucked a sharp breath through gritted teeth and added, "They busted Skinny out of jail!"

"Are they still in town?"

"They broke into one of the saloons—the Wolfwater Inn! Still . . . still there, far as I know . . . Oh . . . oh, *Lordy!*" Bushwhack reached up and wrapped both of his own bloody hands around one of Abel's. "They're killers, Marshal! Don't go after 'em alone." He wagged his head and showed his teeth between stretched-back lips. "Or . . . you'll . . ." He was weakening fast, eyelids growing heavy, barely able to get the words out. ". . . . you'll end up like me—*dead!*"

With that, Bushwhack's hands fell away from Abel's. His head fell back against the floor with a loud *thump*. He rolled onto his back and his head sort of wobbled back and forth, until it and the rest of the man's big body fell still. The eyes slightly crossed and halfway closed as they stared up at Abel Wilkes, glassy with death.

Footsteps sounded behind Abel, and he turned to see Beth striding through the parlor behind him. "I have water heating, Pa! Want I should fetch the doc . . . ?" She stopped suddenly as she gazed down at Bushwhack. Again, she raised her hands to her mouth, her brown eyes widening in shock.

"No need for the doc, honey," Abel said, slowly straightening, gazing down at his deputy. Anger burned in him. "I reckon he's done for, Bushwhack is." Beth moved slowly forward, dropped to her knees, and gently set her hand on the deputy's head, smoothing his thick, curly, salt-and-pepper hair back from his forehead. "I'm so sorry, Bushwhack," she said in a voice hushed with sorrow.

"Stay with him, take care of him as best you can, honey," Abel said, reaching down to squeeze his daughter's shoulder comfortingly. "On my way into town, I'll send for the undertaker."

Beth looked up at her father, tears of sorrow and anger in her eyes. "Who did this to Bushwhack, Pa?"

"Frank Thorson."

Beth sort of winced and grimaced at the same time. Most people did that when they heard the name. "Oh, God," she said.

"Don't you worry, honey," Abel said, squeezing her shoulder once more. "Thorson will pay for what he did here tonight."

Abel gave a reassuring dip of his chin, then turned to start back up the stairs to get dressed.

"Pa!" Beth cried.

Abel stopped and turned back to his daughter, on her knees now and leaning back against the slipper-clad heels of her feet. Beth gazed up at him with deep concern. "You're not thinking about confronting Frank Thorson alone—are you?"

Abel didn't like the lack of confidence he saw in his daughter's eyes. "I don't have any choice, honey." Aimes was his only deputy, and there was little time to deputize more men. He needed to throw a loop around Frank Thorson and the men riding with him before they could leave town. This was his town, Abel Wilkes's town, and he'd be dogged if anyone, including Frank Thorson, would just ride in, shoot and beat his deputy to death, spring a prisoner, then belly up to a bar for drinks in celebration.

Oh, no. Wilkes might not be the lawman he once was, but Wolfwater was still his town, gallblastit. He would not, could not, let the notorious firebrand Frank Thorson, whom he'd had run-ins with before, turn him into a laughingstock.

Trying to ignore his deputy's final warning, which echoed inside his head, Wilkes returned to his room and quickly dressed in his usual work garb—blue wool shirt under a brown vest, black twill pants, and his Colt's six-gun strapped around his bulging waist. He grabbed his flat-brimmed black hat off a wall peg and, holding the hat in one hand, crouched to peer into the mirror over his dresser.

He winced at what he saw there. An old man . . .

His dear wife's death two years ago had aged him considerably. Abel Wilkes, former soldier in the War Against Northern Aggression, former stockman, former stage driver, former stagecoach messenger, and, more recently, former Pinkerton agent, was not the man he'd been before Ethel Wilkes had contracted bone cancer, which they'd had diagnosed by special doctors up in Abilene. Abel's face was paler than it used to be; heavy blue pouches sagged beneath his eyes, and deep lines spoked out from their corners.

There was something else about that face staring back from the mirror that gave Wilkes an unsettled feeling. He tried not to think about it, but now as he set the low-crowned hat on his head, shucked his Colt from its holster, opened the loading gate, and drew the hammer back to half cock, he realized the cause of his unsettlement. The eyes that had stared back at him a moment ago were no longer as bold and as certain as they once had been.

They'd turned a paler blue in recent months, and there was no longer in them the glint of bravado, the easy confidence that had once curled one corner of his mustached upper lip as he'd made his rounds up and down Wolfwater's dusty main drag. Now, as he stared down at the wheel of his six-gun as he poked a live cartridge into the chamber he usually left empty beneath the hammer, his eyes looked downright uncertain. Maybe even a little afraid.

Maybe more than *a little* afraid.

"Don't do it, Pa. Don't confront those men alone," Beth urged from where she continued to kneel beside Bushwhack as Abel descended the stairs, feeling heavy and fearful and generally out of sorts.

Beth wasn't helping any. Anger rose in him and he shifted his gaze to her now, deep lines corrugating his broad, sun-leathered forehead beneath the brim of his hat. "You sit tight and don't worry," he said, stepping around her and Bushwhack, his Winchester in his right hand now. "I'll send the undertak—"

She grabbed his left hand with both of her own and squeezed. "Pa, don't! Not alone!"

Not turning to her, but keeping his eyes on the night ahead of him, the suddenly awful night, Abel pulled his hand out from between Beth's and headed through the door and onto the porch. "I'll be back soon."

Feeling his daughter's terrified gaze on his back, Abel crossed the porch, descended the three steps to the cinder-paved path that led out through the gate in the white picket fence. He strode through the gate and did not bother closing it behind him. His nerves were too jangled to trifle with such matters as closing gates in picket fences.

As he strode down the willow-lined lane toward the heart of town, which lay ominously dark and silent straight ahead, Abel shook his head as though to rid it of the fear he'd seen in his daughter's eyes . . . in his own eyes. Beth's fear had somehow validated his own.

"Darn that girl, anyway," he muttered as he walked,

holding the Winchester down low in his right hand. *She knows me better than I do. She knows my nerves have gone to hell.*

Fear.

Call it what it is, Abel, he remonstrated himself. *You've grown fearful in your later years.*

There'd been something unnerving about watching Ethel die so slowly, gradually. That had been the start of his deterioration. And then, after Ethel had passed and they'd buried her in the cemetery at the east end of town, that darn whore had had to go and save his hide in the Do Drop Inn. The gambler had had Wilkes dead to rights. The marshal had called the man out on his cheating after hearing a string of complaints from other men the gambler had been playing cards with between mattress dances upstairs in the inn.

So Abel had gone over to the inn, intending to throw the man out of town. The gambler had dropped his cards, kicked his chair back, rose, and raised his hands above the butts of his twin six-shooters.

Open challenge.

Let the faster man live.

Abel remembered the fear he'd felt. He had a reputation as a fast gun—one of the fastest in West Texas at one time. "Capable Abel" Wilkes, they'd called him. His dirty little secret, however, was that when he'd started creeping into his later forties, he'd lost some of that speed. His reputation for being fast had preceded him, though. So he hadn't had to entertain many challengers. Just drunks who hadn't known any better or, because of the who-hit-John coursing through their veins, had thrown caution to the wind.

And had paid the price.

The gambler had been different. He'd been one cool customer, as most good gamblers were. As Abel himself once had been. Cool and confident in his speed. That night, however, the gambler had sized Wilkes up, sensed that the aging lawman was no longer as fast as he once had been. Abel hadn't been sure how the man had known that.

Maybe he'd seen the doubt in Abel's own eyes.

The fear. That fear.

Abel had let the gambler make the first move, of course. Over the years, the lawman had been so fast that he'd been able to make up for his opponents' lightning-fast starts. That night, however, Abel would have been wolf bait if the drunk doxie hadn't stumbled against him in her haste to leave the table and not risk taking a ricochet.

She had nudged his shooting arm just as the man had swept his pearl-handled Colt from its black leather holster thonged low on his right thigh. Abel's own Colt Lightning had cleared leather after the gambler's gun had drilled a round into the table before him, between him and his opponent. Abel's bullet had plunked through the man's brisket and instantly trimmed his wick.

Abel had left the saloon after the undertaker had hauled the gambler out feet first. He'd tried to maintain an air of grim confidence, of a job well done, but the other gamblers and the saloon's other customers all knew it to be as phony as he did. If that drunk, little doxie hadn't nudged the gambler's arm at just the right time, the undertaker would have planted Abel in the Wolfwater bone orchard, beside his dearly departed Ethel.

Leaving their old-maid daughter alone in the cold, cruel, West Texas world.

* * *

Now he swung onto Wolfwater's broad main drag, dark except for up at the Wolfwater Inn, half a block ahead and on the street's right side.

Abel felt his boots turn to lead. He wanted to do anything this night, except confront Frank Thorson and Thorson's men. Abel didn't know whom Frank was running with now, but for them to do what they had done to Bushwhack, they all had to be every bit as bad as Frank.

No, Wilkes wanted nothing to do with them. But he couldn't very well ignore them. He wanted to turn tail and run home and hide. Wait for the Thorson storm to pass. That's why he did what he did now. He quickened his pace.

There was only one thing worse than being dead.

That thing was being a laughingstock in front of your whole dang town.